Andersen's Fairy Tales

Andersen's Fairy Tales

Hans Christian Andersen

Illustrated by
E.H. Wehnert
and W. Thomas

This edition published in 1998 by
Redwood Editions
a division of Hinkler Book Distributors
17-23 Redwood Drive, Dingley,
Victoria, Australia 3172.
by arrangement with
Anness Publishing Limited
Hermes House
88-89 Blackfriars Road, London SE1 8HA

ISBN 1-8651-5009-6

Printed and bound in Australia

Contents

COLOUR ILLUSTRATIONS

All the other cockchafers that lived in the tree came to visit her. *(Little Thumb.)*

"But he has nothing on," said at length a little child. *(The Emperor's New Clothes.)*

She cared only for a beautiful little statue of a boy, of pure white marble. *(The Little Mermaid.)*

The Princess could not speak a word. At length, however, she got up and gave John her hand. *(The Travelling Companion.)*

Running up to him, she pressed him closely to her, and cried, "Kay! dear little Kay! So I have found you at last!" *(The Snow Queen.)*

The whole Court was present even to the little kitchen wench. *(The Nightingale.)*

The Hell-horse turned quite giddy and had to leave the table. *(The Elfin-Hillock.)*

Early in the morning the Queen took three hideous toads into the bathroom with her. *(The Wild Swans.)*

PREFACE

Hans Christian Andersen, the author of the world-renowned stories contained in this volume, was born at Odense, a small town in Funen, one of the islands of Denmark. His parents were poor, and could only afford to give him so humble an education that when the lad left school he could not write his own language. Happily, his father was an intelligent man, who spent many of his leisure hours in reading aloud tales and plays to his family, and thus, doubtless, sowed the seed which ripened in the future author.

Hans Christian had many difficulties to contend with, but he fought manfully through them, and has added one more to the list of men who, by energy and perseverance, have won success. The poor, ignorant lad aspired to fame, and famous indeed he has become. In all civilised countries, to both old and young, his name is known, and there is scarcely a language in which "The Ugly Duck" and "The Daisy" are not to be met with. In his own land his stories are read aloud between the acts in the theatres, and monarchs of many countries have delighted to do him deserved honour.

There is no need of an excuse for offering a new translation of his tales, so justly esteemed are they for their freshness of tone, and the simple purity they breathe; but the publishers trust that the many illustrations which Mr. Wehnert has conceived so happily in accordance with the imaginative spirit of the author, will enhance the value of this edition, and make Andersen a greater favourite than ever with children everywhere.

The storks.

The Storks

On the last house in a village was a stork's nest. The stork-mother sat in the nest with her four little ones, which stretched out their heads with the little black beaks, for they had not yet become red. A little way off, on the ridge of the roof, stood the stork-father, quite stiff and rigid, with one leg drawn up under him, so that, at any rate, he might have some trouble in standing as he kept watch. It seemed almost as if he were carved in wood, he stood so still. "It must certainly look quite grand that my wife should have a guard near the nest," he thought, "for no one can know that I am her husband, but they will surely think that I have been ordered to stand here. It looks well!" and he continued to stand on one leg.

In the street below a troop of children were playing; and when they saw the storks, first one of the boldest of them, and afterwards all together, sang the old rhyme about the storks, but they sang it just as it came into the first singer's head:-

"Stork, stork, fly home, I beg,
And don't stay idling on one leg.
There's your wife sits in her nest,
Rocking all her young to rest;

The first he will be hung,
The second roasted young,
They'll come and shoot the third,
And stab the fourth, I've heard."

"Just listen to what the boys are singing," said the little storks; "they say we shall be hanged and roasted."

"You need not mind that!" said the mother; "don't listen to them, and it matters not what they say."

But the boys went on singing, and made game of the storks, pointing at them with their fingers; only one of them, whose name was Peter, said it was wrong to laugh at the poor things, and he himself would not join in. The stork-mother, in the meantime, consoled her young ones, saying, "Do not mind them; just look how unconcerned your father stands there, and on one leg too."

"We are so afraid!" said the young ones, and they drew back their heads into the nest.

On the following day, when the children met together again to play, and saw the storks, they sang their rhyme:–

"The first he will be hung,
The second roasted young."

"Must we be hanged and roasted?" the young storks asked.

"No, certainly not!" said the mother; "you shall learn to fly, which I'll teach you, and then we'll fly out into the meadows and pay the frogs a visit as they sing 'croak, croak!', then we'll eat them up, and that will be fun."

"And what next?" asked the little ones.

"Then all the storks of the whole country will meet together, and the autumn manoeuvring begins, when you must be able to fly well. That is of the greatest importance; for whichever of you does not fly properly, the general will pierce through with his beak, and kill; so take care that you attend to the exercising when it begins."

"So we shall be stabbed after all, as the boy said; and there! listen! – they are singing it again."

"Attend to me, and not to them," said the stork-mother; "after the grand maneouvre we fly away to a warmer country, far, far from here, over mountains and forests. To Egypt we fly, where there are three-cornered stone houses, which rise up into a point above the clouds; these are called pyramids, and are older than a stork has any notion of. In that country is a river, which, overflowing its banks, turns the whole land into slime, and all one has to do is to pick up the frogs."

"Oh, how nice!" cried all the young ones.

"Yes, that is a glorious life! One has nothing to do all day but to eat; and during the time we are living there in such luxury, in this country there is not a single green leaf on the trees; it is so cold here that the clouds freeze, and break to pieces in white flakes." She meant snow, but did not know how to express it better.

"Do the naughty boys, then, freeze and break into pieces too?" the young storks asked.

"No, they do not break into pieces, but are very cold and miserable, and have to huddle together in their dark rooms, whereas you can fly about in a foreign country, where there are flowers, and where the sun gives warmth."

Some time had now passed by, and the young ones had grown so big that they could stand up in the nest, and watch their father from afar, as he brought them beautiful frogs and small snakes, and such-like delicacies. Then what fun it was to watch his tricks! His head he would bend right back, laying it upon his tail, and with his beak he made a noise like a rattle, and told them besides such stories, all about the swamps.

"Listen to me: you must now learn to fly," said the stork-mother one day; and then all the four young ones had to get out of the nest on to the ridge of the roof. Oh, how they waddled, how they balanced themselves with their wings, and yet were near falling down!

"Now watch me," said their mother, "this is the way you must hold your head, and place your feet thus! One, two; one, two; that's the way to get on in the world." Then she flew a little way, and the young ones gave an awkward jump, when, plump, down they went, for their bodies were too heavy.

"I'll not fly," said one of them, and crept back into the nest; "what do I care about going into a warmer country?"

"Do you wish to freeze to death when winter comes? And shall the boys come to hang and to roast you? Well, then, I'll call them."

"No, no!" cried the young stork, and hopped out of the nest again to the others.

On the third day they began to be able to fly a little, and then thought they could float in the air; but, when they tried that, over they went, and were obliged to move their wings again pretty quickly. Then came the boys again, down below in the street, and sang:-

"Stork, stork, fly home, I beg."

"Shall we not fly down and peck out their eyes?" said the young storks.

"No, leave that alone," said the mother. "Attend to me, which is much more important. One, two, three; now we'll fly to the right. One, two, three; and now to the left, round the chimney. Now, that was very well done, particularly the last turn, so that to-morrow you may be allowed to fly with me to the marsh. There we shall find several nice stork families; and mind you show that my childen are the best. You may strut about as proudly as you like, for that creates respect."

"But are we not to be revenged on the naughty boys?" they asked.

"Let them say what they like; you'll fly up into the clouds, and go to the land of the pyramids, whilst they are freezing here, and haven't a green leaf nor a sweet apple."

"We'll be revenged for all that," said they to each other, and then they went on with their exercising again.

Of all the boys in the street, not one was worse with the mocking than just he who had begun the rhyme, and he was quite a little fellow, not more, perhaps, than six years old. The young storks, indeed, thought he must be a hundred years old, for he was so much bigger than their father or mother, and what should they know of the age of human beings, old or young? All their revenge should fall upon this one, for it was he who had begun. The young storks were much enraged, and as they grew bigger the less they could bear it, so that at last their mother was obliged to promise that they should be revenged, but not till the last day of their being in the country.

"We must first see how you get on at the great manoeuvre. If you come off badly, so that the general runs you through with his beak, then the boys are right, at least in one respect. Now let us see how you get one."

"Yes, that you shall," they answered, and took particular pains. They practised so diligently every day, and flew so straight and lightly, that it was a pleasure to look at them.

Now came autumn; and the storks began to meet together, preparatory to migrating to a warmer climate during our winter. Then there was a grand manoeuvre. They had to fly over forests and villages, in order to see how they got on, for it was a serious journey that was before them. The young storks managed so well, that they received a reward of a frog and snake, which they lost no time in eating.

"Now we ought to take our revenge," said they.

"Yes, certainly," said their mother; "and what I have planned is just the very best thing to do. I know where the pond is, in which the children lie till the stork comes and takes them to their parents. The dear little children sleep, and have such delightful dreams as they never have in after-life. All parents are anxious to have such a child, and all children wish to have a brother or a sister. Now, we will fly off to the pond, and fetch a child for each of those that did not sing that naughty song about the storks."

"But what are we to do to him – to that bad, ugly boy who began the song?" cried out the young ones.

"In the pond there lies a dead child, which has dreamed itself to death. That one we will fetch for him, and then he will have to cry, because we have brought him a dead brother; but for the good boy, whom I hope you have not forgotten – the one who said it was wrong to make game of the birds – for him we will fetch a brother and a sister; and as his name is Peter, so shall all storks be called Peter."

What she said was done, and all storks were called Peter, as they are up to this day.

Little Thumb

There was once a woman who had a very strong desire to have a little child of her own, but did not at all know how it was to be managed, and therefore went to an old witch, to whom she said, "I do so heartily desire to have a little, little child; will you not tell me how I am to come by one?"

"Yes, that is easily done," the witch said; "there is a barley-corn, in no way like what the farmers sow, or is given to chickens to eat; set that in a flower-pot, and then you shall see what you shall see."

"I thank you," the woman said, and giving her a shilling, went home, where she set the barley-corn, and immediately there sprang up a magnificent, large flower, which looked like a tulip, but the leaves of the flower were closed, as if it were only in bud.

"That is a pretty flower," the woman said, and kissed the red and yellow leaves, but just as she did so the flower opened with an explosion. It was a real tulip, as now could easily be seen, but seated in the middle of the flower was a quite little girl. She was so pretty and delicate, and not being above the length of one's thumb, she was called Little Thumb.

She had a neat lackered walnut-shell for a cradle, blue violet leaves were her

Little Thumb.

mattress, and a roseleaf her covering. There she slept at nights, but during the day she played on the table, on which the woman placed a plateful of water, with flowers all round the edge, and a lily-leaf floating in the middle. On this Little Thumb could sit and row herself from one side to the other, which looked very pretty. She could sing too, and so sweetly, that the like had never been heard.

One night, as she was lying in her beautiful bed, an ugly toad came hopping through the window, one of the panes of glass being broken. The toad was a big, wet, and frightfully ugly creature, and happened just to hop on to the table on which Little Thumb was asleep, under her roseleaf.

"That would be a charming wife for my son," the toad said, and taking up the walnut-shell in which Little Thumb was lying, hopped with it through the broken window, down into the garden.

There flowed a broad river, the banks of which were muddy and marshy, and it was here the toad lived with her son. Oh, dear! how ugly and disgusting he was too, exactly like his mother. "Koar, koar, croak, croak!" was all that he could say when he saw the pretty little girl in the walnut-shell.

"Do not speak so loud, or she may wake up," the old toad said, "and might escape us, for she is as light as swansdown. We will put her on one of the water-lily leaves out in the river, for, to her, who is so light, that will be just like an island, and from there she cannot get away, whilst we are busy preparing the state-room under the marsh where you are to live."

In the water grew a quantity of water-lilies, with their broad green leaves, which seemed to be floating on the top of the water, and the one which was the furthest out from the banks was also the largest. To this the old toad swam, and placed Little Thumb, with her walnut-shell, upon it.

The little thing awoke early in the morning, and when she saw where she was, she began to cry bitterly, for there was water on all sides of the large green leaf, and there was no reaching the land.

The old toad was busy, down in the marsh, decorating her room with rushes and yellow flowers, for she wanted all to be very smart for her new daughter-in-law; and when she had finished she swam, with her ugly son, out to the leaf, where Little Thumb stood, for she wanted to fetch the pretty bed, to place it in the bridal-chamber. The old toad bowed low to her and said, "Here you see my son, who is to be your husband, and you will live splendidly together, below under the marsh."

"Koar, koar, croak, croak," was all the son could say.

Then they took the pretty little bed and swam away with it, but Little Thumb sat all alone on the green leaf and cried, for she could not bear the idea of living with the disgusting old toad, or of having her ugly son for a husband. The little fish that swam about in the water, had seen the toad and heard all she said, so they popped up their heads to see the little girl, and finding her so pretty, they grieved to think that she should have to live with the ugly toads. "No, that must never be." So they assembled together, round the green stalk of the leaf on which Little Thumb stood, and bit it through, so that the leaf floated down the river, far away, where the toads could not reach it.

Little Thumb floated past many cities, and the little birds, as they sat in the bushes, saw her and sang, "What a lovely little girl!" The leaf swam on with her, further and further, and they got into another country.

A pretty little white butterfly fluttered round her constantly, and at last settled down on the leaf, for Little Thumb pleased him. She was very happy, for the toad could now not reach her, and it was very beautiful all around, the sun shining on the water, so that it glittered like the brightest gold. She now took her girdle, tied one end of it round the butterfly, whilst she fastened the other to the leaf, which glided on much faster, and she as well, for she was standing upon it.

Then came a large cockchafer, and seeing her, instantly caught hold of her slender body with its claws, and flew with her into a tree. The green leaf swam on down the river, and the butterfly too, for it was tied to it and could not get away.

Oh, how frightened poor Little Thumb was when she found herself carried away by the cockchafer, but she felt still more sad, on account of the beautiful white butterfly, which she had fastened to the leaf, for it could not get away and must starve. But the cockchafer did not care a pin about that. He seated himself with her upon the largest leaf of the tree, gave her honey out of the flowers to eat, and said that she was very pretty, though not a bit like a cockchafer. Later, all the other cockchafers that lived in the tree, came to visit her, and the young ladies, turning up their feelers, said, "What can any one see to admire in her! Why, she has only two legs, how ridiculous that looks!" "She has no feelers," another said, "and how small she is in the waist. Oh my! she is like a human being;" "And how ugly she is!" all the young ladies joined in. Now Little Thumb was exceedingly pretty, which the cockchafer that had carried her off knew well enough; but as all the others said she was ugly, he began to believe it himself at last, and would have nothing to do with her, so he carried her down from the tree, and placed her on a daisy. There she sat and cried, because she was so ugly that even the cockchafers would have nothing to do with her, and yet she was the prettiest and most delightful girl that can be imagined, as clear and blooming as the most beautiful roseleaf.

During the whole summer poor Little Thumb lived all alone in a large forest. She plaited herself a bed of grass, and hung it up under a burdock leaf, where she was sheltered from the rain. She ate the honey out of the flowers and drank the dew, that lay every morning upon the leaves. In this manner passed summer and autumn, but now came winter – the cold, long winter. The birds that had sung so sweetly to her flew away; the flowers died and the trees lost their leaves; the large burdock leaf, under which her dwelling was, rolled up, and nothing remained but a yellow, withered stalk, and she was dreadfully cold, for her clothes were worn out, so that she was nearly frozen to death. It began to snow, and each flake that fell upon her was as if a whole shovelful were thrown upon one of us, for she was so little, not more than an inch in height. She wrapped herself up in a dry leaf, but that did not warm her, and she shook with cold.

She wandered out of the forest with difficulty, and came to a cornfield, but the corn had long gone, and only the short dry stubble stood out of the frozen earth, which to her was like another forest. Oh! how she shook with cold. At length she reached the door of the dwelling of a field-mouse. There the mouse lived warm and well, having a whole room full of corn and every comfort. Poor Little Thumb stood inside the door, just like any other poor beggar-girl, and begged for a small piece of a barley-corn, for she had not eaten a morsel of anything for two days.

"You poor little being," the field-mouse said, for at heart she was a good old field-mouse, "come in to my warm room and dine with me."

Now, as Little Thumb pleased her much, she said, "You may remain with me here all the winter, but you must keep my room tidy and clean as well as tell me stories, of which I am very fond;" and Little Thumb did what the good old field-mouse desired, and in return was made uncommonly comfortable.

"We shall now soon have a visitor," the field-mouse said; "my neighbour is in the habit of visiting me once a week. He is still better off than I, has large rooms, and wears the most beautiful black fur coat. If you could only get him for a husband, you would be well provided for, but he cannot see. You must tell him the very prettiest stories that you know."

But Little Thumb was not at all anxious to see the neighbour, for he was a mole.

He came, however, and paid his visit in his black fur coat. The field-mouse said he was so clever and so rich; that his house was more than twenty times larger than hers, and that his learning was very great, but the sun and the beautiful flowers he could not bear, and had little to say of them, for he had never seen them.

Little Thumb had to sing to him, and she sang, "Lady bird, lady bird, fly away home," and, "Sir frog he would a-wooing go," and he fell in love with her on account of her sweet voice, but he said nothing, for he was a very prudent man.

He had lately dug himself a walk underground, from his own house to the field-mouse's, in which she and Little Thumb received permission to walk as much as they liked, but he warned them not to be frightened at the dead bird which lay there, in the walk he had made, for that it was a perfect bird with feathers and beak and all, which could only lately have died and got buried there.

The mole then took a piece of rotten wood in its mouth, for that shines in the dark like fire, and went on in front to light them in the long dark passage. When they came to the place where the dead bird was, the mole, thrusting its broad nose into the roof of the passage, began throwing up the earth till it had worked a large hole, through which the light shone. In the middle of the walk lay a dead swallow, with its beautiful wings pressed close to its sides, and its feet drawn in under the feathers. The poor bird had evidently died of cold. That grieved Little Thumb so much, for she was very fond of all little birds, they having chirped and sung so beautifully to her all the summer; but the mole pushed it on one side with its short legs and said, "We'll sing no more; how miserable it must be to be born a bird! Thank goodness that will not happen to any of my children. What has a bird but its twittering and chirping, and in winter it dies of hunger?"

"Yes, a sensible man like you may well say so," the field-mouse said; "what does a bird get by all its twittering when the winter comes? It must die of cold and hunger; and yet how proud they are!"

Little Thumb said nothing, but as soon as the other two had turned their backs upon the bird, she bent down, and dividing the feathers that covered the head, kissed it on the closed eyes.

"Perhaps it was he who sang so beautifully to me in the summer," she thought. "What pleasure has he not caused me, the dear, beautiful bird!"

The mole now filled up the hole which let in the light, and accompanied the two ladies home. But that night Little Thumb could not sleep, so, getting up, she plaited a beautiful large mat with hay, which she carried with her, and covered up the bird, laying some soft wool, which she had found in the mouse's room, at both its sides so that it might lie warm in the cold earth.

"Farewell, you beautiful little bird," she said; "farewell, and many thanks for the delightful songs during the summer, when the trees were green, and the sun shone warm, down upon us." She then laid her head upon the bird's breast, but was frightened, for it was just as if there were some noise within. It was the bird's heart beating, for he was not dead, but only benumbed by the cold, and being now warmed, had come to life again.

In autumn all the swallows fly away to warmer countries; but if one remains by chance till it is too cold, it falls down like dead, and lies there, where it fell, till the cold snow covers it.

Little Thumb trembled violently, she had been so frightened, for the bird was big, very big compared to her, who was only an inch in height, but she mustered courage, and laid the wool still closer to the bird's sides, fetching, besides, the mint-leaf, which had served her as a bed-covering, and laid it over the bird's head.

The next night she stole away to him again, and found him quite alive, but very weak, so that he could only for a moment open his eyes, and look at Little Thumb, who stood before him with a piece of rotten wood in her hand, for that was the only lantern she had.

"I thank you, my pretty little girl," the invalid said; "you have warmed me so nicely, that I shall soon get my strength back, and shall then be able to fly about again, outside in the warm sunshine."

"Alas!" she said, "it is very cold, it snows and freezes; so you must still remain in your warm bed, and I will nurse you."

She then brought some water in the leaf of a flower, and the swallow drank and told her how it had wounded one of its wings in a thorn-bush, so that it could not fly so well as the others, which had gone off to a warmer country, and that at last it had fallen to the ground, when it could remember no more, and did not know at all how it had got there, or where it was.

The whole winter the swallow remained under ground, and Little Thumb attended to it with the utmost care, without the mole or the field-mouse knowing anything about it, for they could not bear the swallow.

As soon as spring came and warmed the earth, the swallow said farewell to Little Thumb, who opened the hole, which the mole had made above. The sun shone so beautifully down upon them, and the swallow asked, "Will you not go with me, for you can sit on my back, and we will fly far away into the green woods?" But Little Thumb knew that the old field-mouse would feel much hurt if she left in that manner, so she said:-

"No, I cannot go with you."

"Farewell, then, farewell, you good, charming girl," the swallow said, and flew out into the sunshine. Little Thumb looked after it, and the tears came into her eyes, for she was very fond of the swallow.

"Quiwit, quiwit," the bird sang, as it flew away into the wood, and Little Thumb was very sorrowful. The poor little thing could get no permission to go out at all into the warm sunshine, though all was so beautiful; and the corn, which grew over the field-mouse's house, had shot up so high, that it was quite like a forest of tall trees to her who was only an inch high.

"Now, in the summer you must work at your wedding outfit," the field-mouse said to her, for their neighbour, the tedious old mole, with the black fur coat, had proposed to her. "You must have a good stock of woollen, as well as linen clothes, for there must not be anything wanting when you are the mole's wife."

Little Thumb had to work at her spindle, and the field-mouse hired four spiders as well to spin and weave day and night for her. Every evening the mole visited her, and his constant theme was that, when the summer should be over, the sun, which now baked the earth as hard as a stone, would not be nearly so hot, and that then they would be married. The prospect of this did not afford Little Thumb much pleasure, for she could not bear the tedious mole. Each morning, when the sun rose, and each evening when it set, she stole out, outside the door; and when the wind separated the ears of corn so that she could see the blue sky, she thought how light and beautiful it was out there, and wished with all her heart that she could see the dear swallow again; but it did not come back, and was, no doubt, far away in the beautiful green wood.

When autumn came, Little Thumb's wedding outfit was all ready.

"In four weeks time your wedding will take place," the field-mouse said to her. But Little Thumb cried, and said, that she would not have the tedious mole.

"Fiddlededee," the old mouse said. "Don't be perverse, or I'll bite you with my white teeth. Your future husband is a handsome man, and the queen herself has not such a fur coat. His kitchen and cellar are well stored, so bless your stars that you make such a match."

The time for the wedding had now come. The mole had arrived to fetch away Little Thumb to live with him deep under ground, and never to come up to the warm sunshine, which he was not at all fond of. The poor child was very sad, for she was now to bid the beautiful sun good-bye, which she had had permission to look at, from the door at any rate, whilst living with the field-mouse.

"Farewell, you bright sun!" she said, raising up her hand towards it, and she went a few steps outside the door, for the corn was harvested, and there was now only the dry stubble. "Farewell! farewell!" she again said and flung her arms round a little red flower which stood there. "Remember me to the little swallow, when you happen to see it."

"Quiwit, quiwit!" it sounded at that moment from above, and when she looked up she saw the little swallow just flying over her head. When it perceived Little Thumb, it was much rejoiced: and she told her story, how unwillingly she was about to marry the ugly mole, when she would have to live under ground, where the sun never shone, and she could not help crying.

"The cold winter is now coming," the swallow said, "and I am about to fly off to a warmer country. Will you go with me? You can sit on my back; only tie yourself fast with your girdle, and we will fly away from the ugly mole and his dark room, far, far away to a warmer country, where the sun shines more brightly than here; where it is always summer, and there are the most beautiful flowers. Come with me, you dear little girl, you who saved my life, when I lay frozen and buried."

"Yes, I will go with you," Little Thumb said, and seating herself on the bird's back, she tied herself fast with her girdle to one of the strongest feathers, when the swallow flew up high into the air, over forests and seas; high up over mountains that are always covered with snow, and she shivered in the cold air, but she crept under the bird's warm feathers, only having her head out, that she might admire the wonders and beauties below.

They at length reached a warmer country, where the sun shines much more brightly than here, where the sky is twice as deep a blue, and where the most beautiful grapes grow in the hedges. There were forests of orange and citron trees, and the air was sweet with the scent of myrtles and mint, whilst on the roads there were charming children, playing with the most beautifully painted butterflies. The swallow, however, flew on still further, and it grew more beautiful and more beautiful, till they came to a delightful blue lake, where there stood a marble palace, from olden times surrounded by sweet-scented trees. The vine wound round the high columns, and at the top there were many swallows' nests, one of which belonged to Little Thumb's companion.

"This is my house," the swallow said; "but if you choose yourself one of the most beautiful of the flowers that grow there below, I will place you in it, and you may be as happy as the day is long."

"That will be delightful," she cried, and clapped her little hands with joy.

There lay a large white marble column, which had fallen to the ground and broken into three pieces, and from between these grew up the most beautiful large white flowers. The swallow flew down with Little Thumb, and placed her upon a broad leaf of one of these; but how astonished she was, when in the flower she saw a little man sitting, so white and transparent, as if he were of glass. He wore a beautiful gold crown upon his head, and had the most lovely gauzy wings, being scarcely bigger in body than Little Thumb herself. This was the Spirit of the Flowers. In each flower there lived a like little man or woman, but this was the king of them all.

"Oh, how beautiful he is!" Little Thumb whispered to the swallow.

The little Prince was greatly frightened at the swallow, for compared to him, it was a monstrous bird; but, when he saw Little Thumb, he was as much rejoiced, for she was the most beautiful girl he had ever seen. He took off his crown, and placed it upon her head, asking at the same time, what her name was, and if she would marry him, when she should be queen over all the flowers? This was, indeed, a very different being to the toad's son and the mole with his fur coat; so she answered "Yes" to the delightful Prince; and immediately there came a little man or woman from the different flowers, all so charming, that it was quite a pleasure to look at them, and each brought her a present, the best of which was a beautiful pair of wings, taken from a large white fly. These were fastened to her shoulders, so that now she could fly from flower to flower; and all was happiness. The little swallow sat above in its nest, and sang its best to them, but at heart it was sad, for it loved Little Thumb, and wished never to be parted from her.

"You shall not be called Little Thumb," the king of the flowers said, "for that is an ugly name, and you are so beautiful. Your name shall be Maga."

"Farewell, farewell!" the little swallow said, and flew away from the wam country again back to Denmark. There it had a nest, above the window of the man who tells stories, and there it sang, "Quiwit, quitwit!", and that is how we know the whole story.

The angel.

The Angel

"Whenever a good child dies, an angel comes down from heaven, takes the dead child in its arms, and, spreading out its large white wings, visits all the places that had been particularly dear to the child, where it gathers a handful of flowers, flying up again to heaven with them, and there they bloom more beautifully than on earth; but that flower which it loves most receives a voice, so that it can join in the universal chorus of thanksgiving and praise."

Thus spoke an angel whilst carrying a dead child up to heaven; and the child listened as in a dream; and they visited the places that had been most dear to the child whilst alive, and where it had played, passing through gardens full of the most beautiful flowers.

"Which flowers shall we take with us to plant in heaven?" the angel asked.

Now there stood a solitary rose-tree of extraordinary beauty, but a mischievous hand had wantonly broken the stem, so that all the branches, recently of such a beautiful green, laden with half-opened buds, hung down, withered and sad, upon the mossy turf below.

"Oh, that dear little tree!" the child sighed. "Pray take that with you, so that in heaven it may again come to life."

The angel took it, kissing the child at the same time, and the little thing half opened its eyes. They gathered of the beautiful plants, the perfume and colours of which delight mankind; but the despised buttercup, and the wild pansy, they also took with them.

"Now we have flowers," the child said; and the angel nodded. But still they did not fly up to heaven. It was night, and all was quiet; but yet they remained in the large town, hovering over one of the narrowest streets, where there were heaps of straw, ashes, and all manner of rubbish, for it was quarter-day, when many people change their lodgings. There lay broken plates, pieces of plaster, the crowns of old hats, and rags of all sorts – in short, a mass of things in no way pleasing to the eye.

The angel pointed down amongst all this rubbish to some pieces of a broken flower-pot, and a lump of earth which had fallen out of it, held together by the roots of a large dried-up wild-flower, which had been thrown into the street as useless.

"That we will take with us," the angel said, "I will tell you why as we fly on."

And the angel spoke thus:-

"There below, in that narrow street, in a cellar, lived a poor, sick boy, who from his earliest years had been bed-ridden. When at his best, he could manage to walk round the little room a couple of times on his crutches, and that was all. On some few days during the summer, the sun's rays shone upon the floor of the cellar for half an hour; and when the poor boy sat there warming himself in the sun, and wondering at the red blood which he saw through his thin fingers as he held them up to his face, it was said, 'To-day he has been out.' He only knew of the green forest by the son of a neighbour bringing him the first branch of a beech-tree that was out in leaf, which he held over his head, fancying that he was in the forest under the beech-trees, with the sun shining and birds singing. One day in spring the neighbour's son brought him some wild flowers, amongst which there happened to be one that had its roots, and it was therefore set in a pot and placed near his bed. The flower flourished, sending forth new shoots, and blossomed every year, so that it became the sick boy's flower-garden, his greatest comfort and treasure here on earth. He watered and watched it, taking care that it had even the last ray of the sun which glided through the low window. The flower became identified with his dreams, for it was for him alone it blossomed, delighting him by its scent and its beautiful colours, and to it he turned in death. It is now a year he has been in heaven, and for a year the flower has stood, forgotten and dried-up in the window, till, during the moving, it was thrown out into the street. And that is the flower, the poor withered flower, which we have placed in our nosegay, for it has given more pleasure than the most beautiful flower in the garden of a queen."

"And how do you know all this?" the child asked.

"I know it," the angel answered, "because I myself was that poor sick boy who walked on crutches. I know my flower well."

The child now thoroughly opened its eyes, and looked up into the angel's beautiful face, which beamed with happiness, and at the same moment they were in heaven, where joy and bliss reigned. The dead child received wings like the other angel, with whom he flew about, hand in hand. The flowers received renewed life; but the poor withered wild-flower received a voice, and sang with the angels, with whom the whole space of the heavens was filled, in circles, one row behind the other, further and further back, and so on to infinity, all being equally happy.

All sang praises and thanksgivings – the child just received into heaven, and the poor wild-flower, which had been thrown out amongst the rubbish in the narrow, dark street.

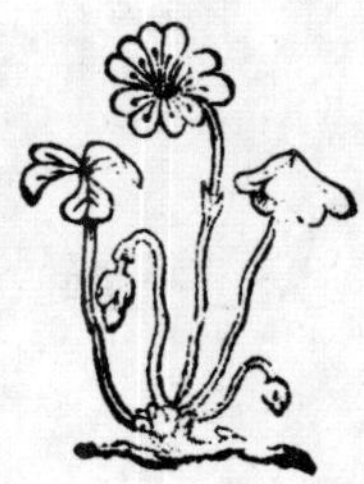

Little Ida's Flowers

"My poor flowers are quite withered," little Ida said. "They were so beautiful yesterday evening, and now the leaves are all dead. What is the reason?" she asked the student, who was sitting on the sofa, for she was very fond of him, as he told her all manner of pretty stories and cut out the most amusing pictures for her – hearts with little ladies dancing inside; flowers, and castles of which the doors opened. He was a lively young man. "Why do the flowers look so wretched to-day?" she asked again, showing him a nosegay, which was quite dead.

"Why, don't you know what's the matter with them?" the student said. "The flowers were at a ball last night, and that's why they hang their heads."

"But how can that be, for the flowers cannot dance," little Ida said.

"And why not?" the student answered. "As soon as it gets dark, and we are all asleep, they jump about merrily enough; almost every night they have a dance.

"Are there no children at the balls?"

"Oh yes," the student said; "there are quite little daisies and May-blossoms."

"And where do the most beautiful flowers dance?" little Ida asked.

"Have you not often been outside the city gates, to the palace, where the king lives in summer and where there is the beautiful garden with such quantities of flowers?

Little Ida's flowers.

You know the swans which swim up to you when you feed them with bread-crumbs. Depend upon it, there are large balls there."

"I was in the garden yesterday with my mother," Ida said, "but all the leaves were off the trees, and there were no flowers whatever. Where are they all? In summer I saw such quantities."

"They are inside the palace," the student said. "You must know that as soon as the king and all the courtiers move into the town, the flowers run off, at once, out of the garden into the palace, and there make merry. You should see that. The two most beautiful of the roses seat themselves upon the throne, and they are then king and queen. The red cockscombs stand bowing on either side, and they are the pages. Then come the prettiest flowers, which represent the maids of honour, and there is a grand ball. The blue violets are midshipmen, and they dance with hyacinths and crocuses, whom they call milady. The tulips and the great tiger-lilies are old ladies who watch that the dancing is good, and that all goes on with propriety."

"And does no one interfere with the flowers going into the palace?" little Ida asked.

"No one knows really anything about it," the student said. "It's true that sometimes the old steward, who has to see that all is right, comes in of an evening, but no sooner do the flowers hear the jingling of his big bunch of keys than they are quite quiet, and hide themselves behind the curtains. 'I smell that there are flowers here,' he says, but he cannot see them."

"Oh, what fun that is!" little Ida said, clapping her hands. "And should I not be able to see the flowers either?"

"Yes," the student answered, "and remember the next time you go out there, that you look through the window, and you will see them plainly enough. I did so to-day, and there lay a long yellow lily stretched upon the sofa. That was one of the ladies in waiting."

"And are the flowers from the botanical garden there? Can they get as far?"

"To be sure they can," the student answered, "for if necessary they can fly. Have you not noticed many beautiful butterflies, red, yellow, and white, that look almost like flowers, which indeed they have been? They have broken off from their stems, flying up in the air, beating about with their leaves as if they were wings; and as they behaved well, they received permission to fly about, and not be obliged to sit quietly fastened down to their stems, till at length the leaves became real wings. All this you may have seen yourself. However, it may be that the flowers from the botanical garden have never been in the king's palace, or even that they do not know what sport goes on there at nights. And now I'll tell you something, how you can astonish the professor of botany, who lives here close by. You know him, do you not? When next you go into his garden, you must tell one of the flowers that there is dancing at the palace every night. That one will tell the others, and away they'll fly. Then when the professor goes into the garden, he will not find a single flower, and he will be nicely puzzled to think what has become of them all."

"But how can the flower tell the others? For flowers cannot speak."

"That is true enough," the student said, "but then they make signs. Have you not often noticed that when the wind blows a little, the flowers bend down, and all the green leaves move? That is as plain as if they spoke."

"And can the professor understand them?"

"Certainly he can. One morning he went into the garden and saw a stinging nettle making signs to a red carnation, which signs meant: You are very pretty and I love you. Now the professor cannot hear anything of that sort, so he gave the stinging nettle a slap on its leaves, for those are its fingers, but he stung himself, and since then he has not ventured to touch a stinging nettle."

"Oh, what fun!" little Ida said, and laughed out loud.

"How can any one talk such nonsense to a child!" the tedious chancery counsellor said, who, having called to pay a visit, was sitting on the sofa. He did not much like the student, and always began to growl when he saw him cutting out the funny pictures: first it was a man hanging on the gallows with a heart in his hand, for he was a robber of hearts, and then an old witch riding on a broom and carrying her husband on her nose. That sort of thing annoyed the counsellor, and he would then say, "How can any one put such foolish notions into a child's head!"

But what the student told little Ida about her flowers, appeared very funny to her, and she thought much of it. The flowers hung their heads, because they were tired, after dancing all the night, and no doubt they felt ill. Then she carried them to her other playthings, which were on a nice little table, the drawer of which, also, was full of pretty things. In the doll's bed lay the doll Sophy, and slept, but little Ida said to her, "You must really get up, Sophy, and be satisfied with passing this night in the drawer, for the poor flowers are ill, and must sleep in your bed, which will perhaps put them right again." She then took the doll out of its bed, and it looked quite fretful, but did not say a word, for it was sulky at having to give up its bed.

Ida laid the flowers in the doll's bed, and covering them up with the clothes, said they must lie quite quiet, and she would make them some tea, so that they might be quite well by the following day and be able to get up; and she then drew the curtains of the little bed, that the sun might not shine in their eyes.

The whole evening she could not helping thinking of what the student had told her; and when it was time for her to go to bed she must needs first look under the curtain that hung at the window, where her mother's beautiful flowers, hyacinths as well as tulips, stood, and she whispered quite low, "I know that you are going to the ball to-night"; but the flowers pretended not to understand her, and did not move a leaf; however, little Ida knew what she knew for all that.

When she was in bed she lay awake a long time thinking how pretty it must be to see all the beautiful flowers dancing in the King's palace. "I wonder whether my flowers were really there?" She then went to sleep, but woke again in the night, having dreamed of the flowers, the student, and the chancery counsellor, who said he was putting foolish fancies into her head. All was quiet in the bedroom where Ida lay;

the night-lamp burned on the table, and her father and mother were asleep.

"I wonder whether my flowers are still lying in Sophy's bed," she thought. "I should much like to know." She raised herself up a little in the bed and looked towards the door, which stood ajar. In the next room lay her flowers and all her playthings, and as she listened it seemed to her as if she heard the piano being played, but quite softly and so beautifully as she had never heard before.

"No doubt all the flowers are now dancing in there," she said. "Oh, dear, how much I should like to see them"; but she could not venture to get up for fear of waking her father and mother.

"If they would but come in here," she said. But the flowers did not come in, and as the music continued playing she could resist no longer, for it was much too pretty; so she crept out of her little bed, gently to the door, and looked into the next room. Oh, how beautiful it was, what she there saw!

There was no night-lamp burning, but yet it was quite light, for the moon was shining through the window right into the middle of the room, and it was almost like day. All the hyacinths and tulips stood in two rows along the room, so that there were none left in the window. The flower-pots stood there empty, whilst the flowers were dancing so prettily on the floor of the room, round each other, forming a regular ladies' chain, and holding each other by the long green leaves as they whirled round. At the piano sat a large yellow lily, which Ida must certainly have seen during the summer, for she remembered quite well that the student had said, "How exactly it is like Miss Line." Every one laughed at him then, but it really seemed to little Ida now, that the long tall yellow flower was indeed like that young lady, and it had the same ways too at the piano. Now it leaned its long yellow face to one side, now to the other, whilst it nodded in time to the beautiful music. Little Ida was not noticed, and she now saw a large blue crocus jump on to the table on which the playthings were, go straight up to the doll's bed, and draw the curtains. There lay the sick flowers, but they got up at once and nodded to the others, as much as to say that they would dance too. The old shepherd, who had lost his under-lip, stood up and bowed to the beautiful flowers, which did not appear at all sick now, for they jumped down to join the others and were as merry as possible.

It sounded as if something fell, and when Ida looked round she saw that it was the little three-legged stool that had jumped down from the table, seeming to think it belonged to the flowers. It was a neat little stool, and on it there sat a little wax doll, with just such another broad-brimmed hat on its head as the chancery counsellor was in the habit of wearing. The stool hopped about on its three legs, stamping heavily, for it was dancing the Mazurka, which the flowers could not dance, for they were too light to stamp.

The wax doll on the stool became, all at once, quite big, and cried out, "How can any one talk such nonsense to a child!" and then it was exactly like the counsellor, looking quite as yellow and fretful. Then it became a little wax doll again, and all this was so droll that Ida could not restrain her laughter. The three-legged stool continued to dance, and the chancery counsellor had to dance with it, whether he would or no, whether he made himself big, or remained the little wax doll with the large black hat. There was now a knocking in the drawer, where Ida's doll, Sophy, was lying with other playthings; and the old shepherd, jumping on to the table, lay flat down, and crept as near as possible to the edge, when he was able to pull the drawer out a little. Then Sophy got up and looked around her, quite astonished. "Why, here is a dance!" she said. "Why did no one tell me that?"

"Will you dance with me?" the shepherd said.

"Oh, yes; you are a pretty fellow to dance," she said, and turned her back upon him. She then seated herself upon the table, expecting that one of the flowers would come and engage her, but none came, and then she coughed "Hem, hem, hem!" but none came for all that. The shepherd danced all by himself, and not so badly either.

Now, as not one of the flowers appeared to see Sophy, she let herself fall from the table on to the floor, with a great noise, which brought all the flowers about her, and they asked her whether she had not hurt herself. They were all so kind and polite to her, particularly those that had lain in her bed. But she had not hurt herself at all, and Ida's flowers thanked her for the beautiful bed, were very attentive to her, and leading her into the middle of the room, where the moon shone, they danced with her. Sophy was delighted, and said they might keep her bed, for she did not at all mind sleeping in the drawer.

But the flowers said, "We thank you from our hearts, but we cannot live so long, for to-morrow we shall be quite dead. Then tell little Ida to bury us where the canary lies, and we shall grow again next summer, when we shall be more beautiful than now."

"No, you must not die," Sophy said, kissing them, and just then a quantity of the most beautiful flowers came dancing in through the door. Ida could not at all imagine where they came from, unless from the King's palace. In front were two beautiful roses, wearing little crowns of gold; these were the king and queen. Then followed the prettiest gilli-flowers and pinks, bowing on all sides. They had music of their own, large poppies and peonies blowing away on pea-shells till they were quite red in the face. The snowdrops and bluebells were ringing, exactly as if they had metal bells, so that altogether it was most extraordinary music. Then came quantities of other flowers, the blue violets and the red amaranths, daisies and Mayflowers, and all danced together, and kissed each other, that it was delightful to look at them.

At length all the flowers wished each other good-night, and then little Ida crept back to her bed, where she dreamed of all she had seen.

As soon as she got up the next morning she went to the little table to see whether the flowers were still there. She drew aside the curtains of the little bed, and yes, there they lay, but quite withered, a great deal more so than the day before. Sophy was lying in the drawer, where she had laid her, and she looked very sleepy.

"Do you remember what you were to tell me?" Ida asked, but Sophy looked quite stupid, and did not answer one single word.

"You are not at all good," Ida said, "when all of them danced with you too." She then took a little paper box, on which the most beautiful birds were painted, and having opened it, laid the dead flowers in it. "That shall be your pretty coffin," she said; "and when my cousins come, they shall help me to bury you in the garden, so that you may grow again next summer, and be more beautiful than ever."

The two cousins were two lively boys whose names were John and Adolphus. Their father had given each of them a crossbow, which they had brought with them to show Ida. She told them of the poor flowers which had died the day before, and invited them to be present at the funeral. The two boys walked on in front, with their crossbows on their shoulders, and little Ida followed with the dead flowers in the pretty box. They dug a small grave in the garden, and Ida, first having kissed the flowers, placed them with the box in the earth, and the cousins fired their crossbows over the grave, for they had neither guns nor cannon.

All the other cockchafers that lived in the tree came to visit her. (Little Thumb.)

"But he has nothing on," said at length a little child.
(The Emperor's New Clothes.)

The tinder-box.

The Tinder-box

A soldier came marching along the highroad – one, two! one, two! He had his knapsack at his back and his sword at his side, for he had been in the wars, and was now going home.

He fell in with an old witch on the road – oh, she was so frightful, for her underlip hung down right upon her breast! "Good day, soldier," she said; "what a beautiful sword and large knapsack you have! You are a real soldier, and shall have as much money as you can possibly wish for."

"Thank you, old witch!" the soldier said.

"Do you see that large tree there?" the witch said, pointing to one which stood by the side of the road. "It is quite hollow, and if you climb to the top you will see a hole, through which you can let yourself down, right to the bottom of it. I will tie a rope around your body, so as to pull you up when you call to me."

"And what am I to do down there, inside the tree?" the soldier asked.

"Fetch money," the witch said. "For you must know, that when you reach the bottom of the tree, you will find yourself in a large hall lighted by more than a hundred lamps. Then you will see three doors which you can open, for the keys are in the locks. If you go into the first room, you will see, in the middle of the floor, a large box on which a dog is seated; it has eyes like big teacups, but you need not mind it. I will give you my blue check apron, which you must spread out upon the floor, then walk straight up to the dog, lay hold of it and place it upon my apron; then you can take out as many pennies as you like. It is all copper money; but if you would rather have silver, you must go into the next room. There sits a dog with eyes as large as the wheels of a water-mill, but do not let that trouble you, for if you place it on my apron, you can take the money. If, however, you prefer gold, you can have that too, and as much of it as you like to carry, by going into the third room. But the dog that is seated on the money-box has two eyes, each one as big as the Round Tower of Copenhagen. That is a dog! But never mind him, only put him upon my apron, and he will not hurt you, and you can take as much gold out of the box as you like."

"That is not so bad," the soldier said; "but what must I give you, you old witch, for of course you want something?"

"No," the witch said, "not a single penny do I want. For me you need only bring an old tinder-box, which my grandmother forgot the last time she was in there."

"Well, then, tie the rope round me at once," the soldier said.

"Here it is," the witch said; "and here, too, is my blue check apron."

Then the soldier climbed up the tree, let himself slip down through the hole, and found himself, as the witch had said, down below, in the large hall where the many hundred lamps were burning.

Now he opened the first door, and, sure enough, there sat the dog with eyes like big cups, staring at him.

"Well, you are a pretty fellow," the soldier said, placed him upon the apron, and filled his pockets with pence, after which he locked the box, and having put the dog back upon it, went into the next room, where he found the dog with eyes like mill-wheels.

"Now, you shouldn't look at me in that way, for it may strain your eyes and injure your sight," the soldier said. He then seated the dog upon the apron; and no sooner did he see all the silver in the box, than he threw away the copper money he had, and filled his pockets and knapsack with the more valuable metal. He then went into the third room, and it was an ugly beast he saw there. The dog's eyes were, indeed, as large as the Round Tower, and kept turning round in its head exactly like mill-wheels.

"Good-day to you," the soldier said, touching his cap, for such a dog he had never seen in all his life, but after examining him for a time, he thought that was enough, so he took him down and opened the box. Good gracious! What a quantity of gold was there! With that he could buy the whole of Copenhagen, and all the gingerbread horses, all the tin soldiers, whips, and rocking-horses in the whole world. There was a quantity of gold! He now threw out all the silver with which he had filled his pockets and knapsack, and replaced it by gold. Yes, his pockets, the knapsack, his cap, and even his boots, were filled with it, so that he could scarcely walk. He was now rich, so he put the dog back on the box, shut the door, and called out to the old witch:-

"Now pull me up."

"And have you got the tinder-box?" the old witch asked.

"Well to be sure, that I had clean forgotten," the soldier said, so he went back and fetched it. The witch pulled him up, and there he stood again on the highroad, but with his pockets, his knapsack, cap, and boots filled with gold.

"And what do you intend to do with the tinder-box?" he asked.

"That is no business of yours," the witch said. "You have got your gold, so give me my tinder-box."

"What does this mean?" the soldier cried; "tell me at once what you want to do with the tinder-box, or I'll draw my sword and cut off your head."

"No," the witch said.

So the soldier cut off her head, and there she lay. But he tied up all his gold in her apron, slung it across his shoulder, and thrusting the tinder-box into his pocket, walked on, straight to the town.

That was a beautiful town, and he turned into the very grandest hotel, where he took the best rooms, and ordered his favourite dishes, for he was rich now that he had so much money.

It certainly struck the servant, as he cleaned his boots, that they were most wretched things to belong to so rich a gentleman, for he had not yet bought any new ones, but the next day he got good boots and fine clothes. Now the soldier had become a gentleman of rank, and he was told of all the wonders that were to be seen in the town, of the King, and what a pretty princess his daughter was.

"How can one get to see her?" the soldier asked.

"She is not to be seen at all," they all said, "for she lives in a brass castle surrounded by many walls and towers. No one but the King himself can go in and out there, it having been prophesied that she will be married to a common soldier, to which the King cannot consent."

"I should like to see her," the soldier thought, but nohow could he gain permission to do so.

Now he led a merry life, visited the theatre, drove about in the King's garden, and gave a great deal of money to the poor, which was very good of him; but he recollected from former times, how miserable it is not to possess a penny. He was now rich, had beautiful clothes and many friends, who all said that he was a first-rate fellow and a real gentleman, which the soldier liked to hear. But as he spent money every day and never received any, it happened after a while that he only had a shilling left; so he was obliged to give up his splendid rooms, where he had lived, and go into a small garret under the tiles, and clean and mend his own boots; and no more of his friends came to see him, for there were so many stairs to mount.

It had grown quite dark and he could not even buy a candle, but then he bethought himself that there was a small taper in the tinder-box which he had got out of the hollow tree. He got the flint and steel out of the box, and no sooner had he struck a few sparks, than the dog, which had eyes as big as a tea-cup and which he had seen in the tree, stood before him, and said, "What are your commands, sir?"

"How is this?" he said. "That is a good sort of tinder-box, if I can so easily get all I want by means of it. Procure me some money," he said to the dog. In an instant it was gone, and almost at the same moment was back again, with a purse of money in its jaws.

Now the soldier knew what a valuable tinder-box it was. If he struck the flint once, the dog that sat on the box containing the copper money appeared; if twice, that which had care of the silver; and if three times, there came the dog that guarded the gold. The soldier now moved back to his splendid rooms, and reappeared in fine clothes, when all his friends immediately recognised him again, and made much of him.

It occurred to him once, that it was something very extraordinary there was no seeing the Princess. By all accounts it appeared she was very beautiful, but what was the good of that if she was always to be shut up in the brazen castle with the many towers? "Cannot I get to see her anyhow?" he said; "where is my tinder-box?" He struck fire, and on the instant the dog with eyes like a tea-cup appeared.

"It is true it is the middle of the night," the soldier said, "but I should so very much like to see the Princess, only for a moment."

The dog was gone in an instant, and before the soldier thought it possible, was back again with the Princess. She was lying asleep on its back, and so lovely, that every one could see at once she was a real princess. The soldier could not possibly resist kissing her, for he was a true soldier.

Then the dog ran back with the Princess, but the next morning, when the King and Queen were taking their breakfast with her, she said she had had a most extraordinary dream of a dog and a soldier. That she had ridden on the dog, and the soldier had kissed her.

"That is a pretty story indeed!" the Queen said.

It was now settled, that the next night one of the old ladies of the court should sit up by the Princess's bed-side, in order to see whether it was really a dream, or how it might be.

The soldier had an irresistible desire to see the Princess again, so the dog came in the night, took her up, and ran off as fast as possible, but the old lady immediately put on a pair of magic boots and followed quite as quickly, and when she saw that they disappeared in to a large house, she thought, "Now I'll know where it is." So she made a large cross on the door with a piece of chalk. She then went home to bed, and the dog returned with the Princess. But the dog had seen that a cross was chalked on the door of the house where the soldier lived, so he took a piece of chalk too, and made a cross on all the doors of the town, which was cleverly done, for now the old lady could not find the proper door, as there were crosses on them all.

Early the next morning, the King and Queen, the old lady and all the officers of the court, came to see where the Princess had been.

"Here it is," the king said when he saw the first door with the cross upon it.

"No, there it is, my dear husband," the Queen said, seeing the second door with the cross.

"But here is one, and there is one," they all said, for whichever way they looked, there was a cross on the doors, so they saw well that their looking would be of no avail.

The Queen, however, was a very clever woman, and could do more things than drive in her carriage, so she took her large golden scissors, cut up a large piece of silk, and made a pretty little bag, which she filled with buckwheat meal, and tied it round the Princess's neck. When this was done, she cut a small hole in the bag, so that the meal falling out would strew the road the whole way the Princess might take.

In the night the dog came again, took the Princess on his back, and carried her to the soldier, who loved her dearly, and wished so much he were a prince that he might marry her.

The dog did not notice how the meal strewed the whole of the way, from the castle to the soldier's window, where he ran up the wall with the Princess. The following morning the King and Queen saw plainly where their daughter had been, so they had the soldier taken and put in prison.

There he was, and oh! how dark and frightful it was there, nor was it cheering when he was told, "To-morrow you are to be hanged." It was not pleasant to hear, and his tinder-box he had left behind him at the hotel. In the morning he could see, through the bars of his prison window, how the people were hurrying to the place of execution to see him hanged. He heard the drum, and saw the soldiers marching. All were running to get out of the town in time, and amongst the rest was a shoemaker's boy with his apron on, and in slippers, one of which flew off as he ran along, right against the wall where the soldier was looking out through the prison window.

"Here, you shoemaker's boy," the soldier said to him, "you need not hurry so, for there will be nothing to see till I come; but if you will run to where I lived, and fetch me my tinder-box, you shall have a shilling. But you must make good use of your legs." The boy was willing enough to earn the shilling, so he ran and fetched the tinder-box, which he gave the soldier, and – yes, now it comes!

Outside the town a high gallows was erected, and all round it stood soldiers, besides several hundred thousand people. The King and Queen sat upon a beautiful throne, and opposite to them sat the judges and all the council.

The soldier stood already on the top of the ladder, but when they were about to put the rope around his neck, he said that the condemned were always granted any innocent desire before undergoing their punishment. He wished so much to smoke one pipe of tobacco, the last he should get in this world.

This the King did not like to refuse, so the soldier took out his tinder-box and struck fire. One – two – three, and immediately the three dogs stood before him, the one with eyes like a tea-cup, that with eyes like a mill-wheel, and the one with eyes like the Round Tower of Copenhagen.

"Help me now, that I may not be hanged," the soldier said; and the dogs fell at once upon the judges and the council, catching one by the legs and another by the nose, and threw them up so high in the air, that when they fell down they were all smashed to pieces.

"You must not touch me," the King said, but the biggest of the dogs caught hold of him as well as the Queen, and threw them after the others. Then the soldiers were frightened, and all the people cried, "Good soldier, you shall be our king, and marry the beautiful Princess."

They then seated him in the King's carriage, and the dogs sprang on in front, crying, "Hurrah!" The boys whistled with their fingers, and the soldiers presented arms. The Princess came out of the brazen tower, and was elected Queen, which pleased her well enough. The marriage-feast lasted a whole week, and the dogs sat at table with the others, making eyes at those around them.

The princess on the bean.

The Princess on the Bean

There was once a Prince who wished to marry a Princess, but it must be a real Princess. So he travelled about the whole world to find such a one, but everywhere there was something in the way. Princesses there were plenty, but whether they were real Princesses he could not satisfy himself, for there was always something that did not seem quite right. He therefore came home again and was quite sad, for he wished so very much to have a real Princess.

One night a terrific storm came on; it thundered and lightened, and the rain poured down, so that it was quite dreadful. There was then a knocking at the gate of the town, and the old King went to open it.

It was a Princess who stood outside at the gate. And, good heavens! what a state she was in. The water ran down from her hair and her clothes, in at the toes of her shoes and out at the heels, but she said she was a real Princess.

"Well, that we'll soon find out," the old Queen thought. She said however nothing, but went into the bed-room, and having taken all the things off the bed, laid a small bean upon the slabs, upon which she heaped twenty mattresses, and then twenty eider-down beds upon the mattresses.

There the Princess was to lie that night.

In the morning she was asked how she had slept.

"Oh, abominably badly!" she answered. "I have scarcely closed my eyes the whole night. Heaven knows what there may have been in the bed! But I lay upon something hard, so that I am black and blue all over my body. It is quite dreadful."

It was evident, then, that she was a real Princess, since she had felt the bean through the twenty mattresses and the twenty eider-down beds. No one could have so very fine a sense of feeling but a real Princess.

So the Prince married her, for he knew that now he had a real Princess; and the bean was placed in the royal museum, where it may still be seen if no one has taken it away.

Now, this is a true story.

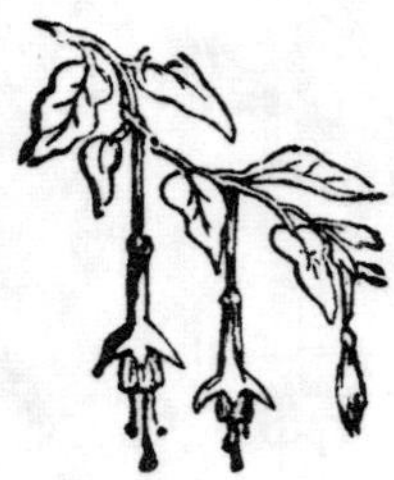

The Emperor's new clothes.

The Emperor's New Clothes

Many years ago there lived an Emperor who was so excessively fond of new clothes, that he spent all his money in order to be well dressed. He did not care about his soldiers, nor did he care for the theatre, neither was he fond of driving out, excepting for the sake of showing his new clothes. He had a different coat for every hour of the day, and just as one says of a King, he is in the council, so it was here always said, "The Emperor is in his dressing-room."

In the large city where he lived, it was very gay, for every day fresh visitors arrived; and one day there came amongst others two impostors, who pretended to be weavers, and that they had the secret of weaving the most beautiful fabrics that could be imagined. Not only were the colours and designs pretended to be uncommonly beautiful, but that the fabric possessed the wonderful peculiarity of being invisible to every one who was either unfit for his situation, or unpardonably stupid.

"Clothes made of that material would be inestimable," the Emperor thought. "If I had such on, I could discover which men in my empire are unfit for the offices they hold, and could at once distinguish the clever from the stupid. That stuff must be at once woven for me." So he gave an order to the two imposters, and a large sum of money, in order that they might begin their work at once.

They set up two looms, and did as if they were working, but there was nothing at all on the looms. Straightway they required the finest silk, and the most beautiful gold thread to work into their stuffs, which they put into their pockets, and worked away at the bare looms till late at night.

"I should like to know how they have got on with the stuff," the Emperor thought; but at the same time he was greatly embarrassed when he thought of it, that he who was stupid or ill-fitted for his situation, could not see it. Now, he had no doubts about himself, but yet he thought it as well, first to send some one else, to see how it was getting on. Every one in the city knew the peculiarity of the fabric, and every one was anxious to see how unfit for his situation, or how stupid his neighbour was.

"I will send my old, honest minister to the weavers," the Emperor thought. "He will be best able to judge how the fabric succeeds, for he has sense, and no one is better fitted for his office than he."

So the good old minister went to the room where the two impostors were working at their bare looms. "Heaven preserve me!" the old minister thought, and he opened his eyes wide. "Why, I cannot see anything." But that he did not say.

Both impostors begged of him to step nearer, and they asked whether he did not think the design pretty and the colours beautiful? They then pointed to the bare loom, and the poor old minister opened his eyes still wider, but yet he could see nothing, for there was not anything to see. "Can it be possible," he thought, "that I am stupid? That I would never have believed, and no one must know it. Or is it that I am not fit for my office? It will never do to tell that I cannot see the stuff!"

"Well, you say nothing to our work," one of the weavers said.

"Oh, it is very pretty! quite beautiful!" the old minister said, looking through his spectacles. "The design and the colours – Yes, I shall not fail to tell the Emperor that it pleases me very much."

"We are delighted to hear it," both the weavers said; and then they mentioned all the different colours, and explained the curious design. The old minister paid great attention, that he might use the same words when he returned to the Emperor; and he did so.

The impostors now applied for more money, more silk, and more gold, to be used in their weaving, which they put in their pockets, for not a single thread was put upon the looms, though they continued their pretended work as heretofore.

The Emperor soon after sent another able statesman to see how the weaving got on, and whether the stuff would soon be ready. With him it was exactly as with the other; he looked and looked, but as there was nothing besides the bare loom, he could see nothing.

"Well is not that beautiful stuff?" the two impostors asked; and they explained the magnificent design which did not exist.

"I am not stupid," the man thought, "so it must be my good appointment that I am unfit for. That would be funny enough, but it must never be suspected." So he praised the fabric which he did not see, and assured them he was highly pleased with the beautiful design and colours. "Oh, it is lovely," he said to the Emperor.

Every one in the city spoke of the mangificent fabric.

The Emperor was now desirous of seeing it himself, whilst still on the loom, so with a host of chosen followers, amongst whom were also the two honest statesmen who had been before, he went to the two artful impostors, who now worked away with all their might, though without a fibre or thread.

"Is that not magnificent?" the two honest statesmen asked. "Will not your Majesty look more closely into it and examine the design and beautiful colours?" And they pointed to the bare loom, for they thought that the others could see the fabric.

"How is this?" the Emperor thought. "Why, I see nothing at all, it is quite dreadful. Can it be that I am stupid, or am I not fit to be Emperor? That would be the most dreadful thing that could happen to me. Yes, it is very beautiful!" he said. "It has my highest approbation;" and he nodded with apparent satisfaction at the bare loom, for he would not confess that he did not see anything. All his followers looked and looked, seeing no more than the others, but they said the same as the Emperor, "Yes, it is very beautiful!" and they advised him to wear the clothes of that magificent fabric at the approaching grand procession. "It is delightful, charming, excellent!" passed from mouth to mouth, and all seemed really delighted. The Emperor decreed an order to each of the impostors to wear in their button-holes, with the title of Court weaver.

The whole night before the day on which the procession was to take place, the impostors were up, and had more than twenty lights burning. Every one could see that they were very busy getting the Emperor's new clothes ready. They made appear as if they took the stuff off the loom, cut away in the air with large shears, and sewed with needles without thread, and said at length, "See, now the clothes are ready."

The Emperor himself came with his chief nobility, and both impostors raised one arm, exactly as if they were holding something up, and said, "These are the small-clothes; this is the coat; here is the mantle," and so on; "all as light as a cobweb, that one might think one had nothing on; but just in that consists the beauty."

"Yes," all the nobility said; but they saw nothing, for there was nothing.

"If your Imperial Majesty will please to take off your clothes," the impostors said, "we will put the new ones on for you here, before the looking-glass."

The Emperor took off all his clothes; and the impostors pretended to help him on with one article after another of the new garments; and the Emperor bent and turned his body about before the looking-glass.

"Oh, how becoming they are! How beautifully they fit!" all said. "The pattern and colours are perfect; that is a magnificent costume."

The chief usher said, "The canopy, which is to be carried over your majesty in the procession, is waiting for your majesty without."

"Well, I am ready," the Emperor said. "Do not the things fit well?" And then he turned again to the looking-glass, for he wished to appear as if he were examining his attire carefully.

The pages, who were to carry the train, stooped, and pretended to lay hold of something on the ground, as if they were raising the train, which they pretended to hold up, for they would not have it appear that they could not see anything.

So the Emperor walked in the procession, under the magnificent canopy; and all the people in the street and in the windows said, "The Emperor's clothes are not to be equalled; and what a magnificent train he has!" No one would let it appear that he did not see anything, for if so, he would have been unfit for his situation, or very stupid. No clothes of the Emperor's had ever had so much success as these.

"But he has nothing on," said at length a little child.

"Good heavens! Listen to the innocent thing's voice!" its father said. And one whispered to the other what the child had uttered.

"But he has nothing on!" all the people cried at last.

This perplexed the Emperor, for it appeared to him that they were right; but he said to himself, "Now that I have begun it, I must go on with the procession." And the pages continued to carry the train which had no existence.

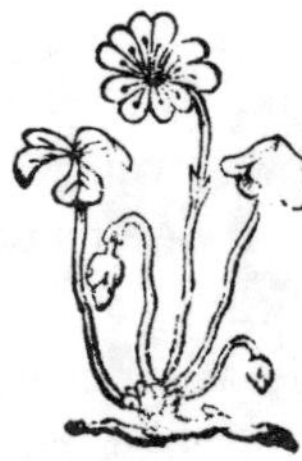

The Little Mermaid.

THE LITTLE MERMAID

Far out in the sea the water is as blue as the most beautiful cornflower, and as transparent as the clearest glass; but it is very deep – deeper than any ship's cable can reach – and many church-spires would have to be placed one on the top of the other to reach from the bottom above the surface of the water. There below live the people of the sea.

Now it must not be imagined that the bottom is merely bare white sand; no, the most curious trees and plants grow there, the stems and leaves of which are so pliant, that the slightest agitation of the water moves them, just as if they were alive. All the fish, large and small, slip through the branches like the birds here, in the air above. In the very deepest part lies the Sea-King's palace, the walls of which are of coral, the long, pointed windows being of the purest amber, and the roof is formed of mussel-shells, that open and shut according to the flowing of the waters, which has a very beautiful appearance, for in each lie glistening pearls, of which either would be the chief ornament in the crown of a queen.

The Sea-King there below had been a widower for many years, and his old mother conducted his household for him. She was a clever woman, but very proud of her birth, on which account she wore twelve oysters on her tail, whereas the highest of the nobles were allowed to wear only six. In other respects she deserved the highest praise, particularly for her great care of her granddaughters. These were six beautiful children. But the youngest was the most beautiful of all; her skin was as clear and smooth as the leaf of a rose, and her eyes as blue as the deepest sea; but, like her sisters, she had no feet, her body ending in the tail of a fish.

The whole day they could play in the large halls of the palace, where living flowers grew out of the walls. When the amber windows were thrown open, the fish swam in, as with us the swallows fly into the room; but the fish swam straight up to the Princesses, eating out of their hands, and allowing themselves to be stroked by them.

In front of the palace was a large garden, with deep red and dark blue trees, the fruit of which shone like gold, and the flowers were like the brightest fire, the stems and leaves being in perpetual movement. The ground was the finest sand, but blue, like the flame of burning sulphur, and, indeed, a peculiar blue tint pervaded everything, so that one would have thought one was high up in the air, with sky above and below, rather than at the bottom of the sea.

During very calm weather the sun could be seen, looking like a purple flower, from the calyx of which streamed all the light.

Each Princess had a little piece of ground in the garden, where she could dig and plant as best pleased her. The one gave her garden the form of a whale, whilst another preferred hers looking like a mermaid; but the youngest made hers round, like the sun, and planted it only with flowers of the same colour as the sun. She was a strange child, quiet and thoughtful; and whilst her sisters delighted in all the beautiful things they got from wrecked vessels, she, besides her flowers that were like the sun, cared only for a beautiful little statue of a boy, of pure white marble, which had fallen down from some vessel to the bottom of the sea. She planted a rose-coloured weeping willow by the side of her statue, which it covered with its branches, hanging down towards the blue sand, where they cast violet shadows, in constant movement like the branches themselves. It had the appearance as if the top of the tree and the roots were playing, and wished to kiss each other.

Nothing gave her so much pleasure as to hear about the world above, and her old grandmother had to tell all she knew of ships, cities, men and beasts; but of all things it seemed to her most delightful that the flowers on the earth had scent, which those of the sea had not; that the woods were green; and that the fish, which were there seen amongst the trees, sang so loud and beautifully that it was a pleasure to listen to them. These were the birds, which the grandmother called fish, for otherwise they would not have understood her, as they had never yet seen a bird.

"When you have reached your fifteenth year," the grandmother said, "you will be allowed to rise up to the top of the sea, where, seated on a rock in the moonlight, you will see the large ships sail past, and also see cities and forests." The following year the eldest sister would be fifteen, and as there was a year's difference in all their ages, the youngest would consequently have five full years to wait before being allowed to come up from the bottom of the sea, and see how all looked with us. But the eldest promised to tell the others what she should see, and find the most beautiful on the first day, for their grandmother did not tell them near enough, and there remained much they wished to know about.

Not one had such a strong desire after this knowledge as the youngest, just the one that had the longest to wait, and who was so quiet and thoughtful. Many a night she stood at the open window watching the fish, how they moved their fins and tails about in the water. She could see the moon and stars, which certainly appeared paler than with us, but through the water they seemed much larger than appears to our eyes; and when anything dark, like a cloud, passed between them and her, she knew that it must be either a whale-fish, or a ship full of human beings, into whose heads it certainly did not enter that a pretty young Mermaid was standing below, raising up her white hands towards them.

The eldest Princess was now fifteen years old, and might rise up to the surface of the sea.

On her return she had a hundred different things to tell, but the most beautiful of all, she said, had been lying on a sandbank in the calm sea, with the moon shining, and looking at a large city on the coast close by, where the lights glittered like hundreds of stars; to hear the music, and the noise made by the men and the conveyances of different sorts; to see the church-spires, and to listen to the ringing of the bells, and she felt the greater longing for all these, just because she could not get there.

Oh! how attentively the youngest sister listened, and as she, later in the evening, stood at the open window looking up through the dark water, she thought of the large city and the noise, and then she thought she heard the ringing of the bells.

The following year, the second sister's turn came to rise up through the water and to swim whither she felt inclined. She rose to the top just as the sun was going down, and this sight she thought the most beautiful. The whole sky looked like gold, she said, and the beauty of the clouds she could not describe, as they sailed over her head, red and violet-coloured, but still faster than these flew a flock of wild swans, across the water towards where the sun was. She herself swam in the same direction, but the sun went down, and the rose-coloured tint faded from the water and the clouds.

The next year the third sister rose to the surface of the water, and she was the boldest of them, for she swam up a broad river which flowed into the sea. She saw beautiful green hills covered with vines; she saw castles and farm-houses appearing from amongst magnificent forests; and heard how the birds sang, the sun shining so hot that she often had to dive under the water, in order to cool her burning face. In a little creek she came upon a number of children, who were splashing about in the water quite naked. She wished to play with them, but they ran away frightened, and a little black animal, namely a dog, came and barked so fiercely at her, that she was quite afraid and sought the open sea again. She could never forget the magnificent forests, the green hills, and the pretty children that could swim, although they had no fishes' tails.

The fourth sister was not so bold, remaining out in the middle of the vast sea, and she maintained that just there it was the most beautiful, for one could see for miles around, with the sky above like a glass bell. She had seen ships, but only far off in the distance, looking like little dark specks, and the funny dolphins turning somersaults, and the large whales throwing up the water through their nostrils, so that it looked like hundreds of fountains.

Now the fifth sister's turn came, and, as her birthday happened to be in winter, she saw what the others had not seen the first time. The sea looked quite green, and round about large icebergs were floating, which, she said, looked like pearls, but were much larger than the church-steeples that men build. They were of the most extraordinary forms, and sparkled like diamonds. She had seated herself upon one of the largest, the wind playing with her long hair, and towards evening the sky became overcast; it thundered and lightened, whilst the black sea raised the large blocks of ice high up, and they glittered with the reflection of the red lightning. On all the vessels the sails were taken in, and there was fear and trembling, as they sought to steer clear of the huge masses of ice, but she sat calmly watching the lightning passing in zig-zags through the air, till it was lost in the sea.

The first time that either of the sisters came up to the top of the water, she was delighted with the beauty and novelty of all she saw, but now, since as grown-up girls they could rise up when they chose, it became indifferent to them; and after the lapse of a month, they said that down below it was most beautiful, as there they felt at home.

Often of an evening the five sisters, arm in arm, rose to the surface of the water. They had beautiful voices, far more beautiful than any human being; and when a storm was coming on, and they might expect the ships to be wrecked, they swam before them, singing so delightfully how beautiful it was at the bottom of the sea, and begging the sailors not to fear going down; but these could not understand their words, thinking it was the storm, nor did they ever see the splendour there below, for when the ship sank they were drowned, and as dead bodies only reached the Sea-King's palace.

When the sisters rose thus, arm in arm, from their dwelling below, the little sister stood alone watching them, and she felt as if she must cry, but a Mermaid has no tears, and therefore she suffers far more.

"Oh, were I but fifteen!" she would say. "I know that I shall love the world above, and the beings that inhabit it, with all my heart."

At length she was fifteen.

"Well, now you are grown up," her grandmother, the old widowed queen, said, "come that I may decorate you like your sisters;" and she placed a wreath of lilies on her head, of which each leaf was the half of a pearl, and let eight large oysters stick fast on the princess's tail, in order to show her rank.

"Oh, how it hurts!" the Little Mermaid said.

"Yes, rank has its inconveniences," the old Queen answered.

She would so gladly have thrown off all this magnificence, for the red flowers of her garden would have become her better, but she could not help herself. "Farewell!" she cried, and rose up in the water, as light as a bladder.

The sun had just gone down, as her head appeared above the water, but the clouds still glittered like roses and gold, and in the midst of the light red sky the evening star sparkled so bright and beautiful, the air was mild and the sea quite calm. There lay a large ship with three masts, she had all her sails spread, for scarcely a breath of air was stirring, and the sailors sat about in the rigging. On board there was music and singing, and as the evening grew darker hundreds of variegated lamps were lighted, which looked like the flags of all nations waving in the air. The Little Mermaid swam right up to the cabin window, and each time that she rose with a wave, she could look into the room, where there were several richly dressed men, but by far the handsomest of all was a young Prince, with large black eyes. He could not be more than sixteen years old, and this being his birthday was the cause of all the splendour. The sailors were dancing, and when the young Prince appeared on deck, more than a hundred rockets rose up in the air, which threw light around like day, so that the Mermaid was very much frightened, and dived down under the water; but her head soon appeared again, and it was just as if all the stars of heaven were falling down upon her. She had never seen any fireworks before. Splendid suns whirled round, and serpents of fire rose up in the air, all being reflected in the clear calm sea. On the vessel itself it was so light, that one could see every rope, and much more the men. Oh! how handsome the young Prince was, and smiling he pressed the sailors' hands, whilst the music sounded through the clear night.

It was growing late, but the Little Mermaid could not turn her eyes away from the ship and the handsome Prince. The lamps were put out, no more rockets rose up in the air, nor did the cannon sound any longer; but deep down in the sea there was a rumbling and rolling noise, whilst she was rocked up and down on the waves, so that she could see into the cabin window. The ship now began to make more way, one sail after the other was unfurled, the waves rose higher, and black clouds began to appear whilst it lightened in the distance. It threatened to be bad weather, and the sailors therefore again furled the sails. The large ship rocked to and fro in its rapid course on the wild sea, and the water rose like black mountains, threatening to overwhelm it, but it dived down like a swan between the high waves, appearing again on the heaped-up waters. The Little Mermaid thought this most delightful, but it did not seem so to the sailors, for momentarily the ship's distress increased. The thick planks began to yield to the pressure of the waves, and the water burst into the vessel, the mast now snapped in two as if it were only a reed, and the ship lay entirely at the mercy of the waves. The Little Mermaid now saw that they were in danger, and she had to be on her guard against beams and pieces of the ship which were floating on the water. One moment it was so pitch-dark that she could see nothing, but when it lightened it became so light again that she could recognise all on board the vessel. In particular she sought the young Prince, and she saw him, as the ship disappeared, sink into the depth of the sea. Her first feeling was that of delight, for he would now come down to her, but then she bethought herself that human beings could not live in the water, and that he would not reach her father's palace otherwise than dead. Die he must not, and therefore she swam between beams and planks which were floating on the sea, without a thought that she might be crushed by them, dived down deep under the water, rising again between the waves, and thus at length reached the spot where the Prince with difficulty kept himself afloat. He was nearly exhausted, his beautiful eyes closing, and he must have died had not the Little Mermaid come to his assistance. She held his head above the water, and allowed herself to be borne along with him at the will of the waves.

In the morning the storm had subsided, but of the ship not a splinter was to be seen; the sun rose red and bright, and it appeared as if life returned to the Prince's cheeks, but his eyes remained closed. The Mermaid kissed his beautiful, high forehead, stroking back his wet hair, and it seemed to her that he resembled the marble statue down below in her little garden. She kissed him, and wished he might come to life again.

She now saw land before her with high blue mountains, on the tops of which lay the snow as if it were swan's down. Below on the coast were beautiful green woods, and in front stood a church or convent, she did not know exactly which, but it was a building at any rate. In the garden there grew lemon and orange-trees, and before the gates stood high palm-trees. The sea here formed a little creek, where the water was calm but very deep, and under the cliffs were firm white sands. To these she swam with the handsome Prince, and laid him in the sand, taking care that his head lay high in the warm sunshine.

Now the bells began to ring in the large white building, and many young girls came through the garden, when the Little Mermaid swam further out behind some rocks that rose from the water, and she laid some of the foam of the sea on her hair and her breast, so that she might not be noticed. Then she watched to see who would come to the poor Prince.

Not long after, a young girl came to the spot where he lay; at first she seemed frightened, but only for a moment; then she called several others, and the Mermaid saw that the Prince came to life, smiling on all around him, but on her out in the sea he did not smile, for how should he know that it was she who had saved him? She felt quite sorrowful, and when he was led into the large building, she dived down under the water, in sadness returning to her father's palace.

She had always been quiet and thoughtful, but she was now much more so. Her sisters asked her what she had seen, but she did not answer them.

Many an evening and morning she returned to where she had left the Prince. She saw how the fruit of the garden ripened and was gathered, she saw how the snow on the high mountains melted, but the Prince she did not see, and sadder and sadder she returned home. It was now her only consolation to sit in her little garden, with her arms around the beautiful marble statue, but her flowers she did not attend to, so that they grew wild across the paths, winding amongst the branches of the trees till it was quite dark there.

At length she could bear it no longer, and told one of her sisters; then the others knew it too, but none besides these and a couple of other mermaids, who spread it no further than amongst their intimate friends. One of them knew who the Prince was; she had seen the rejoicing on board the vessel, and told whence he came and where his kingdom lay.

"Come, little sister," the other Princesses said, and arm in arm they rose with her, swimming to where they knew the Prince's palace stood.

This was built of a light yellow sparkling stone, with large marble steps which ran down into the sea. Splendid gilt domes rose above the roof, and between the pillars, which quite surrounded the building, were marble statues, which looked as if they were alive. Through the clear glass in the high windows, the most magnificent rooms could be seen, with costly silk curtains, and the walls all hung with beautiful paintings which were delightful to behold. In the middle of the largest room a fountain threw up its sparkling waters to the glass dome in the roof, through which the sun shone upon the water and the beautiful plants which grew in the basin.

She now knew where he lived, and there she was on the water many an evening and many a night; she swam much nearer the land than either of the others had ventured to do, and even made her way along the whle length of the canal, up to the magnificent marble terrace, which threw a long shadow over the water. Here she sat and watched the young Prince, who thought himself quite alone in the clear moonlight.

She saw him many an evening, sailing with music in his beautiful boat; she listened from amidst the green reeds, and when any one saw her long silvery veil, waving in the air, he thought it was a swan spreading out its wings.

At night, when the fishermen were out by torchlight, she heard them say so much in praise of the young Prince, that she felt delighted she had saved his life when, half dead, he could no longer struggle with the waves, and she thought how his head had rested on her bosom, and how she had kissed him, but of that he knew nothing, and could not even dream of her.

She began to love the human race more and more, and more and more she wished she could dwell amongst them, for their world appeared much larger to her than hers. They could cross the seas in ships, and they could climb the high mountains high up above the clouds, and the territory they possessed with forests and fields stretched further than her eye could reach. There were so many things she wished to know, but her sisters could not answer all her questions, and therefore she had to ask her grandmother, who knew the upper world well, and called it the lands above the sea.

"If men are not drowned," the Little Mermaid asked, "do they live for ever? Do they not die, as we here below in the sea?"

"Yes," the old grandmother answered, "they must die, too; and their life is even shorter than ours. We may live for three hundred years; but then, when we cease to exist, we only turn to foam on the water, and have not even a grave here below amongst those we love. We have no immortal soul, we never come to life again; we are like the green reeds, which, if once broken, can never become green again; whereas men have a soul which lives for ever – lives after the body has turned to dust. It takes its flight through the clear air up to the shining stars, and the same as we rise up out of the water and behold the lands of men, so they rise to beautiful, unknown places, which we shall never see."

"Why did we not receive an immortal soul?" the Little Mermaid said sadly. "I would gladly give my hundreds of years that I have to live to be a man for only one day, and have part in the heavenly kingdom."

"You must not think of that," the old grandmother said; "we feel much happier and are better than the men above."

"I must die, then, and become foam on the top of the water, and not hear the music of the waves, nor see the beautiful flowers and the red sun. Can I not do anything to gain an immortal soul?"

"No," was the answer; "only if a man were to love you so that you would be more to him than father or mother; if he clung to you with all his thoughts and all his love, and let the priest lay his right hand in yours, with the promise of fidelity now and to all eternity, then his soul would flow into your body, and you would have part in the felicity of mankind. He would give you a soul, and still keep his own. But that can never be. Just that which is a beauty here in the sea – namely, your fish's tail – is thought ugly on earth. They know no better; and to be beautiful one must have two sturdy props, which they call legs."

Then the Little Mermaid sighed, and looked down sadly upon her fish's tail.

"Let us be happy," the old grandmother said. "We will jump and dance during the three hundred years we have to live, which is long enough in all conscience, and then we shall rest all the better. To-night there is a state ball."

There was splendour, such as is never seen on earth. The walls and the ceiling of the large dancing-hall were of thick but clear crystal. Several hundred colossal mussel-shells, red and green, stood in rows on either side, with a blue burning flame, which lighted up the hall, and shone through the walls, so that the whole sea around was bright. Innumerable shoals of fish, large and small, were seen swimming about, the scales of some being scarlet, and of others like silver and gold. In the middle, through the hall, flowed a broad stream, and in this the mermaids and men danced to their own lovely singing. The beings on earth have not such beautiful voices. The Little Mermaid sang more beautifully than any of them, so that she was very much applauded, and for a moment she experienced a feeling of pleasure, for she knew that she had the most beautiful voice of all on earth or in the sea. But soon again she thought of the world above her. She could not forget the handsome Prince, and her sorrow at not possessing an immortal soul. Then she stole out from her father's palace, and whilst all within was merriment and happiness, she sat in deep sorrow in her little garden. She now heard a horn sound through the water, and she thought,

"That is no doubt the Prince sailing there above, he for whom I care more than for father or mother, he in whom all my desires centre, and in whose hands I would trust my life's happiness. I will venture everything to gain him and an immortal soul. Whilst my sisters are dancing in my father's palace I will go to the Water-witch, of whom I have always been so afraid; but she can, perhaps, advise and help me."

Now the Little Mermaid left her garden, and went to the roaring whirlpool, beyond which the Water-witch dwelled. She had never been that way before. No flowers grew there – no sea-grass – only the naked grey sand stretched towards the whirlpool, where the water whirls round like boisterous water-wheels, dragging everything it lays hold of down into the depths below. Through the middle of this all-destroying whirlpool she had to pass in order to reach the domains of the Water-witch; and part of the way she had to cross hot bubbling slime; this the witch called her peat-bog. Behind this lay her house, in the midst of a most extraordinary forest. All the trees and bushes were polypi – half-animal and half-plant – which looked like hundred-headed snakes growing out of the earth. All the branches were long slimy arms with fingers like pliant worms, and every limb from the root to the highest point moved. Everything in the sea that they could catch they laid hold of and never let it go again. The Little Mermaid was quite frightened; her heart beat with fear, and she nearly turned back again; but then she thought of the Prince and of the human soul, which gave her fresh courage. Her long, flowing hair she fastened up tight round her head, that the polypi might not catch her by it; and, with her hands crossed over her bosom, she swam swiftly between the hateful polypi, which stretched out their pliant arms after her. She saw how each of them held something or other, that it had caught, with hundreds of little arms like strong iron bands. Human beings, that had been drowned and sunk deep down in the sea, remained as skeletons in the arms of the polypi. They held boxes and rudders of ships, and the skeletons of animals, besides a little mermaid which they had caught and smothered; and this was to her the most horrible sight of all.

Now she came to a large swampy spot in the forest, where huge fat water-snakes twisted and twirled about; and in the middle of this spot was a house built of the bones of wrecked human beings, and there sat the witch, feeding a toad out of her mouth, just as we give a canary sugar, and the snakes hung round her neck.

"I know already what you want," the witch said; "it is foolish of you, but you shall have your wish, since it will bring you to misery, my pretty Princess. You want to get rid of your fish's tail and have two legs instead, like a man, so that the young Prince may fall in love with you, and you may gain him and an immortal soul." Saying this, the witch laughed so loud and repulsively that the toad and the snakes fell to the ground, where they rolled over together. "You come just in time," she continued, "for to-morrow, after the rising of the sun, I could not have helped you for another year. I will prepare you a draught with which, before the sun rises, you must swim to the land and there drink it. Then your tail will disappear, shrinking into what men call legs, but it will give you pain, just as if a sword were being thrust through you. All who see you will say you are the most beautiful being they have seen; you will retain a floating gait, such as no dancer can equal, but every step you take will be as if you trod on sharp knives, and as if your blood must flow. If you consent to suffer all this, I will help you."

"Yes," the Little Mermaid answered quickly, and she thought of the Prince and of an immortal soul.

"But, consider," the witch continued, "after you have once assumed the human form you can never become a mermaid again. You can never return to your sisters or to your father's palace; and if you do not gain the Prince's love, so that for you he forgets father and mother, clinging to you with body and soul, and if the priest does not join your hands together so that you are man and wife, you will not gain an immortal soul. The first morning after his marriage with another, your heart will break and you will turn to foam on the water."

"I agree," the Little Mermaid said, and she was as pale as death.

"But I must be paid," the witch resumed, "and it is not little I require. You have the most beautiful voice of any here at the bottom of the sea; with that you trust to fascinate him, but that voice you must give me. The best you possess I require for my invaluable draught, for it is some of my own blood I must give you, so that it may be sharp like a two-edged sword."

"But if you take my voice, what have I left?" the Little Mermaid said.

"Your beautiful person, your floating gait, and your speaking eyes, and these are enough to gain any heart. Well, have you lost your courage? Come, put out your little tongue, which I will cut off in payment for the powerful draught!"

"So be it," the Little Mermaid said, and the witch put her kettle on the fire to boil the magic draught. "Cleanliness is a good thing," she said, as she scoured out the kettle with the snakes which she tied in a knot. She then cut open her breast, and let the black blood drop into the kettle, the steam of which formed such extraordinary figures, enough to frighten any one. Each moment she threw fresh things into the kettle, and when it boiled thoroughly it was like the crying of a crocodile. At length it was ready and looked like the clearest water.

"There it is," the witch said, and cut off the Little Mermaid's tongue, so that she was now dumb, and could neither sing nor speak.

"If the polypi should lay hold of you as you pass through my forest," the witch continued, "throw only one drop of this draught upon them and their arms and fingers will break into a thousand pieces." But that was not necessary, for they drew back frightened when they saw the sparkling draught, which shone like a star, so she passed quickly through the forest, the bog, and the roaring whirlpool.

She could see her father's palace. The lights were extinguished, and no doubt all were long past asleep, but she dared not go to them now that she was dumb, and on the point of leaving them for ever. She felt as if her heart would break with grief. She stole into the garden, took a flower from each of her sisters' beds, and kissing her hand, she rose up through the dark blue sea.

The sun had not yet risen when she reached the Prince's palace, and the moon was still shining brightly. She drank the magic draught, and it felt as if a two-edged sword were cutting through her tender body, so that she fainted and lay there as dead. When the sun shone upon the sea she awoke, feeling a cutting pain, but immediately before her stood the handsome young Prince, who fixed his coal-black eyes upon her, so that she cast hers down, and then she perceived that her fish's tail had disappeared, and in the place of which she had the prettiest little white legs that any girl can have. But she was quite naked, and she therefore covered herself with her long hair. The Prince asked who she was and how she came there, and she looked at him mildly, yet at the same time so sadly, with her dark blue eyes, but speak she could not. He then took her by the hand and led her into the palace. Every step she took was, as the witch had foretold, as if she were walking on the edge of sharp knives, but she bore it willingly, and led by the Prince she mounted the steps so lightly that he and every one marvelled at her lovely, floating gait.

She had now costly clothes of silk and muslin, and was the most beautiful of all in the palace, but she was dumb and could neither speak nor sing. Beautiful female slaves, dressed in silk and gold, sang before the Prince and his royal parents, and one sang more delightfully than all the others, so that the Prince clapped his hands and smiled, which made the Little Mermaid quite sad, for she knew that she had sung much better, and she thought, "Oh, did he but know that in order to be near him I have sacrificed my voice for ever."

The slaves now danced to beautiful music, and the Little Mermaid rose, stood on the points of her toes, and then floated across the boards so that none had danced like her, her beauty becoming more striking at every movement, and her eyes spoke more touchingly to the heart than the singing of the slaves.

All were delighted with her, particularly the Prince, who called her his little foundling, and she danced more and more, though each time she put her foot to the ground it was as if she trod on knives. The Prince said that she should always remain with him, and she received permission to sleep on a velvet cushion at his door.

He had man's clothes made for her so that she might accompany him on horseback, and they rode together through the fragrant groves where the green boughs touched their shoulders and the little birds sang behind the fresh leaves. She climbed with the Prince up the highest mountains, and though her tender feet bled so that he could see it, she only laughed, and still followed him till they saw the clouds floating beneath them, like a swarm of birds flying to another country.

At night, when the others slept, she would go down the broad marble stairs and cool her burning feet in the cold sea, and her thoughts then flew back to those below in the deep.

One night her sisters came arm in arm, and they sang so sadly as they floated on the water. She made signs to them, and when they recognised her they told her into what grief she had plunged them all. After that they came every night, and once she saw, far out in the sea, her old grandmother, who for many years had not risen to the surface of the water, and also the Sea-King with the crown upon his head. They stretched out their hands towards her, but did not venture so far inland as her sisters.

She daily became dearer to the Prince, who loved her as one loves a good, dear child, but to make her his queen never once entered his head; and unless she became his wife she would not receive an immortal soul, but the morning after his marriage with another must become foam upon the sea.

"Do you not love me more than them all?" the little Mermaid's eyes seemed to say, when he took her in his arms and kissed her beautiful forehead.

"Yes, you are the dearest to me," the Prince said, "for you have the best heart and are the most devoted to me, besides that you are like a young girl whom I saw once, but shall never see again. I was on board a ship that was wrecked, when the waves cast me on land near a holy temple, which was tended by several young girls, of whom the youngest found me on the shore and saved my life. I saw her only twice, and she is the only one in this world whom I could really love, but you are like her and have nearly driven her image from my heart. She belongs to the holy temple, and therefore my good fortune has sent you to me, and we will never more be parted."

"Oh, he does not know that it was I who saved his life, carrying him through the sea to where the temple stands," the Little Mermaid thought. "I sat behind the foam, watching till some one should come, and I saw the pretty girl whom he loves more than me. The girl belongs to the temple, he has said, so they can never meet, whereas I am with him, and see him daily. I will tend him, love him, and sacrifice my life for him."

"The Prince is about to marry our neighbouring king's beautiful daughter, and therefore so magnificent a ship is got ready," was said on all sides. "It is announced that he is going to travel, but it is in reality to see the king's daughter, and a large retinue is to accompany him." The Little Mermaid smiled, for she knew the Prince's thoughts better than they. "I must travel," he had told her. "My parents desire that I should see the beautiful Princess, but they will not force me to marry her. I can never love her, for she is not like that beautiful girl in the temple whom you resemble, and if I must ever choose a wife it would be you rather, my dumb foundling with the speaking eyes;" and he kissed her rosy lips, played with her long hair, and laid his head on her heart, so that it dreamed of human happiness and of an immortal soul.

"You are not afraid of the sea, my dumb child?" he asked, as they stood together on the deck of the magnificent vessel which was to carry him to the neighbouring king's country; and he told her of storms and calms, of the curious fish in the deep, and of what the divers had seen below. She smiled at what he told her, for she knew better than all what it was like at the bottom of the sea.

In the moonlight night, when all, even the pilot who stood at the rudder, were asleep, she sat at the side of the vessel staring down into the clear water, and she thought she saw her father's palace, with her grandmother looking up towards her. Then her sisters appeared above the water, and looking at her sadly, wrung their

She cared only for a beautiful little statue of a boy, of pure white marble. (The Little Mermaid.)

The Princess could not speak a word. At length, however, she got up and gave John her hand.
(The Travelling Companion.)

white hands. She nodded to them, and, smiling, wished to tell them that all was going well and happily for her, but the cabin-boy came near, so that her sisters dived down, and he thought what he had seen was the foam of the waves.

The next morning the ship entered the harbour of the neighbouring king's splendid city. All the church-bells rang, the trumpets sounded from the high towers, and the soldiers presented arms. There was some new fête every day. Balls and parties followed one upon the other, but the Princess was not yet there. She was far away, it was said, being educated in a holy temple where she was learning all royal virtues. At length she arrived.

The Little Mermaid was very anxious to see her, and was obliged to acknowledge her beauty, for a more lovely apparition she had never beheld. Her skin was so clear and transparent, and from beneath the long dark lashes smiled the most honest eyes of a deep blue.

"It is you," the Prince said, "you, who saved me when I lay as dead on the shore;" and he pressed his blushing bride to his breast. "Oh, I am too happy!" he said to the Little Mermaid. "My fondest hopes are realised. You will rejoice in my happiness, for you take more interest in me than any of them." The Little Mermaid kissed his hand, and began to feel already as if her heart were breaking. Was not the morning after his marriage to bring death to her and to change her into foam on the sea?

All the church-bells rang, and heralds rode about the street announcing the betrothal. On all the altars sweet-scented oil was burning in beautiful silver lamps. The priests swang the censers, and the bride and bridegroom received the bishop's blessing. The Little Mermaid stood there, clothed in silk and gold, holding the bride's train, but she did not hear the beautiful music, nor did she see the holy ceremony; she only thought of her death and of all she had lost in this world.

The same evening the bride and bridegroom went on board the vessel. The cannon thundered, the flags were flying, and in the middle of the ship's deck a magnificent tent of purple and gold was erected, furnished with the most beautiful cushions, and there the newly-married couple were to pass the night.

The sails swelled with wind and the ship glided smoothly through the calm sea.

When it grew dark, lamps of all colours were lighted, and the sailors danced merrily on the deck. The Little Mermaid could not help thinking of the first time she rose to the surface of the sea, when she witnessed the same magnificence and rejoicing, and she whirled round in the dance so that all applauded her, for she had never danced so beautifully. It was as if sharp knives were cutting into her tender feet, but she did not feel it, for her heart was cut still more painfully. She knew it was the last night she would see him for whom she had left her home and relations, for whom she had sacrificed her lovely voice and had suffered daily tortures, and of all this he knew nothing. It was the last night that she should breathe the same air with him, or behold the sea and the sky studded with stars. An eternal night without thoughts or dreams awaited her, who had no soul and could not gain one. All was joy and merriment till long past midnight, and she laughed and danced with death in her heart. The Prince kissed his beautiful bride, whilst she played with his black hair, and hand in hand they retired to rest in their magnificent tent.

All was silent and quiet on board, only the pilot stood at the helm, when the Little Mermaid laid her white arms on the side of the vessel looking towards the east, for she knew that the first ray of the sun would kill her. She now saw her sisters rise from the waves as pale as herself. Their beautiful long hair did not now float in the air, it was cut off.

"We have given it to the witch to purchase help for you," they said, "so that you may not die this night, and she has given us a knife – here it is – see how sharp it is. Before the rising of the sun you must bury it in the Prince's heart, and when the warm blood falls upon your feet, they will turn into a fish's tail, and you will again be a Mermaid. You can then return to us and live your three hundred years, before you become the dead salt sea-foam. Make haste, for he or you must die before the sun rises. Your old grandmother has fretted so that her white hair has fallen off, like ours has fallen by the witch's scissors. Kill the Prince and return to us, but make haste, for do you not see the red streak in the sky? in but a few minutes the sun will rise and you must then die." They heaved a heavy sigh and disappeared in the waves.

The Little Mermaid drew back the curtain from the tent and saw the beautiful bride resting with her head on the Prince's breast. She bent down and kissed him on the forehead, then looked at the sky which was becoming redder and redder. She examined the sharp pointed knife, and agains fixed her eyes on the Prince, who in his dreams murmured his bride's name. She only was in his thoughts, and the knife trembled in the Little Mermaid's hand, but then she threw it far out into the sea, which shone red where it fell, as if drops of blood bubbled up from the water. Once more she looked upon the Prince with dying eyes, then threw herself from the vessel into the sea, and felt her body dissolving into foam.

The sun now rose above the water, the rays falling warmly upon the cold sea-foam, and the Little Mermaid felt nothing of death. She saw the bright sun, and just above her floated hundreds of transparent, beautiful beings, through whom she could see the white sails of the ship and the red clouds in the sky. Their voices were delightful melody, but so spiritual that no human ear could hear them, nor could the eye of man perceive them, and they were so light that they floated in the air without wings. The Little Mermaid saw that she had a body like these, which rose higher and higher out of the foam.

"To whom am I carried?" she asked, and her voice sounded like that of the other beings, so spiritual that no earthly music could imitate it.

"To the daughters of the air," the others answered. "Mermaids have no immortal soul, and can never have one unless they gain a man's love, so that their future existence depends upon another power. The daughters of the air have no immortal soul either, but by good acts they can gain one for themselves. We fly to the warm countries where the plague is in the burning air, and there we fan coolness, we impregnate the air with the scent of flowers, and give relief and health. When we have striven for three hundred years to accomplish all the good we can, we then receive an immortal soul, and share in the eternal bliss of mankind. You, poor Little Mermaid, have had the same lofty aspirations, you have suffered and endured, and thus raised yourself to the equal of the spirits of the air, so that you can now, after three hundred years of good works, earn an immortal soul."

The Little Mermaid raised her hands towards the glorious sun, and now for the first time refreshing tears filled her eyes. On the vessel there was again life and bustle, and she saw the Prince with his beautiful bride looking for her. Sadly they looked down upon the waves as if they knew that she had thrown herself into the water, when, invisible, she kissed the bride's forehead, smiled upon her and rose with the other children of the air upon the red cloud into the ethereal regions.

"After three hundred years we shall thus glide into heaven."

"And we may even get there earlier," one of the daughters of the air whispered. "Invisibly we glide into the dwellings of man where there are children, and for each day on which we find a good child that pleases its parents and deserves their love, the Lord shortens the time of our probation. The child does not know that we pass through the room, but if it draws from us a smile of pleasure, one year is taken off the three hundred; but if, on the contrary, we have to shed tears of sorrow over a bad child, each tear adds one day to the time of our probation."

Little Klaus and big Klaus.

Little Klaus and Big Klaus

In a village there lived two men of the same name, both being called Klaus, but one had four horses, whereas the other only possessed one; and to distinguish them from each other, the one that had four horses was called Big Klaus, and he who had only one horse, Little Klaus. Now we will see what happened to both of them, for this is a true story.

The whole week through Little Klaus had to plough for Big Klaus and lend him his single horse, for which Big Klaus in return helped him with his four horses, but only once a week, and that was on Sunday. Hurrah! How Little Klaus clacked with his whip over the five horses, for they were as good as his on that one day. The sun shone so beautifully, whilst the bells tolled for church, and the people dressed in their best, with their hymn-books under their arms, went to hear the clergy man preach. Now when they saw Little Klaus ploughing with the five horses, he was highly delighted, and again clacking his whip, cried, "Gee, woh! all my horses!"

"You must not speak thus," Big Klaus said, "for only one of the horses is yours."

But when the next person passed, Little Klaus forgot that he was not to say it, and again cried, "Gee, woh! all my horses!"

"Now I'll trouble you not to try that again," Big Klaus said, "for if I hear it once more, I'll knock your horse on the head that it will fall down dead on the spot, and there'll be an end of that."

"Well, now, indeed, it shall not escape me again," Little Klaus said, but no sooner did another come by and wish him good day, than he thought how grand he looked ploughing his field with five horses, and then he clacked his whip, crying, "Gee, woh! all my horses!"

"Oh, it is to be, then?" Big Klaus said; and taking up a large stone, struck Little Klaus' horse on the head, so that it fell over and was quite dead.

"Oh, dear, now I have no horse at all," Little Klaus said, and began to cry. He then took the skin off his dead horse, and after it had thoroughly dried in the wind, packed it in a sack, which he slung over his shoulder, and started off to the town to sell it there.

He had far to go, besides having to pass through a great dark forest, and the weather came on very bad. He now quite lost his way, and before he found it again it was growing dark, and he was too far off from the town or his home to be able to reach either before night thoroughly set in.

Close by the road-side there stood a large farm-house, and though the shutters were closed, the light could still be seen shining above them. "There I shall no doubt obtain permission to pass the night," Little Klaus thought, so he went and knocked at the door.

The farmer's wife opened it, but when she heard what he wanted, she said he might trudge on, for that her husband was not at home, and she could not admit any strangers.

"Well, then, I suppose I must stop outside," Little Klaus said, and the woman slammed the door in his face.

Close by there was a large hay-stack, and between that and the house a small shed with a flat straw roof.

"I can lie up there," Little Klaus said when he saw the roof, "and a first-rate bed it will be, but I hope the stork won't come down and bite my legs." For on the roof of the house there stood a live stork, which had its nest there.

Little Klaus now climbed up on to the shed, where he turned and turned till he made himself comfortable, and it so happened that just as he lay he could see right into the room of the farm-house, for the wooden shutters did not close at the top.

He saw a large table laid with wine and roast meat, besides a magnificent fish, and the farmer's wife and the sacristan sitting there all alone, and she filled his glass whilst he stuck his fork into the fish, for that was his favourite dish.

"If I could but have some of that," Little Klaus thought, and he stretched out his neck to see further into the room. There was also a beautiful cake. That was, indeed, a feast.

Just then he heard some one come riding along the road towards the house, which was the farmer coming home.

He was the very best-natured man, but had one peculiarity, that he could not bear to see the sacristan at his house. If he even met a sacristan he at once got into a rage. That was the reason why the sacristan had gone in to wish the woman a good evening, knowing her husband was from home, and she in gratitude had put all that good cheer before him; but when she heard her husband, she was frightened and begged the sacristan to get into a large empty box that stood in the room, as she well knew her poor husband would be in a great rage if he saw him. The woman hastily hid all the eatables as well as the wine in the oven, for it her husband had seen them he would certainly have asked the reason for all those preparations.

"Oh, dear!" Little Klaus sighed from the top of his shed when he saw all the good things disappear.

"Is any one up there?" the farmer asked, looking up. "Why are you lying there? it will be better to go into the house with me."

Little Klaus then told him how he had lost his way, and begged for a night's lodging.

"Certainly," the farmer answered; "but the first thing to do will be to get something to eat."

The wife received them cheerfully, laid the cloth for them, and brought a large bowl of oatmeal porridge. The farmer was hungry and ate with a right good appetite, but Little Klaus could not help thinking of all the delicacies which he knew to be in the oven.

Under the table at his feet, he had thrown the sack with the horse's skin, to sell which he had come out, as we already know.

The porridge was not at all to his taste, so he pressed his foot upon the sack, and the dry skin made a loud crackling noise.

"Be quiet, there!" Little Klaus said to his sack, but as he pressed his foot more heavily upon it at the same time, it crackled louder than before.

"What have you got in your sack?" the farmer asked.

"Oh, it's a sorcerer," Little Klaus answered; "and he says we should not be eating porridge, for that by his witchcraft he has filled the oven with roast meat, fish, and cake."

"Bless me, can it be possible?" the farmer exclaimed, and opening the oven, he discovered all the dainties his wife had hidden there, but which he believed the sorcerer in the sack had provided for them. His wife dared not say anything, so she placed all on the table, and they ate of the fish, meat, and cake. Little Klaus trod again upon the sack till it cracked.

"What does he say now?" the farmer asked.

"He says," Little Klaus answered, "that there are three bottles of wine for us in the oven." The farmer's wife was obliged to fetch the wine, and her husband drank and grew as merry as possible. Such a sorcerer as Little Klaus had in his sack he would give anything to possess.

"Can he call up the devil?" he asked, "for I am right merry now and should like to see him."

"Yes, my sorcerer can do all I ask him. Can't you?" he said, pressing his foot upon the sack, and when it crackled he continued, "Don't you hear? He says the devil is so ugly that we had better not see him."

"Oh, I am not at all afraid! I wonder what he looks like!"

"Why, he looks exactly like a sacristan."

"Whew!" the farmer cried, "that is ugly; for you must know that, of all things, I hate a sacristan. But it doesn't matter, for I shall know it is only the devil, and shall be the better able to bear the sight. Now I have courage for it; but he must not come too near me."

"Well, I'll ask my sorcerer," Little Klaus said, and treading on the sack, held down his ear.

"What does he say?"

"He says you may go and open the box that stands there in the corner, and you will see the devil huddled up in it; but you must not raise the lid too high, or he'll escape."

"Pray help me to hold it," the farmer begged; and he went to the box where the real sacristan was hidden, who sat there in a great fright.

The farmer opened the lid a little, and looked in. "Whew!" he cried, and sprang back. "Now I've seen him, and he's exactly like our sacristan. That was dreadful."

After that they must have another glass, so they went on till late in the night.

"You must sell me the sorcerer," the farmer said. "Ask whatever you like. I'll give you a whole bushel of money."

"No, I can't sell him," Little Klaus said, "for just consider the great use he is to me."

"I should so much like to have him," the farmer said, and he went on importuning him.

"Well," Little Klaus at length said, "since you have been so good as to give me shelter this night, I consent, and you shall have the sorcerer for a bushel of money, but I must have the bushel heaped up."

"That you shall," the farmer said; "but you must take yonder box as well, for I won't keep it a minute longer in the house. How should I know – perhaps he is in there still?"

Little Klaus gave the farmer his sack with the dry skin, and received a bushel heaped up with money in return. The farmer besides made him a present of a large wheelbarrow to carry his money and the box.

"Goodbye," Little Klaus said, and he wheeled off his money and the box, in which the sacristan was still huddled up.

On the other side of the forest was a broad, deep river, which ran so rapidly that it was scarcely possible to swim against the stream, and over this river a new bridge had been built, in the middle of which Little Klaus stopped, saying out loud, so that the sacristan in the box might hear him:-

"What am I to do, I wonder, with this stupid box? It is as heavy as if it were full of stones, and I'm only tiring myself to death by wheeling it along with me. I'll throw it into the river, and if it floats on to my house, well and good, and if it does not, it is no great matter."

He then laid hold of the box with one hand, and lifted it up a little, just as if he were going to throw it over the side of the bridge.

"Don't do that!" the sacristan cried from inside the box. "Let me get out first."

"Whew!" Little Klaus cried, pretending to be frightened; "he is in still. I must be quick and throw him into the river, so that he may be drowned."

"No, no!" the sacristan screamed. "I'll give you a whole bushel of money if you let me out."

"Well, that's quite another thing," Little Klaus said, and opened the box. The sacristan made haste to get out, pushed the empty box into the river, and went home, where he gave Little Klaus a bushel of money, so that, with the one he had already received, he now had his barrow full.

"I am not badly paid for my horse," he said to himself, when he had got back to his room and heaped the money up in a pyramid in the middle of the floor. "What a rage Big Klaus will be in when he hears how rich I have become through my single horse, but I'll not tell him all at once!"

He then sent a boy to Big Klaus to borrow a bushel measure.

"What can he want with it?" Big Klaus thought; and he smeared some tar at the bottom of the bushel, so that some of whatever was measured might stick to it, which indeed happened, for when he got the bushel measure back, he found three new shilling pieces sticking to the bottom.

"How is this?" Big Klaus cried, and ran immediately to the little one. "How did you come by all that quantity of money?"

"Oh, that I got for my horse's skin, which I sold yesterday evening."

"That was well paid," Big Klaus said; and, having run home quickly, he took an axe, knocked all his four horses on the head, and, having taken their skins off, drove with them to the town.

"Hides! hides! who will buy hides?" he cried through the streets.

All the shoemakers and tanners came running, and asked how much he wanted for them.

"A bushel of money for each," Big Klaus said.

"Are you mad?" all the people cried. "Do you think that we have money by the bushel?"

"Hides! hides! who will buy hides?" he cried again. And to all those who asked the price of them, he answered, "A bushel of money for each."

"He is making fools of us," the people cried. And the shoemakers took up their thongs, and the tanners their leather aprons, and set to thrashing Big Klaus with them. "Hides! hides! Yes, we'll tan your hide for you," all cried after him. "Out of the town with you as quickly as possible!" And Big Klaus had to hurry his best. He had never been so thrashed in his life before.

"Wait a bit," he said, when he got home. "Little Klaus shall pay for this, for I'll certainly kill him."

Now Little Klaus' old grandmother was just dead, and though she had always been cross and malicious he was quite sad, and taking the dead body, he laid it in his warm bed, to see whether that would restore life. There she should lie the whole night, whilst he sat in the corner and slept in a chair as he had often done before.

As he sat there in the night, the door opened and Big Klaus came in with his axe. He knew well where Little Klaus' bed stood, so he went straight up to it, and knocked the old grandmother on the head, thinking that it was Little Klaus.

"Now we'll see," he said, "whether you'll make a fool of me again," and he went home.

"Well, that is a bad man," Little Klaus said, "for he intended to kill me; it was well for my old grandmother that she was already dead, or he certainly would have taken her life."

He then dressed his dead grandmother in her Sunday's best, borrowed a horse from his neighbour, which he put to the cart, and seated her upon the back seat so that she could not fall. Having arranged all this they rolled off through the forest, and by the time the sun rose had reached a large inn where Little Klaus stopped and went in to get some refreshment.

The landlord had a great, great quantity of money, and was a very good man, but so hot, as if he had been made up of pepper and tobacco.

"Good morning," he said to Little Klaus. "Why, you are early on the stir."

"Yes," Little Klaus answered, "I am going to the town with my old grandmother, who is outside in the cart. I wish you would take her out a glass of mead, for she will not come in, but you must speak very loud, as she is rather deaf."

"Most willingly," the landlord answered, and having poured out a large glass of mead, took it to the dead woman, who was seated upright in the cart.

"Here is a glass of mead from your grandson," the landlord said; but the dead woman did not answer a word, sitting perfectly quiet.

"Do you not hear?" he cried as loud as he could. "Here is a glass of mead from your grandson."

Once more he shouted the same words, and then again, but as she did not take the slightest notice nor stir in the least, he got in a passion and threw the glass in her face, so that the mead trickled down her nose, and she fell back into the cart, for she was only seated upright, but not bound.

"What is this?" Little Klaus cried, and, rushing out, seized the landlord by the throat. "You have killed my grandmother! Do you not see there is a great hole in her forehead?"

"Oh, what a misfortune!" the landlord cried, wringing his hands. "That comes of my hot temper. My dear Little Klaus, I will give you a bushel of money, and have your grandmother buried as if she were my own mother, but do not say a word about it, or I shall lose my head, which would be too bad."

So Little Klaus got a bushel of money, and the landlord buried his grandmother just as if she were his own mother.

As soon as Little Klaus reached home with all that quantity of money, he sent to Big Klaus again to borrow a bushel measure.

"How is this?" Big Klaus said. "Have I not killed him? Then I must go myself and see how that is;" so he went himself to Little Klaus with the bushel measure.

"Why, where did you get all that money?" he asked, opening his eyes wide at the sight of the addition to his treasure.

"You killed my grandmother and not me," Little Klaus said, "so I sold her body for a bushel of money."

"That was a good price," Big Klaus said, and hurrying home he took an axe with which he killed his old grandmother, and laying her in a cart drove to the town where the apothecary lived, whom he asked whether he would buy a dead body.

"Who is it, and where did you get it?" the apothecary asked.

"It is my grandmother," Big Klaus said, "and I killed her in order to get a bushel of money for her body."

"The Lord forbid!" the apothecary said. "Surely you are rambling. Don't talk that way or you'll lose your head." He then told him what a sinful act it was, and what a bad man he must be, threatening him besides with punishment, so that Big Klaus was frightened, and jumping at once into his cart, he lashed the horses and drove home as fast as possible. The apothecary and all the people thought he was mad, and therefore let him go his way.

"You shall pay for this," Big Klaus said, on his road home. "Yes, Little Klaus, dearly shall you pay"; and as soon as he reached home he took the largest sack he had, and going with it to Little Klaus' house, said, "You have made a fool of me a second time. First I knocked my horses on the head, and now I have killed my grandmother. This is all your fault, but you shall not make a fool of me a third time." Thereupon he seized Little Klaus round the body, and having put him into the sack, threw it across his shoulder, saying, "Now I am going to drown you."

He had a long way to go before reaching the river, and Little Klaus was not so light a weight to carry. He had to pass close by a church in which the organ sounded, and the people were singing so beautifully that Big Klaus thought he might as well go in and hear a hymn before going further, so he put down the sack, with Little Klaus in it, by the side of the church-door, and went in. He knew well that Little Klaus could not get out, and as all the people were in church, there was no one to help him.

"Oh, dear me! Oh, goodness me!" Little Klaus sighed as he turned and twisted in the sack, but it was impossible to undo the rope that tied the mouth of it. Then an old drover, with snow-white hair, and a long staff in his hand, came that way. He was following a drove of cows and oxen, which ran up against the sack in which Little Klaus was, so that it was upset.

"Oh, dear me!" Little Klaus sighed, "I am still so young, and must already go to heaven."

"And I, poor wretch," the drover said, "am so old and yet cannot get there."

"Open the sack, then," Little Klaus cried, "and get into it instead of me, and you will soon be in Heaven."

"That I will do, with pleasure," the old man said, and no sooner had he unfastened the sack than Little Klaus jumped out.

"Will you take care of the cattle for me?" the old man asked as he crept into the sack, and Little Klaus having fastened it, went on with all the cows and the oxen.

Soon after Big Klaus came out of church and took up the sack, which appeared to have grown much lighter, for the old drover was not more than half the weight of Little Klaus. "How light it has grown! That comes of having heard a hymn," he said, and went on to the river, which was both wide and deep. He then threw the sack with the drover in it into the water, and called out, "Now I think you will not make a fool of me again."

After this he returned towards home, and when he got to where the roads crossed, he met Little Klaus driving his cattle along.

"How is this?" Big Klaus said. "Did I not drown you?"

"Yes," Little Klaus answered, "it's scarcely half-an-hour ago since you threw me into the river."

"But how came you by all that beautiful cattle?" Big Klaus asked.

"It is sea cattle," Little Klaus answered. "I will tell you the whole story, and must thank you for having drowned me, for now I am up in the world and am really rich. I was so frightened in the sack, and the wind whistled through my ears when you threw me off the bridge into the cold water. I sank to the bottom immediately, but I was not hurt, for the most beautiful soft grass grows down there. On that I fell and immediately the sack was opened; then a most lovely girl, dressed in snow-white garments, with a green wreath round her wet hair, took me by the hand, saying, 'Are you there, Little Klaus? For the present, here are a few head of cattle for you, but about a mile further on the road you will see a whole drove, which I give you.' Then I perceived that the river formed a large road for the people of the sea. Down below they were walking and driving straight from the sea as far inland as the river runs. There were such lovely flowers, and such beautiful fresh grass grew by the side of the road, and the fish swimming about in the water shot past my ears like the birds here in the air. What beautiful people they are, and, oh, what magnificent cattle!"

"But why did you come up again to us so soon?" Big Klaus asked. "I would not have done so, if it is as beautiful down there as you say."

"Well, you shall see how politic that was on my part," Little Klaus said, "for as I told you, the girl said that about a mile further on the road there is a whole drove of cattle for me, and by the road she of course meant the river, for she can walk on no other. Now I know what turns the river takes, first here and then there, so that it is a long way round, and it is much shorter to cut across the dry land here and get to the river again. By that I save at least half a mile, and shall all the sooner come into the possession of my cattle."

"Oh, you are a lucky man," Big Klaus said. "And do you think I should get some sea cattle too, if I were down there at the bottom of the river?"

"No doubt about it," Little Klaus answered; "but I cannot carry you in the sack as far as the river; you are too heavy for me. If you like to walk there and then get into the sack, I will throw you in with the greatest pleasure imaginable."

"Thank you," Big Klaus said, "but if I do not get any cattle when I am down there, take my word for it, I will cudgel you well."

"Oh, no, you won't use me so ill as that." With this, they walked towards the river, and as soon as the cattle, which were very thirsty, saw the water they ran as fast as they could to get some to drink, and Little Klaus continued, "Just look, what a hurry they are in to get to the bottom again!"

"Yes, I see," Big Klaus said, "but you had better make haste and help me, or you'll feel my stick," and he got into the sack which lay across the back of one of the oxen.

"Put a stone in as well," Big Klaus said, "or I fear I may not sink."

"It will do as it is," Little Klaus said; but for all that he put a large stone in the sack, secured the mouth well, and then pushed it in. Plump! and Big Klaus sank at once to the bottom.

"I'm afraid he won't find the cattle," Little Klaus said, and he went home with that which he had.

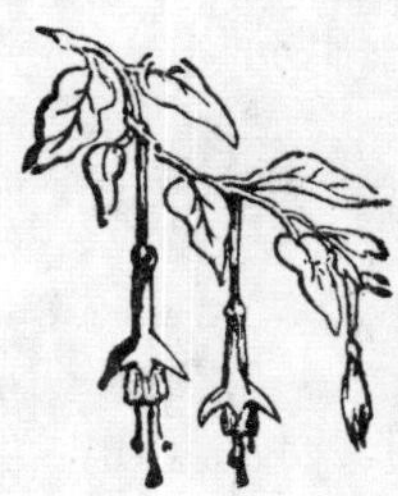

The travelling companion.

The Travelling Companion

Poor John was very sad, for his father was so dangerously ill that there were no hopes of his recovery. Besides those two there was no one in the little room, where the lamp on the table was near going out, as it had grown late.

"You have always been a good son, John!" his sick father said, "and the Lord will help you on in the world." He looked at him with mild, earnest eyes, and drawing a deep breath, died. It was just as he were asleep. John cried, for now he had no one in the whole world, neither father nor mother, brother nor sister. Poor John! He knelt by the bedside and kissed his dead father's hand, crying many bitter tears, but at last his eyes closed, and he fell asleep with his head resting on the edge of the bed.

He then had a curious dream. It was as if the sun and moon bowed down before him, and he saw his father brisk and well, and heard him laugh as he always laughed when he was particularly joyous. A beautiful girl with a golden crown on her shining hair held out her hand to him, and his father said, 'See what a beautiful bride you have. She is the most beautiful in the whole world.' He awoke, and all the splendour was gone, his father lay dead and cold in the bed and there was no one with them. Poor John!

The next week the dead body was buried; John followed close behind the coffin, and in this world never again was he to see his good father who had loved him so much. He heard how they threw the earth down upon the coffin, he still saw one corner of it; but the next spadeful that was thrown down, that too disappeared, and he felt as if his heart would break, he was so wretched. All around hymns were being sung which sounded so beautiful, and the tears came into his eyes; he cried, and that lightened his sorrow. The sun shone brightly on the green trees, as if to say, "You must not be sad, John! See how beautifully blue the sky is, and your father is now up there in heaven, praying to God that all may go well with you."

"I will always be good," John said, "and then I shall go to heaven to my father. What delight it will be when we see each other again, and how much I shall have to tell him, and he will show me so many things, instructing me in all the splendour of heaven, exactly as he taught me here on earth. Oh, how delightful that will be!"

All this assumed such reality in his thoughts, that he smiled whilst the tears still ran down his cheeks. The little birds sat above in the chestnut-trees and twittered "Quiwit! quiwit!" They were so joyous, though they had been present at the funeral, but they knew that the dead man was now in heaven and had wings, larger and more beautiful than theirs, that he was now happy because he had been good on earth, and at this they rejoiced. John saw how they flew away from the green trees far into the world, and he longed to go there too, but first he made a large wooden cross to place upon his father's grave, and when in the evening he took it there, the grave was decorated with sand and flowers. Strangers had done that, for all thought so highly of his dear father who was now dead.

Early the next morning John packed his small bundle, and secured his inheritance, consisting of ten pounds and a couple of pence, in his girdle; and with this he was about to wander forth into the world, but first he went to the churchyard, to his father's grave, where he prayed and said, "Farewell, my dear father. I will always be good, and therefore you may beg of the Lord that it may go well with me."

Out in the fields, where he now went, the flowers stood so fresh and beautiful in the warm sunshine, and they nodded in the wind, just as if they meant to say, "Welcome out here in the green fields! Is it not beautiful?" But John turned once more to look at the old church, where, as a little child, he had been christened, and where he had gone every Sunday with his father to divine service. High up in the tower he saw the church sprite standing at one of the openings with his pointed red cap on, and with his bent arm shading his eyes from the sun. John nodded him a farewell, and the little sprite waved his red cap, and, with one hand on his heart, kissed the other to him, to show how well he wished him, and that he might have a happy journey.

John thought how many beautiful things he should see in the large magnificent world, and he went on and further on – further than he had ever been. The places through which he passed he did not know at all, nor the people whom he met.

The first night he had to sleep on a haycock in the open field, for he had no other bed; but just that he thought delightful. No king could be better off. The field, with the river, the haycock, and the blue sky above, was a splendid bed-room. The green grass, with the little red and white flowers, was the carpet; the elder-trees and the rose-bushes were nosegays, and his wash-basin was the river, with the clear, fresh water, in which the rushes nodded him a good night and good morning. The moon was a large lamp, high up in the ceiling, which would not set fire to the curtains. He might sleep in perfect security, which he did, and did not wake till the sun rose, and the little birds all around sang, "Good morning! Good morning! Are you not up yet?"

The bells rang for church, for it was Sunday, and the people went to hear the clergyman. John followed them, sang a hymn, and listened to the word of God, and it seemed to him exactly as if he were in the church where he had been christened, and where he had sung hymns with his father.

In the churchyard were many graves, some of them covered with high grass, and he thought of his father's grave, which would some day become like one of these, now that he could not weed and attend to it. He therefore seated himself, and pulled up the grass, raised the crosses that had fallen, and put back the wreaths which the wind had blown off the graves, thinking, "Perhaps some one will attend in like manner to my father's grave, now that I cannot do it."

Outside the church-door there stood an old beggar, supporting himself on his crutches, to whom John gave the pence which he had, and then went on happy and cheerful.

Towards evening a storm was blowing up, so that he hurried on to get under cover, and as it grew quite dark he reached a small church that stood by itself on a slight eminence, the door of which standing fortunately open, he slipped in, intending to remain till the storm should have passed over.

"I will seat myself here in a corner, for I am tired and need rest." he said; and, folding his hands, he repeated his evening prayer, but before he knew it he was asleep and dreaming, whilst it thundered and lightened without.

When he awoke it was the middle of the night, but the storm was over, and the moon shone in through the window. He now saw an open coffin, with a dead man in it, standing in the middle of the church, but he was not in the least frightened, for he had a good conscience, and he knew that the dead never do any injury to any one; it is the living bad people who do harm. Two such evil-disposed persons stood close by the side of the dead man, who had been placed here in the church previous to being buried. It was their intention to take the poor dead man out of his coffin and throw him outside the church-door.

"Why would you do that?" John asked. "That is a bad act. In the Lord's name let him rest."

"Oh, stuff of nonsense!" the two wicked men said. "He has cheated us. He owed us money, which he could not pay, and now he must needs die, so that we shall not get a penny; but we will have our revenge, for he shall lie outside the church-door like a dead dog."

"I have only ten pounds," John said; "that is my whole inheritance, but that I will give you with pleasure if you promise me faithfully to leave the poor dead man in rest. I shall no doubt get on without the money. I have strong, healthy limbs, and God will at all times help me."

"Well," the two wicked creatures said, "if you pay his debt we will not do anything to him, you may rely upon that;" and they took the money which John offered them, laughing at him for his good nature, and they went away. John now put the dead man in order in his coffin again, folding his hands, then took his departure, and wandered contentedly through the forest that lay before him.

On all sides, where the moon could shine through the trees, he saw the prettiest little elves playing merrily; and they did not allow themselves to be disturbed, for they knew that he was a good, innocent fellow, and it is only the wicked who can never see the elves. Some of these were no bigger than the breadth of a finger, and they had their long, yellow hair fastened up with golden combs. Two and two they were rocking on the large dew-drops which hung to the leaves and the high grass. Occasionally one of the drops would burst, and they then fell down amongst the grass, which caused laughter and confusion amongst the other little beings. It was delightful to watch them. They sang; and John recognised all the pretty songs which he had learnt as a little boy. Large speckled spiders, with silver crowns on their heads, spun hanging bridges and palaces from one hedge to another, which looked like shining glass in the clear moonlight, as the fine dew fell upon them. This continued till the sun rose, when the little elves crept into the flower-buds, and the wind, seizing their bridges and palaces, swept them through the air.

John had now left the forest, when a man's voice called after him, "Hallo, comrade! Where are you going to?"

"Out into the wide world," John answered. "I have neither father nor mother, and am a poor lad; but the Lord will help me."

"I am going into the wide world, too," the stranger said, "so let us go together."

"With all my heart," John said. So they went on in company, and soon grew friends, for they were both good fellows. John very soon found out that his companion was by far more clever than he, for he had travelled nearly all over the world, and knew something of everything.

The sun was already high up when they seated themselves under a large tree to have their breakfast, and just then an old woman came by. Oh, she was so old that she walked quite double, supporting herself with a stick, and on her back she carried a bundle of wood, which she had gathered in the forest. Her apron was tucked up, and John saw that she had three large fern-leaves in it. When she had got close up to them her foot slipped, and she fell, uttering a loud cry, for she had broken her leg – the poor old woman!

John proposed at once that they should carry her home; but the stranger opened his knapsack, and, taking out a small jar, said that he had a salve in it which would immediately set her leg, making it as strong as if it had never been broken, so that she could walk home alone. For this, however, he required that she should give him the three fern-leves which she had in her apron.

"That will be paying somewhat dear," the old woman said, nodding her head in a peculiar manner, and she did not seem at all inclined to part with the leaves; but then it was not agreeable to lie there with a broken leg, so she gave them to him; and as soon as he had applied the salve to her leg she got up and walked better than she had done before. Such were the effects of the salve; but that was not to be bought at an apothecary's.

"What do you want with the fern-leaves?" John asked his travelling companion.

"They will make capital brooms," he answered, "which I am very fond of, for I am a queer fellow."

Then they went on a considerable distance further.

"How overcast the sky is becoming!" John said, pointing before him; "those are immensely heavy clouds."

"No," his companion said, "those are not clouds, but mountains. Oh, the beautiful high mountains! At the top of those one is high above the clouds, in the purest air. That is delightful, and by to-morrow we shall be there."

They were not as near as appeared, and had a whole day to walk before they reached the mountains, which were partly overgrown with black forests, and there were rocks as large as a town.

It threatened to be hard work to get over these, and therefore John and his companion went into the inn to have a good rest and gather strength for the next day's walk.

Down below, in the public room of the inn, were a great many people assembled, for there was a man there who performed plays with dolls. He had just erected his little theatre, and the people sat all around to see the play, but right in front, in the very best place, was a big butcher with a large bulldog – oh, what an ugly beast! – seated by his side, and staring before it just like all the others.

Now the play began, and a very pretty play it was, with a King and Queen sitting on a beautiful throne, with gold crowns on their heads and with long trains; for why should they not? The very prettiest wooden dolls with glass eyes and large mustaches stood at all the doors, opening and shutting them to let fresh air into the room. It was the prettiest possible play, and not at all doleful; but no sooner did the Queen rise and walk across the room, when – heaven only knows what the great bulldog could have been thinking of, but as the butcher did not hold it, it made a spring right on to the stage and seized the Queen round her slender waist, so that it went "krick, krack!" How dreadful it was!

The poor man who owned the dolls was quite frightened and sad, for the Queen was the very prettiest of all his dolls, and now the ugly bulldog had bitten off her head; but when all the people had gone, the stranger who had come with John said he would put her to rights again. Hereupon he took out his jar, and rubbed the Queen with the salve with which he had cured the old woman when she broke her leg. As soon as the doll was salved it was not only whole again, but it could move all its limbs of his own accord; there was no longer any necessity for pulling a string. Indeed the doll was a living human being in everything, excepting that it could not speak. The master of the dolls was delighted, for now he had not to touch this one at all, but she danced of her own accord, which none of the others could do.

Now, late at night, when all were in bed in the inn, there was some one sighing so dreadfully, and for so long a time, that all got up to see who it could be. The man who had performed the play went to his little theatre, for from there the sighing came, and he found all the dolls lying about, the King with all his vassals, and they were all sighing so piteously, and staring with their glass eyes, for they too wanted to be salved a little, the same as the Queen, so that they might move as she. The Queen kneeled down, and, holding up her beautiful crown, prayed, "Take this from me, but salve my husband and all my court." The poor man could not help crying, for he sincerely pitied them, and he promised the stranger all the receipts from the next performance if he would only salve four or five of the prettiest dolls; but the stranger would accept nothing but the large sword which the man wore at his side, and no sooner had he received this than he rubbed six of the dolls with his salve, and they immediately began to dance so prettily that all the girls – the live girls - danced with them. The coachman and the cook danced, the waiter and the housemaid and all the strangers danced, as did likewise the fire-shovel and the tongs, but they fell over the very first step they took – that was a merry night.

The next morning, John and his companion went away from them all, up the high mountain and through the large pine-forests. They mounted so high that at last the church-roofs below looked like little red berries amongst all the green, and they could see so far, many, many miles, where they had never been. So many beauties of nature John had never before beheld at once, and he heard amongst the mountains the huntsman's horn, blown so delightfully, that tears of pleasure came into his eyes, and he exclaimed, "Oh God, how grateful we ought to be for all thy goodness, and for all the beauties in this world!"

His companion stood there also, with folded hands, looking down upon the forest and the towns, and just then there was a delightfully sweet sound above their heads. They looked up and saw a large white swan floating in the air and singing, as they had never heard a bird sing before; but the sounds became fainter and fainter, and the beautiful bird, drooping its head, sank slowly down at their feet, where it lay quite dead.

"Two such beautiful wings," the travelling companion said, "so large and so white, are worthy any money, and I must take them with me. Now you see how useful the sword is"; and with one stroke he cut off the two wings of the dead bird, which he carried with them.

They travelled many, many miles further, over the mountains, till at last they saw a large city before them, with more than a hundred towers, which sparkled like silver in the bright sunshine; and in the middle of the city there stood a magnificent marble palace with a roof of pure gold, and there the King lived.

John and his companion would not enter the town at once, but remained in an inn outside, for they wished to smarten themselves up before appearing in the streets. The innkeeper told them that the King was a very good man, who would never hurt any one, but that his daughter was – oh, such a wicked Princess! Beauty she had enough, for there was no one to compare to her; but what use was that, for she was a wicked cruel witch, and was the cause of so many excellent young Princes losing their lives? She gave permission to all to woo her, be it Prince or beggar, it was all the same to her, and he need only guess three thoughts of hers, at the time of her asking them. If he could do this she would marry him, and he should be King of the whole country after her father's death; but if he could not guess them, she then had him hanged or beheaded. All this made the old King, her father, very sad, but he could not interfere, for he had once said that he would have nothing to do with her lovers, and that she might do as she liked. Now each time a Prince came and she asked him her thoughts, he could not guess them, so that he was hanged or beheaded, for he had been warned of the consequences and might have left the wooing alone. The King was in such deep sorrow on account of all this mourning and misery, that for one whole day in the year he lay on his knees, with all his soldiers, praying that the Princess might be less wicked, but she would not alter. The old women who drank brandy coloured it black before drinking it. That was their way of mourning, and what more could they possibly do?

"The hateful Princess!" John said; "she ought to be whipped, which would do her good. If I were but the old King she should smart!"

They then heard the people without shouting "Hurrah!" The Princess was passing, and she was so beautiful that all forgot how wicked she was, and therefore they shouted "Hurrah!" Twelve beautiful maidens, all dressed in white silk, holding a golden tulip in their hands, rode by her side, mounted on coal-black horses. The Princess herself rode a snow-white horse, decorated with diamonds and rubies, and her riding-dress was of pure gold, whilst the whip she had in her hand was like a ray of the sun. The golden crown on her head looked like stars from the heavens above, and her mantle was made of more than a thousand butterflies' wings, but for all that she was much handsomer than all her clothes.

When John saw her he turned as red as a drop of blood, and he could scarcely utter a word. The Princess was exactly like the beautiful girl with the gold crown of whom he had dreamed the night of his father's death. She was so very beautiful that he could not help loving her. "It cannot possibly be true," he said to himself, "that she is a wicked witch, who has the people hanged or beheaded if they cannot guess what she asks them. Every one is allowed to woo her, even the poorest beggar, and I will therefore go to the palace, for I cannot help it." Every one advised him not to do so, for that he would be sure to share the fate of all the others. His travelling companion also tried to dissuade him, but John said all would be right, and having brushed his boots and coat, washed his face and hands, and combed his beautiful yellow hair, he went into the town, all alone, straight to the palace.

"Come in," the old King said when John knocked at the door, and as he opened it, came to meet him in his dressing-gown, and with worsted-work slippers on his feet. He had his gold crown on his head, his sceptre in one hand, and the imperial globe in the other. "Wait a minute," he said, and he put the globe under his arm, so that he might be able to give John his hand, but when he heard the object of his visit, he began to cry so that the sceptre and the globe fell on the floor, and he had to dry his eyes with the corner of his dressing-gown. The poor old King!

"Have nothing to do with her," he said, "you will come to grief, like all the others. But come and see." He then led John out into the Princes's pleasure-garden, and it was horrible what he saw there. Up aloft in each tree were hanging three or four sons of kings, who had wooed the Princess, but had not been able to guess her thoughts. At every breeze the skeletons rattled and frightened the little birds so that they never ventured into the garden again. The flowers were tied to human bones insteads of sticks, and in the flower-pots were grinning skulls. That was certainly an extraordinary garden for a Princess.

"Here you see,' the old King said, "and you will fare just the same as all the others whose bones you behold here. Do not persist therefore. Indeed you make me quite unhappy, for I take it so to heart."

John kissed the good King's hand and said it would all be right, for that he was quite enchanted with the beautiful Princess.

She just then came riding into the court-yard with all her ladies, so they went out to meet her and wish her a good morning. She was so lovely, and when she shook hands with John, he loved her more than ever. It was quite impossible she should be the wicked witch all the people said she was. They then went up into the drawing-room, where little pages handed them preserves and gingerbread nuts, but the old King was so sad that he could not eat anything, and the gingerbread nuts were besides too hard for his old teeth.

It was settled that John should come to the palace again the following morning, when the judges and the whole council would be present to hear how he succeeded with his guessing. If he answered correctly he would have to come twice more, but no one yet had got over the first visit.

John felt in no way troubled about how he should succeed, but was in high spirits, thinking only of the beautiful Princess. He firmly believed the Lord would help him, but how he did not know and would rather not think at all about it.

He seemed never to grow tired of talking about the Princess, how kindly she had behaved to him, and how beautiful she was, and he longed for the following day, that he might see her again and try his fortune at the guessing.

But his travelling companion shook his head and was quite depressed. "I have grown so fond of you," he said, "and we might still have remained a long while together, but now I am to lose you. My poor, dear John, I could cry, but I will not trouble the last evening very likely that we are to spend together. Let us be merry, right merry, and to-morrow morning, when you are gone, I can cry quite undisturbed."

It was known all over the city that a new pretender to the Princess's hand had arrived, and sorrow reigned everywhere, for it was not likely John would succeed better than the others had done. The theatre remained closed, the old cake-women tied crape round their ginger-bread, and the King with all the priests remained on their knees in the churches all day long.

Towards evening the travelling companion prepared a large bowl of punch, saying, "Now we will be very merry and drink the Princess's health!" But when John had drunk two glasses he became so sleepy that it was quite impossible to keep his eyes open, and he sank into a sound sleep. His companion then took him gently off his chair and put him to bed, and as soon as it had grown dark he took the two large wings which he had cut off the dead swan, and fastened them to his shoulders. He also took the largest of the fern-leaves he had received from the old woman who fell and broke her leg; he put it into his pocket and flew out of the window, over the city, straight to the palace, where he seated himself in a corner above the window of the Princess's bedroom.

All was quiet in the city, and it had just struck a quarter to twelve when the window opened, and the Princess, in a long white cloak and with black wings, flew away to a large mountain. The travelling companion made himself invisible and flew after her, whipping her with the fern-leaf till the blood came. Oh, that was a flight through the air! The wind seizing her cloak, which spread itself out, like a large sail, and the moon shining all the white.

"How it hails, oh, how it does hail!" the Princess cried at every stroke from the fern-leaf; but she got to the mountain, where she knocked. There was a rolling noise like thunder as the mountain opened, and the Princess went in, John's companion following her, for no one could see him, as he was invisible. They went along a wide passage, the sides of which glittered in a very peculiar manner, owing to thousands of spiders running up and down the walls, and they shone like fire. They now came to a large hall, built of silver and gold; and red and blue flowers, as large as sunflowers, grew out of the walls, but no one could pluck them, for the stalks were ugly, poisonous snakes, and the flowers were fire coming out of their throats. The whole ceiling was covered with glow-worms and sky-blue bats, constantly fluttering their wings, which had a very extraordinary effect. In the middle of the floor stood a throne supported by four skeletons of horses with harness made of the red fiery spiders. The throne itself was of milk-white glass, and the cushions were little black mice holding each other by the tail. Above the throne was a covering of rose-coloured cobweb, spotted with the prettiest little green flies which shone like jewels. On the throne sat an old magician with a crown on his ugly head, and a sceptre in his hand. He kissed the Princess on the forehead, made her sit by his side on the splendid throne, and then the music began. Large black grasshoppers played the Jew's harp, and the owl struck itself on the stomach, for it had no drum, so that it was a strange concert, during which little black goblins with *ignes fatui* in their caps danced about the hall. No one could see John's companion, who had taken his station immediately behind the throne, where he heard and saw everything.

The courtiers who now entered were very fine and grand, but whoever examined them closely could see at once that they were only broom-handles with cabbages for heads, to which the Magician had given life and embroidered clothes. But that did not matter as they were only used for show.

After the dancing the Princess told the Magician that there was a new pretender to her hand, and consulted him about what she should think of, so that she might ask him when he came to the palace the following morning.

"Attend," the Magician said, "and I will tell you. You must choose something very easy, and then he is sure not to hit upon it. Think of one of your shoes, and that he will never guess. Then have his head cut off, and do not forget, when you come to-morrow night, to bring me his eyes, for those I will eat."

The Princess bowed low and said that she would not forget the eyes, whereupon the Magician opened the mountain, and she flew back home, her follower whipping her so hard all the time that she sighed heavily over the violent hail, and hastened as much as possible to get through the window into her bedroom. The travelling companion then flew back to the inn where John was still asleep, took off his wings and went to bed too, for he might well be tired.

It was quite early in the morning when John awoke, and his companion, who got up at the same time, told him that he had had a most strange dream about the Princess and her shoe, wherefore he begged him to ask her whether it was not of her shoe she was thinking.

"I may as well ask that as anything else," John said. "It may be all right what you dreamed, for I put my trust in God, who will help me. I will, however, say goodbye to you, for if I guess wrong I shall never see you again."

They then embraced each other, and John went to the palace. The whole hall was full of people, the judges sitting in their arm-chairs with eiderdown pillows behind their heads, for they had so much to think of. The old King got up and dried his tears with a white pocket handkerchief, and just then the Princess entered. She was more lovely than the day before, and saluted all so kindly, but to John she gave her hand, wishing him a good morning.

The time had come for John to guess what she was thinking of, and – oh, goodness! – how lovingly she looked at him, but as soon as she heard him pronounce the one word "shoe", she turned as white as a sheet, and her whole frame trembled; but that was of no use, for he had guessed right.

Oh, gracious! How delighted the old King was; he turned head over heels, that it was a pleasure to see him, and all the people applauded both him and John, who had guessed right the first time.

His companion was pleased also when he heard how well all had gone off, but John folded his hands and thanked God, in whom he put his trust, to help him the other times as well. The next day he was to guess again.

That evening passed the same as the evening before, and when John was asleep, his travelling companion flew after the Princess to the mountain, whipping her harder than the first time, for he had now two of the leaves. No one saw him, and he heard everything. The Princess was to think of her glove, and that he told John, as if he had dreamed it, so that there was no difficulty in guessing right, and there was rejoicing all through the palace. The whole court turned head over heels, just as they had seen the King do it the day before; but the Princess lay on the sofa and would not utter a syllable. It was now the question whether John would guess correctly the third time. If he succeeded he was to have the beautiful Princess, and after the old King's death inherit the whole kingdom, but if he guessed wrong he was to lose his life, and the Magician would eat his beautiful blue eyes.

That night John went to bed betimes, said his prayers and slept soundly, whilst his companion fastened on the wings, hung the sword at his side, and taking the three fern-leaves flew off to the palace.

The night was as dark as pitch, and the wind blew so that the tiles from the roofs flew in all directions, and the trees in the garden where the skeletons hung were bent like reeds in a storm. It lightened every moment, and the thunder rolled as if it were one clap that lasted the whole night. The window was now thrown open and the Princess flew out. She was as pale as death, but she laughed at the bad weather, saying that it might as well blow a little harder. Her white cloak was whirled about in the air, whilst the travelling companion whipped her with the three leaves till the blood dripped down upon the earth and she could scarcely fly, but she reached the mountain at last.

"It hails and blows," she said. "I have never before been out in such weather."

"One may have too much, even of a good thing," the Magician said. She then told him that John had again guessed right, and that if he should do so for the third time on the morrow, he would then have won, and she could never again come to the mountain or practise magic as during the past, and that she was therefore quite sorrowful.

"But he shall not guess it," the Magician said. "I will set him something that he will never think of, or he must be a greater magician than I am. Now let us be merry"; and taking the Princess by both hands, they danced about with all the little goblins, whilst the red spiders ran up and down the wall so quickly that it seemed to be on fire. The owl beat the drum, the crickets whistled, and the black grasshoppers played the Jew's harp. It was a merry ball!

When they had danced long enough the Princess had to go home, for fear she might be missed, and the Magician said he would accompany her, so that they might be as long together as possible.

They flew off through the storm, and the travelling companion broke his three rods upon their backs; never had the Magician been out in such hail. When they reached the palace he said goodbye to the Princess, whispering to her, "Think of my head." But the travelling companion heard it, and at the very moment that the Princess entered her bedroom window, and the Magician turned to go home, he caught him by his long black beard and with the sword cut his ugly head off his shoulders, without the Magician once seeing him. His body he threw into the sea to the fish, but the head he only dipped in the water, and tying it up in the silk pocket handkerchief, he carried it to the inn with him and went to bed.

The next morning he gave John the handkerchief, and told him that he must not undo it till the Princess should ask him what her thought was.

There were so many people in the great hall at the palace, that they were packed as closely together as radishes tied up in a bundle. The judges sat in their arm-chairs with the soft pillows, and the old King had new clothes on, and his crown and sceptre had been polished up, so that he was quite smart, but the Princess was very pale and wore a black dress, as if she were going to a funeral.

"What is my thought?" she asked John, who immediately untied the handkerchief, and was himself quite frightened when he saw the hateful head. All shuddered, for it was frightful to look at, but the Princess sat there exactly like a statue and could not speak a word. At length, however, she got up and gave John her hand, for he had guessed right. She looked neither to the right nor to the left, but sighed heavily and said, "You are now my master, and this evening our marriage shall take place."

"Well, that's right," the old King said, "and just as it should be." All the people shouted "Hurrah!", the royal guard played on their instruments, and the cake-women took the crape off their gingerbread, for joy now reigned. Three whole oxen, stuffed with chickens and ducks, were roasted in the market-place, so every one might cut himself a piece off; the fountains ran with wine, and whoever bought a penny loaf at the baker's received six buns as well, with plums in them, too.

At night the whole town was illuminated, and the soldiers fired off the cannon, whilst the boys did the same with crackers, and there was eating, and drinking, and dancing, everywhere.

But the Princess was still a witch and could not bear her husband John, which his travelling companion happening to think of, he gave him three feathers out of the swan's wings with a bottle containing three drops, and told him to have a large tub of water placed by the side of the Princess's bed, and that just as she was getting in he should give her a little push, so that she might fall into the water, in which he was previously to put the three feathers and the drops out of the bottle; he was then to dip her down three times, and she would lose her witchcraft and love him dearly.

John did everything just as his travelling companion advised him, and the Princess screamed when he dipped her under the water. As she struggled in his hands she appeared as a black swan with flaming eyes, but when she rose the second time above the water the swan was white, with only a black ring round its neck. John prayed fervently, and when the water for the third time covered the bird, it was changed into the most beautiful Princess. She was more lovely than before, and with tears in her delightful eyes thanked him for having disenchanted her.

The next morning the old King came with his whole court, and the congratulations lasted till late in the day. John's travelling companion came also, with his stick in his hand and his knapsack on his back. John embraced him over and over again, and said that he must not go, but stay with him, for he was the cause of his good fortune. But his companion shook his head, saying in a mild and friendly voice, "No, now my time is up. I have only paid my debt. Do you remember the dead body which the wicked men were going to throw out of its coffin? You gave all you possessed that he might have rest in his grave. I am that dead man."

The same moment he disappeared.

The marriage festivities lasted a whole month, John and the Princess loving each other with all their hearts; and the old King lived to enjoy many a happy day, letting his grandchildren ride on his knees and play with his sceptre, but John ruled over the whole kingdom.

THE SWINEHERD

There was once a Prince who was poor, for his kingdom was very small, but still it was large enough for him to think of getting married, and think of it he did.

It was certainly rather bold of him that he ventured to say to the Emperor's daughter, "Will you have me?" But he ventured for all that, for his name was celebrated far and near, and there were hundreds of Princesses who would readily have said "Yes"; but did she say so?

Now we shall hear.

On the grave of the Prince's father there grew a rose-tree – oh, such a beautiful rose-tree! – for, though it blossomed only every fifth year, and then bore but one rose, that was a rose, with such a delicious scent, that whoever smelt it forgot all care and trouble. He also had a nightingale, which sang as if all the most beautiful melodies were congregated in its little throat. This rose and this nightingale the Princess was to have, and they were therefore put in silver boxes and sent to her.

The Emperor had them carried before him into the great hall, where the Princess was playing at "puss in the corner" with her ladies in waiting, and when she saw the large boxes with the presents, she clapped her hands with delight.

The swineherd.

"I hope it's a little kitten," she said; but the rose-tree with the beautiful rose appeared.

"Oh, how pretty it is done!" all the ladies cried.

"It is more than pretty; it is beautiful," the Emperor said.

"Faugh, papa!" the Princess cried, "it is not artificial, it is natural."

"Faugh!" all the ladies cried, "it is natural."

"Let us first see what is in the other box before we grow angry," the Emperor said; and then the nightingale made its appearance, singing so beautifully that nothing could be said against it.

"Superbe, charmant!" all the ladies cried, for they all jabbered French, one worse than the other.

"How the bird reminds me of the musical box of the late Empress," an old courtier said. "It is exactly the same tone, the same execution."

"Yes," the Emperor said, and he cried like a little child.

"I hope that at least is not natural," the Princess said.

"Yes, it is a natural bird," those who brought it answered.

"Then let the bird fly," the Princess resumed; and she would by no means listen to the Prince's coming.

But he came for all that. He painted his face with brown and black, pulled his cap down over his eyes, and knocked at the gate.

"Good day, Emperor," he said. "Can I not meet with some employment here in the palace?"

"Yes, certainly," the Emperor answered. "I want some one to look after the pigs, for we have a great many."

So the Prince was appointed imperial swineherd. He had a miserable little room down below, near the pigsty, and there he had to live; but the whole day he sat working, and when night came he had made a pretty little iron pot with bells all round, and as soon as the pot boiled they rang so prettily, and played the old tune, "Home, sweet home." But the most curious part was, that by holding one's finger in the steam of the boiling pot, one could immediately smell what food was being prepared in every house in the town. Now, that was a very different thing to the rose.

The next time the Princess went out with her ladies she heard the beautiful melody, and was quite delighted, for she, too, could play "Home, sweet home" – it was the only thing she could play, and that she played with one finger.

"That is the very same tune that I play," she said; "and he must be a very well-informed swineherd. Just go down one of you, and ask him the price of the instrument."

So one of the ladies had to go down, but she put on wooden clogs.

"What do you want for the iron pot?" the lady asked.

"I must have ten kisses from the Princess," the swineherd answered.

"Heaven forbid!" the lady cried.

"I cannot take less," he replied.

"He is a rude fellow," the Princess said, and she went on, but had not gone many steps when the bells sounded so prettily, "Home, sweet home."

"Go again, and ask him whether ten kisses from my ladies will not do."

"I am very much obliged," he answered, "they must be ten kisses from the Princess herself, or I keep my instrument."

"What rubbish all this is!" the Princess said. "Now you must all stand round me, so that no one may see it."

Then the ladies stood round her, spreading out their dresses; and the swineherd got the ten kisses, and the Princess the iron pot.

Never did anything give so much pleasure. The whole evening, and the whole of the following day, the iron pot had to keep boiling, so that there was not a single hearth in the whole town that they did not know what had been cooked on it – at the Prime Minister's as well as at the shoemaker's. The ladies danced about, clapping their hands.

"We know who will have sweet soup and omelettes for dinner, and who will have broth and sausages. Oh, how interesting that is!"

"Yes; but you must not blab, for I am the Emperor's daughter."

"The Lord forbid!" all cried.

The swineherd, that is, the Prince – but no one knew he was anything more than a real swineherd – did not pass his time idly. He had now made a rattle, which, when swung round, played all the waltzes and quadrilles that had been heard from the beginning of the world.

"Oh, that is superb!" the Princess said as she passed. "I have never heard a more beautiful composition. Go and ask him how much the instrument costs; but I will not kiss again."

"He asks a hundred kisses from the Princess," the lady said who went in to ask.

"I believe he is mad," the Princess said, and she went on, but had not got many yards when she stopped. "The arts must be encouraged," the continued; "and am I not the Emperor's daughter? Go and tell him that he shall have ten kisses from me, the same as the last time, and the rest he can have from my ladies."

"Oh, but we are very unwilling!" the ladies cried.

"What rubbish that is!" the Princess said. "When I can kiss him I should think you can, too; and remember that I feed you and pay you wages."

So what could they do but go again?

"A hundred kisses from the Princess," he said, "or let each keep his own."

"Stand there," she said. The ladies stood round her, and the kissing began.

"What is all that commotion at the pigsty?" the Emperor cried, as he stepped out on the balcony. He rubbed his eyes, and put on his spectacles. "Why, it is the court ladies, who are up to some of their tricks! I suppose I must go and look after them." So he pulled his slippers up at the heel, for they were shoes the heels of which he had trodden down.

What haste he did make to be sure!

When he reached the yard he walked quite softly, and the ladies were so busily engaged counting the kisses, to make sure all was fair, that they did not notice him. He stood on tiptoe.

"What's this?" he cried, when he saw them kissing, and he hit them on the head with his slipper, just as the swineherd was receiving the eighty-sixth kiss.

"Get out with you!" he said, for he was very angry; and the Princess, as well as the swineherd, was banished from the Empire.

There she now stood, crying; the swineherd grumbled, and the rain came pouring down.

"Oh, miserable wretch!" the Princess cried. "Had I but accepted the handsome Prince! Oh, dear, how unhappy I am!"

The swineherd now went behind a tree, washed the black and brown from his face, threw off the shabby clothes, and appeared in his Prince's costume, so handsome that the Princess curtsied to him.

"I only despise you now," he said. "You refused an honest Prince, and did not understand the value of the rose and the nightingale, but were ready enough to kiss the swineherd for a plaything. Now you see what you get for it all."

He then went into his kingdom, and shut the door in her face. Now she might well sing, "Home, sweet home."

Running up to him, she pressed him closely to her, and cried, "Kay! dear little Kay! So I have found you at last!" (The Snow Queen.)

The whole Court was present even to the little kitchen wench. (The Nightingale.)

Kay and Gerda. (The Snow Queen.)

STORY THE FIRST

THE SNOW QUEEN

A Looking-glass and the Broken Pieces

Well now we are going to begin, and when we have got to the end of the story we shall know more than we do now, for it is of a wicked sorcerer, one of the very worst of sorcerers. One day he was in high glee, for he had made a looking-glass which possessed this peculiarity, that everything good or beautiful reflected in it dwindled down to almost nothing, but whatever was worthless and unsightly stood out boldly, and became still worse. The most beautiful landscapes, when seen in it, looked only like cooked spinach, and even handsome people became repulsive, or stood on their heads and looked ridiculous. The faces were so distorted that they could not be recognised, and if any one had a freckle, never mind how small, it was sure to spread over nose and mouth. That was highly amusing, the sorcerer said. When anything good or innocent entered a man's head, there was a grin on the face of the looking-glass, and the sorcerer laughed heartily at his ingenious invention. All who attended his school of magic related everywhere that a miracle had happened, and that now, for the first time, one could see what man and the world really were. They ran about everywhere with the looking-glass, till at last there was no man and no country that had not been distorted by it. Not satisfied with this, they flew up towards heaven with it; but the looking-glass shook so violently with its own grinning that it slipped out of their hands; and having fallen down to the earth it broke into hundreds of millions of billions of pieces, and still more, which caused greater mischief than ever, for some of the pieces were no larger than dust, and these flying about in the air, whoever got them in his eyes saw the whole human race distorted, for each particle, however small, retained the peculiarity of the whole looking-glass. Some men even got a small piece of the glass in their hearts, and that was dreadful, for the heart became like a lump of ice. Some of the pieces were so large that they were used for panes of window glass, but it would not do to look at one's friends through them. Other pieces got made into spectacles, and then indeed all went wrong, particularly when people put them on in order to see right and to be just.

And some of the dust of the broken glass is still flying about in the air, as is seen, unfortunately, every day.

Story the Second

A Little Boy and a Little Girl

In a large city, where there were so many people and houses that there was not room enough for all to have even a little garden, and where they were mostly, therefore, obliged to be satisfied with flowers in flower-pots, there lived two poor children who had a garden a little larger than a flower-pot. They were not brother and sister, but were as fond of each other as if they had been so. Their parents lived exactly opposite in two attics, for where the roof of the one house would have joined the other, only that they were separated by the gutter running between the two, there was in each house a small window, and one had but to take a step across the gutter to reach from the one to the other.

Outside each window was a large wooden box, in which grew some kitchen-herbs and a rose-tree, flourishing equally well in the two. It occurred to the parents to place the boxes crossways over the gutter, so that they reached nearly from one window to the other, looking like two walls surmounted by flowers. Peas hung down over the sides of the boxes, and the branches of the rose-trees bent forward towards each other, so that it looked almost like a triumphal arch of leaves and flowers. As the boxes were very high, and the children not allowed to climb upon them, they often received permission to get out of the windows, where, seated on their little stools under the rose-trees, they used to play together.

In winter there was an end to this amusement, for the windows were often frozen quite over, but then the children warmed halfpence on the stove, and laying the warm coin against the frozen glass made a beautiful peep-hole – so round – and behind each there shone a bright sparkling eye, that of the little girl and the little boy. His name was Kay, and hers Gerda. In summer, with one jump they could be together, but in winter they had to run down the many stairs of the one house and up the others, whilst the snow was falling without.

"Those are the white bees swarming," the old grandmother said.

"Have they a queen, too?" the little boy asked, for he knew there was such amongst the real bees.

"Yes, they have," the grandmother said. "She is flying there, where they are swarming the thickest; she is the largest of them all, and never rests quiet on the ground, but flies up again into the black cloud. Often during the winter night she flies through the streets of the town and looks in through the windows, which are then covered with frost, in such strange forms as if they were so many flowers."

"Yes, that I have seen!" both children said, and they now knew that it was true.

"Can the Snow Queen come in here?" the little girl asked.

"Let her come," the boy said, "and I will put her on the stove, so that she will melt."

But the grandmother smoothed his hair and told them other stories.

That evening, when little Kay was at home and half undressed, he climbed into a chair by the side of the window and looked through the hole. Some flakes of snow were falling, and one amongst them, the very largest, remained lying on the rim of the flower-box. It increased more and more, till at last it became a woman, dressed in the finest white crape, as if formed by millions of star-like flakes. She was so beautiful, but of ice – dazzling, glistening ice; and yet she was alive. Her eyes sparkled like two bright stars, but they were restless and unsteady. She nodded towards the window and beckoned with her finger, which frightened the little boy, so that he jumped down from the chair; and just then it seemed as if a large bird flew past the window.

The next day it was a clear frost. Then came spring; the sun shone, the trees began to bud, the swallows built their nests, the windows were opened, and the little children again sat in their small garden, high up in the gutter of the roof.

The roses blossomed more beautifully than ever this summer, and the little girl having learnt a hymn, in which there was mention of roses, it reminded her of her own, and she sang the hymn to the little boy, he joining in:-

"The rose blooms but its glory past,
Christmas then approaches fast."

The little ones held each other by the hand, kissed the roses, and stared up into the sky, into the clear sunshine.

What delightful summer-days those were! And how pleasant it was to be out-of-doors near the fresh rose-trees, which seemed as if they would never have done blossoming!

Kay and Gerda were seated, looking over a picture-book of animals and birds, when, just as the church clock struck five, Kay exclaimed, "Oh, something sharp has run into my heart! And now something has flown into my eyes."

The little girl took him round the neck, and looked in his eyes, but no, there was nothing to be seen.

"I think it has gone again," he said; but it was not gone. It was just one of the pieces of the magic glass, which, we recollect, fell and was broken – the hateful glass, that made everything great and good reflected in it appear small and contemptible, but what was bad and mean was made the most of, and the faults in anything were very perceptible. Poor Kay had got one of those pieces in his heart, and soon it will become a lump of ice. It no longer hurt him, but it was there.

"Why are you crying?" he asked. "It makes you look so ugly, and there is nothing whatever the matter with me." Then, all at once, he exclaimed, "Look there, how nasty that rose is! It is all worm-eaten; and this one is quite out of shape. They are ugly flowers, like the box in which they grow," and he kicked the box, and tore off some of the roses.

"What are you about, Kay?" the little girl cried; and as he saw her fright he tore off another rose and clambered in through his window, running away from the dear little girl.

Now, when she came with the picture-book, he said it was only fit for babies; and when the old grandmother told stories, he would constantly interrupt her with a "but"; and when he could manage it, he got behind her, and putting a pair of spectacles on his nose, imitated her so exactly, that all who saw him laughed. Soon he could mimic all the inhabitants of the whole street, taking off their peculiarities and defects, so that people said, "That boy has a good head"; but it was only the glass that had got into his eyes, the glass that was in his heart, and that was the reason why he teased even little Gerda, who loved him with all her heart.

His play was now quite different to what it used to be, it was so sensible. One winter's day, when it was snowing, he came with a large magnifying glass, and holding out a corner of his blue coat, let the snow-flakes fall upon it.

"Look through the glass, Gerda!" he said, and the snow-flakes appeared much larger, looking like beautiful flowers or ten-cornered stars; they were quite beautiful to look at. "Now, are not these more interesting than the real flowers?" Kay said. "See, there is not a single fault in them, they are all so accurate, if they could but remain without melting."

Soon after Kay appeared with large gloves on, carrying his sledge on his back, and he shouted in Gerda's ear, "I have got permission to go to the great square, where the other boys play!" and he was gone in an instant.

There, in the square, the boldest of the boys fastened their sledges behind the farmers' carts, and went a good way with them. All was life; and when they were at the height of their games there came a large sledge, painted all white, and in it sat a figure muffled up in shaggy white fur, with a white cap on. The sledge drove ten times round the square, and Kay quickly fastened his little sledge to it. It drove faster and faster, and then turned into one of the streets that ran out of the square. The person driving turned round and nodded so friendly to Kay, just as if they knew each other; and each time he was on the point of unfastening his sledge the person nodded to him again, so that he remained as he was, and they drove out through the city gates. The snow began to fall so thick that the little boy could not see his hand before him, and then he undid the string with which he had fastened himself to the large sledge; but that was of no use, for his little sledge remained attached to the other, and on they flew as fast as the wind. He called out as loud as he could, but no one heard him, and the sledge seemed to drive over hedges and ditches. He now grew quite frightened, and tried to say his prayers, but could think of nothing but his multiplication tables.

The snow-flakes became larger and larger, till at last they appeared like white chickens, when of a sudden they turned on one side and the large sledge stopped. The person driving it stood up, and Kay now saw that it was a lady, tall and slim, and dazzlingly white. It was the Snow Queen.

"We have had a good drive," she said; "but how is it that you are cold? Come, creep under my bear's-skin"; and she seated him by her side, in the sledge, covering him up with the skin, but it appeared to him as if he were sinking into a snowdrift.

"Are you still cold?" she asked, and kissed him on the forehead. Oh, that was colder than ice, and seemed to penetrate to his very heart, which was already half a lump of ice. He felt as if he were going to die, but only for a moment, after which he was particularly comfortable and did not in the least feel the cold around him.

"My sledge! Do not forget my sledge!" Of that he thought first, and it was fastened to one of the white chickens, which now followed with the sledge on its back. The Snow Queen kissed Kay again, and he then forgot little Gerda, her grandmother, and all at home.

"You must now have no more kisses," she said, "or else I shall kiss you to death."

Kay looked at her; she was so beautiful, and a more intelligent, lovely face he could not imagine. She no longer appeared of ice, like when she sat outside on the window-sill and beckoned to him. In his eyes she was perfection, and he felt no fear; he told her that he could reckon in his head, and knew the number of square miles in the country as well as the number of its inhabitants, and she smiled at all he said. It then seemed to him as if he did not yet know enough, and he looked up into the vast expanse of air. She flew up with him, high, high, on to the black cloud; and the storm whistled and howled, as if it were singing old songs. They flew over forests and lakes, over seas and continents. Beneath them the cold wind whistled, the wolves howled, the snow sparkled; but high above them the moon shone brightly, and on this Kay's eyes were fixed the whole long winter night. During the day he slept at the feet of the Snow Queen.

Story the Third

The Flower Garden of the Enchantress

But how did little Gerda get on, Kay not returning? What could have become of him? No one knew, no one could give any information. The boys could only tell that they had seen him fasten his sledge to a magnificent large one, which had driven along the street and out of the city gates. No one could tell where he was; many tears where shed, and little Gerda cried more than all. It was then said he was dead, that he had fallen into the river which flowed past the town. Oh, what long, dreary winter days those were!

Now came spring and warmer sunshine.

"Kay is dead and gone!" little Gerda said.

"I do not think so," the sunshine said in reply.

"Kay is dead and gone!" she said to the swallows.

"We do not think so," these answered; and at last little Gerda did not think so either.

"I will put on my new red shoes," she said one morning, "those which Kay has never seen, and I will go down to the river and ask it about him."

It was still early. She kissed her old grandmother, who was not awake yet, and having put the red shoes on, she went all alone out at the city gates and down to the river.

"Is it true that you have taken my little playfellow? I will give you my red shoes if you restore him to me."

It seemed to her as if the waves nodded in a peculiar way, and she then took her red shoes, the things she like best, and threw them both into the river; but they fell near the side, and were washed on to land again. It was exactly as if the river would not take what was so dear to her, for it had not little Kay to give in return; but she thought she had not thrown the shoes out far enough, so she got into a boat, which was there amongst the rushes, and going to the farthest end of it she from there threw the shoes into the water again. Now the boat was not fastened, and the motion she caused in it drove it off from land. She noticed it and hastened to get back, but it was already more than a yard from land, and now drifted fast out into the river.

Then little Gerda was frightened and she began to cry, but no one heard her excepting the sparrows, and they could not carry her on to land, but they flew along the banks singing, as if to console her, "Here we are! here we are!" The boat glided down the stream, and little Gerda sat there quite quiet, in her bare stockings, whilst her little red shoes floated after, but they could not overtake the boat.

It was very pretty on both sides; there were beautiful flowers, old trees and meadows with sheep and cows, but not a human being was to be seen.

"Perhaps the river will carry me to little Kay," she thought; and then she grew more cheerful: she stood up, and for hours she admired the beautiful green banks. At length she came to a large orchard full of cherry-trees, in which there stood a little house with strange red and blue windows. It had a straw roof, and in front stood two wooden soldiers, which shouldered arms as Gerda passed.

She called to them, thinking they were alive; but they returned no answer, as was quite natural.

Gerda cried still louder, and then there came an old, a very old, woman out of the house, supporting herself on a hooked stick. She wore a large straw hat, painted all over with the most beautiful flowers.

"You poor little child!" the old woman said, "how did you get on to the rushing stream, thus carried out into the world!" And she walked right into the river, caught hold of the boat with the hook of her stick, and having drawn it to land, lifted little Gerda out.

Gerda was delighted to feel herself on dry land again, though a little bit frightened at the strange old woman.

"Come, and tell me who you are, and how you came here," she said.

And Gerda told her all. The old woman shook her head mumbling "Hem! hem!", and when Gerda asked her whether she had seen little Kay, she said that he had not passed yet, but that he would be sure to come, and that therefore she must not be sad, but had better taste her cherries, and look at her flowers, which were more beautiful than any picture-book, and that each could tell a story. She then took Gerda by the hand, and having led her into the house, locked the door.

The windows were up very high, and the panes of glass red, blue, and yellow, so that the light came in of various colours, which looked very strange. On the table were the most delicious cherries, of which Gerda ate as many as she felt inclined, for she had permission to do so. Whilst she was eating the old woman combed her hair with a golden comb, and the beautiful yellow hair shone so bright, and curled round her pretty, cheerful, little face, which was as round and blooming as a rose.

"I have always longed to have a dear little girl like you," the odl woman said, "and you shall see how well we will get on together." As she combed Gerda's hair, the little girl more and more forgot her playfellow Kay, for the old woman practised magic, but she was not a wicked witch, and only conjured a little just for her own amusement, and she wished to keep Gerda with her. On this account she went into the garden, and touching all the rose-trees with her stick, they sank down into the black earth, so that there was no trace left of where they had stood. The old woman was afraid, that when Gerda saw the rose-trees she might think of her own, and remembering little Kay, run away.

She then took Gerda into the flower-garden. Oh, what a perfume, and what splendour! There were all imaginable flowers of every season of the year, so that no picture-book could be more showy or prettier. Gerda jumped with delight and played till the sun went down behind the high cherry-trees, when she had a beautiful bed with red silk pillows, stuffed with violets, and she slept and dreamed as delightfully as any queen on her wedding-day.

The next day she again played with the flowers in the warm sunshine, and thus many days passed by. Gerda knew every flower, but as many as there were, it seemed to her as if one were wanting, though she did not know which. Now, one day, she was sitting looking at the old woman's painted hat, and just the most beautiful of the flowers was a rose. The old woman had forgotten to blot that out when she banished the others into the earth, for so it is when one has not one's thoughts constantly about one. "What!" Gerda cried, "are there no roses here?" She looked in all the beds, but none was to be found; and she then sat down and cried, and it so happened that her tears fell just on one of the spots where a rose-tree was buried, and as the warm tears watered the ground the tree sprang up in as full and beautiful blossom as it had ever been. Gerda threw her arms round it, kissed the roses, and thought of her own rose-tree at home, as well as of little Kay.

"Oh, how I have been delayed!" the little girl said. "I came to look for Kay. Do you know where he is?" she asked the flowers. "Do you think he is dead?"

"He is not dead," the Roses said; "for we have been in the earth, where all the dead are, but Kay was not there."

"Thank you," Gerda said, and she went to the other flowers, looked into their calyx, and asked, "Can you not tell me where little Kay is?"

But each flower stood there in the sunshine, dreaming its own story, which Gerda had to listen to, but of Kay they knew nothing.

And what did the Tiger-lily say?

"Do you hear the drum? – drum! drum! – only two notes, always the same drum, drum! Listen to the funeral song of the women, to the call of the priests! The Hindoo-woman stands in her long red mantle on the funeral pile; the flames flicker around her and her dead husband; but the Hindoo-woman thinks of a living one there in the crowd, of him from whose eyes the fire burns hotter, and troubles her heart more than the flames which will soon burn her body to ashes. Will the flame of the heart be consumed in the flame of the funeral pile?"

"I do not understand a word of that," little Gerda said.

"That is my story," the Tiger-lily answered.

What says the Convolvulus?

"At the end of a foot-path rises an old castle. The ivy climbs up the old red walls, thickly covering the terrace, and there stands a beautiful girl. She leans over the balustrade, looking eagerly down the path. No rose is fresher than she; no apple-blossom carried from the tree by the wind moves more gracefully. Now her magnificent satin dress rustles. Is he not coming yet?"

"Do you mean Kay?" little Girda asked.

"I am speaking only of my story, my dream," the Convolvulus answered.

What says the Snow-drop?

"A board hangs on a rope fastened between two trees. That is a swing, and two pretty little girls, with dresses as white as snow, and long green ribbons fluttering from their hats, are seated on it swinging. Their brother, who is bigger than they, is standing in the swing, with one arm round the rope to keep himself up; for in one hand he holds a cup, and in the other a clay pipe: he is blowing soap-bladders. The swing is moving, and the bladders fly with beautiful constantly-changing colours; the last still hangs to the pipe, and is wavering in the wind. A little black dog is standing on its hind-legs, wanting to get into the swing, too. The bladder flies, the dog falls and barks, for it is angry. The dog is teased, and the bladders burst. A swinging-board, and a bursting airy vision, are my song."

"I dare say your story is very pretty, but you tell it in such a melancholy voice, and there is not a word of little Kay."

What do the Hyacinths say?

"There were three sisters, so lovely and fragile. The dress of the one was red, of the other blue, and of the third entirely white. Hand in hand they danced by the side of a lake in the bright

moonshine. They were not fairies, but human beings. There was a sweet scent, and the girls disappeared in the forest. The scent became stronger, and three coffins, in which lay the three beautiful girls, glided out of the forest, and floated across the lake, the glow-worms flying around them. Are the girls asleep, or are they dead? The scent from the flowers says they are dead, and the vesper-bell tolls for their funeral."

"You make me quite sad," Gerda said. "You have such a strong scent that I cannot help thinking of the dead girls. Can it be that Kay is really dead? The roses have been buried, and they say no."

"Ding, dong!" sound the Hyacinth-bells. *"We do not toll for little Kay – we do not know him: we only sing our song, the only one we know."*

Gerda went to the Buttercup, which shone from amongst its glittering green leaves, and said, "You are a little clear sun. Tell me if you know whether I shall find my playfellow."

The Buttercup shone so beautifuly, and looked at Gerda, but its song was not of Kay either.

"In a small yard the sun shone so warmly the first day of spring; the rays were reflected from the white wall of the house, and close by stood the first yellow flower, shining like gold in the sun. The old grandmother was sitting out-of-doors in her chair, and her granddaughter, a poor beautiful servant-girl, was parting from her, after a short visit. She kissed her grandmother. In that kiss there was a blessing. Well, that is my little story."

"My poor old grandmother!" Gerda sighed; "she is no doubt longing for me, and is sad about me, as she was about Kay. But I will soon be back home, and bring Kay with me. It is of no use my asking the flowers, for they only know their own song, and can give me no information." She then tucked up her dress, in order to be able to run the faster; but, as she jumped over a white tulip, it struck her across the legs. So she stopped, looked at the long white flower, and said, "Perhaps you have something to tell me"; and she bent down her ear to the flower. Now what did the Tulip say?

"I see myself! I see myself! Oh, how beautiful I am! Up above, in a small attic, stands a little dancer, half dressed. She stands first on one leg, and then on two. She is nothing but a dazzling of the eyes. She is pouring water out of the tea-pot upon a piece of stuff that is her stays. Cleanliness is a good thing. And the white dress which hangs upon the nail has also been washed in the tea-pot, and dried on the roof. She puts it on, and, tying a yellow handkerchief round her neck, makes the dress look whiter still. With one leg out, is she not standing on a stalk? I see myself! I see myself!"

"I care little about that," Gerda said. "You need not tell me that"; and she ran off to the end of the garden.

The door was locked; but she pressed heavily against the rusty hinges, and it sprang open, and out she ran in her bare feet, out into the wide world. She looked back three times, but there was no one following her. When she could run no longer, she seated herself upon a large stone, and, looking round her, saw that the summer was gone; it was late in autumn; but that could not be perceived in the beautiful garden, where the sun was always shining, and where there were flowers of all seasons.

"Oh, goodness! how long I have delayed!" little Gerda said. "Why, it has grown autumn, and now there is no time to rest!" So she got up again to go on.

Oh, dear! How sore and tired her little feet were! And all around her it looked cold and comfortless. The long leaves of the willow were quite yellow, and the dew dripped from them. One leaf fell after the other, and only the sloe-tree bore fruit, but that was so rough that it drew the mouth on one side. How grey and depressing it was in the wide world!

Story the Fourth

The Prince and the Princess

Gerda was obliged to rest again, where, just opposite the spot where she was sitting, a large Raven was hopping about on the snow. It had been watching her some time, shaking its head, and now it cried, "Caw! Caw! How do? How do?" It could not express itself better, but meant well with the little girl, and asked where she was going all alone into the wide world. Gerda felt how much there lay in that one word "alone", and then she told her whole story and fortunes, asking whether it had not seen Kay.

The Raven nodded quite knowingly, and said, "It may be, it may be!"

"What? You think you have seen him?" the little girl cried, and hugged the Raven so that she nearly squeezed it to death.

Gerda and the ravens. (The Snow Queen.)

"Gently, gently!" the Raven said. "I think I know; I think it may have been little Kay; but, for certain, by now the Princess has driven you out of his thoughts."

"Does he live with a Princess?" Gerda asked.

"I understand what you say," the Raven replied, "but I find it difficult to express myself in your language. If you understand Raven's language it will go better."

"No, I never learnt that," Gerda said; "but my grandmother knew it. Oh, had I but learnt it!"

"It does not matter," the Raven said, "I will tell the story as well as I can, though it will be badly done"; and then it related all it knew.

"In this kingdom in which we are now sitting, lives a Princess, who is so immoderately clever; but then she has read all the newspapers that are in the world, read and forgotten them again, so clever is she. Lately she was sitting on her throne, which is said not to be over-pleasant, when she began to sing, and the theme of her song was, 'Why should I not marry?' 'Well, there is something in that,' she said, and so she determined to get married; but she must have a husband who knew how to answer when spoken to, not one who could only stand there and look grand, for that is too stupid. She now had all her court-ladies drummed together, and when they heard what her intention was, they were much delighted. 'That would suit my fancy very well,' one said; and 'I have been thinking of that too,' said another. You may believe every word of what I tell you," the Raven said, "for I have a tame sweetheart who wanders at liberty all over the palace, and it is she has told me all."

The sweetheart was, as a matter of course, a raven too.

"The newspapers appeared with a border of hearts and the Princess's monogram. Therein might be read, that every good-looking young man was at liberty to go to the palace and converse with the Princess, and that she would marry him who spoke the best and who appeared to feel at home there. Yes, yes!" the Raven said, "you may believe what I say, for it is as true as that I sit here. There was a fine stream of people, a crowding and pushing; but it did not succeed, either the first or second day. They could all speak well enough out in the street, but when they got into the palace and saw the guards in silver, and the stairs lined with footmen in gold, and saw the splendid rooms, they were quite bewildered, so that when they stood before the throne on which the Princess sat, they could say nothing but repeat the last word she had uttered, and that she did not particularly care about hearing again. It was exactly as if the good people had swallowed snuff and fallen asleep till they were in the street again, when they could talk fast enough. There was a string of people all the way from the city gates up to the palace, and I was there myself to see them," the Raven said. "They grew hungry as well as thirsty, but in the palace they did not get as much as a glass of water. Some, it is true, had prudently taken some bread and butter with them, but did not share it with their neighbours, for they thought, let him look hungry, and certainly the Princess will not have him."

"But Kay, little Kay!" Gerda asked. "When did he come? Was he amongst the crowd?"

"Patience, patience! For we are just coming to him. It was on the third day; there came a little person without horse or carriage, but walking merrily straight up to the palace. His eyes were bright like yours, and he had beautiful long hair, but he was poorly dressed."

"That was Kay!" Gerda shouted with delight. "At last I have found him!" and she clapped her little hands.

"He had a little knapsack on his back," the Raven continued.

"No, that must have been his sledge," Gerda said, "for he went away with his sledge on his back."

"That may be," the Raven replied, "for I did not pay particular attention to it; but this I know from my sweetheart, that, when he got inside the palace and saw the body-guard in silver, and the footmen in gold on the stairs, he was not in the least abashed, but nodded and said to them, 'That must be tedious work to stand there on the stairs, so I will go in at once.' The rooms were splendidly lighted, and there were lords and excellencies walking about barefoot, whereas his boots creaked awfully, but he was not in the least concerned."

"That was certainly Kay," Gerda said, "for I know he had new boots on, and I heard them creak."

"Yes, creak they did," the Raven continued; "but merrily he walked straight up to the Princess, who was sitting on a pearl as large as a spinning-wheel, and all the court ladies with their maids, and their maids' maids, and the courtiers with their servants and their servants' servants, who kept a boy in turn, were standing around, and the nearer they stood to the door the prouder they looked. The servant's servant's boy, who always wears slippers, stands so proudly in the door that one dare scarcely look at him."

"That must be horrible," little Gerda said; "but Kay has gained the Princess for all that."

"If I had not been a raven I would have had her myself, for all I am engaged. My tame sweetheart says, that he spoke as well as I speak, when I am talking the raven's language. He was gay and well-behaved, but had not come at all to pay court to the Princess, but only to hear how clever she was. He had every reason to be satisfied with her, and she no less so with him."

"Oh, for certain that was Kay," Gerda said, "for he was always so clever. Will you not introduce me into the palace?"

"Well, that is easily said," the Raven answered, "but how are we to manage it? I must talk it over with my tame sweetheart, and she will no doubt be able to advise us; for I must tell you, that a little girl like you will never obtain permission to enter in the ordinary way."

"Oh, yes, I shall," Gerda said, "for as soon as Kay hears that I am there, he will come out directly and fetch me."

"Wait for me there at the railing," the Raven said, wagged its head, and flew off.

The Raven did not return till late in the evening, when it said, "She sends you all sorts of kind messages, and here is a small loaf for you, which she took from the kitchen, where there is plenty of it, and no doubt you are hungry. It is impossible for you to be admitted into the palace, for you are barefooted. The guards in silver and the footmen in gold would never allow it; but do not cry, for get in you shall. My sweetheart knows a little back staircase which leads up to the bedroom, and she knows where to find the key."

So they went into the garden, into the great avenue, where one leaf was falling off after the other; and when the lights in the palace were put out, one after the other, the Raven led Gerda to a back-door, which stood ajar.

Oh, how Gerda's heart beat with fear and anxiety! She felt exactly as if she were going to do something wrong, and yet she only wanted to know whether little Kay was there, and there he must be. So vividly she called to mind his clear eyes and long hair, and it seemed as if she saw him smiling, as he used to do when at home they sat together under the roses. He would surely be pleased to see her and to hear what a long way she had come for his sake, as also to know how they had all fretted at home at his not returning. Oh, what fear, and, at the same time, delight!

They were now on the stairs, where a small lamp was burning, and on the floor stood the tame Raven, turning her head first on one side and then on the other, looking at Gerda, who courtesied as her grandmother had taught her to do.

"My future husband has spoken to me so much in your praise, and your story, too, is very touching," the tame Raven said. "If you, my little lady, will please to take the lamp, I will lead the way. We are going the straight way, for there we shall not meet any one."

"It seems to me as if some one were coming just behind us," Gerda said, and then there was a rustling past them. It was like shadows on the wall, horses with flowing manes and thin legs, huntsmen, and ladies and gentlemen on horseback.

"Those are only dreams," the Raven said, "and come to carry the ladies' and gentlemen's thoughts off to the chase; which is well, for we can the better examine them in bed. But I hope that when you have risen to honour and dignity you will show a grateful heart."

"It is quite unnecessary to talk about that," the Raven from the forest said.

They now entered the first room, the walls of which were hung with rose-coloured silk and artificial flowers. Here the dreams rushed past them again, but went so fast that Gerda could not catch a sight of them. Each room was more splendid, as they passed from one to the other – almost enough to make one giddy; and now they reached the bed-room. That ceiling was like large palm-leaves, made of the most beautiful glass, and from the centre were suspended, by a golden branch, two beds in the form of lilies. The one was white, and in that lay the Princess; whilst the other was red, and in that Gerda was to look for little Kay. She bent one of the red leaves on one side and saw a brown neck. Oh, that was Kay! She called his name out loud, holding the lamp towards him. The dreams rushed back out of the room; he awoke and turned his head round – it was not little Kay!

The Prince's neck only was like Kay's, but he was young and handsome. At the same time the Princess's face appeared from amongst the white-lily leaves, and she asked what the matter was. Little Gerda then cried and told her whole story, and all that the Ravens had done for her.

"Poor child!" the Prince and Princess said, praising the Ravens for what they had done, and saying they were not at all angry, but that they must not repeat it. A reward was promised them.

"Will you go free?" the Princess asked, "or will you have a fixed appointment as court-ravens, with all the kitchen remains?"

The two Ravens made their bows and begged they might have a fixed appointment, for they thought of their old age, saying, "It is so nice to have something for the old man," as they called it.

The Prince then got out of his bed and let Gerda sleep in it; more he could not do. She folded her little hands and thought, "How good men and beasts are!" and then closing her eyes, she slept soundly. The dreams came flying back, and they looked like angels drawing a sledge, on which sat Kay and nodded. But the whole was only a dream, and was therefore all gone again as soon as she awoke.

The next day she was clothed from head to foot in silk and velvet, and she received the offer to remain at the palace and enjoy herself; but she only begged for a little carriage with a horse, and for a pair of boots, when she would go out again into the wide world and look for Kay.

And she not only got the boots but a muff; and when she wished to leave, a new coach of pure gold drew up at the door, with the Prince's and Princess's coats-of-arms upon it, like shining stars. The coachman, footmen, and outriders, for there were outriders too, wore golden crowns. The Prince and Princess themselves helped her into the carriage and wished her success. The Raven of the forest, who was now married, accompanied her the first ten miles, sitting by her side, for riding backwards disagreed with him, whilst the other Raven stood at the door flapping her wings. She could not go with them as she suffered from headache, since she had a fixed appointment at the palace and got too much to eat. The inside of the carriage was lined with cakes and sweets, and in the seat were fruits and gingerbread nuts.

"Farewell! Farewell!" the Prince and Princess said, whilst little Gerda cried, and the Raven cried too. They went on for ten miles, and then the Raven had to say farewell, which was the saddest parting of all. He flew up into a tree and flapped his black wings as long as he could see the carriage, which shone like the sun.

Story the Fifth

The Little Robber-Girl

They drove through the dark forest, but the carriage gave light like a torch, which affected the robbers' eyes so that they could not bear it.

"That is gold! that is gold!" they cried, rushed forward, seized the horses, killed the little jockeys, coachman, and servants, and then dragged little Gerda out of the carriage.

"She is nice, she is fat, she has been fed upon nuts!" the old robber-woman said, who had a long bristly beard, and eyebrows which hung down over her eyes.

"Why, she is as good as a fat lamb! How nice she will taste!" and she then drew out her long knife, which shone so that it was horrible to look at.

"Ow!" the woman cried at the same time, for she was bitten in the ear by her own daughter, who was hanging at her back, and who was so wild and wicked that nothing could be done with her. "You hateful imp!" the mother cried, and now had not time to kill Gerda.

"She shall play with me," the little robber-girl said. "She shall give me her muff and her beautiful dress, and shall sleep with me in my bed;" and she then bit her mother again, so that the woman jumped and twisted herself about, and the robbers laughed, shouting, "See how she dances with her cub!"

"I will get into the carriage"; and she would have her own way, for she was so obstinate and spoiled, so she and Gerda sat in it, and were driven over stones and through holes deeper into the forest. The little robber-girl was as tall as Gerda, but stronger, with broader shoulders and a dark skin. Her eyes were black, and had rather

The little robber-girl. (The Snow Queen.)

a melancholy expression. She laid hold of Gerda round the waist and said, "They shall not kill you, as long as I am not angry with you! You are a Princess, I suppose?"

"No," Gerda said, and told her all she had undergone, and how much she loved little Kay.

The robber-girl looked at her quite seriously, nodded her head slightly, and said, "They shall not kill you, if even I am angry with you; but I'll do it myself then." She dried Gerda's eyes, and then put both her hands in the beautiful muff, which was so soft and warm.

The carriage now stopped, and they were in the yard of a robber's castle. It was all in ruins, and the ravens and crows flew out of the holes, and large bulldogs, of which each looked as if it could devour a man, sprang towards them; but they did not bark, for that was forbidden.

In the large, old, smoke-coloured hall, in the middle of the stone floor, a huge fire was burning, and the smoke, rising to the roof, had to find itself an outlet. Soup was boiling in a caldron, and hares as well as rabbits were roasting on spits.

"Tonight you shall sleep with me, with all my animals," the robber-girl said; and after they had had something to eat and drink they went into a corner, where there was straw and a piece of carpet. More than a hundred pigeons sat above upon laths and sticks, and they all seemed to be asleep, though they did turn round a little at the approach of the two little girls.

"They all belong to me," the robber-girl said; and catching hold of one of the nearest by the feet, shook it till it flapped its wings. "Kiss her," she cried, and she struck Gerda in the face with it. "There, behind those bars, there are two that would fly away directly if they were not properly secured; and here stands my dear old Bae!" As she said this she pulled the horns of a reindeer, which was fastened by a bright copper ring it had round its neck. "We have to keep him a prisoner, too, or he would be off. Every evening I tickle his throat with my sharp knife, which frightens him dreadfully." The little girl drew a long knife out of a crack in the wall and let it glide across the reindeer's throat, which made the poor beast tremble and kick, and the little robber-girl, laughing, drew Gerda into the bed with her.

"Are you going to keep that knife in bed with you?" Gerda asked, and looked rather nervously at it.

"I always sleep with the knife," the robber-girl said; "one can never tell what may happen. But let me again hear what you said about little Kay, and why you came out into the wide world." And Gerda told all again from the beginning, and the wood-pigeons fluttered in their cage, but the others slept. The little robber-girl put one arm round Gerda's neck, holding the knife in the hand of the other, and soon fell asleep, but Gerda could not close her eyes, she did not know whether she was to live or whether death awaited her. The robbers sat round the fire, drinking and singing, whilst the robber-woman turned somersaults. It was quite horrible for the little girl to watch them.

The Wood-pigeons said, "Kourrou! Kourrou! We have seen little Kay. A white chicken carried his sledge, and he sat in the Snow Queen's carriage, which drove close over the forest, as we lay in our nest. She blew upon us young ones, and all excepting us two died. Kourrou! Kourrou!"

"What are you saying, up there?" Gerda asked. "Where was the Snow Queen going to? Do you know anything about it?"

"She was most likely going to Lapland, for there is always snow and ice there. Ask the Reindeer that is tied up there."

"There is ice and snow, and there it is delightful and healthy," the Reindeer said. "There one can jump and run about. There the Snow Queen has her summer tent, but her palace is up towards the North Pole, on the island which is called Spitzbergen."

"Oh, Kay! Dear little Kay!" Gerda sighed.

"You must now lie quiet," the robber-girl said, "or I will run the knife into you."

The next morning Gerda told her all that the Wood-pigeons had said, and the little robber-girl looked quite serious, but nodding her head said, "It doesn't matter! It doesn't matter! Do you know where Lapland is?" she asked the Reindeer.

"Who should know better than I?" the animal answered, its eyes sparkling. "I was born and bred there, and there I have run about on the snow-field."

"Listen!" the robber-girl said to Gerda. "You see that all the men are gone; my mother, however, is still here, and she will remain; but about midday she drinks out of the great flask, and then sleeps a little. I will then do something for you." She now jumped out of bed, rushed to her mother, and pulling her beard, said, "My own beloved goat, good morning!" Her mother in return filliped her on the nose, so that it was red and blue; but that was from sheer love.

As soon as her mother was asleep, after having drunk out of the flask, the robber-girl went to the reindeer, and said, "I might still have a good deal of fun, tickling you with the sharp knife, for then you are very odd; but that doesn't matter. I will unfasten you, and let you out, so that you may run back to Lapland; but you must make good use of your legs, and carry this little girl to the Snow Queen's palace, where her playfellow is. You heard what she said, for she spoke loud enough, and you were listening."

The reindeer jumped high up in the air with delight. The robber-girl lifted little Gerda on to its back, having taken the precaution to tie her fast, and even to give her a little cushion to sit upon. "It doesn't matter," she said. "There are your fur boots, for it will be cold; but the muff I shall keep, for it is too pretty. You shall not freeze, however, for you shall have my mother's large, warm gloves, which will reach up to your elbow. There, put them on. Now, as to your hands, you look exactly like my ugly mother."

Gerda cried with joy.

"I won't have you blubbering," the little robber-girl said; "you ought now to look particularly happy. Here are two loaves and a ham, so you will not die of hunger." Both were fastened behind her; and the little robber-girl opened the door, having chained up all the big dogs, cut the rope with her sharp knife, and said to the reindeer, "Now run; but take great care of the little girl."

Gerda stretched out her hands, with the large gloves on, towards the robber-girl, and cried, "Farewell!" And the reindeer flew as fast as possible through the great forest, and over heaths and marshes. The wolves howled, and the birds of prey screamed, "Atsche! Atsche!" It sounded from the sky exactly like sneezing.

"Those are my old northern lights," the Reindeer said; "see how they shine!" And then it ran even faster than before. It ran day and night. The loaves were demolished, and the ham also, and then they were in Lapland.

Story the Sixth

The Lapland Woman and the Finland Woman

They stopped at a small house, and a miserable place it was. The roof reached down to the ground, and the door was so low that the inmates had to crawl on their stomachs when they wanted to go in or out. There was no one at home, excepting an old woman, who was cooking fish by the light of a train-oil lamp, and to her the Reindeer told Gerda's whole story, but his own first, for this appeared to him by far the most important, and the cold had nipped Gerda, so that she could not speak.

"Oh, you poor creatures!" the old woman said, "you have far to run still. You must go more than a hundred miles into Finland, for there the Snow Queen lives. I will write a few words on a dried haberdine, for I have no paper, and that I will give you for the Finn up there, for she can give you more accurate information than I."

Now, as soon as Gerda was warm, and had got something to eat and drink, the old woman wrote a few words on a dried haberdine, begged Gerda to take great care of it, and having tied her on the reindeer again, off it started. "Atsche! Atsche!" it sounded from above, in the air, and the whole night long the northern lights shone the most beautiful blue. They arrived in Finland, and knocked at the Finn's chimney, for she had no door at all.

There was such a heat within, that the woman was nearly naked. She was little, and very dirty. She immediately undid Gerda's things, taking off her gloves and boots, for it would otherwise have been too hot for her; laid a lump of ice on the reindeer's head; and then read what was written on the haberdine. She read it three times, when she knew it by heart, so put the fish in the soup-pot, for it was good to eat, and she never wasted anything.

The Reindeer then told, first, its own story, and then Gerda's; and the little woman blinked with her clever eyes, but said nothing.

"You are so clever," the Reindeer said; "I know that you can bind all the winds of the world together with one piece of string, so that, when the sailor unfastens the one knot, he has a fair wind; if he unties the other, it blows freshly; but if the third and fourth, the wind rages that it overthrows the trees of the forest. Won't you prepare the little girl a drink to give her the strength of twelve men, so that she may vanquish the Snow Queen?"

"The strength of twelve men!" the little woman said. "That would help her a great deal." And then she went to a cupboard, from which she took a large rolled-up skin. As she unrolled it there appeared strange letters written, and she read till the water dripped down from her forehead.

But the Reindeer begged again so hard for Gerda, and she looked at the little woman with such beseeching eyes, full of tears, that she again began to blink her eyes, and, drawing the reindeer into a corner, whispered to him, whilst she put fresh ice upon his head.

"Little Kay is still with the Snow Queen, and finds everything there to his taste, so that he thinks it the best place in the world; but this is caused by his having a piece of broken glass in his heart, and another piece in his eyes. These must come out, or he will never be a man, and the Snow Queen will retain full power over him."

"But can you not give little Gerda something, so that she may obtain power over all?"

"I cannot give her greater power than she already possesses, and do you not see how great that is? Do you not see that men and beasts must serve her, and how, barefooted as she is, she has got on so well in the world? She cannot receive her power from us, that is in her own heart, and consists in her being a good, innocent child. If she cannot herself get into the Snow Queen's palace and free little Kay from the glass, we cannot help her. Ten miles from here the Snow Queen's garden beings, and there you must carry the little girl. Set her down at the large bush, which stands there in the snow, covered with red berries; and do not waste many words, but make haste

Gerda and the Finland woman. (The Snow Queen)

back here." The little woman then placed Gerda upon the reindeer, which ran off as fast as ever it could.

"Oh, I have not got my boots! I have not got my gloves!" little Gerda cried out, for this she noticed in the piercing cold; but the reindeer could not venture to stop, and it ran on till it came to the bush with the red berries. It there put her down, kissed her on the mouth, and large clear tears ran down the animal's cheeks when it started off back again. There stood poor Gerda, without boots and without gloves, in the middle of that fearfully cold Finland.

She ran forwards as fast as possible, and was soon met by a whole regiment of snow-flakes, which did not fall from heaven, for that was quite clear, but they ran straight along the ground, and the nearer they came the larger they grew. Gerda remembered how large and beautiful those looked which she saw through the magnifying glass; but these were much larger, and far different: they were living, and dreadful to look at – they were the Snow Queen's guards. They had the strangest shapes, some looking like frightful porcupines, others like knots of living snakes stretching out their heads, and others like fat little bears with bristly hair, but all were a glittering white – they were all living snow-flakes.

Little Gerda then prayed, and the cold was so great that she could see her own breath coming like smoke out of her mouth. The breath became denser and denser, at length assuming the forms of little angels, which grew larger and larger as they touched the ground. They all wore helmets on their heads, and held spears and shields in their hands, and their number was constantly increasing, so that, by the time Gerda had finished her prayer, she was surrounded by a whole legion. They thrust their spears into the frightful snow-flakes, breaking them into hundreds of peices, and Gerda went on joyously and in safety. The angels kissed her hands and feet, so that she felt less how extremely cold it was; and quickly she hastened on to the Snow Queen's palace.

But now let us first see what Kay was doing. He was certainly not thinking of little Gerda, and, least of all, that she was then standing outside the palace.

Story the Seventh

The Snow Queen's Palace

The palace walls were of driven snow, and the doors and windows of the cutting winds. There were more than a hundred rooms, as the snow had formed them, the largest extending several miles, and all were lighted by the bright northern lights. They were all so large, so empty, and so icy-cold and shining. There was never any amusement here, not even a bears' ball; for which the storm could have provided music, and the polar bears could have shown off their antics, walking on their hind feet. Never any card-parties, with tea and scandal, but empty, vast, and cold, were the rooms in the Snow Queen's palace. In the middle of the empty, immense snow-room there was a frozen lake, cracked into a thousand pieces, but each piece was so like the others that it appeared a master-work of art, and in the middle of this sat the Snow-Queen when she was at home. She used to say that she then sat in the mirror of reason, and that it was the only one in the world.

Little Kay was quite blue with cold – indeed almost black; but he did not know it, for she had kissed away the frost-shiver, and his heart was like a lump of ice. He was dragging some sharp-edged, flat pieces of ice about, and these he fitted together in all possible ways, just as we do small pieces of wood which we call the Chinese puzzle. Kay was also forming figures of the most wonderful description, and that was the ice-game of the understanding. In his eyes the figures were perfect, and of the highest importance, for the piece of broken glass which was in his eye made him think this. He formed whole words, but he could never succeed in the one word he wished to have – the word Eternity – for the Snow Queen had said to him, "If you can succeed in forming that one word you shall be your own master, and I will give you the whole world, together with a new pair of skates." But he could not.

"I am now going to pay a visit to the warmer countries," the Snow Queen said, "and intend giving a peep into the black caldrons"; she meant the volcanoes Etna and Vesuvius. "I will cover them with white, which will also do good to the orange-trees and vines." The Snow Queen then flew away, and Kay was left alone in those vast empty rooms, staring at the pieces of ice, and thinking and thinking, till his brain almost cracked. He sat there quite stiff and still, so that it appeared as if he were frozen.

Just then little Gerda came through the large gate into the palace. Here were cutting winds, but she said her evening prayer, and the winds were lulled as if they wanted to go to sleep, and she entered the large, empty, cold rooms. She then saw Kay, recognised him at once, and running up to him pressed him closely to her, and cried, "Kay! Dear little Kay! So I have found you at last!"

But he sat quite still, stiff and cold, and little Gerda cried bitter, burning tears, which fell upon his breast, and penetrating to his heart thawed the lump of ice, and dissolved the piece of broken glass. He looked at her, and she sang the hymn:-

"The rose blooms, but its glory past,
Christmas then approaches fast."

Kay then burst into tears, and cried till the pieces of glass were washed out of his eyes, when he recognised her, and exclaimed in delight, "Gerda! Dear little Gerda! Where have you been all this time? And where have I been?" He looked all around, and continued, "How cold it is here! And how vast and empty!" He pressed closely to her, and she laughed and cried in turns. There was such joy, that even the pieces of ice danced, and when they were tired and lay down again they formed the letters of the word which, when discovered, the Snow Queen said he should be his own master, and she would give him the whole world, besides a pair of new skates.

Gerda kissed his cheeks, and the colour came back into them; she kissed his eyes, and they were as bright as her own; she kissed his hands and feet, and he was himself again. The Snow Queen might now return, for his discharge was there written in sparkling ice.

They took each other by the hand, and wandered out of the palace. They spoke of their grandmother, and of the rose-trees upon the roof, and wherever they went the winds were lulled and the sun burst forth; and when they got to the bush with the red berries they found the reindeer waiting for them, and another with it. These carried them first to the little woman, in whose hot room they warmed themselves, and got information about their homeward journey, and then to the old Lapland-woman, who had made new clothes for them and got a sledge ready.

The two reindeer took them quickly to the borders of the country, and there the first green was springing up. Here they parted from the reindeer and the old Lapland-woman, and all cried "Farewell!" The little birds began to twitter, the buds were green on the trees in the forest, and out of it came riding a young girl on a beautiful horse which Gerda knew, for it was one that had been harnessed to the golden carriage. This was the robber-girl with a red cap on her head, and pistols in her belt. She had enough of home, and was now travelling towards the north, and to take another direction later, if that did not please her. She and Gerda immediately recognised each other, and there was great rejoicing.

"You are a pretty fellow," she said to little Kay; "I should like to know whether you deserve that one should run to the end of the world after you."

But Gerda tapped her on the cheek, and asked after the Prince and Princess.

"They have gone to a foreign country," the robber-girl said.

"And the Ravens?" Gerda asked.

"The Raven is dead," she answered, "and his wife, now a widow, goes about with a piece of black cotton round her leg, and laments dreadfully; but that is nothing but words. But now tell me how it fared with you, and how you managed to catch him."

Gerda and Kay told her all.

The robber-girl took them both by the hand, and promised that if ever she should pass through their town she would mount up to visit them, and then she rode on into the wide world. Gerda and Kay continued their way hand in hand. It was delightful spring, with green leaves and beautiful flowers; the church-bells rang, and they recognised the high steeples and the large city; it was that in which they lived: so they entered it and went to the grandmother's house, up the stairs, and into the room, where everything was just as it used to be, the clock going "tick, tick!" and the hands moving, but they then noticed that they were no longer children. The roses from the roof gutter, in full bloom, hung in at the open window; and there stood the two children's stools, and Gerda seated herself on hers, and Kay took his, holding each other still by the hand. The cold, empty splendour in the Snow Queen's palace was forgotten like a disagreeable dream. The grandmother sat in the clear sunshine, and read aloud out of the Bible, "Whosoever shall not receive the kingdom of God as a little child, shall in no wise enter heaven."

Kay and Gerda looked at each other, and both thought of the old hymn:-

"The rose blooms, but its glory past,
Christmas then approaches fast."

There they sat, grown up and yet children; for in their hearts they were children, and it was summer – warm, delightful summer.

The Nightingale

In China, you know, the Emperor is Chinese, and the people whom he has around him are all Chinese. It is many years ago since the events of my story took place, but on that very account they deserve the more to be listened to, before they are forgotten. The Emperor's palace was, with good reason, considered the most magnificent in the whole world, for it was built entirely of the finest porcelain, so costly, but at the same time so fragile, and so dangerous to be touched, that one could not be sufficiently on one's guard with it. In the garden there were the scarcest flowers, the most beautiful of which had silver bells hanging to them, and these rang melodiously, of their own accord, so that no one might pass them without duly admiring such wonders from the vegetable kingdom. Everything was of the most extraordinary kind in the Emperor's garden, which was of such extent, that even the gardener did not know exactly where it ended. If, however, one walked straight on, one came at last to a beautiful forest, with high trees and deep lakes. This forest bordered immediately on the most picturesque shore of infinite extent, which the bottomless sea sprinkled with its snow-white foam. Large ships could sail in close under the branches of the trees, and here, amongst the shady foliage, lived a Nightingale, which sang so sweetly, that even the poor fisherman, who must not

The Nightingale.

neglect a single minute, if, in the Celestial Empire, he would, by the most untiring industry, gain the merest pittance on which to subsist, was accustomed to rest there for a moment to listen with delight as soon as the Nightingale sang, when he was out at night drawing in his nets. "Oh, heavens, how beautiful it is!" he often involuntarily exclaimed. But more than one instant he must not indulge in such delights, for his hard work had to be done, and during the labours of the day he forgot the bird in the grove; but the next night, when the Nightingale sang, and the fisherman, as usual, came to that part, he again exclaimed, "Oh, heavens, how beautiful it is!"

From all countries travellers flocked to the Imperial city, and in amazement admired it, as well as the palace and the garden; but when they heard the Nightingale, they all with one voice exclaimed, "The Chinese magic bird is the most wonderful of all."

When the travellers returned to their countries, they narrated all they had seen, and the learned wrote many thick books describing the city, the palace, and the garden. Neither did they forget the Nightingale, which indeed was made most of; and those who could write poetry coupled the most ingenious verses together, in praise of the feathered wonder of the Chinese forest by the side of the deep sea.

By degrees these books and verses got spread over the world, and fate, which has a hand in everything, carried some of them even to the Emperor of China. The ruler of the "Celestial Empire" sat reading in his armchair of gold, and every two or three minutes nodded his head, for it gave him unbounded pleasure to read the pompous descriptions of his city, palace, and garden, as he most condescendingly turned over the leaves. "But the Nightingale is the best of all." This he found written in several places.

"What can that mean?" the Emperor said. "The Nightingale that I do not know at all. Can it be possible that there is such a bird in my empire, and that, too, in my garden? The like is only learnt by reading."

He now ordered his cavalier, or gentleman-usher, before him, who was so high a personage, that when any one who was beneath him in rank ventured to address him, or ask him a question, he need give no other answer than "Pah!" and that means nothing at all.

"There is said to be here a most extraordinary bird, called the Nightingale," the Emperor uttered, with much gravity. "It is said that this little creature is the most remarkable curiosity in the whole of my unbounded states. Why have I never been told anything whatever about it?"

"May your Majesty please to excuse me, but never before have I heard such a creature mentioned," the cavalier answered. "Such a person, at least, has never been presented at court," he added.

"It is my will that she appears tonight, and sings before me. Here, all the world knows what I possess, and I myself know nothing of it."

"I have never, till now, heard the name," the cavalier humbly assured his

The Hell horse turned quite giddy and had to leave the table. (The Elfin-Hillock.)

Early in the morning the Queen took three hideous toads into the bathroom with her. (The Wild Swans.)

Imperial Majesty. "But I will seek the person, and will find her."

But where was the wonderful songstress to be found? The cavalier ran up and down the stairs, rushed through halls and passages, but none of those whom he met had heard speak of the Nightingale. So the cavalier ran back to the Emperor, and said that it certainly must be one of the many fables that are frequently found in books.

"Your Majesty must not believe everything that is printed or written," he said, touching the earth with his forehead. "This is a mere invention, such as is called the black art."

"But the book in which I have read it," the Emperor said, "has been sent me by the mighty Emperor of Japan, so there can be nothing that is untrue in it. In short, I am determined to hear the Nightingale. She must be here this evening, for it is my intention to show her my utmost favour. And if she does not appear at the proper time in my palace, then, at supper-time, the whole court shall receive a sound bastinadoing on their empty stomachs."

"Tsing-tza!" the cavalier groaned, as he again rushed up and down the stairs, through halls and passages; and half the court ran with him, for the good people were most anxious to spare themselves the threatened bastinadoing on an empty stomach. There was a seeking and inquiring after the Nightingale, which all the world, excepting the people at the Imperial court, knew so well.

At last, in the kitchen, they fell upon a poor little girl, the daughter of one of the lowest of the cooks. She exclaimed, "Oh, dear me! yes, the Nightingale I know well. Oh how she sings! Every evening I have permission to carry home a little of the remains from the table, to my sick mother, who lies down on the shore, and when returning tired, I rest in the forest, I hear the dear Nightingale sing. Tears then come into my eyes; yes, I feel just as if my good mother were kissing me."

"Little kitchen wench," the cavalier said, "I will obtain you a permanent appointment in the kitchen, besides the permission to see the Emperor sup, if you lead us to the Nightingale, for she is invited here this evening."

Then they all wandered together into the forest, where the Nightingale was in the habit of singing. Half the court, at the very least, were present, and when they had got about half way, a cow began to low.

"Oh," said the chief page, "now we have her! It is certainly a remarkable power of voice for so small a creature. But it strikes me that I have heard this sound before, somewhere or another."

"No, those are the cows lowing," the little girl said. "We are still far from the place."

The frogs then croaked in the pond.

"Delightful! Truly delightful!" the commander of the bodyguard said: "now I hear her, the celebrated singer. It sounds like church bells, only subdued."

"No!" the little girl again said, "those are the frogs; but I think we shall now soon hear her."

Immediately after the Nightingale struck up with a long, long shake.

"That is she," the little girl whispered, pointing with her finger to a little ash-grey bird sitting high up amongst the branches. "Listen, listen! And there, you can see her!"

"Can it be possible?" the cavalier said. "I should never have imagined her like that. How plain she is! No doubt she has lost her colour, seeing so many noble persons before her."

"Little Nightingale," the girl cried out, quite loud, "our most gracious Emperor desires so much that you will sing before him."

"With the greatest pleasure," the Nightingale answered, and sang so sweetly, that it was real delight to listen to her.

"It is exactly as if a number of glass bells were ringing harmoniously together. Upon my honour, like harmoniously tuned glass bells," the cavalier asserted. "And how she exerts her little throat! It is strange, indeed, that we never heard her before. For certain she will have great success at court."

"Shall I sing any more to the Emperor?" the Nightingale said, under the impression that the Emperor was present.

"My most esteemed little lady," the cavalier said, "I have the – to me so flattering – commssion, to invite you this evening to a party at court, where you will delight our most gracious Emperor with your charming singing."

"That sounds better in the open air," the Nightingale said. She, however, went willingly with them, as she understood that the Emperor wished it.

The palace was set off to the greatest advantage; the walls and floors, which were both of more or less transparent porcelain, glittered with the reflection of many thousand golden lamps, like the sparkling stars of the milky way. The rarest flowers, which failed not to use their bells, stood in rows, ranged along the ante-room. There was much running backwards and forwards, and a strong draft; but the bells rang all the more melodiously, so that people could scarcely hear even themselves talk.

Across the middle of the great hall, where the Emperor sat, there might be seen a golden rod, which was to be the Nightingale's seat of honour. The whole court was present, even the little kitchen wench, who had received permission to stand behind the door, now that she held the appointment of a court cook. All were dressed out to the best, and every one looked with curiosity at the little unsightly grey bird, to which the Emperor nodded most graciously.

The Nightingale sang so sweetly and affectingly, that large tears came into the Emperor's eyes. The tears rolled down his cheeks, and the Nightingale sang more and more enchantingly. Did it touch his heart, I wonder? Yes, the Emperor was so affected, that he said the Nightingale should wear his golden slipper round its neck. But the Nightingale thanked him modestly, and declined the great honour, as she felt herself sufficiently rewarded by the Emperor's approbation.

"I have seen tears in the Emperor's eyes; those are the most valuable treasures. The tears of a monarch possess a wonderful virtue; heaven knows, I am rewarded enough." And now she sang again, with her sweet, enchanting voice.

"It is the most delightful accomplishment that I know of," each of the ladies said, as they sat around in a circle, and each took water in her mouth, that she might warble when spoken to, and then they thought that they were nightingales also. What will not female vanity do, particularly when supported by the imagination! Even the footmen and maids expressed their satisfaction; which is a great thing, for to do anything to please them rightly, is the most difficult of all tasks. The Nightingale had, indeed, wonderful success.

She was now to pass her life at court, was to have a cage of her own, with liberty to take an airing twice in the day, and once at night. Twelve servants, however, were to accompany her, each holding her by a silken string, fastened round her slender leg. These excursions afforded no particular pleasure, as they reminded her too much of the restricted walks of a state-prisoner.

The whole town, in the meantime, spoke with its many hundred thousand tongues of the indigenous, but till then, unknown wonderful bird; and when two people met in the street, the one said "Night", the other "In", when they understood each other without the "Gale". Even eleven children of the highest families, boys and girls, were named after the feathered songstress, but not one of them could ever sing.

One day a large parcel, with "The Nighingale" written on the outside, was delivered to the Emperor.

"Here we have another book about our celebrated bird," the Emperor said. It was, however, no book, but an automaton of inexpressible value, a costly little plaything, which lay securely packed, in a neat box. It was a Nightingale of most ingenious mechanism, resembling the real bird in every respect, excepting that it was nearly weighed down by a covering of diamonds, rubies, and sapphires. When this bird was wound up like a watch, it sang one of the real Nightingale's songs, imitating the shakes most accurately; and then its tail wagged up and down, sparkling with gold and silver. Round its neck was a scarlet ribbon with these words embroidered, symbolic of the flowery manner of speech of those countries: "The Nightingale of the Emperor of Japan is poor compared to that of the Emperor of China."

"That is splendid!" the ladies and gentlemen said; and the bearer of the ingenious bird received his patent in a sealed letter, with the title of "First Imperial Nightingale bearer".

"Now they must sing together. Oh, what a duet that will be!"

This was done, but they did not get on well together, for the real Nightingale sang in its own peculiar manner, whereas the other sang methodically, and the practised ear of a musician might easily have detected a grating sound of the machinery. But the reader must recollect that they were only Chinese.

The leader of the Imperial band assured them all, "The noble lady in the box keeps perfect time, and is quite of my school."

The artificial bird was then made to sing alone, and had equal success to the real one. With what splendour, too, it presented itself, glittering like diadems, necklaces, and bracelets of precious stones! Thirty-three times it sang off the same piece as accurately as clockwork, and yet it was not tired. The people would gladly have heard it once more from the beginning, but the Emperor thought that, for a change, the real Nightingale should be heard a little. However, she was nowhere to be found. No one had noticed how, taking advantage of being unobserved, she had flown out of the open window, away into the green forest, where the sea-breeze blew.

"What is the meaning of this?" the Emperor grumbled, offended at the unceremonious departure of the grey lady. All the courtiers scolded, and were of opinion that the Nightingale was a most ungrateful creature, utterly unworthy of having basked in the sunshine of the Imperial favour.

"However, the better bird remains with us," they said, and the artificial bird had to sing again. This was the thirty-fourth time that, as taken out of the box, the bird sang the same piece to them, but did not yet know the end of it, it was so difficult. The leader of the Imperial band bestowed unbounded praise upon the bird, and assured them, on his honour as a musician, that it was better than the little grey lady herself, not only with respect to outward appearance, on account of the many beautiful diamonds, but also as to its inner worth.

"For note, my lords and ladies, your Majesty in particular, that with the real Nightingale one can never calculate as to her song, neither how it will begin, continue, nor end; whereas, all in the artificial bird goes by rule: so it will be, and no otherwise. One can with certainty tell beforehand how every part will be; and indeed the mechanism will prove how one part must necessarily follow another, as clearly as a correctly worked arithmetical sum."

"That is exactly how I think," each said at the same time; and the leader of the band had permission to exhibit the bird to the public on the following Sunday, for the good Emperor said, "Why should I not give my poor subjects a treat, particularly as it will cost me nothing?" So all heard the glittering bird, and were as delighted as if they had intoxicated themselves with drinking tea, which is the custom in China, and all cried out, "Oh!" at the same time holding up one finger, nodding and wagging their heads from side to side. But the poor fisherman, who had heard the real Nightingale in the forest, shook his head and said to himself, "That sounds pretty enough, it is true, and is very like, but there is something wanting, I don't know rightly what."

The real Nightingale was for ever banished from the Imperial states, but she troubled herself little about that, keeping quietly in her shady grove.

The artificial bird had its place on a satin cushion by the side of the Emperor's bed; all the presents that were made it, ornaments and jewels, were spread out around it. In title it had risen to "Imperial Nightingale Singer", and in rank to "Number One on the left side", for the Emperor considered the left side the noblest, where the heart is, and an Emperor's heart is on the left side, the same as other people's. The worthy leader of the band wrote twenty-five volumes full, respecting the bird. They were so learned and far-fetched, and so lavishly interlarded with the very most difficult Chinese words, that all at once said, they had read, and understood them too, for if not they would be stupid, and the bastinado on a full stomach was the punishment for proved stupidity.

So matters went on for a whole year. His majesty, the court, and all other Chinese knew every shake, however insignificant, in the song of the nobled jewelled lady by heart, and just for that reason they liked the bird all the better, for they could now join in, which they did not fail to do. The boys in the streets sang "Pipipi, gluck – gluck – gluck!" and the Emperor sang the same, though, perhaps, in a different tone of voice. Now what could be more delightful?

One evening, however, when the bird had been singing its very best, and the Emperor lay in bed listening, it went "Kur-r-r" inside the bird. Something had snapped, the wheels whirled round, and there was an end to the music.

The Emperor jumped out of bed in an instant, and had the court surgeon called, but what good could he do in such a case? The court watchmaker was next called, who, after long consideration and examination, at last succeeded in putting it to rights, in a certain measure; but he said at the same time that the greatest possible care must be taken of it in future, for that, from constant use, many parts of the works were very much worn, and that these could not be put in new without destroying the harmony of the whole. This misfortune caused great sorrow, as may be imagined; and henceforth the now half-pensioned-off, after-dinner, imperial singer was allowed to sing only once a year, and then only with great risk and precautions; but the leader of the band then delivered a short and most incomprehensible address, proving that, with respect to the singer's celebrity, there could be no possible difference between past and present, and that the bird was therefore as good as ever.

Five years had now passed over, when the whole land was unexpectedly thrown into the deepest distress, by the startling news that the old Emperor was so seriously ill that his death might momentarily be expected, for all were sincerely attached to their magnanimous monarch, by whose decease they would in fact gain nothing, but might be much worse off under his successors. A new Emperor was already chosen, and a countless mass of people thronged the streets of the capital, but more particularly the large court of the palace. From all corners the poor, fagged cavalier was overwhelmed with the thousand-times-repeated question, "How is our Emperor?"

"Pah!" he said, and shrugged his shoulders.

Cold and pale the Emperor lay in his large, magnificent bed; the whole court thought him dead, and all hastened to pay their humble respects to his successor. The footmen ran out to chat about it out-of-doors, and the maids had large tea-parties within. In all parts, in the passages and the halls, matting had been laid down, so that no footstep might be heard, and it was therefore doubly quiet. But the old Emperor had still a little life in him, though he certainly lay there, stiff and pale in his splendid bed, with the long satin curtains and the heavy gold tassels. There stood a window open, and the moon shone in, as if in pity, upon the sick Emperor and the artificial bird.

The poor Emperor could scarcely breathe, he felt as if some weight lay on his chest. With difficulty he opened his eyes, and saw with horror that Death had made his oppressed chest its throne. On its bare skull it had placed the golden crown, in one hand holding the Emperor's sword of state, and in the other his magnificent flag; and on all sides, out of the folds of the full satin bed-curtains, peeped the most extraordinary heads, some very ugly, but others, on the contrary, most lovely and mild. These were the bad and good actions of the Emperor, which, now that Death had possession of him, were looking deep into his heart, like stern, unbending judges.

"Do you remember?" sounded from one side. "Do you remember?" sounded from another, and drops of cold perspiration stood upon his forehead.

"That I never knew!" groaned the tortured Chinese Emperor. "Music, music, the large drum!" he cried in despair, "so that I may not hear all these impertinent visions are preaching."

They, however, continued, and Death nodded each time that anything new was said, like a real Chinese.

"Music, music!" the Emperor cried; "sing, you delightful little jewelled bird! Sing, sing! I have given you gold and precious stones, and I, myself, have hung my golden slipper round your neck, so sing, pray sing!"

But the bird stood immoveable, for there was no one present to wind it up, and without that it could not sing, Death in the meantime staring at the Emperor with its hollow eye-sockets, and all was still – so fearfully still.

All of a sudden, close to the window, there sounded the most delightful song. It was the little live Nightingale, sitting on a branch without, for she had heard of her Emperor's distress, and had come to sing him hope and consolation; and as she sang the spectral visions became fainter and fainter, the stagnant blood began to flow again, through the weak limbs of the gradually reviving body, and Death itself listened with astonishment, saying, "Go on, go on, little Nightingale, go on!"

"Yes, if you will give me the beautiful golden sword, if you will give me the rich flag, and the Emperor's crown."

Death gave up each bauble for a song, and still the Nightingale went on. She sang louder and louder and more irresistibly; she sang of the quiet burial-ground, where the white roses grow, where sweet marjoram scents the air, and where the grass is bedewed with the tears of mourners. Death was seized with an irresistible longing for his garden, and, like a cold white mist, floated out at the window.

"Thanks, thanks," the Emperor sighed, breathing more freely. "I know you well, you heavenly bird. I, fool, banished you from my empire, and yet you have sung the frightful visions away from my bed, and have driven Death from my heart! How can I reward you?"

"I have received my reward, above my deserts, beforehand," the Nightingale answered, "for, the first time I sang I drew tears into my Emperor's eyes, which I shall never forget. These are the jewels a singer's heart delights in. Now go to sleep and awaken refreshed and well! In the meanwhile I will continue to sing to you."

The sun was shining through the stained window, when he awoke refreshed and strengthened. As yet none of the servants had returned, for they thought him dead, but the Nightingale was at her post singing.

"You must remain with me for ever," the Emperor said. "You shall sing only when you feel inclined, and the artificial jewelled bird I will break into a thousand pieces."

"No, do not do that," the Nightingale said, "for it has done as much as it could. Keep it the same as ever. Besides, I cannot live in the palace, but let me come when I am inclined, and then of an evening I will sit in the branches, there at the window, and sing my best, so that you shall be happy, and at the same time thoughtful. I shall sing of those that are happy, and of those that suffer, but bear their troubles with patience; in fact, I shall sing of the good and the evil, which unfortunately is but too often unknown to you. The little bird flies far around, to the poor fisherman, to the peasants' thatched huts, to all who are far away from you and your court. I love your heart more than your crown, although the crown has a certain almost sacred halo around it. I will come, then, from time to time, and sing to you as much as you wish, but one thing you must promise me."

"Everything!" the Emperor cried, and standing there in his imperial splendour with which he had clad himself unaided, he held the point of his heavy gold sword to his heart, in confirmation of his promise.

"One thing I beg of you. Tell no living soul that you have a little bird that tells you everything, and all will go on well."

Therewith the Nightingale flew away.

At length the servants appeared to look after their dead Emperor; yes, there they stood, and the Emperor said, "Good morning."

The little lovers.

The Little Lovers

A Whipping-top and a Ball lay next to each other in a drawer, amongst a quantity of other playthings, and the Whipping-top said to the Ball, "Why should we not be lovers, since we are lying together in the same drawer?" But the Ball, which was made of satin, and thought as much of itself as any pretty girl, deigned no answer.

The following day, the little boy, to whom the playthings belonged, went to the drawer, and painted the Top red and yellow, quite smart, and drove a bright brass-headed nail through the middle of it. It looked quite magnificent, as the Top turned round and round, with the velocity of a whirlwind.

"Look at me attentively, I pray," he said to the Ball, with a self-satisfied air. "Why should we not be engaged as well as others? We are admirably suited to each other, for you jump and I dance. We should be as happy as the day is long."

"What are you thinking of?" the fine little lady, the Ball, answered pertly. "Perhaps you do not know that my father and my mother were real satin slippers, and that I have a ball of Spanish cork in my body."

"Yes, but then I am of mahogany wood," the Top answered, "and the town-clerk himself turned me, for he has his own turning-lathe, and the work gave him the greatest possible pleasure."

"Well, but may I confidently trust to that?" the Ball said, incredulously.

"May I never be whipped again if I tell a falsehood," the Top said, impressively.

"There is no denying that you speak well," the Ball replied; "but still I cannot say yes, for, in fact, I am half engaged, and that to a most charming Swallow. Every time that I fly up in the air, he thrusts his head out of his nest, and whispers 'Will you?' And now I have fully made up my mind, which is nearly the same as an engagement. However, I promise that I will never forget you."

"That is a pretty consolation to me," the Top grumbled, and they spoke no more together.

Some days later the Ball was taken out of the drawer. The Top saw with astonishment how, like a lively bird, she flew high up in the air, until the eye could scarcely reach her, but soon returned from the upper regions, and when she touched the ground always gave a high jump. This was either from buoyancy of spirits, or because she had a cork in her body. But the ninth time the Ball did not return at all. The boy looked and looked, but it was gone.

"I know well where the charming creature is," the Top sighed. "She is in the Swallow's nest, and has married him."

The more the Top thought of it, the more strongly he felt himself attracted by the lost Ball. Just because he could not gain the object of his love, his consuming passion increased tenfold, and her marriage with another only added fuel to the fire, constantly increasing the flame. As formerly, the Top danced round and round, but his thoughts were perpetually with the Ball, who, waking or dreaming, appeared to him constantly in a new light of increased perfection.

Thus many years passed over, till by degrees it became an old love.

Neither was the Top young any longer, and therefore he was one day gilt all over, so that he had never before seen himself, nor had any one else seen him, in such splendour. He was now a golden Top, and sprang doubly high. It can be imagined that the dancing went well; but once he jumped too high, and was gone.

Where was he? Guess who can.

Quite unintentionally he had sprung into the dust-bin, where all manner of useless things had been thrown, and lay heaped together, forming a strange medley enough. There were old cabbage-stalks, potato-peelings, lettuce-leaves, bits of dirty rag and dust, together with sand, lime, and small stones, which had fallen off the roof.

"Well, I have got into nice quarters," he moralised, pretty loud. "Here I shall soon lose my gilding. And what tag-rag I have fallen amongst!" he grumbled, as he looked with contempt upon a long cabbage-stalk without a vestige of leaf, and which had not even the grace to be ashamed of its disgusting nakedness. His eyes then rested upon a most extraordinary round thing, which, from its appearance, looked like a half-rotten, shrivelled old apple. It was, however, not an apple, but an old, soaked through, torn ball, which lay for several years in the roof-gutter, till at length it had been washed down by a heavy fall of rain.

"Thank goodness that a decent being has come, with whom one can have a little talk!" the Ball said, looking with admiration at the gilt Top. "The fact is, that I am made of satin," the now no-longer pretty little lady continued after a while; "I was sewn by delicate maiden hands, and have a ball of real Spanish cork in my body, though no one would guess it to look at me now. I was on the point of being married to a Swallow, when I fell into the roof-gutter, where I lay, unfortunately, a whole eternity of five years without pleasure; indeed, without a covering, exposed to bad weather and dampness, whilst my best years were flying past. Believe me, such a hard fate was not promised me in my cradle."

But the Top made no answer. He thought of his old love, and the more he heard the more evident it became that this was she and no one else.

Then the cook came to empty something into the bin.

"Well, I never! If this is not Master Rudolph's gold Top," she cried.

And the Top appeared again in the drawing-room, where it was held in great honour and esteem; but of the Ball nothing more was heard, neither did the Top talk at all about his old love. What love, indeed, would bear an eternity of five years' lying in a wet, dirty gutter, exposed to all weathers and all sorts of mishaps? Why, no one would recognise the object of his deepest veneration if met with in a dust-bin.

The Flying Trunk

There lived once, in a certain town, which you would now look for in vain on a map, a merchant, who was so rich that he could have paved the whole street in which his house stood with silver money, and perhaps the little street that ran into it as well; but he did nothing of the sort, for he knew how to make better use of his money. If he parted with a shilling it came back to him a pound; that is the sort of merchant he was; but he died at last.

Now his son inherited all this money, and he led a merry life, going every night to masquerades, and making kites with bank-notes, besides amusing himself with throwing ducks and drakes on the glassy surface of the lake, just below his window, with gold pieces instead of stones. By such means the money might well disappear; and so it did, till at last he possessed no more than four shillings, and had no other clothing but a pair of slippers and an old dressing-gown. His friends now naturally took no notice of him, since they could no longer walk in the streets together; but one of them, who was particularly good-natured, sent him an old trunk, with the well-meant advice, "To pack up as soon as possible." That was all very well; but the poor spendthrift had nothing to pack up, so he put himself in the trunk.

A most curious piece of furniture it was. When the lock was pressed the trunk

The flying trunk.

could fly. So it happened, to the no slight astonishment of the young man, who now flew up the chimney, high above the clouds, as if in a balloon. Further and further he flew, the bottom of the box giving an occasional crack, as if it would break in pieces; and the venturesome traveller was dreadfully frightened, for in that case he would have a pretty fall. That, however, did not happen, and at length he reached the country of the Turks. The trunk he carefully hid in the forest, under some dry leaves, and went straightway to the city, near to the gates of which he had arrived in so extraordinary a manner. There was no impropriety whatever in this, for the Turks all go about in slippers and dressing-gowns, like himself. On his way he met a nurse with a little Turkish child in her arms.

"Listen to me, you Turkish woman," he said, "what castle is this, close to the city, with the high windows?"

"The king's daughter lives there," she answered. "It has been prophesied that a lover will cause her much heart-ache, and therefore no one is allowed to go near her, unless accompanied by the king and queen."

"Many thanks," said the merchant's son, and hastened back into the forest, seated himself in his trunk, and flew up on to the roof of the castle, whence he crept through a window into the room where the Princess was.

She was lying on a sofa asleep, and she was so wonderfully beautiful, that the young man could not resist kissing her on the instant. She awoke quite frightened, but he said he was the God of the Turks, who had flown through the air down to her, to honour her with his company, and to this she had nothing to object.

So they sat side by side, in confidential conversation, and he told her stories of her eyes, how they were the most beautiful dark lakes, in which the thoughts swam about like alluring mermaids! He told her stories of her forehead, how it was a proud mountain of snow with magnificent chambers and paintings! And he told her of the storks, how they brought the pretty little children.

These were, indeed, delightful stories! And then, in well-chosen words, he besought the Princess to marry him, to which she immediately said yes.

"But you must come again next Saturday evening," she said. "Exactly at six o'clock the king and queen are here to tea, and they will certainly feel highly flattered to have the God of the Turks for a son-in-law. But be prepared, my friend, to tell us a really pretty story, for my parents dote on such. For my mother, it must be moral and exalted, but to suit my father it must be merry – something very laughable."

"Well, I will bring a story, and that will be my only wedding present," he answered, embracing her. Herewith they parted, the Princess having buckled a magnificent sabre round his loins, the sheath of which was adorned with gold coins, and gold coins were particularly useful to him.

He now flew away, bought himself a new dressing-gown, and a few hours later was seated in the forest composing a story to be ready by Saturday, which was no such easy matter.

After much thought and consideration it seemed to be in a fair way, and was ready on Saturday exactly at six o'clock.

The king, the queen, and the whole court were waiting for their tea at the Princess's, and they received the strange suitor most civilly.

After tea the queen begged he would tell them a story. "I pray," she said, "let it be very profound and instructive."

"But let us have a good hearty laugh, too," the king put in.

"Most certainly," the stranger assured them, and he began after hemming only three times.

Now listen attentively.

"There was once a bundle of Matches, and they scarcely knew what to do with themselves for very pride, for they considered themselves of remarkably high descent. The head of the family, that is a mighty pine-tree, of which they were small splinters, had been formerly a large old tree in a northern forest. The Matches were now lying on a rather bare hearth in the kitchen, between a Tinder-box and an old Iron-pot, to whom they were telling the most remarkable events of their youth. 'You may believe us,' they said, 'whilst we were still a green branch – we were, in fact, a green branch – every morning and evening we had diamond tea,' that was the dew, 'and the whole day we had sunshine, when the sun shone, and all the little birds had to sing to us, or amuse us with interesting stories. We could plainly see that we were rich, for the other trees had decent clothing only during the summer, whereas our whole family wore, even during the hardest winter, a beautiful green dress, which neither wind nor frost could rob us of. At last, however, in the midst of this pleasant life, the woodcutters came – that was the dreadful revolution that cut up our family. The head of the family was appointed to the post of main-mast on a magnificent ship, which could sail round the world if it would. The branches were otherwise disposed of, and it is our tedious, though undoubtedly honourable, employment to give light to the lower orders, on which account we are banished here into the kitchen, away from the society of the great.'

"'Well, it has been different with me,' said the Iron-pot, next to which the Matches lay. 'From the very beginning of my life I have been first put on the fire, and then scoured. The solids are my care, and I am, in fact, the first person in the house. My only pleasure is after dinner to stand neat and clean upon the shelf, and have some sensible conversation with my comrades. With the exception of the Pail, which sometimes gets out into the yard, we, however, lead a more secluded life here than in a convent. Our only news-purveyor is the Market-basket; but he talks too freely of the government and of the people. Why, it was only yesterday, I think, that an old jug fell off the shelf from sheer fright, and broke into pieces.'

"'You chatter too much,' the Tinder-box interrupted her, and the flint and steel came in such violent contact that sparks followed. 'Let us now have a merry evening of it.'

"'Let us discuss which of us is of the noblest birth,' the Matches said.

"'No, I do not like talking about myself,' a Dish said. 'Let us rather have a general friendly conversation. I will make a beginning, and tell things such as every one has experienced, for then one can enter so thoroughly into the story, and it becomes really amusing. Well, on the coast of the German Ocean, under the shade of the Danish beech forests – '

"'What a delightful beginning!' the Plates exclaimed with one voice. 'That will certainly be a story after our own hearts!'

"'Well, there I spent my youth in a quiet family. Each piece of furniture was dazzlingly bright, that one might see oneself in it. Every morning the floor of hard, white wood, most tastefully laid down in a pattern, was scoured clean, and regularly every fortnight clean curtains were put up.'

"'My gracious! How interestingly you do tell the story!' the Broom interrupted. 'One can see at once that it is a lady who is talking, for there is something so neat and tidy in it all.'

"'Yes, indeed, one feels that without a doubt,' the Pail asserted; and it gave a little hop of delight, that it went splash on the floor.

"The Dish now went on with its story, and the end was in no way inferior to the so much promising beginning.

"All the Plates rattled with delight, whilst the Broom fetched some dry flowers out of the dust-hole and crowned the Dish with a wreath, for she knew it would vex the others; and she said to herself, 'If I crown her to-day she will crown me tomorrow.'

"'Now I'll dance,' the Tongs said, and she did dance. Oh dear, how she lifted up one leg in the air, nearly as high and much more gracefully than Mademoiselle Elsler! The old chair-cover in the corner split with staring at her. 'Am I not to be crowned too?' the Tongs asked, and she was crowned.

"'They are only low people,' the Matches thought.

"Now the Tea-urn was asked to sing, but she excused herself, saying she was cold, and could only sing when very hot, which, however, was her pride, for she would only sing when she was grand, standing on the drawing-room table.

"In the left-hand corner of the window there lay an old Pen the cook was in the habit of writing with, and in which there was nothing particularly remarkable, excepting that it had gone down too deeply in the inkstand, but just this it was proud of. 'If the Tea-urn won't sing,' it said, 'she is quite welcome to leave it alone. Outside, in a cage, there is a Nightingale, who is a little musical too. It is true that she hasn't a note of school-learning, but this evening we will be particularly lenient.'

"'Well, I think it highly improper that a stranger should be heard,' the Tea-kettle said, who was the kitchen-singer, and half-brother to the Urn. 'Is that patriotic? I appeal to the Market-basket, who is a man of experience; let him decide.' 'What a rage it puts me in to hear all this nonsense,' the grumbling old Market-basket said; 'would it not be more sensible to turn the house topsy-turvey, and then, perhaps, some of us would get into their proper places? That would be another sort of fun.'

"'Yes, let us have a regular row,' all cried together; but at that very moment the door opened and the servant came in, when all were immediately as quiet as mice. Not a syllable was uttered, but there was not one of them, the smallest or the meanest, that did not feel what he or she could do. "'Yes, if I had wished,' they thought, 'it would certainly have been a merry night.'"

"The servant lighted the Matches. Oh, how they fizzed, and with what a blue flame they burned!

"'Now,' they thought, 'every blockhead amongst them can see that we are the first. What splendour! what a light!' And then all was over, for they were burned out."

"That was a delightful story," the Queen said. "I felt exactly as if I were in the kitchen with the Matches. You shall certainly have my daughter."

"That, as a matter of course," the King said, nodding approval. "Monday next you shall have our daughter; so now, my friend, you may consider yourself one of the family."

The wedding-day was fixed, and the night before the whole city was illuminated. Biscuits and cracknels were showered down upon the eager crowd, the boys climbed into the trees, shouting "Hurrah!" and whistling through their fingers, so that altogether it was a scene of splendour.

"Well, I must see whether I cannot do something to add to the general festivity," the merchant's son thought, so he bought some rockets, wheels, and serpents, not forgetting a good supply of squibs and crackers. In short, he provided all that belongs to the most splendid fireworks, and, having laid all in his trunk, he ascended into the air.

What a cracking and whizzing there was!

The Turks all sprang up in the air with excitement at the enchanting sight, till their slippers flew about their ears. Such an aerial spectacle they had never witnessed. There could not now be the shadow of a doubt that it was the God of the Turks himself who was to have the Princess.

As soon as the merchant's son had got back into the forest with his trunk, he thought, "I must go into the city just to ascertain what effect it produced!" Was it not perfectly natural that he should have this fancy?

And what wonders he heard!

Every one whom he asked had a different account to give, but all agreed that it was incomparably beautiful.

"I saw the God of the Turks himself," one said, "and he had eyes like sparkling stars, and a beard like the foaming sea."

"He floated on a fiery mantle," another asserted, "and the heads of blessed cherubs peeped forth from the folds."

All these accounts he received from the enthusiastic people, and the next day his marriage was to take place.

He now hurried back into the forest, to seat himself in his trunk; but what had become of it? The trunk was burned. A spark from the fireworks had, through his carelessness, remained in it, so that the dry wood took fire, and the trunk lay there in ashes. The poor lover could no longer fly, and therefore could not get to his future bride.

She stood the whole day on the roof waiting for him. She is waiting still, whilst he wanders homelsss about the world telling stories, which, however, are nothing like as good as the story of the Matches.

The Daisy

Now attend.

In the country, close by the road-side, stands a beautiful villa, built in the pure Italian style. You have no doubt seen it yourself. In front of the house is a garden which, though not large, is exceedingly pretty with all sorts of flowers, enclosed by a neat freshly-painted railing. Close to it, at the edge of a ditch, in the midst of the most beautifully green grass, there grew a little Daisy, which the sun shone on as warmly and refreshingly as on all the luxuriant, splendid flowers in the garden, and in consequence it grew stronger from hour to hour. One morning it appeared quite in bloom, with its tender, dazzlingly white little leaves, like rays from the yellow sun which they surrounded. It did not think at all about it, that here, in the high grass, no one would notice it, nor that it was only a poor despised flower. It felt so thoroughly happy, for it might turn its pretty little face towards the glorious sun, looking up at it without any opposition, and could besides listen to the lark as, high up in the blue air, it sang its melodious songs, the harbingers of spring.

The poor little Daisy felt as happy as if it were a high festive day, though it was no more than a commonplace Monday. The children were all at school, and whilst they sat on their benches, deep in study, the little flower sat on its slender green stalk,

The Daisy.

learning also, for the dear sun and all around taught it how good God is, and it seemed as if the little lark sang plainly and prettily all its own sensations, though it could not express them. And the little Daisy looked up, with a sort of veneration, at the happy bird which could sing and fly, though not sad that it could not do so itself. "Can I not see and hear?" it thought. "The sun shines upon me, and the wind kisses me. Oh, how favoured I am!"

Within the railing there stood many stuck-up, grand flowers; the less scent they had, the more proudly they held themselves. The Peonies, puffed up with pride, tried all they could to look larger than a rose, but what has the size, more or less, to do with it? The Tulips were of the most splendid colours, and they knew it well enough, for they held themselves stock upright that they might attract the eye. They did not pay the slightest attention to the modest little Daisy, but the Daisy looked at them with admiration and thought, "How rich and beautiful they are, and to visit them, no doubt, the charming bird will come down. How glad I am that I am so near, for I shall be able to see their happy meeting!" Just then there sounded from above "Quirevit". The Lark came down in its rash flight, but its visit was not to the Tulips and Peonies in the villa-garden, but to the poor little flower in the green grass, which was so frightened with sheer delight, that it did not know at all what to think.

The merry little bird danced round it and sang, "Oh, what beautiful soft grass, and what a sweet little flower with its golden heart and silver dress!" The yellow centre of the Daisy looked, indeed, like gold, and the surrounding leaves were of a silvery white.

The surprise and the delight of the Daisy at this greeting can in no way be described, and the bird kissed it with its beak and sang to it in the most beautifully soft tones, when it again flew up into the blue spring air. It was, at the very least, a full quarter of an hour before the flower recovered itself. Half ashamed, yet inexpressibly delighted, she glanced across at her courtly sisters in the garden, who had been involuntary spectators of the honour that had been done her, and who would surely share her pleasure, but the Tulips looked more stiff than ever, and their faces were so sharp and so red, that it was evident they were in a rage. As for the thick-headed Peonies, they seemed ready to burst with rage, and looked only the more stupid.

It was fortunate that they could not speak, or they would have well exercised their poisonous tongues upon the timid little Daisy. The poor flower saw plainly that they were in a bad humour, and she was much grieved at it. At that very moment a girl came into the garden from the house; a large, sharp knife glittered in her hand, and hurrying straight to where the Tulips stood, she cut one after the other. "Oh, dear!" the Daisy sighed, "how dreadful that was, and now it is all over with them." After this, the cruel girl went away with the Tulips. Now, had not the Daisy every reason to be grateful that it stood without, in the green grass, and that it was only a little unpretending field flower? It felt, too, a flow of the warmest gratitude, and when the sun went down it folded its leaves as if in prayer, slept softly, and dreamed the whole night through of the sun and of the charming bird.

The next morning, when the little flower stretched out its white leaves, like longing little arms, to the air and light, it heard the bird's voice, but what it sang sounded quite melancholy. The poor lark had but too good a reason for losing its cheerfulness, for it had been caught, and was now in a cage hanging close by the open window. It sang how delightful it was to fly about freely and joyously through the wide expanse of smiling nature. It sang of the young, green corn in the fields, and of its past delightful flights. The so-much-to-be-pitied bird too much missed the soft elasticity of the air, in which it had been accustomed to rock itself, as also its lost freedom – the choicest of treasures, to be able to resign itself patiently to its fate. Imprisoned it sat there, behind the brass bars, and bitterly bemoaned its misfortune.

The tender, good-natured Daisy wished so much to be of assistance; but how to set about it? That was a difficult problem. She forgot entirely how beautiful all around her in the vast creation was; forgot how warm the sun was, and how white her own leaves were. Her thoughts were constantly with the imprisoned bird, whom, as much as she wished it, she could not help.

Just then two little boys came running out of the garden, one of whom held a knife, large and sharp, like that with which the girl had cut the flowers. They ran directly towards the spot where, sad and silent, the little Daisy, with drooping head, gave way to her thoughts, little dreaming what their intentions were.

"Here we can cut a beautiful piece of turf for our lark," one of the boys said; and he began to cut in a square, deeply into the earth around the Daisy, so that it stood pretty near in the middle of the piece of turf.

"Pluck that flower," the one boy said; and the Daisy trembled with fear, for to be plucked was to lose its life, and just now it particularly wished to live, for it was to go into the cage to the Lark.

"No, let it remain," the other said, "for it makes it look pretty." So it remained, and was put into the cage to the Lark.

Loudly the poor bird lamented its lost freedom, striking its prison bars with its wings, and the little Daisy could not speak. Not a word could it utter, as much as it wished to console the poor prisoner. Thus passed the whole morning.

"No water," the Lark complained. "They are all gone out, and have forgotten me. They have not given me a single drop to drink. My throat is parched and burning. It is as if I were all ice and fire; and the air is so oppressive. I shall die, and must part for ever from the warm sun, from the fresh green, and from all the beauties God has created." And in despair it bored its little beak deep into the cool turf. Its eyes then fell upon the Daisy, to which the bird nodded, and, kissing it, whispered, "You, too, must wither here, you poor, innocent flower! They have given you and the little clod of grass to me instead of the whole world, which I possessed. Each blade of grass shall be a green tree to me, and each of your white leaves a sweet-smelling flower. Oh, you only recall to me how much I have lost!"

"Oh, could I but console the charming singer!" the little Daisy thought. But it could not move a leaf. The scent, however, which the tender leaves exhaled was much stronger than is usual in this wild flower. The bird noticed this, too; for although it was dying of thirst, and in its sufferings bit off the blades of grass, it took care not to do the flower any injury.

It was evening, and still no one came to give the poor bird any water. It stretched out its beautiful wings, which shook convulsively. Its once-so-joyous song was now only a melancholy "Pip-pip". Its head drooped down towards the flower, and the dear little bird's heart broke from longing and from want. The flower could not, as the previous evening, fold its leaves and sleep quietly; no, it hung on a withered stalk, drooping to the earth.

The next morning only the boys appeared, and when they saw the bird lying dead in the cage they cried bitterly. They dug a grave under a rose-bush, and strewed it with the leaves of flowers, but the dead bird they put in a pink box, for it was to have a regal funeral. Whilst it was alive and sang they forgot it, and let it die shamefully of want in its close prison; but, now that it was dead, they thought to honour it with tears and pomp.

The clod of turf with the Daisy in it was thrown into the road in the dust, and no one thought of the modest, affectionate little flower, which, however, had felt most for the bird, and, not able to give consolation and relief, had died with it.

The Fir-tree

Out in the forest there stood such a pretty little Fir-tree; it had a good place, for there was sun, plenty of air, and all around grew many larger comrades, spruce as well as larch, but the little tree thought of nothing but growing. It did not trouble itself about the sun or the fresh air, nor about the children who came into the forest to gather strawberries and raspberries. Often they seated themselves close to the little fir-tree; and then they would say, "How charmingly little that tree is!" which it did not at all like to hear.

The next year it was a long joint bigger, and the year following another; for with fir-trees one can always tell, by the number of joints, how many years they have been growing.

"Oh, were I but a large tree like the others!" the little thing said, plaintively, "for then I could stretch out my branches far around, and look out into the world. The birds would build nests in my branches, and when the wind blew I could nod as proudly as the others."

It took no pleasure in the sunshine, in the birds, and in the red clouds which sailed over it night and morning.

In winter, when the snow was lying all around so glitteringly white, a hare would

The Fir-tree.

frequently come running that way, and, without troubling itself to turn to the right or to the left, would jump over the little tree. Oh, how annoying that was! But two winters passed, and the third the Tree was so tall that the hare had to run round it. Oh, to grow, to grow, to become big and old, was the only thing worth living for!, the Tree thought.

In autumn the woodcutters always came and cut down some of the largest trees. This happened every year, and the young Tree, which had considerably sprung up, shuddered at the sight, for the great, magnificent trees fell with a crash to the ground, when their branches were cut off, and the trees looked so long and thin, that they could scarcely be recognised; but they were then laid upoin carts, and horses dragged them away out of the forest.

Where were they going to? What awaited them?

In spring, when the Swallows and Storks came, the Tree asked them, "Do you not know where they are carried to? Have you not met them?"

The Swallows knew nothing, but the Stork looked thoughtful, nodded his head, and said, "Yes, I should think so; for we met many new ships when we left Egypt, and the ships had magnificent masts. We may suppose those were they, for they had a smell of turpentine, and they looked so fine, that I must congratulate you."

"Oh, were I but big enough to cross the sea too! But what is the sea really, and what does it look like?"

"That would take rather long to explain," the Stork said, and went its way.

"Rejoice in your youth!" the Sunbeams said; "rejoice in your power of growing, and in your young life."

And the Wind kissed the Tree, and the Dew shed tears over it, but the Fir-tree did not understand them.

Towards Christmas some quite young trees were cut down, many that were not even as big or old as this Fir-tree, that had neither peace nor rest, but was constantly longing to get away. These young trees – and they were just the most beautiful – always retained their branches, and thus put upon waggons, were drawn out of the forest.

"Where are they going to?" the Fir-tree asked. "They are no bigger than I; indeed, there was one considerably smaller; and why do they keep all their branches? Where can they be going to?"

"We know all about that," the Sparrows twittered. "Down there in the town we were looking through the windows of the houses, and we know where the young trees are carried to. Oh, the greatest splendour that can be imagined awaits them! When we looked through the windows we saw that they were stood up in the middle of the warm room, and adorned with the most beautiful things – gingerbread, gilt apples, playthings of all sorts, and hundreds of wax-tapers!"

"And then?" the Fir-tree asked, trembling all over; "and then? What happens then?"

"We did not see more, but that was incomparably beautiful."

"I wonder whether I am destined to enjoy all this splendour?" the Fir-tree thought. "That is still better than crossing the sea. Oh, I am consumed by an inward longing! Were it but Christmas-time! For I am now as tall, and stretch out as far as those that were carried away last year. Oh, were I but on the waggon! Were I but in the warm room with all the splendour! and then – Yes, then something still better and more beautiful must come, or why should they adorn me so? Oh, yes! Something by far better must follow. But what? Oh, how unsettled I feel! How I suffer! I do not know what is the matter with me!"

"Rejoice in us!" the Air and Light cried. "Rejoice in your youth, out in the open air!"

But it did not rejoice at all; it grew and grew; winter and summer it stood there equally green, and all who saw it said, "That is a beautiful tree!" When Christmas came, it was the very first to be cut down; and as the Tree fell with a sigh, it felt a sharp pain – a feeling of faintness. It could not think of any happiness, for it was sad at having to leave the place of its birth, that it would never see its dear old comrades again, nor the little bushes nor flowers that grew round about, nor perhaps even the birds. The start was anything but cheerful.

The Tree did not recover itself till it was being unpacked with others, and it heard a man say, "This is a magnificent one! We shall not want any other."

Two servants in grand livery then came out and carried the Fir-tree into a large and beautiful room. The walls all around were hung with pictures, and by the side of the stove stood two large Chinese vases, with lions on the lids. There were rocking-chairs, satin sofas, and large tables covered with picture-books, besides playthings, which cost large sums of money. The Fir-tree was put into a large tub filled with sand, but no one could see that it was a tub, for it was covered with green cloth, and stood upon a gay carpet. Oh, how the Tree trembled! What is going to happen now? The servants, as well as the young ladies, helped to decorate it. They hung little baskets, cut out of coloured paper, upon the branches, and each basket was filled with sweets. Gilt apples and walnuts hung there, as if they had grown on the Tree; and more than a hundred little red, blue, and white tapers were fixed among the branches. Dolls, exactly like human beings, such as the Tree had never seen before, were swinging in the air, and at the very top of the Tree there was a star of gold tinsel. It was beautiful – truly beautiful!

"Won't it be bright to-night?" all said.

"Oh, were it but night," the Tree thought, "and the tapers lighted! And what will happen then, I wonder? Will the Trees come from the forest to see me, and the Sparrows fly against the panes of glass? I should like to know whether I shall grow here, and remain decorated like this summer and winter."

It thought and thought, till its bark ached, and that is the same for a tree, and quite as bad as the headache with us.

The tapers were now lighted. What brilliancy and splendour! The branches of the Tree trembled, so that one of the lights set fire to the green leaves, and it burned up. "Good gracious!" the young ladies exclaimed, and hastily extinguished it.

After this the Tree suppressed its emotion, for it was so afraid of losing any of its splendour, but it felt quite giddy with all the glare. The folding-doors were now thrown open, and a number of children rushed in, whilst the older people followed more steadily. For a moment the young ones stood still in admiration; but then their joy broke forth again, and they danced round the Tree.

"What are they doing, and what will happen now?" the Tree thought, as one present after the other was torn off. The tapers, too, began to burn down to the branches; and as they did so they were put out, when the children received permission to plunder the Tree. They fell upon it, that all the branches cracked; and if the top with the gold star had not been fastened to the ceiling, the whole Tree would certainly have been thrown over.

The children danced about with their beautiful playthings, and no one looked at the Tree, excepting the nursery-maid, who only looked to see whether a fig or an apple had been forgotten.

"A story! A story!" the children cried, and they dragged a little fat man up to the Tree. He seated himself under it, "For now we are in the green," he said, "and what I tell you may be of use to the Tree. But I shall only tell you one story. Which will you have, the one about Ivede-Avede, or that about Klumpe-Dumpe, who fell down the stairs but was still exalted, and married the Princess?"

"Ivede-Avede!" some cried; "Klumpe-Dumpe!" cried the others. Then there was a shouting and noise, only the Fir-tree was quiet, and thought, "Shall I not have anything more to do in the evening's amusement?"

The little man told the story of "Klumpe-Dumpe, who fell down the stairs, but was still exalted, and married the Princess"; and the children clapped their hands, crying, "Go on! Go on!" They wanted to have the story of Ivede-Avede as well, but got no more than Klumpe-Dumpe. The Fir-tree stood perfectly quiet and thoughtful. The birds in the forest had never told such stories as that of how Klumpe-Dumpe fell downstairs and yet married the Princess. "That is how things go on in the world," the Fir-tree thought, believing that the story was true, since so decent a man told it. "Who can tell? Perhaps I may fall down-stairs and marry a Princess!" It rejoiced in the thought that the next night it would be adorned again with lights and playthings, fruits and gold.

"Tomorrow I shall not tremble," it thought. "I will enjoy all my splendour thoroughly, and shall hear the story of Klumpe-Dumpe again, and, perhaps, that of Ivede-Avede." The Tree stood in deep thought the whole night.

The next morning the servants came in.

"Now it's going to begin again," the Tree thought; but they carried it out of the room, upstairs to the loft, and there they put it in a dark corner, where the daylight never reached. "What can this mean?" the Tree thought. "What am I to do here, and what shall I hear, I wonder?" It leaned against the wall, and thought and thought, and for that it had plenty of time, for days and nights passed without any one coming up, and when at last some one did come, it was to bring up some large boxes to stand in the corner. The Tree was quite hidden, and it seemed as if it were forgotten as well.

"It is now winter!" the Tree thought. "The ground is hard and covered with snow, so that they cannot plant me; and therefore I am to be taken care of here till spring. How good and thoughtful men are! If it were but a little less dark and lonely here. Not even a hare. Oh, how beautiful it was out in the forest, when the snow lay on the ground, and the hare came running past, even when it jumped over me, though then I did not like it! It is dreadfully lonely up here!"

"Squeak! squeak!" a little Mouse said, cautiously coming forward. Then another came, and having snifted at the Tree, they crept between its branches.

"It is awfully cold here!" the little Mice said, "or else it would be well enough. Is it not true, you old Fir-tree?"

"I am by no means old!" the Fir-tree said. "There are many who are much older than I."

"Where do you come from?" the Mice asked, "and what do you know?" They were so mightily inquisitive. "Tell us all about the most beautiful place in the world. Have you been there? Have you been in the store-room, where the cheeses lie on the shelf and the bacon hangs from the ceiling; where one runs about on candles, and into which one goes in thin and comes out fat?"

"I have not been there," the Tree answered; "but I know the forest, where the sun shines and the birds sing." And then it told them all about its youth; and the little Mice, who had never heard anything of the sort before, listened with all their ears, and said, "What a deal you have seen! How happy you must have been!"

"Why happy?" the Fir-tree said, and thought over all it had been telling. "Yes, after all, those were happy times"; but then it told them about Christmas-eve, when it was covered with cakes and tapers.

"Oh!" the little Mice exclaimed. "How happy you have been, you old Fir-tree!"

"I am not at all old," the Tree answered. "It was only this winter I was brought from the forest, and I am just in the prime of life."

"How well you talk!" the little Mice said; and the next night they came again with four others to listen to it; and the more it talked of the past, the more clearly it remembered all itself, and thought, "Yes those were happy times, but they may come again – may come again! Klumpe-Dumpe fell down stairs, and yet married the Princess, and so may I marry a Princess." The Tree then remembered a pretty little Birch-tree that grew in the forest, and that seemed a real Princess.

"Who is Klumpe-Dumpe?" the little Mice asked; and the Fir-tree told them the whole story, every word of which it remembered perfectly well; and the little Mice were so delighted, that they were ready to jump right into the top of the Tree. The following night still more Mice came; and on Sunday even two Rats, who did not think the story pretty, which vexed the little Mice, and they now thought less of it themselves.

"Do you only know that one story?" the Rats asked.

"Only that one," the Tree answered, "and that I heard the happiest night of my life; but then I did not properly feel how happy I was."

"It is a most miserable story," the Rats said. "Do you not know any store-room story about bacon or tallow?"

"No," the Tree answered.

"We are very much obliged to you, then," they said, and went away.

After a time, the little Mice did not come either, and the Tree sighed. "It was quite pretty as they sat round me and listened, and now that is over, too; but I will not forget to enjoy it thoroughly when I am again taken out from here."

But when was that to happen? Well, one morning people came and rummaged about in the loft. The boxes were taken away, and the Tree, too, was dragged out from the corner. It is true they threw it down rather roughly upon the floor; but one of them then dragged it to the stairs, where it was light.

"Now life will begin again," the Tree thought. It felt the fresh air and the first rays of the sun, for it was now in the yard. There was so much to see all around, that the Tree quite forgot to look at itself. The yard adjoined a garden, where everything was beautiful and fresh. The roses smelt so delicious, and the lime-trees were in blossom, and the Swallows flew about, saying, "Quirre-virre-vit, my husband has come!" But it was not the Fir-tree they meant.

"Now I shall live!" the Tree cried with delight, and it spread out its branches; but – oh, dear! – they were quite dry and yellow; and there it lay in the corner, amongst nettles and rubbish. The gold star was still fastened to the top of it, and glittered in the sun.

A couple of the merry children that had danced round the Fir-tree on Christmas-eve were playing in the yard, and one of them, seeing the star, ran and tore it off.

"Look here! What was left on the ugly old Fir-tree," he said, and trod upon the branches, so that they cracked under his boots.

The Tree looked on all the splendour of the flowers in the garden, and then, looking at itself, wished it were back again in its dark corner in the loft. It thought of its fresh youth in the forest, of the merry Christmas-eve, and of the little Mice listening so attentively to the story of Klumpe-Dumpe.

"All is over now!" the poor Tree said. "Oh, had I but enjoyed myself whilst I could! All is over!"

Then a servant came and chopped the Tree into pieces, which he laid in a heap. Brightly the fire was burning under the large kitchen-kettle; and as one piece of wood after another was thrown in it sighed heavily, and each sigh was as the report of a small pistol. The children came running into the kitchen to listen, and, seating themselves before the fire, they cried, "Puff, puff!" But at each report, which was a sigh, the Wood thought of a bright summer's day in the forest, or of a winter's night, when the stars twinkled; it thought of the Christmas-eve and of Klumpe-Dumpe, the only story it had ever heard or could tell – and then the Tree was consumed!

The children played in the garden again, and one of them had the gold star on his breast, which had been on the Tree the happiest night of its life. That was passed; with the Tree all was over too; and with the story it is over. So it must be with all stories.

The brave tin-soldier.

THE BRAVE TIN-SOLDIER

There was once twenty-five Tin-soldiers, who were all brothers, for they were born of the same old tin-spoon. They looked straight before them, shouldering their muskets in military style, and their uniforms were blue and red, of the most splendid description. "Tin-soldiers" was the very first word they heard in this world, when the lid was taken off the box in which they lay. That was the exclamation of a little boy who had received them as a birthday present; he clapped his hands, and stood them up on the table. One soldier was the very image of the other, with the exception of one single one, who had only one leg, for he had been cast last, when there was not tin enough remaining; but he stood as firmly on his one leg as the others on their two; and it is just he whose adventures we have to relate.

On the table, on which they were placed, there were several other playthings; but that which attracted the eye the most was a pretty castle made of cardboard. One could see through the windows into the rooms, and in front there were several small trees, standing round a piece of looking-glass, which represented a lake, reflecting the wax swans that swam upon it. It was all pretty, but the prettiest of all was a little girl, who stood in the middle of the open door. She was also made of cardboard, but had a dress of the thinnest muslin, and a piece of blue ribbon across her shoulders for a scarf, fastened at the neck with a brooch quite as big as her whole face. The little girl held both her arms stretched out, for she was a dancer, and one leg was raised so high, that the Tin-soldier could not discover it, so that he thought she, like himself, had only one leg.

"That would be just the wife for me," he thought; "but she is rather grand, living in a castle, whereas I have only a box, and that I have to share with twenty-four others. That is no place for her; but yet I must try to make acquaintance with her." So he laid himself down flat behind a snuff-box that was upon the table, from whence he could watch the pretty little lady, who continued to stand on one leg without losing her balance.

At night all the other tin-soldiers were put in their box, and the people of the house went to bed. Now the playthings began to play on their own account, at all manner of games, and the Tin-soldiers made a commotion in their box, for they wanted to share the fun, but they could not raise the lid. The Nut-crackers turned somersets, and the Pencil had fine sport on the slate, so that there was such a noise that the canary woke up, and began to join in. The only two that did not move from their places were the Tin-soldier and the little Dancer. She stood still on the tip of her toe, with her two arms stretched out, and he did not turn his eyes from her for one instant.

It now struck twelve, and all of a sudden the lid flew off the snuff-box, but it was not suff that was in the box, no! It was a little black imp, such as children call a "Jack-in-the-box".

"Tin-soldier," the Imp said, "keep your eyes to yourself!"

But the Soldier pretended not to hear him.

"Well, just wait till tomorrow," the Imp said.

The next morning, as soon as the children were up, the Tin-soldier was stood in the window, and it was either the black Imp's doing or the draught – anyhow, the window flew open, and the Soldier went head over heels from the second story down into the street. That was a dreadful fall, and he reached the ground head first, so that the bayonet stuck in the ground between two paving-stones.

The servant and the little boy came running down immediately to look for it, but though they were near treading upon it, they could not find it. If the Soldier had cried out, "Here I am!" they would have found him, but he did not think it becoming to call out, as he was in uniform.

It now began to rain, and the drops fell faster and faster, till it came down in torrents.

When the rain was over, two boys came that way, and one of them exclaimed, "Look! Here lies a Tin-soldier, he shall have a sail down the gutter."

So they made a boat of a piece of newspaper and put it, with the Soldier standing in the middle, into the water, which after the heavy rain rushed down the street. The paper boat was tossed about, and occasionally whirled round and round, that the Soldier quite shook, but yet he did not move a feature, looking straight before him and shouldering his musket, and the boys ran by the side clapping their hands.

All at once the gutter turned under the pavement, which thus formed a stone bridge, and here the Soldier was as utterly in darkness as if he were in his box.

"Where am I going to now?" he thought. "This is certainly the black Imp's doing; but if only that dear little girl were here in the boat with me, it might be twice as dark, for aught I care."

Now a large Water-rat suddenly appeared, for it lived under the bridge.

"Have you a pass?" it cried. "Come, show your pass!"

But the Tin-soldier was silent, holding his gun still firmer.

The boat rushed on, and the Rat after it. Oh, how it showed its teeth, and shouted to the wooden beams and to the pieces of straw, "Stop him! Stop him! For he has not paid toll; he has not showed his pass."

The rushing of the water grew stronger and stronger, and already could the Soldier see light at the further end, but at the same time he heard a noise which might have frightened the bravest man. Only imagine: where the bridge ended the gutter emptied itself into a canal, a descent as dangerous to him as it would be to us, were we carried down a high waterfall.

He was so near upon it that there was no help, and down the boat rushed, the poor Soldier holding himself as steady as he possibly could. No one should be able to say, that he as much as blinked his eyes. Four times the boat was whirled round and round, and was filled with water nearly up to the top, so that it was evident it must sink. The water already reached up to the Soldier's shoulders, and momentarily the boat sank deeper and deeper, and more and more the paper became unfastened. The water was now over his head, and he thought of the pretty little dancer, whom he should see no more. Then the paper tore, and he fell through, but at the very moment he was swallowed by a large fish.

Oh, how dark it was! Worse than under the bridge, and there was no room to move; but the Tin-soldier's courage did not forsake him, and he lay there his full length with his musket in his arm.

Soon after, the fish made the most frightful contortions and struggling, and was then quite quiet. Suddenly light appeared, and a voice exclaimed, "The Tin-soldier!" The fish had been caught, and taken to the market, where it was bought and carried into the kitchen, and the cook cut it open with a large knife. With two fingers she laid hold of the Soldier round the body and carried him into the room, for all to see the extraordinary man who had been swallowed by a fish, but the Soldier was not at all proud. He was placed upon the table, and – wonder of wonders! – the Tin-soldier was in the same room he had been in before, where he saw the same children and the same playthings on the table. The beautiful castle was there, and the pretty little dancer, still standing on one leg, with the other raised high up in the air. He could have cried if it had been becoming, and he looked at her and she at him, but neither spoke a word.

Then one of the boys took the Soldier and threw him into the fire, without giving any reason for doing so, but no doubt the Jack-in-the-box had something to do with it.

The Tin-soldier stood there in the midst of flames, and the heat was something dreadful, but whether it was the heat of the fire or of his love, he did not know. His colour had clean gone, but whether caused by his travels or by grief, no one could tell. He looked at the little girl, and she looked at him, when he felt that he was melting, but still he stood firmly with his musket at his shoulder. A door was then opened suddenly, and carried away by the draught, the little dancer flew like a sylph into the fire, to the Tin-soldier. She blazed up and was gone. The Soldier now melted down into a lump, and the next morning, when the servant cleared out the ashes, she found a tin heart. Of the little dancer nothing remained but the brooch, which was burnt quite black.

The Shepherdess and the Sweep.

The Shepherdess and the Sweep

~

Have you ever seen a very old wooden cabinet, quite black with age and carved all over with leaves and filigree-work? Such a one stood in a sitting-room, and had been in the family from the great-grandmother's time. It was covered from top to bottom with carved roses and tulips, amongst which there were the most extraordinary flourishes, and from these sprang the antlered heads of stags, whilst on the top, in the middle, stood a whole figure. He was ridiculous enough to look at, with goat's legs, short horns on his head, and a long beard, besides which he was constantly grinning, for it could not be called a laugh. The children christened him the GoatslegHighadjutantgeneralmilitarycommandant, for that was a difficult name to pronounce, and a title not conferred upon many. To carve him cannot have been easy work, but there he stood, constantly looking at the table under the looking-glass, for there was the lovliest little china Shepherdess. Her shoes were gilt, and her dress neatly fastened up with a red rose, and then she had a gilt hat and a shepherdess's crook. She was, indeed, lovely. Close to her stood a Sweep, as black as any coal, but he, too, was entirely made of china; he was quite as neat and clean as any one else, for that he was a Sweep was, of course, only to represent something, and the porcelain-manufacturer could just as well have made a prince of him.

There he stood, with his face red and white, just like a girl, and that was a mistake, for it might have been blackened a little. He was close to the Shepherdess, and they had both been placed where they stood, which, being the case, they were naturally engaged to each other, and well suited they were, for they were made of the same china, and were both little.

Not far from them there was another figure, but three times as big, a Chinese, who could nod his head. He was also made of china, and pretended to be the Shepherdess's grandfather, though he could not prove it, so claimed authority over her, and had promised her to the GoatslegHighadjutantgeneralmilitarycommandant.

"You will have a husband," the old Chinese said, "who I almost believe is made of mahogany, and he has the whole cabinet full of plate, besides the valuables that are in the hidden drawers."

"I will not go into the dark cabinet," the little Shepherdess said, "for I have heard that he has eleven china wives in there."

"Then you will make the twelfth," the old Chinese said, "for this very night your marriage shall take place." He then nodded his head and fell asleep.

The little Shepherdess cried and looked at her dearly beloved china Sweep.

"I must ask you," she said, "to go with me out into the wide world, for here we cannot stay."

"Your will is my will," the little Sweep said. "Let us go at once, and I have no doubt that by my calling I shall gain sufficient to keep you."

"Were we but safely down from the table," she said, "for I shall never be happy till we are out in the wide world."

He consoled her, and showed her where to put her little feet, on the projections and ornaments within their reach, and they got safely on to the floor, but when they looked towards the old cabinet, all was confusion there. The stags stretched their heads further out, raising their antlers, and turned their necks from side to side. The GoatslegHighadjutantgeneralmilitarycommandant jumped high in the air, and cried as loud as he could to the old Chinese, "They are now running away! They are now running away!"

At this they were frightened, and they jumped into the cupboard under the window-seat.

Here lay three or four packs of cards, which were not complete, and a little doll's theatre, in which a play was being acted, and the Queen of hearts, diamonds, clubs and spades, sat in the front row fanning themselves with their tulips, whilst behind them stood the Knaves, who seemed to be their pages. The plot of the play was the difficulties thrown in the way of two persons who wished to be married, and the little Shepherdess cried, for it was her own story.

"I cannot bear this," she said, "I must get out of the cupboard." But when they were out and looked up at the table, they saw that the old Chinese was awake and his whole body shaking.

"Now the old Chinese is coming," the little Shepherdess cried, and fell down upon her china knees, she was in such a fright.

"I have an idea," the Sweep said. "Let us get into the potpourri jar which stands there in the corner, where we can lie on rose-leaves and lavender, and throw salt in his eyes, if he comes."

"That cannot help us," she said; "besides, I know that the old Chinese and the Potpourri jar were once engaged to each other, and there always remains some sort of tie between people with whom such a connexion has existed. No, there is nothing left for us but to go out in the wide world."

"Have you really courage to go out with me into the wide world?" the Sweep asked. "Have you considered how large it is, and that we can never come back here?"

"Yes, I have," she answered.

The Sweep looked at her intently, and then said, "My way lies up the chimney, and that way I know well enough, and if you really have courage to go with me, we shall soon mount up so high, that they will never be able to reach us."

And he led her to the grate.

"How black it looks up there!" she said, but still she went with him, and they had not gone far when he exclaimed, "Look, what a beautiful star is shining there above!"

It was a real star in the heavens, shining down upon them, as if to show them the way. They crept on and climbed, and a dreadful way it was – so high, so high, but he held and lifted her, and showed her where to place her little china feet, till at last they reached the edge of the chimney, where they seated themselves, for they were very tired, as well they might be.

The sky, with all its stars, was above them, and lower there were all the roofs of the city, and they could see so far around, so far out into the world. The poor Shepherdess had never imagined anything like it, and laying her little head on her Sweep's breast, she cried so that the gold was washed off her girdle.

"That is too much," she sobbed. "That I can never bear. The world is too large; oh, were I but back again on the table under the looking-glass! I shall never know happiness till I am back there. I have followed you into the world, and if you care for me you must now go back with me."

The Sweep spoke most reasonably and sensibly to her, spoke of the old Chinese, and of the Goatsleg Highadjutantmilitarycommandant, but she sobbed so violently, that he was obliged to do as she wished, though it was foolish.

They therefore climbed down again with much trouble and difficulty, and when they got near the bottom they stopped to listen, but all being quiet they stepped into the room. There lay the old Chinese on the floor; he had fallen off the table when he attempted to follow them, and there he lay broken into three pieces. His whole back had come off in one piece, and his head had rolled far off into a corner of the room.

"That is horrible!" the little Shepherdess said. "My old grandfather is broekn to pieces, and it is our fault. Oh, I shall never survive it!" And she wrung her little hands.

"He can be riveted," the Sweep said. "He can very well be riveted. Do not you give way so, for if they put a good strong rivet in his back and neck he will be as good as new again, and will be able to say many unpleasnt things to us yet."

"Do you think so?" she said, and they then got on to the table again where they had always stood.

"It was of much use going all the way we did," the Sweep said; "we might just as well have saved ourselves that trouble."

"Oh, if my poor old grandfather were but riveted," the Shepherdess said. "Will it cost very much?"

The family had him riveted, and he was in every way as good as new again, excepting that, owing to the rivet in his neck, he could no longer nod his head.

"You have grown proud since you were broken to pieces," the Goatsleg-Highadjutantgeneralmilitarycommandant said, "but I do not see any good reason for it. Now, am I to have her, or am I not?"

The Sweep and the little Shepherdess looked so beseechingly at the old Chinese, fearing that he would nod, but he could not. He did not choose to tell a stranger that he had a rivet in the back of his neck, so he was quiet, and the Shepherdess and the Sweep remained together, loving each other till they got broken.

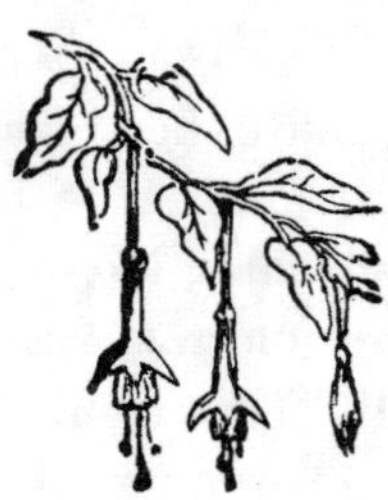

The red shoes.

The Red Shoes

There lived a little girl, who was very pretty, but in summer she had to go bare-footed, for she was poor, and in winter she wore heavy wooden shoes, which made her little feet so red that it was dreadful to see them.

In the middle of the village, the old shoemaker's wife sat sewing, as well as she could, at a pair of small shoes, made out of pieces of old red cloth; they were very clumsy, but it was well meant, for they were intended for the little girl. The little girl's name was Karen.

On the very day that her mother was buried she received the red shoes and wore them for the first time, though they were certainly not suited for mourning; but she had no others, and in them, without stockings, she followed the miserable coffin.

Just then came a large, old carriage, and in it sat a fat old lady, who, having looked at the little girl, felt pity for her, and said to the clergyman, "Give me that little girl, and I will adopt her."

Karen thought that certainly the red shoes were the cause of this, but the old lady thought them hideous, and they were burned. Karen was clothed neatly and cleanly, and people said she was pretty, but the looking-glass said, "You are more than pretty, you are beautiful!"

The Queen then passed through the land, having her little daughter with her, who was a Princess, and the people crowded to the palace, and Karen with them, where the little Princess, in fine white clothes, stood on a balcony and let herself be stared at. She had neither train nor crown, but wore magnificent red satin shoes, which were much more beautiful than those the old shoemaker's wife had made for Karen. Certainly nothing in the world can be compared with red shoes.

Karen had now grown old enough to be confirmed, for which occasion she had new clothes, and was to have new shoes too. The rich shoemaker in the town took her measure, and that was in his own shop, where there were glass cupboards full of pretty shoes and shining boots. They looked very pretty, but the old lady could not see well, nor did she take much pleasure in looking at them. Now, amongst the shoes, were a red pair, exactly like those the Princess had worn, and the shoemaker said, "They had been made for a Count's daughter, but did not fit her." They were very beautiful.

"I suppose those are patent leather, they are so shiny," the old lady said.

"Yes, they do shine," Karen answered, and as they fitted her they were bought, but the old lady knew nothing about their being red, for she would never have allowed Karen to be confirmed in red shoes, which, however, happened.

Every one looked at her feet, and as she walked across the church to the altar, it seemed to her as if even the pictures of the bishops and saints had their eyes fixed upon her shoes; and it was of these only she thought when the clergyman laid his hand upon her head, and spoke of her christening, and that now, as a grown-up Christian, she took the covenant made with God upon herself. The organ was played so solemnly whilst the pretty voices of the children sang, and the old clergyman sang too, but Karen only thought of her red shoes.

In the afternoon the old lady learnt that the shoes were red, and she said that it was very wrong and unbecoming, and particularly told Karen that she should always wear black shoes when she went to church, even if they were old.

The next Sunday Karen was to take the sacrament, and she examined her black shoes: she looked at the red ones – and looked at them again, and put the red ones on.

It was a beautiful sunshiny day, and she and the old lady walked along the footpath across a cornfield, where it was rather dusty.

At the door of the church stood an old soldier with a crutch and a wonderfully long beard, which was more red than white, and he bowed down to the ground, asking the old lady whether he should wipe the dust off her shoes. Karen stretched out her little foot as well, and the old soldier said, "See, what beautiful dancing shoes! They will keep on when you dance," and he gave the sole a slap with his hand.

The old lady then gave the soldier some money and went into the church with Karen.

And all the people inside looked at Karen's red shoes, and all the pictures looked at them, and when she knelt before the altar and had the golden cup at her lips, she thought only of her red shoes, and it seemed to her as if she saw them floating in the cup. She forgot to sing the hymns and forgot to say her prayers.

Now all the people left the church, and the old lady got into her carriage. Karen lifted up her foot to get in also, when the old soldier said, "See, what beautiful dancing shoes!" and Karen could not resist dancing a few steps; but, now she had begun, her feet continued to dance: it was exactly as if the shoes had power over them. She danced round the churchyard wall, and could not stop herself, so that the coachman had to run after her and lay hold of her, and he lifted her into the carriage, but her feet went on dancing so that she kicked the old lady, and her legs had no rest till the shoes were off.

When they got home the shoes were put into a cupboard, but she could not resist looking at them.

The old lady was now taken ill, and it was said she could not survive. She had to be watched and waited upon, and no one was more attentive than Karen, but there was a great ball in the town, to which Karen was invited; she looked at the old lady, who could not recover, and she looked at the red shoes, thinking there could be no sin in that; she then put them on, and in that there was no harm; but then she went to the ball and began to dance.

When she wanted to dance to the right, the shoes danced to the left, and when she wanted to dance up the room, the shoes danced down, down the stairs, through the streets, and out at the city gates. She danced and could not help dancing, across the fields into the dark forest.

There was light between the trees, and she thought it was the moon, for there was a face, but it was the old soldier with the red beard, who nodded and said, "See, what beautiful dancing shoes!"

She was now frightened, and wished to throw off the red shoes, but they stuck fast. She tore off her stockings, but the shoes seemed to have grown to her feet, and she danced across the fields and meadows, in rain and sunshine, by day and by night, but at night it was the most dreadful.

She danced into the churchyard, but the dead there did not dance; they had something better to do; for her, however, there was no rest; and when she danced up to the open church door, she saw an angel in white garments, with wings reaching from the shoulders down to the ground. His countenance was serious and severe, and in his hand he held a sword, which was broad and shining.

"Thou shalt dance," he said, "dance in thy red shoes till thou art pale and cold, till thou shrinkest away to a skeleton. Dance shalt thou from door to door, and where proud children dwell shalt thou knock, so that they may hear and fear thee. Thou shalt dance, dance – "

"Mercy!" Karen cried, but she did not hear the angel's answer, for the shoes carried her on, across the fields and roads, and incessantly she had to dance.

One morning she danced past a door which she knew well. From within sounded the singing of hymns, a coffin was carried out covered with flowers, and she then knew that the old lady was dead, and felt that she was forsaken by all, and condemned by the angel of God.

She danced – could not help dancing. The shoes carried her through brambles and thorns, till the blood ran down her lacerated limbs, and she danced across the heath towards a little lonely house. She knew that the executioner lived there, and knocking at the window with her knuckle; she said:-

"Come out! – come out! – I cannot come in, for I am obliged to dance!"

And the executioner said, "I suppose you do not know who I am? I cut wicked people's heads off, and I now hear my axe ring."

"Do not cut my head off," Karen said, "for then I could not repent of my sin, but cut off my feet with the red shoes."

She then confessed her whole sin, and the executioner cut off her feet with the red shoes, but the shoes danced with the little feet in them, across the fields far into the forest.

He made feet of wood for her, and a pair of crutches, teaching her the hymn which condemned criminals always sing, and she kissed the hand which had wielded the axe, and went her way across the heath.

"I have now suffered enough for the red shoes," she said, "and I will go into the church that the people may see me"; but when she got near the church the red shoes danced before her, and, frightened, she turned back.

The whole week she was sad, and shed many bitter tears, but when Sunday came she said, "Now, surely, I have striven and suffered enough, and I believe I am as good as many of those who sit in church and think so much of themselves. I will go there too." But she got no further than the churchyard, for there she saw the red shoes and was frightened, and, turning back, truly repented of her sins.

She then went to the clergyman's house, and begged that she might be taken into service, promising that she would be industrious and do all she could. Wages she did not care for, but only sought a roof to cover her, and to be with good people. The clergyman's wife had pity on her and took her into her service, and she was steady and industrious. She sat perfectly still and listened when of an evening the clergyman read the Bible out loud, and all the little ones were very fond of her, but when they spoke of dress, show, or beauty, she shook her head.

The following Sunday all went to church, and they asked her whether she would not go with them, but sadly, and with tears in her eyes, she looked towards her crutches, and then the others went there to hear the Word of God; but she went all alone to her little room, which was only large enough for her bed and one chair, and there she seated herself with her Prayer book; and as she read in it with pious earnestness, the wind carried the sound of the organ across to her from the church, and raising her eyes filled with tears, she cried, "O Lord, have mercy upon me!"

The sun then shone in so brightly; and immediately before her stood the angel she had seen at the church door, not holding, as then, a sharp sword, but a green branch covered with roses, and he touched the ceiling with it, which was immediately raised, a golden star glittering where he had touched it, and he touched the walls which spread themselves out, and she saw the organ, the old pictures of saints and bishops, and the whole congregation singing out of their hymn-books, for the church had come to the poor girl into her little room, or she had been transported there. She sat among the rest of the congregation, who looked up when the hymn was ended, and nodding to her, said, "It was right of you to come, Karen."

"It is an act of grace," she said.

The notes of the organ vibrated through the church, and the voices of the children sounded so soft and beautiful. The clear, bright sunshine streamed in through the window upon Karen, and her heart was so filled with sunshine, peace, and joy, that it broke. Her soul took its flight up to heaven, and no one there asked after the red shoes.

The Elfin-hillock

Several large lizards were running about quickfootedly in the clefts of an old tree, and they understood each other well enough, for they all spoke the Lizard language.

"What a rumpus and confusion there is in the old Elfin-hillock!" one of the Lizards said. "I have not been able to close my eyes for two nights with the noise, so that I might just as well have had the toothache, for then I cannot sleep either."

"There is evidently something afloat there," another Lizard said, "for the hillock stands raised up on four red poles all night till the cock crows. It is being thoroughly aired, and the Elfin-maidens have been learning new dances. There is something in the wind."

"Yes; I was speaking with a Worm, who is an acquaintance of mine," a third Lizard said, "just after it had come out of the hillock, where it had been burrowing day and night. It had heard a good deal – see it can't, the miserable creature! But feeling and hearing it is up to. Strangers are expected in the Elfin-hillock – grand strangers – but who they are the Worm would not tell, and very likely did not know itself. All the Will-o'-the-wisps are ordered for a torch-light procession, as it is called, and the silver and gold, of which there is plenty in the hillock, is being

The Elfin-hillock.

polished up, and laid out in the moonshine."

"I wonder who the strangers can be?" all the Lizards said. "What can be going on there? Listen! What a humming and buzzing there is!"

Just then the Elfin-hillock opened, and an old Elfin-maiden came tripping out. She was the old Elfin-king's housekeeper, and was distantly related to the family, on which account she wore an amber heart on her forehead. How quickly her legs moved! Trip! Trip! Good gracious! How she trips along, and that straight to the Carrion Crow!

"You are invited to the Elfin-hillock for tonight," she said; "but will you not first do us a great service, and undertake the invitations? You know that you ought to do something, as you do not give parties yourself. We expect some grand people, magicians, who are of great importance, and on that account the Elfin-king intends to show himself."

"Who is to be invited?" the Crow asked.

"Why, to the ball all the world may come, even human beings, if they do but talk in their sleep, or can do something of that sort; but the dinner is to be very select, to consist only of the very highest. I have had a dispute with the King about it, for it is my opinion that we cannot even admit ghosts. The Water-nix and his daughters must be the first, and, though they will not much like coming on dry land, they shall have a wet stone to sit upon, or, perhaps, something better, and so I think they will not refuse for this once. We must have all the old Demons of the first class with tails, Cobolds and Witches; and I think we can scarcely leave out the Hill-man, the Skeleton-horse, the Kelpies, and the Pixies."

"All right," the Raven said, and flew off to give the invitations.

The Elfin-maidens were already dancing on the Hillock, and they wore shawls made of mist and moonshine, which look very pretty to those who like them. The great hall in the middle of the hillock was beautifully got up, the floors had been washed with moonshine, and the walls rubbed down with witches' fat, so that in the light they shone like tulip-leaves. In the kitchen there were plenty of frogs on the spits, there were snails' skins, with children's fingers inside, and salads of mushroom, the snouts of mice, and hemlock, and, to drink, sparkling saltpetre-wine; everything of the best. The dessert consisted of rusty nails and broken church-window glass.

The old Elfin-king had his golden crown fresh polished, and in the bedroom clean curtains were put up, fastened with snails' horns. What a noise and confusion there was!

"Now the whole place must be fumigated with burnt horse-hair and hog's bristles, and then I think I shall have done my part," the old Elfin-maiden said.

"My own sweet father!" the youngest daughter said, coaxingly, "may I not now know who the noble strangers are?"

"Well, I suppose I must tell," he said. "Two of my daughters must be prepared to marry, for certainly two will be married. The old Cobold from Norway, he who lives in the Dovre-rock, and possesses many stone-quarries and a gold-mine, which is worth more than is generally supposed, is coming with his two sons, who are to choose themselves wives. He is a right-down honest northern old Cobold, merry and straightforward; and I know him from olden times, when he was down here, seeking himself a wife; she was a daughter of the Rock-king of Moen, but she is now dead. Oh, how I long to see the old Cobold again! His sons are said to be pert, forward boys, but, perhaps, it is not true, and, no doubt, they will improve as they grow older. Let me see you girls teach them manners."

"And when are they coming?" another of the daughters asked.

"That depends upon wind and weather," the Elfin-king said, "for they travel economically, and come by water. I wished them to come through Sweden, but my old friend does not fancy that. He does not advance with the age, and that I do not like."

Just then two Will-o'-the-wisps came hopping along, the one faster than the other, and it therefore arrived first.

"They are coming! They are coming!" they cried.

"Give me my crown, and let me stand in the moonshine," the King said.

His daughters raised their shawls, and bowed down to the ground.

There stood the old Cobold of Dovre, with his crown of hardened ice and fir-cocks, dressed in a bear-skin and snow-boots. His sons, on the contary, had bare necks, without any handkerchief, for they were hardy young men.

"Is that a mound?" the youngest of them asked, pointing to the Elfin-hillock. "In Norway, we call that a hole."

"Boys!" the old man said, "a hole goes inwards, a mound upwards. Have you no eyes in your head?"

The only thing they wondered at, they said, was that they could understand the language down there without any trouble.

"Mind what you are about," their father said, "or people will think you half fools."

They then went into the Elfin-hillock, where the high and polite company were assembled, and that in such haste, that one might almost have thought they had been blown together. All the arrangements were perfect; the Water-nixes sat at table in large water-tanks, and they said it was exactly as if they were at home. All behaved with the most perfect refinement of manners, with the exception of the two young northern Cobolds, who stretched their legs upon the table; but they thought everything became them.

"Feet off the table!" the old Cobold said, and they obeyed; but they did not do so at once. They made the ladies, who sat by their sides, tickle them with fir-cocks, which they carried in their pockets, and gave them their boots to hold, which they took off to be more at their ease. But their father was very different; he talked so well of the proud northern rocks, and of the waterfalls rushing down with a white foam, and a noise like thunder and the notes of an organ. He talked of the salmon that leap up into the falling waters when the Nix plays on her golden harp. He told of the bright winter nights, when the bells on the sledges tingle, and the young men with burning torches skate across the ice, which is so clear that they can see how they frighten the fish beneath their feet. Yes, he talked so well, that one seemed to see what he described; it was just like the clapper of a sawmill.

The Elfin-maidens then danced together, and that showed them off to great advantage; then singly, or the *pas seul*, as it is called. Oh, dear! How they stuck out their legs; there was no telling where the beginning or end was, nor seeing which were the arms and which the legs; and then they whirled round like tops, so that the Skeleton-horse turned quite giddy and had to leave the table.

"Prrrrr!" the old Cobold cried. "What a commotion there is amongst the legs; but what else can they do besides dance, stick out their legs and raise a whirlwind."

"You shall soon see," the Elfin-king said, and he called his youngest daughter. She was very active, and transparent as moonshine; she was the most delicate of all the sisters, and when she took a white chip in her mouth she disappeared altogether. That was her art.

But the old Cobold said it was an art he would not like in a wife, and he did not think that his sons cared about it.

The next could walk by her own side, just as if she had a shadow, which the Elves have not.

The third was of quite a different stamp, for she had learnt to brew, bake, and cook, and knew how to lard the Elfin-dumplings with glow-worms.

"She will make a good housewife," the old Cobold said, and he drank to her, but with his eyes only, for he wished to remain sober.

Then the fourth came, and she had a large harp, on which she played, and when she struck the first string, all lifted up their left legs, for the Cobolds are left-legged; and when she struck the second string, they were obliged to do whatever she wished.

"That is a dangerous woman," the old Cobold said, whilst both the sons went out, for they found the amusements tedious.

"And what can the next do?" the old Cobold asked.

"I have learnt to like the north, and I shall never marry unless it is to go to Norway."

But the youngest of the girls whispered to the old man, "That is only because she has heard from a northern song, that when the world is destroyed, the rocks of the north will still remain, and therefore she wishes to go there, for she is so dreadfully afraid of death!"

"Ho, ho! Is that her meaning?" he answered. "And what can the seventh and last do?"

"The sixth comes before the seventh," the Elfin-king said, for he could count, but the sixth kept herself in the background.

"I can only tell people the truth," she said, "and therefore no one cares for me, so the best thing I can do is to prepare my shroud."

Then came the seventh, and what could she do? Why, she could tell stories, as many as any one would listen to.

"Here are all my five fingers; tell me a story of each," the old Cobold said.

She laid hold of his wrist, and he laughed till he almost choked, but when she came to the ring-finger, which had a gold ring on, as if it knew there was to be a betrothal, he said, "Keep tight hold of what you have, the hand is yours, for you shall be my wife."

The maiden said the story of the ring-finger and of the little finger still remained to be told.

"We will have those in winter," the old Cobold said, "and have stories of the Fir-tree, and the Birch-tree, of the Fairy-gifts, and of the Frost. You shall tell stories enough, for there no one understands that properly. We will sit in the warm room, where the pine-logs are burning, and drink mead out of the golden cups of the old northern Kings, and the Echo will visit us and sing you all the songs of the Shepherdesses in the mountains. That will be glorious, and the salmon will leap in the water-fall and beat against our stone walls, but he shan't come in. Oh, it is delightful in dear old Norway, but what has become of the boys?"

Ah, where were they? They were running about the fields, blowing out the Will-o'-the-wisps, who had been so good-natured to come and serve as torches.

"What are you up to here?" the old Cobold said. "I have chosen a mother for you, and you may choose yourselves an aunt."

But the boys said they would rather make a speech and then drink healths, for they had no fancy for marriage, so they made speeches and drank healths, turning their glasses upside down to show that they left no heel-taps. They then took off their coats and laid themselves on the table, to sleep, for they did not stand much upon ceremony. But the old Cobold danced about the room with his future wife, and changed boots with her, which is better manners than changing rings.

"The cock is crowing," the old Elfin-maiden, who attended to the house duties, said. "We must now shut the shutters, so that the sun may not scorch us up."

The hillock then closed up.

But outside the Lizards ran about in the split tree, and the one said, "Oh, how much I did like the old Cobold!"

"I like the boys betters," the Worm said, but then it could not see, the miserable creature!

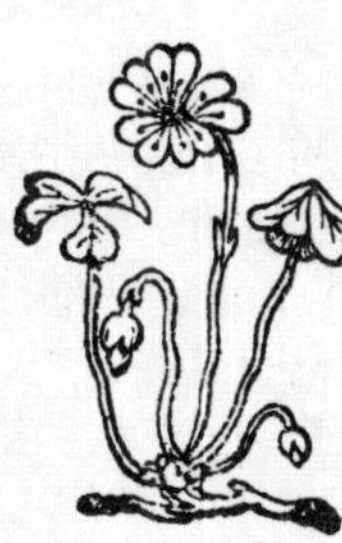

Holger Danske

~

In Denmark there stands an old castle, which is called Kronburg; it stands in the Sound, where the large vessels pass daily by hundreds, English as well as Russian and Prussian, and they salute the old castle with cannon: "Boom!" and the old castle answers with cannon: "Boom!" For that is the way the cannon say "Good day!" and "Many thanks!" In winter no vessels sail past there, for it is then all ice, right across to the Swedish coast; but it is like a regular road, where the Danish and Swedish flags are displayed, and the Danish and Swedish people say to each other: "Good day!" and "Many thanks!" Not with cannon, however, but with a friendly shake of the hand; and they buy cakes and biscuits from each other, fancying they taste better than their own. But the most remarkable of all is old Kronburg, and beneath it, in a deep, dark cellar, which no one ever enters, sits Holger Danske. He is clad in iron and steel, and rests his head on his strong hands, whilst his long beard hangs down upon the marble table, into which it has grown fast; he sleeps and dreams, but in his dreams he sees all that goes on in Denmark. Every Christmas-eve an angel comes down from heaven and tells him, that all he has been dreaming is perfectly right, so that he may go to sleep again in peace, as Denmark is in no actual danger. But should it be in danger, then old Holger Danske will arise, breaking the

Holger Danske.

table as he draws out his beard, and he will lay about him with his sword, so that it shall be heard in all parts of the world.

An old grandfather was telling all this about Holger Danske to his little nephew, and the little boy knew that all his grandfather told him was true. And whilst the old man sat talking – he was carving at a large wooden image, representing Holger Danske, intended to serve as figure-head to a ship, for the old grandfather was a wood-carver, that is, a man who carves the figures after which the vessels are named. He had now carved Holger Danske, who stood so proudly with his long beard, holding a battle-axe in one hand, whilst the other rested on the Danish coat-of-arms.

And the old grandfather told so many stories of celebrated Danish men and women, that at last it appeared to the little nephew as if he knew as much as Holger Danske himself, who, after all, only dreamed it; and when the little fellow was in bed, he thought so much of it that he pressed his chin against the bed-covering and imagined he had a long beard, which had grown fast to it.

But the old man went on with his work which he was just finishing, for he was carving at the Danish coat-of-arms; and when he had done, he examined the whole, thinking of all he had read and heard, and had himself been telling his little nephew. He then nodded his head, wiped his spectacles, and putting them on again, said, "During my lifetime Holger Danske will probably not come again, but that boy in bed may perhaps see him, and be present when there is really something to do"; and he nodded his head again; and the more he looked at his work, the more evident it appeared to him that what he had done was good. It seemed to him as if it actually had colour, and that the armour glittered like iron and steel. The hearts in the Danish coat-of-arms grew redder and redder, and the lions sprang forward with the golden crowns on their heads.

"That is certainly the most beautiful coat-of-arms in the whole world," the old man said. "The lions represent strength, and the hearts mildness and love." He looked at the top lion, and thought of King Canute, who joined mighty England to the Danish throne. He looked at the second lion, and thought of Waldemar, who united the whole of Denmark and subdued Sclavonia; and as he looked at the third lion, he thought of Margaret, who joined Sweden and Norway to Denmark. But when he looked at the red hearts, they shone stronger than before; they became moving flames, and his mind followed each.

The first flame led him into a narrow, dark prison; there sat a prisoner, a beautiful woman, Elenor Ulfeld, the daughter of Christian the Fourth, and the flame settled like a rose upon her bosom, becoming one with the heart of the best and noblest of Danish women.

"Yes, that is a heart worthy of the Danish coat-of-arms," the old man said.

And his mind followed the second flame, which led him out on to the sea, where the cannon thundered and the ships lay veiled in smoke, and the flame settled as a cross of honour on the breast of Hvitfeldt, when to save the fleet he blew up his ship and himself.

And the third flame led him to Greenland's miserable huts, where the preacher, Hans Egede, by word and act performed a duty of love, and the flame was a star on his breast, a heart for the Danish coat-of-arms.

The old man's mind now went before the flitting flame, for he knew its destination. In the midst of poverty, in the room of the peasantess, stood Frederick the Sixth, and wrote his name with chalk on a beam. The flame flickered on his breast, flickered in his heart, and in the peasant's room became a heart for the Danish coat-of-arms. And the old man dried his eyes, for he had known King Frederick with his silvery hair, and his honest blue eyes, and folding his hands he sat in thought. His daughter-in-law then came and said it was time to rest, as it was late, and the table laid for supper.

"What you have done is beautiful, my dear grandfather," she said; "Holger Danske and the whole coat-of-arms. It seems to me as if I have seen that face."

"No, you have scarcely seen it," he said, "but I have, and have striven to carve it in wood, just as I bear it in memory. It was when the English ships lay in our roads, on the Danish second of April, when we showed that we were the Danes of old. When I was in Steen Bille's company, a man stood by my side. It was as if the balls were afraid of him. Merrily he sang old songs, and fired and fought as if he were more than man. I remember his face well, but where he came from, or whither he went, I do not know, and no one knows. I have often thought that was, perhaps, old Holger Danske himself, who had swam down from Kronburg to help us in our danger. That was an idea of mine, and there is his likeness."

The figure threw its large shadow on the wall, and on part of the ceiling, and it seemed as if it were the shadow of Holger Danske himself, for it moved; but that might have been in consequence of the flame of the candle not burning steadily. The young woman kissed her old father-in-law, and led him to a large arm-chair standing at the table, and she and her husband, who was the old man's son, and father of the little boy, then in bed, sat down to supper. The old man spoke of the Danish lions and of the Danish hearts, of strength and mildness, and he explained quite clearly, that there was other strength besides that which lay in the sword. He pointed to a shelf on which stood some old books, and amongst them Holberg's Plays, which have been so often read because they are so interesting; and it seems as if one can recognise all the people of past days.

"He knew how to strike, too," the old man said, "and did not spare the follies and vices of the world." He then pointed to the almanack, on which was a picture of the Copenhagen Observatory, and said, "Tycho Brahe was also one who wanted the sword, not to cut into flesh and bone, but to cut out a clear way amongst the stars of heaven. And then there is he, whose father belonged to my calling, the old wood-carver's son, whom we have seen whith his white hair and broad shoulders, he whose name is celebrated all over the world: Bertel Thorwaldsen. Yes, Holger Danske may come in many shapes, so that Denmark's strength is heard of in all countries of the world. Let us now drink Bertel's health."

In the meanwhile the little boy in bed saw old Kronburg quite plainly, and the real Holger Danske, who sat below with his beard grown fast in the marble table, dreaming of all that happened above. Holger danske dreamed also of the little room where the wood-carver was at work; he heard all that was spoken there, and nodding in his dream, said:-

"Yes, think of me, you Danish people! Keep me in your memories! I shall come in the hour of need!"

Above Kronburg the sky was clear and the wind carried the sound of the huntsman's horn from the neighbouring land, and the ships saluted as they passed, "Boom! Boom!" and from Kronburg was answered, "Boom! Boom!" but Holger Danske did not wake up, as loud as they fired, for it was no more than "Good day!" and "Many thanks!" The firing must be different before he awakes, but awake he will, for there is faith in Holger Danske.

The Rose-elf.

THE ROSE-ELF

Many, many years ago, in a large garden, there grew an enormous rose-tree, which was literally covered with roses, and in one of these, the most beautiful of them all, lived an Elf. He was so very small that he was not perceptible to any human eye, but, at the same time, so delightful and so beautifully made, as one can only imagine an angel to be; and two transparent wings, which reached from his shoulders to the soles of his feet, made him still more like an angel. Beneath each rose-petal he had a soft chamber, and, oh! what a delicious scent filled all his apartments, and how beautifully clear and bright were the walls, for they were the delicate, pale red rose-leaves themselves.

The whole day long he luxuriated in the warm sunshine, and danced on the wings of the roving butterflies, and sometimes in the dreamy hours of idleness he would sportively calculate the number of steps he would have to take to walk along all the high-roads, by-roads, and footpaths, on a single lime or horse-chestnut leaf. Those by us so-called veins in a leaf he looked upon as roads; and, indeed, they were interminable roads to him, for one day, before he had accomplished that long-meditated journey, the sun unfortunately went down. He should have begun earlier, but the first dawn of morning had failed to wake him.

It was growing cold, the dew fell and the wind blew, and the most prudent thing for the delicate little gentleman to do, was to get home as fast as possible. He hurried as much as he could, but before he reached the tree the roses were closed, so that he could not get in, and – alas! – there was not a single rose within his reach open for his reception. The poor Elfin-prince was dreadfully frightened, for he had never been out so late before, but at that hour had always been safely slumbering behind the sweet rose-leaf walls. Passing a night in the open air would, no doubt, cause his death in the bloom of youth, and the very thought of it gave him a shivering fit.

At the other end of the garden, he knew there was a bower of splendid honeysuckles, and in one of these he determined to pass the night.

Quickly he flew thither – but softly! In the bower were two beings anxious to hide from every obtrusive eye; the one, a handsome young man, and the other, the most charming girl. They were sitting side by side, and their sincerest wish was never to be parted, for they loved each inexpressibly, but the young man said, with a heavy sigh:-

"We must part, for your brother is not well-disposed towards me, and, therefore, he now sends me on a disagreeable commission, far from here, across mountains and rivers. Farewell, my dearest, my own beloved!"

They kissed each other again and again, the young girl crying bitterly, and, at parting, she gave him a rose; but, before doing so, she pressed a kiss upon it, so fervently, that the flower opened. The little Elf immediately slipped in amongst the leaves and, exhausted, rested his head against the soft, sweet-smelling walls; but he could hear that "Farewell! Farewell!" was said, and he felt that the rose had its place on the young man's heart. Oh, how that heart beat! So violently, indeed, that the little Elf could not sleep.

The rose did not long remain quiet in its resting-place, for the young man drew it forth, and as he walked alone through the dark forest he kissed it so often and so passionately, that the Elfin-prince was near being squeezed to death. But too sensibly could he feel, through the, at least, ten-leaf-thick covering, how the youth's lips burned, and the rose had completely unfolded itself as in the heat of the midday sun.

Another man then appeared, with a fierce, sinister-looking countenance, and this was the wicked brother of the beautiful girl. He held a large, sharp knife in his hand, and whilst the other was kissing the rose, treacherously stabbed him in the back. He then cut off his victim's head, which, together with the body, he buried under a large lime-tree, where the ground was soft.

"Now he is gone, and will be forgotten," the villain said. "He was to go a long journey, across rivers and mountains, and, travelling, one may easily lose one's life. He will never return, and never will my sister dare to ask me about him."

With his foot he then drew some dead leaves together over the newly-dug grave, and in the dark night returned home, but not alone, as he thought. The little Elf accompanied him, seated in a withered, curled-up lime leaf, which had fallen into the murderer's hair whilst he was digging the grave, for he had taken off his hat, and when he resumed it the leaf was underneath. The Elf was now in the most terrifying darkness, which made him tremble doubly with fear and anger at the horrible crime.

The wicked man reached home early in the morning, and having taken off his hat, went at once into his sister's bedroom. The beautiful girl was asleep, dreaming of him she loved so inexpressibly, and who, she thought, was then wandering over the mountains; but her unnatural brother, guessing her thoughts as he bent over her, laughed as one would imagine a fiend only could laugh, and, as he did so, the withered leaf fell out of his hair upon the bed. He did not notice it, but left the room to seek a few hours' rest in his own. The little Elf now left the leaf, and cautiously creeping into the sleeping girl's ear, told her, as if it were a dream, of the horrible murder, minutely describing the place where her lover was buried, and finally said, "That you may not think what I tell you is a mere dream, you will, on awaking, find a withered leaf upon your bed." She awoke immediately and found it there.

Oh, what bitter tears she shed! And to no one dared she discover the cause of her sorrow and despair, which bordered upon insanity. The whole day her window stood open, and easily could the tender-hearted Elfin-prince have flown out to the roses and other flowers, but he would not leave the poor girl in her sorrow, so he seated himself in a rose that stood in the window, and watched her. Her brother came into the room several times during the day, and the poor girl was obliged to hide the grief which was consuming her heart; but as soon as night approached she stole quietly out of the house and hurried into the forest, which was familiar to her, where she sought the lime-tree under which the darling of her heart lay buried. With her tender hands she dug up the earth, and soon found the lifeless body of her lover. How she cried, and prayed to God that she, too, might soon die!

Gladly would she have carried the body home, but, unable to do that, she raised the head, kissed its cold lips, and, having filled up the grave again, took it with her, as well as a twig of jasmine which grew near the spot where the murder had been committed.

Having reached her quiet little room, she took a large empty flower-pot put the head in, and, having covered it with mould, planted the jasmine-twig.

"Farewell, farewell!" the little Elf whispered, and, finding it impossible to witness so much sorrow, he flew into the garden to his rose-tree, but the roses had withered; and as he sought another dwelling he sighed, "Oh, how quickly all that is beautiful and great passes away!"

Every morning, early, he flew to the poor girl's window, and there he always found her crying by the side of the flower-pot in which, watered incessantly by her tears, the jasmine-twig took root; and as, day after day, she grew paler and paler, it sent forth shoots, and at length the little white buds became flowers. But her wicked brother could not imagine why she was always crying over the "foolish-flower pot", and he scolded, asking, since when she had lost her senses, for he did not know what treasure it contained. One day, when the little Elfin-prince came from his rose to pay her a visit, he found her dozing, and creeping into her ear, he told her of the night in the bower, of the scent of the rose, and the love of the Elves. She dreamed so delightfully, and during the dream her life passed away; she had died an easy death, and was now in heaven with him whom she loved beyond everything.

The jasmine-flowers opened their white bells and sent forth such a delightfully sweet perfume, for that was the only way they could cry over her who was dead.

The wicked brother thoughtfully examined the beautiful tree, now in full blossom, which he had placed in his bedroom close to the bed, for it was so very pretty, and the scent so delightful; but the little Elf went with it, fluttering from flower to flower, for in each flower dwelt a spirit, and he told of the young man whose head was now earth under the earth; he told of the wicked brother and his poor sister.

"We know it already," the spirit answered from each of the flowers; "we know it, for have we not sprung up from between the lips and out of the eyes of the dead man? We know it! We know it!" And as they said this they nodded their heads in a peculiar manner.

The Rose-elf could not imagine how it was they remained so quiet, and he flew away to the bees, who were gathering honey. He told them the story of the wicked brother, and the bees told their Queen, who immediately ordered that they should kill the hateful murderer the next morning.

But that very night – it was the first night after the sister's death – whilst the brother was lying in bed asleep, close to the jasmine-tree, every flower opened suddenly, and from each issued the spirit of the flower, invisible, but armed with a poisoned spear. The first whispered horrible dreams into his ear, and then, flying across his lips, pricked the sleeper's tongue with their spears. "Now we have avenged the murdered man," the said, and returned to their flowers.

As soon as it was morning, the window was violently thrown open from the inside, and the Rose-elf, with the Queen-bee and the whole swarm, flew in to hold judgment on the murderer.

But he was already dead, and by his bed-side people were standing who said, "The strong scent from the jasmine has killed him."

The Rose-elf then understood the revenge of the flowers, and he told it to the Queen-bee, who with her whole swarm surrounded the mysterious flower-pot. They could not be driven off, and when one of the bystanders took it up to carry it away, the bees stung him so severely in the hand that he let it fall, and the broken pieces rolled about the floor.

With astonishment and horror the people saw the white skull, and they now knew that he who was lying dead in his bed was a murderer.

And the Queen of the bees flew out into the open air, humming the revenge of the flowers, the praise of the Rose-elf, and how that beneath the smallest leaf dwells one who can expose and avenge crime.

The Wild Swans

Far from here, in the favoured country whither the swallows fly, when with us all is covered with snow, there lived a King, who had eleven sons and one daughter, named Eliza. The eleven brothers, all born princes, went to school with stars on their breasts and swords at their sides, and wrote with diamond pens on gold tablets. It could be seen at once that they were of royal blood. The sister, Eliza, sat in the meanwhile on a little stool of looking-glass, turning over the leaves of a picture-book which had cost half a kingdom.

Oh! those children were very happy, although their good mother was no longer living; but that was not to last.

Their father, who reigned over the whole land, married a wicked Queen, who could not bear the dear little children. Already, on her wedding-day, she plainly showed her unnatural, inimical feelings towards them, for although there was great feasting and rejoicing going on in the palace, she gave the childen only a little sand in a tea-cup, telling them to imagine that was something nice, whereas they had been accustomed to have as much sweet cake and as many roasted apples as they could eat.

The very next week, the wicked step-mother sent little Eliza into the country, to rough peasants, and before long she had told the weak King so much that was

The wild swans.

bad of the hated princes, that he no longer troubled himself about them.

"Fly out into the wide world," the wicked Queen said, "and take care of yourselves. Fly away as large birds without voices." However, it did not happen quite as she wished, for they were changed into eleven beautiful wild swans, and with a peculiar scream they flew out of the palace across the park and the forest.

It was still quite early in the morning when they came to the peasant's hut where their sister Eliza was lying fast asleep. They flew repeatedly round the roof, turning their long necks first to one side and then to the other, looking for their sister, and flapped with their wings; but no one heard them nor saw them, and they had to continue their flight, high up towards the clouds, and far, far into the vast boundless world.

Poor little Eliza, in the meantime, sat in the peasant's room playing with a green leaf, for she had no other plaything. She pricked a hole in the leaf with a pin, and looked through it up at the sun, when it seemed to her as if she saw her brothers' clear, bright eyes, and whenever the warm rays of the sun fell upon her cheeks, she thought of all their affectionate kisses.

One day passed exactly like the others, and when the wind blew through the rose-bush hedge, by the side of the hut, it whispered to the Roses, "Who can possibly be more beautiful than you?" And the Roses answered, "Oh, Eliza is more beautiful!" And when, on Sundays, the old woman sat at her door reading the Psalm-book, the wind turned over the leaves and said, "Who can be better than you?" "Oh, Eliza is better!" the Psalm-book answered. And what the Roses and the Book said was true.

At the age of fifteen she was fetched home, but when the Queen saw how beautiful she had grown, she was inflamed with envy and anger, and hated her lovely step-daughter twice as much as before. She would gladly have changed her into a wild swan, like her brothers, but she dared not, for the King wished to see his daughter.

Early in the morning the Queen took three hideous toads into the bathroom with her, which was built of marble, and most extravagantly furnished and decorated, and affectionately kissing the nasty creatures, she said to the one, "Seat yourself on Eliza's head when she gets into the bath, so that she may be as stupid and sleepy as you are." "Take your seat," she said to the second, "on her forehead, that she may be as ugly as yourself, and that her father may not recognise her." And to the third she said, "Seat yourself upon her heart, so that she may have a bad, spiteful disposition, which will consume her like slow poison." She then threw the toads into the clear water, which immediately assumed a green tinge, and having called Eliza to her, with cruel delight helped her to undress and get into the water. No sooner did the unsuspecting princess dip under the water, than the three toads took their appionted places, the first in her hair, the second on her forehead, and the third on her breast; but she did not seem to notice it. When she rose from the water, three red poppies floated on its surface. If the creatures had not been poisonous and kissed by the witch, they would have been changed into red roses, but flowers they still became, because they had rested upon Eliza's head and heart. She was much too good and innocent for the charm to take any effect upon her.

When the wicked step-mother saw this, she rubbed Eliza all over with walnut-juice, so that her skin, formerly as white as snow, became a dark-brown colour. She then smeared her lovely face over with an offensive salve, and rubbed it into her beautiful soft hair till it was inextricably entangled, so that it was utterly impossible to recognise the charming Eliza.

Her father was horrified, when the Queen, with ill-concealed delight, led her to him, and the deceived monarch disowned her as his daughter; nor was there any one found who would acknowledge knowing her. Only the house-dog and the swallows, in their own particular ways, greeted the discarded Princess as an old and loved acquaintance; but what good could they do, poor creatures?

Poor Eliza wept, and thinking of her eleven lost brothers, with a heavy heart stole out through the castle-gate, and after wandering the whole day over fields and through swamps, entered a large, dark forest. She had not the slightest idea which way to turn her steps, but she was so dejected, and felt such an inexpressible longing after her brothers, who, no doubt, like herself, were now wandering about the world, that to seek and find them must henceforth be the task of her whole life.

She had been only a short time in the forest when it became night, and having lost all trace of a path, despondingly she stretched herself upon the soft moss, and having said her evening prayer, leant her head against the stump of a tree, which had in all probability been destroyed by lightning. A soft, melancholy stillness reigned through the whole of nature; the air was so mild, and all around shone hundreds of glow-worms, which fell down upon her like shooting-stars when she touched one of the branches which formed a covering to her.

The whole night she dreamed of her brothers; they were again playing joyfully together like children, wrote with their diamond pencils on the gold tablets, and turned over the leaves of the splendid picture-book which had cost half a kingdom. But her grown-up brothers no longer scribbled mere noughts and strokes, but wrote down, in intelligible words, all their deeds, and all that they had experienced and seen. The tablet assumed a new and far greater importance, and in the picture-book all was alive. The different figures stepped out from the book, kindly speaking to Eliza and her brothers, but as each leaf was turned over they went back to their places, so that the order and story of the pictures might not be interefered with. For order rules the world.

When she awoke from her refreshing sleep the sun was already high up in the heavens. She could not see it, indeed, for the branches of the trees formed so close a covering over her head, but here and there a ray broke through like burnished gold. A balmy scent filled the air, and the birds seated themselves upon her shoulders. She heard the splashing of water, for several running streams emptied themselves together into a lake, the bottom of which was strewed with the most inviting sand. The luxuriant creepers and bushes here formed an impenetrable barrier; but in one place the deer had made an opening, and through this Eliza crept to reach the water, which was so clear, that if the wind had not moved the branches and leaves, she would have almost thought the reflection of them a skilful imitation, painted at the bottom, so clearly was each leaf reflected, as well that on which the bright sun shone as that which was in sombre shade.

When she saw her own face in the clear water, she started back in surprise and horror, she was so brown and ugly; but when she wetted her little hands and rubbed her eyes and forehead, her snow-white skin shone gradually brighter and brighter through the nasty coating. Eliza was so delighted at this, that she did not hesitate to throw off her clothes and entrust herself to the clear, refreshing water. And a more beautiful daughter of royalty than she was never seen in the world.

No sooner was she dressed again, and had simply but prettily plaited her hair, than she went to one of the bubbling springs, and having drunk out of the hollow of her hand, wandered joyously deeper and deeper into the forest, without knowing where she was going. She thought of her brothers, and of her heavenly Father, who would certainly not forsake her, for He made the wild fruits grow to feed the hungry. She soon found a tree of beautiful apples, which hung nearly down to the ground, and of these she made her morning meal. When she was satisfied, she gratefully put props under the heavy, hanging branches, and pursued her way through the darkest part of the forest. All was so still that she plainly heard her own footsteps and the rustling of each leaf as she lightly trod upon it; not a single bird was to be seen, and no ray of the sun could penetrate the thick leafy covering. The high trunks of the trees stood so close together, that they looked like the bars of a railing, and here reigned a solitude such as she had never before known.

It grew darker and darker, till it was quite night; not a single glow-worm was to be seen, and, quite sad, Eliza laid herself down to sleep. Then it seemed to her as if the branches above her head were suddenly drawn back, and she saw an angel looking kindly down upon her from heaven.

When she awoke the next morning, she did not know whether she had merely dreamed this, or whether it was really true.

She went on a few steps, when she met an old woman with all sorts of wild berries in a basket. She gave Eliza some of them; and to her question, whether she had happened to see eleven Princes ride through the forest, she answered:-

"No; but yesterday I saw eleven swans, with golden crowns upon their heads, swim down the brook that runs close by here."

She led Eliza a short distance towards some sloping ground which was a little less thickly wooded; and there, indeed, she saw a stream below. The trees on the banks of this stream stretched forth their branches as if lovingly striving to meet; and where the natural growth of the trees would not allow this, their roots had torn themselves from the earth, and spread over the quiet surface of the water.

Eliza wished the old woman a friendly farewell, and followed the windings of the stream till it flowed into the sea.

The grand expanse of sea was majestically spread out before the young girl's eyes, but no sail was to be seen, and how should she now go further? She examined the innumerable stones on the shore, and all had been polished smooth and round by the water. Glass, iron, stones, and all that had been thrown up there was ground to one form by the waves, although the water was much softer than her tender hands.

"It rolls incessantly backwards and forwards, and thus the hard edges are gradually ground off," she uttered, involuntarily. "I also will have untiring perseverance, and my heart tells me that some day I shall find my dearly beloved brothers. Many thanks, you clear-rolling waves, for the lesson!"

On the sea-weed that had been washed on to shore lay eleven white swans' feathers, which she quickly picked up and tied together. Single, clear drops of water hung upon them like pearls, as if, by their purity, to heighten the charm of the beautiful feathers; but whether those drops were the morning dew or tears, no one could distinguish. It was solitary there on the shore, but Eliza scarcely felt it, for the sea offered constant variety; yes, more in a few hours than a dozen of the most picturesque lakes can show in a year. When a large, dark cloud came floating along in the air, it seemed as if the sea said, "I can look black too." And then the wind blew, and the waves threw up their white foam. If, on the contrary, the clouds were red and transparent, the sea looked like a gigantic rose-leaf; but soon it changed colour, as if it were fading, for at one time it was green, then blue, and then white; and, however calm and quiet the water was, there was a constant noise, like breathing, on the shore, and the waves rose gently, like the breast of a sleeping child.

When the sun was going down, Eliza saw eleven wild swans, with gold crowns upon their heads, flying towards her. They floated high up in the air, one behind the other, forming in appearance a fluttering silver ribbon. Eliza then mounted an eminence that was near, and hid herself behind a bush, and soon the swans alighted by her side, flapping their large white wings.

The very instant that the sun had entirely disappeared behind the water, the swans' feathers fell off, and, behold! there stood eleven handsome Princes by Eliza's side. These were her brothers. She uttered a loud cry; for although they had altered much, she knew them, and felt that it must be they. She threw herself into their arms, calling each by his name, and they were no less filled with delight to see their little sister, who had grown so tall and so wonderfully beautiful. They laughed and cried by turns at this unexpected meeting, and soon they had related to each other how cruel their step-mother had been to them all.

"We eleven," the eldest said, "fly about as wild swans as long as the sun is up in the heavens; but when it has gone down, we regain our human form; and, therefore, we must be careful to find a resting-place for our feet towards evening; for should the sun set whilst we were high up in the clouds, we should, as human beings, fall down to our destruction. We do not live here, but on the other side of the sea, where there is a country as beautiful as this, which is, however, very far, and there is not a single island where we can pass the night, only a small rock rises from amidst the rolling waves. This rock is merely just large enough for us to lie upon, close, side by side; and when the sea is rough, the water is thrown up over us; but yet we are thankful for that dangerous resting-place. There we pass the night in our human forms; and without that place of refuge we should never be able to visit our own dear country, for it requires two of the longest days in the year to accomplish the distance. Only once a year are we allowed to visit the land of our birth; and then we can remain eleven days and fly over this vast forest, from whence we can see the proud palace where we were born, and where our father lives, and the high steeple of the church where our dear mother lies buried. Here it seems as if the trees and bushes were related to us; here the wild horses race with joyous leaps across the grassy plains, just like during the days of our happy youth; and here the charcoal-burners sing their old songs, to which, as boys, we delighted to dance. This is our country, to which we are irresistibly drawn, and here we have at last found you, our own dear, beautiful sister! We have still two days to remain; but then we must fly across the sea to a country which, though beautiful, is unfortunately not our home. How can we take you with us, for we have neither ship nor boat?"

"Oh, how can I save you?" the Princess said, sighing.

They passed nearly the whole of the night talking to each other, and only a couple of hours before daybreak were devoted to sleep.

Eliza was waked by the noise of the swans' wings, and, already high above her, she saw her brothers, who had been again changed, flying in wide circles, till they were lost in the distance. But one, the youngest of them, remained behind; and the swan laid its head in her lap, whilst she stroked his white plumage, and the whole day the brother and sister were side by side. Towards evening the others returned; and when the sun had fully gone down, they all appeared again in their natural forms.

"Tomorrow we fly away from here," the eldest said; and the other ten confirmed these words, spoken with evident emotion; "but we cannot thus forsake you. If you have the inclination and courage to go with us, we certainly shall have strength enough in our wings to carry you across the sea."

"Yes, take me with you!" Eliza said, beseechingly.

That whole night, without once closing their eyes, the eleven brothers spent in unremitting industry over the difficult task of making a net sufficiently large and strong, of the peel of the young willow-branches and of tough reeds. On this they laid Eliza; and when the sun rose, and they had been changed into swans, they laid hold of the net with their beaks and flew high up towards the clouds with their dear sister, who was still asleep. One of the swans constantly flew over her head, in order to shade her, with his large wings, from the rays of the sun.

They were already far from land when Eliza awoke, and it seemed to her as if she must still be dreaming, so strange it was to be floating in the air above the sea. By her side, on the net, lay a branch covered with delicious berries, and a handful of sweet-tasting roots, which her youngest brother had gathered for her; and she smiled him her thanks, for she guessed it was he who was flying above shading her with his wings.

They were up so high, that the first ship which they saw under them looked only like a white gull floating on the water. A huge cloud, like a mountain, hung in the air behind them, and on this magic background she saw the shadow of herself and the eleven swans of a gigantic size. She thought she had never seen so beautiful a painting; but, as the sun rose higher, and they left the cloud further behind them, the picture gradually faded.

With untiring exertion they sped through the air during the whole day, like the whizzing of the swiftest arrow; but yet, having their sister to carry, their flight was not so fast as usual. A storm was blowing up towards evening, and with fear Eliza saw the sun sinking, when there was yet no rock to be seen. She thought the swans' wings moved quicker; that they could not get on faster she knew was her fault. When the sun had disappeared, they would be changed to human beings, and, falling into the sea, be drowned. The thought of this almost killed her, and then she prayed most fervently to God, but still her strained eyes could not discover the saving rock. The dark clouds came lower and lower, till at last they seemed to form one black mass with the element below, which rolled on like a sea of lead. One flash of lightning followed rapidly upon the other.

The sun was now close upon the edge of the water. Oh, how Eliza's heart beat! Then the swans shot down with such velocity that she thought they were falling; but they floated in the air again, and, now that the sun had half disappeared, she saw the point of the rock below, no larger than the head of a porpoise, rising above the sea. The sun sank so swiftly, and now it only appeared as a star when Eliza felt her foot touch the firm rock. Then the sun disappeared like the last spark in smouldering paper, and the terrified Princess saw her eleven brothers, arm-in-arm, standing in a close circle around her; but there was only just room for the twelve. The sea broke furiously against the rising rock, throwing its spray over the half-fearing and half-hoping sister and brothers. The thunder continued to roll, and the sky seemed as if on fire; but the twelve stood hand-in-hand, joined in the bond of the truest love and affection, and they fervently sang some hymns in praise of their heavenly Father, which filled them with renewed hope and courage. With the break of day the sky became clear, and as soon as the sun rose the swans flew away with Eliza from their little resting-place. The sea was still rough; and, from the height they were flying, the white foam on the dark green water looked like a number of swans floating along its surface.

When the sun had risen high up in the heavens, Eliza saw beneath her, floating in the air, a mass of mountains with ice-covered rocks, and in the midst of them a place miles in length, with one row of columns rising above another. There were also forests of palm-trees, and the most wonderful flowers, as large as the wheels of a water-mill. She asked if that were the country to which they were going; but the swans shook their heads, for what she saw was the splendid, constantly-changing Palace of the Fairy "Morgana", which no human being might enter. Eliza kept her eyes immovably fixed on the splendour below her, when mountains, palace, and forests fell together in one chaotic mass, and in their places stood twenty proud churches, exactly like each other, with pointed windows and high steeples. She thought she heard the organs, but it was the melodious murmuring of the sea. They were now close upon the churches, which, however, changed into a fleet of stately ships, and when she looked down upon them these were again changed into a sea-mist, which, like swelling sails, swept along the surface of the water. A constant change was going on before her eyes, one picture taking the place of the other; and now she at length saw the real land, which for a time was to be her and her brothers' abode. There arose, in soft outlines, the most wonderful blue mountains, cedar forests, cities, and palaces; and long before the sun had gone down, Eliza sat before a cave covered inside and out with luxuriant green creepers, as if decorated by the hand of Nature with the most costly tapestry.

"Now we shall see what you dream here to-night," her youngest brother said, as he showed her her sleeping apartment.

"Oh, may I but dream how I can disenchant you!" she said, and this thought occupied her incessantly till she retired to rest. She then prayed fervently to God for assistance, and even in sleep her prayer continued, till it seemed to her as if she were floating high up in the air, towards the cloud palace of the Fairy "Morgana", when the Fairy herself came towards her, so beautiful and luminous, and yet resembling the old woman who had given her the berries in the forest, and told her of the eleven swans with the golden crowns.

"Your brothers can be saved," the Fairy said; "but will you have sufficient courage and perseverance to accomplish the difficult task? Certainly the sea is softer than your delicate hands, and yet it polishes the hard stones; but then it does not feel the pain your tender fingers will have to experience; it has no heart, and therefore cannot suffer from the anxiety and agony you must necessarily endure. Do you see these stinging-nettles in my left hand? Of these there are quantities growing round the cave in which you sleep; such only, and those which are sometimes seen on the graves in churchyards, will serve the purpose for which they are required – remember this. You must gather them yourself, if even they raise blisters on your skin. These you must crush with your naked feet, and you will obtain yarn, with which you must make eleven shirts with long sleeves, and throw them over the wild swans. If you succeed in this, as I trust you will, the charm will be immediately broken; but, of all things, do not forget what I am about to say. From the moment that you begin your work up to the hour – the very minute – that the task is accomplished, you must not speak a single word, if even years should pass by, for the first syllable your lips should utter would penetrate your brothers' hearts like a dagger. On your tongue hang their lives. Remember all this!"

The Fairy then touched the sleeping girl's hand with the nettles, and she was awakened by the burning pain. It was broad daylight, and close by her side lay a nettle, just like those she had seen in her dream. She fell upon her knees, thanked her heavenly Father for His mercy, and left the cave, in order to begin her work.

She thrust her tender hands amongst the nasty nettles, which burned like red-hot coals, so that her hands and arms were covered with blisters; but that she would cheerfully bear, if she could but save her dear brothers. She crushed each nettle with her naked feet, and with her blistered fingers wound the yarn.

Immediately after sunset her brothers came, and they were greatly frightened to find her apparently dumb. They thought, at first, it was a new charm of their wicked step-mother's; but when they saw the dreadful state of their noble sister's hands, and the nettles by her side, they understood what she was doing for their sakes, and the youngest cried bitterly over her. Wherever his tears fell she felt no pain, and the burning blisters disappeared.

The whole night she continued her work without ceasing, for she could have no rest till she had saved her dear brothers; and the whole of the following day, whilst the swans were absent, she sat at work in her solitude, and never had the time flown so quickly. One shirt was finished, and instantly she began another.

All of a sudden she heard the merry sound and echo of huntsmen's horns amongst the mountains, and the young Princess was filled with fear and dread. The noise came nearer and nearer, till she plainly heard the barking of the dogs, and, trembling with anxiety, she withdrew into the cave, and, having tied the nettles, which she had gathered and crushed, into a bundle, she seated herself upon it, as if to protect this her most valuable treasure from all danger.

The next moment a large, fierce-looking dog broke through the bushes, and immediately after a second, and then a third. They barked furiously, ran back, and then appeared again, and in a few minutes all the huntsmen stood before the cave, of whom the handsomest was King of the land. Quickly he advanced towards Eliza – never had he seen so beautiful a girl.

"How did you get here, you lovely child?" he asked; but Eliza shook her head sadly, for she dared not speak, as her brothers' lives depended upon it, at the same time hiding her hands under her apron, that the King might not see what she was suffering.

"Follow me," he said; "for here you must not remain; and if you are as good as you are beautiful, I will clothe you in silk and satin, place the golden crown upon your head, and you shall dwell in my splendid palace." With these words he lifted the fainting and struggling Princess upon his horse; and as she continued to cry and wring her hands, he said, "Calm yourself, you lovely girl! For it is only your good I wish, and some day you will thank me with all your heart." He galloped off over the beautiful mountains, carrying his lovely burden before him on his horse, and the huntsmen followed.

Towards sunset the mangificent, regal city, with its churches and domes, rose from the valley, forming an inimitable panorama; and the King hastened to conduct his charming companion to the palace, where sparkling fountains played in the lofty marble halls, decorated with paintings and curiosities; but she had no eyes for all the splendour, as, buried in grief, she continued to cry. Unresistingly she allowed the ladies' maids to array her in princely garments, put pearls in her hair, and draw silk gloves on her blistered hands.

As she now appeared, her beauty was so dazzling, that the whole court bowed down before her, and the King at once declared her his future bride, although the Archbishop shook his head, whispering to his friends that the beautiful forest maiden was no doubt a witch, who blinded and deceived the King.

But the King shut his ears to such suspicions, the music sounded louder, the most delicious refreshments were provided, and he hastened the preparations for more splendid festivities. Through the most delightful gardens Eliza was conducted to splendid apartments, where the loveliest girls surrounded her with joyous dances; but no smile parted her lips, nor ray of merriment lighted up her eyes; no, every feature, and her whole expression, denoted the deepest, all-consuming sadness. The King then opened a small room, by the side of her sleeping apartment, which was painted and fitted up in exact imitation of the cave in the forest where he had found her. On the floor lay the yarn which she had made from the nettles, and which, in spite of her surprise and fear, she had so carefully made up into a bundle, and from the ceiling hung the one shirt she had already finished.

"Here you can, in imagination, return to your former home," the King said. "Here is the work at which you were occupied; and it may, perhaps, in the midst of all the present splendour, afford you pleasure to think sometimes of the past."

When Eliza saw these things, which were of such inestimable value to her, a happy smile played around her lovely mouth, and the blood returned to her cheeks. She thought of the time when she could save her brothers, and in the overflowing of her gratitude she kissed the King's hand. He pressed her to his beating heart, and ordered all the church bells to proclaim their speedy marriage. The charming dumb girl of the forest was Queen of the country.

The suspicous Archbishop whispered evil words into the King's ear, but they did not sink as deep as his heart. The marriage took place, and the Archbishop himself had to place the crown upon the bride's head, which, in his with-difficulty-concealed vexation, he pressed down so heavily, that it hurt her forehead; but grief and anxiety for her brothers caused her heart much more intense suffering. What was bodily pain? Her mouth remained dumb, for a single word would have destroyed her brothers' lives, but her eyes expressed the deepest love for the good, handsome King, who left nothing untried to cheer her. Daily she became more devoted to him; oh, could she but have confided in him, and told him all her grief! But she must remain dumb till her task should be completed. For this she stole away from his side at nights, and hurried to the little room, like the cave in the forest, of which she always carried the key with her. Here she worked, finishing one shirt after the other, but when she wanted to begin the seventh she had no more yarn.

She knew that in the churchyard the same sort of nettles grew, which she might use, but she must gather them herself, and how could she do that unnoticed?

"Oh! what is the pain in my fingers," she thought, "compared to the agitation of my heart? It must be ventured, and my heavenly Father will not withdraw His protection from me in this hour of trial." With fear and trembling, as if she were about to commit a bad action, she stole down into the garden, through the avenue and along the deserted streets to the churchyard. With horror, she there beheld a circle of the most revolting witches, who threw off their disgusting rags, and began digging with their long, bony fingers down into the newly-made graves. She had to pass close by the side of them, and they fixed their evil eyes upon her, but, praying to herself, she hastily gathered the burning nettles and carried them home to the palace.

Only one human being had seen her during her night expedition, and that was the Archbishop, who was up and awake whilst others were sleeping. There could be no doubt now that his suspicions were well founded, that all was not right with the Queen. She was evidently a wicked sorceress, who had bewitched the King and all the people.

In the confessional he told the King his suspicions, and all that he had seen; and as his venomous tongue, with cruel eloquence, uttered the words, the carved images of the saints shook their heads, as if to say, "It is not so, Eliza is innocent." But the Archbishop explained it otherwise, maintaining that they confirmed his words. Two large tears rolled down the King's cheeks, and with the first seeds of suspicion sowed in his breast, he returned to the palace. At night he pretended to be asleep, but watched Eliza as she got up. Every night she repeated this, and each time he followed her noiselessly and saw her enter the little room, the door of which she immediately locked after her.

Day after day the King's countenance became more sombre, and Eliza, in secret, fretted at this change, the reason for which she could not guess; and her heart was, besides, torn by the most acute suffering on account of her unfortunate brothers, who, as wild swans, were still wandering about far from her. Bitter tears fell upon the satin and velvet of her regal attire, where they lay like glittering diamonds; but all the people, seeing such splendour, only envied her. Her task was at length nearly accomplished; only one shirt still remained to be done; but she had no more yarn, and not a single nettle of which to make any. Once more, therefore, and now for the last time, she must go to the churchyard to gather a few handfuls. She shuddered at the thought of that lonely walk and the hateful witches, but her will was as firm as her trust in the Ruler of the destiny of man.

Eliza went, but followed at a distance by the King and the Archbishop, who lost sight of her as she disappeared through the churchyard-gate, which they no sooner reached than they saw the witches as Eliza had seen them. Shuddering, the King averted his face from the scene of horror, for in the midst of the group he imagined her whose head but a short time back had rested on his breast.

"The people shall judge her," he said, in a scarcely audible voice; and the people condemned her to be burned.

She was dragged from her magnificent rooms to a damp hole, where the wind whistled incessantly through the window, but ill secured by the rusty iron bars. Instead of velvet and satin, they gave her the bundle of nettles she herself had gathered in the churchyard, for her to lay her head upon; and for a covering they gave her the harsh burning shirts she had made. Nothing could have been so welcome to her, and immediately she resumed her painful work, praying at the same time with increased fervour. The rabble sang songs in derision of her, and there was not one being to console her with a single word of pity.

Towards evening she heard the "whirring" of a swan's wings close to the grating of her window. It was her youngest brother, who at length had found her, and she smiled with delight and happiness, though there was scarcely a doubt but that this would be her last night. But now her work was nearly finished, and her brothers were at hand.

The Archbishop came to pass the last hours with her, as he had promised the King; but she shook her head, and by signs gave him to understand that she wished to be left alone. In this, the most important night of her life, her work must be finished, or all would have been in vain, all – her sufferings, tears, silence, and sleepless nights. The Archbishop went away uttering angry words, but poor Eliza knew that she was innocent, and without ceasing she continued her work.

The little mice ran about the floor quite tame and fearlessly; they dragged the nettles and laid them at her feet, that they might be of some use to her, and a thrush sat on one of the iron bars of her window, singing, as merrily as it possibly could, during the whole night, that the prisoner might not lose her courage.

It was just the break of day, an hour before the rising of the sun, when the eleven brothers appeared at the palace gate and desired earnestly to be conducted to the King, but they were answered that it was impossible, as it was still night, and they dared not wake the King from his sleep. They begged, they threatened; then the guards came, and at length the King himself. Just then the sun rose, and no longer where any brothers to be seen, but eleven wild swans flew over the palace.

An innumerable concourse of people crowded together to witness the burning of the witch. A miserable horse, a walking skeleton, dragged the cart in which she sat. A loose smock of sackcloth had been thrown over her, and her beautiful long hair hung down upon her shoulders, surrounding her noble face, childishly pious, like that of an angel. She was as pale as death, and there was scarcely perceptible movement of her lips, whilst her fingers with strained velocity strove to finish the almost-accomplished task, which she would not give up, even on her way to death. At her feet lay the ten finished shirts.

"Look at the witch!" the rabble cried, "how she presses her lips together. There is no hymn-book in her hands – no, she is going on with her horrid sorcery. Let us tear the Satanic work into a thousand shreds."

They began to press upon her, intending to deprive her of the fruits of the noblest sisterly sacrifice and love, when eleven white swans surrounded her, and the crowd fell back in terror.

"That is a sign from heaven of her innocence," many whispered, but they dared not say it out loud.

The executioner now laid hold of the unfortunate Princess's hand, when hastily she threw the eleven shirts over the swans, and in their places there suddenly stood eleven handsome Princes; but the youngest of them had a swan's wing instead of one of his arms, for one sleeve was wanting to his shirt, though his good sister Eliza had striven with unexampled industry to finish it.

"Now I may speak," she said. "I am innocent!"

And the people, who saw what had happened, bowed down before her, as before a saint, whilst she sank lifeless into her brothers' arms, so violently had anxiety, fear, and pain affected her.

"Yes, she is innocent!" her eldest brother exclaimed, and whilst he was relating all the events that had occurred, a sweet scent, as of thousands of roses, filled the air, for each stick of the pile that was to consume the Princess had taken root, and they formed a high thick hedge of dark red roses. But higher than the rest was one flower of dazzling whiteness, which shone as a silver star, crowning the red tint of a fine sunrise. This flower the King plucked and laid it upon Eliza's breast; then animation, for a short time suspended, returned, and peace and happiness filled her heart.

All the bells rang of their own accord, whilst innumerable flights of birds gathered around, and there was a bridal procession, back to the palace, such as had never before been witnessed.

The Sandman.

The Sandman

~

No one in the whole world knows so many stories as the Sandman; yes, he is an incomparable master in story-telling.

Of an evening, as soon as it begins to grow dark, and the children are sitting quietly at the table, or in their little chairs, the Sandman comes; he comes up the stairs without the slightest noise, for he walks in his stockings only; gently he opens the door, and throws sand into the children's eyes – fine, fine sand, but so much of it that they can keep their eyes open no longer, and therefore they cannot see him. He steals close behind them, and as soon as his warm breath touches the back of their necks, their heads become heavy and sink foward. But it does not hurt them – oh no! – for the good Sandman only plays off that joke upon them, which is in reality his serious earnest for the good of his young charges. He only wishes them to be quiet, and it is best for them to be taken to bed. He wants them to be silent, in order to tell them stories, quite undisturbed, as he sits on their beds after they are asleep.

The Sandman's dress, although not according to the last fashion, is handsome, and even elegant. His coat, resembling rather a loose tunic, is of a rich silk, but it is impossible to say what colour, for it is green, red, or blue, according to how the gentleman turns. Under each arm he carries an umbrella, the one of which is lined through and through with the most beautiful pictures, and this he holds over the good children, so that during the whole night they dream the most delightful stories, whereas in the other there is nothing whatever to be seen, and that he opens over the naughty children, so that they sleep heavily, and when they awake of a morning have not dreamed anything.

Now we shall see how the Sandman, during a whole week, came regularly every night to a little boy whose name was Fred; and hear also what he told him. There are exactly seven stories, for the week has seven days.

MONDAY

"Now, pay attention," the Sandman said at night, after he had covered Fred up warm in his soft bed, "for I will show you something worth looking at." Suddenly all the little plants in the china flower-pots grew to large trees, which spread out their long branches picturesquely across the walls of the room, forming a leafy dome at the top, so that it had the appearance of a beautiful green-house. The branches were thickly covered with flowers and buds, and each of the thousands of flowers were more beautiful than a rose, they had such a delightful scent; and if one wished to eat them, were sweeter than any of the preserved fruits which the confectioner has in his shop. The fruits themselves shone like pure gold, and altogether it was a scene of splendour such as, perhaps, only Aladdin saw in the enchanted cave. Nor was there any want of the most delicious cakes and tartlets, so full of jam that they could scarcely contain it. That was, indeed, a state of happiness; but at that moment there arose a dreadful moaning and sighing in the table-drawer, where Fred's school-books were kept.

"What can that be?" the Sandman said, going up to the noisy table, the creaking drawer of which he pulled out at once. The moaning and sighing proceeded from a slate, set in a wooden frame, with metal corners, for a wrong figure had got into the sum, which was, in consequence, near upon falling to pieces. The hopping and jumping of the slate-pencil, fastened with a piece of string to the frame, like a chained dog, were truly deafening, in its strained but fruitless efforts to correct the gross mistake in the algebra sum. Then Fred's copy-book began complaining so bitterly, that it was quite distressing to listen to it. At the beginning of each line, all the way down the leaves, was written a capital letter of the alphabet, and the small letter next to it, as copies, written, no doubt, by the master, and all along the lines were unreadable hieroglyphics, thinking themselves, in their unpardonable vanity, exact representations of the copies. Fred had scratched these down, and they were all falling, head first, over the lines, which were intended for them to stand upon.

"Look, this is the way you should hold yourselves," the Copies cried, impatiently. "Look here! In this manner, with a graceful bend to one side."

"We would willingly do so," Fred's letters answered, "but we cannot, we are so badly made."

"You must feel the edge of the knife, then," the Sandman said, threateningly holding up his finger.

"Oh, no!' they cried, entreatingly, and they stood upon the line, so straight, and with such ease, that it was quite a pleasure to look at them.

"There will be no stories tonight," the Sandman said, "for I must drill these crazy letters. One, two!" And he drilled them so thoroughly that they stood as gracefully as only the best writing-master could accomplish; but when he had gone, and Fred looked at them in the morning, they were as bad as ever.

TUESDAY

As soon as Fred was in bed, the Sandman touched the different pieces of furniture, and all began to chatter; but each only talked of itself, without paying any attention to what the others said. Over the drawers there hung a large painting in a gilt frame, representing a landscape with high, old trees, flowers in the grass, and a large river, which wound round the wood, past several castles, till it was lost in the wild, raging sea.

The Sandman only gently touched the picture, and immediately the birds in it began to sing, the branches of the trees moved, set in motion by the wind, and the flight of the clouds was evident, for their shadows could be plainly seen gliding across the landscape.

The Sandman now held little Fred up towards the frame. Fred put out one leg into the painting, right into the grass, and there he stood. The sun shone through the fresh, green leaves, as if smiling upon him. He ran down to the water, and seated himself in a little boat which lay there, as if on purpose for him. Painted red and white, the little craft looked almost like a Dutch tulip; the sails glittered like silver; and six swans, all with gold crowns on the lower part of their necks and a bright blue star on their heads, drew the boat swiftly past the green forests, in which the trees spoke eloquently of robbers and witches, and the flowers of the most beautiful little elves, as well as of other things which their sisters, the butterflies, had told them.

The most beautiful fishes, with scales like gold and silver, swam after the boat, one occasionally venturing on a jump into the air, and then going splash into the water again, whilst birds, blue and red, large and small, followed in two long rows. The gnats danced in the air, and the cock-chafers hummed, "Whoooo! whoooo!" and each had its own particular story to tell.

That was, indeed, a joyous trip along the flowing stream. At one time the forests were thick and dark, then like the most delightful garden, with sunshine and flowers, and to the right and left were vast palaces of glass and marble. Splendidly-dressed Princesses leaned over the gilt railings on the terraces, all little girls whom Fred knew well, having formerly played with them, and each of them stretched out her hand towards him, smilingly offering the dearest little sugar-pig that any cake-woman ever sold. As he sailed past, Fred laid hold of one end of the pig, whilst the Princess held tight hold of the other, so that each had a piece; but Fred had the largest. By the side of each palace little Princes kept watch, shouldering their gold swords, and throwing regular showers of figs and tin-soldiers, so that there was no doubt about their being real Princes.

Now he passed through forests, and then, as it were, through large rooms or imperial cities, till he came to the village where his nurse lived – she who had carried him as a baby in her arms, who, depriving herself, had stilled his hunger and thirst, and who had loved him almost as a mother. She nodded to him, and sang the pretty little verse which she herself had composed and sent to him:-

"I think of you, so oft, so oft!
You know, my love, my darling Fred!
I've kissed your little lips, so soft,
Your forehead, and your cheeks so red!
I heard you utter your first word,
Then was I forced to say farewell!
But ever, ever, may the Lord
Bless you, my Fred, where'er you dwell!"

And all the birds sang too, the flowers dangled backwards and forwards on their stalks, and the old trees nodded as if the Sandman had been telling them these stories. What will not people imagine!

WEDNESDAY

In what torrents the rain came down, so that Fred could hear it even in his sleep; the whole town seemed one lake, and when the Sandman opened the window the most magnificent ship lay anchored close to the house where the good little boy's parents lived.

"Will you sail with me, little Fred?" the Sandman asked. "You can visit far, far distant foreign lands during this night, and be back in time for school tomorrow morning."

Then suddenly Fred stood upon the deck of the vessel, the rain left off, and the sky became clear; in short, it could not be more favourable or beautiful than it was.

Quickly they sped on, through straight and crooked streets, and, as if flying, turned round to the left of the church, and then there was nothing to be seen but the vast, wild sea, with waves and foam. They had long lost sight of land, when they saw above them, in the air, a numerous body of pilgrims, nothing but long-legged storks, who, like themselves, came from their distant home, bound for a warmer country. One stork flew immediately after the other, in a close column; and they had already left several hundred miles behind them, in consequence of which one of them was so tired that his wings could scarcely carry him any further; he was last in the row, and gradually he remained further and further behind, at the same time sinking lower and lower. He made a few more desperate efforts, but in vain. Already his feet touched the cordage of the ship, and, shaking with fear, he slid down the sail, till – plump! – he stood quite confused upon the deck.

He was immediately seized by the ship-boy, who, dancing with delight at his catch, put him into the chicken-house, with the chickens, geese, and ducks. The poor Stork did not know how he ought to behave, whether with dignity, according to his rank, or whether quite humbly, and for consideration his feathered companions left him neither peace nor time.

"Do just have a look at this one," the Chickens said.

And the proud Cock, making himself as tall as he could, asked the newcomer, with the airs of a policeman, who and what he really was. The Ducks waddled backwards, and most awkwardly knocking against each other, cried, with a nasal twang, "Be quick! Be quick, will you?"

Then the Stork told them about hot Africa, and the Pyramids, and of the ostrich that races across the desert like a wild horse; but the Ducks did not understand a word he said, and again sidling and backing against each other, mumbled, "We are all agreed that the newcomer is a stupid and impertinent Monsieur."

"Yes, he is stupid – as stupid as an owl!" the Cock cried, letting his shrill voice have unrestrained play. "Stupid, stupid, stupid!" Then the Stork was quite silent, and thought of his dear Africa.

"What inimitable, thin legs you have!" cackled a fat Goose; "how much are they a yard?"

"Quack! Quack! Quack!" the Ducks sneered, but the Stork pretended not to hear.

"You may as well laugh with the rest, Monsieur Longleg," the Goose said, "for it was very wittily spoken; but, perhaps, it is too low for such a high gentleman. Cackle! Cackle! Cackle!" and the Ducks joined in, "Quack! Quack! Quack!" as if they had to help the Geese in watching the ship, like another Capitol.

But Fred, who was considerably annoyed by the uproar, and the injustice of the whole feathered company to the interesting Egyptian guest, made an attack upon the chicken-house and released the Stork, who had been driven into a corner by his numerous persecutors. The Stork, hearing himself called by name, hopped joyfully on to the deck, and, having now recovered from his fatigue, spread out his wings and flew away, nodding to his little champion, as if to thank him for his assistance. He flew off to a warmer country, where he, no doubt, hoped shortly to be married to a young lady of the same old, noble race; for it could easily be seen that he was carried on the wings of love. The Ducks continued to "quack", the Geese to "cackle", and the Cock crowed, so that his comb was as red as fire with the exertion.

"Tomorrow we will make soup of you, you stupid, narrow-minded set!" Fred said, and spoke so loud that it waked him. Only half awake, he rubbed his eyes, as he lay in his soft, warm bed, when the church clock struck seven, and at eight o'clock, exactly, he had to be in school, so he had not much time to waste.

It was certainly a wonderful voyage the Sandman had taken him that night.

THURSDAY

"Do you know what?" the Sandman said; "but do not be frightened; you shall now see a little Mouse"; and he stretched out his hand, in which he held the pretty, nimble creature towards the boy, smiling sweetly in his sleep. "The little Mouse has come to invite you to a wedding, for two little but stately Mice are going to be married to-night. It is true they live somewhat low down, namely, under the flooring of your mother's store-room, but it is said to be a most convenient place."

"But how shall I get through the little Mouse's hole in the floor?" Fred asked, in alarm.

"Leave that to me," the Sandman said, with the self-satisfied air of the most perfect confidence. "I shall have no difficulty in making you small enough"; whereupon he touched Fred, who became smaller and smaller, till he was nothing near as big as a finger. 'You can now borrow the Tin-soldier's clothes, which, I think, will just fit you, for it always looks well to wear uniform in the company of ladies."

"That is true," Fred said, and the same moment he was dressed in the clothes of the smartest of the Tin-soldiers.

"Will you have the goodness to seat yourself in your mother's thimble?" the pretty little Mouse said with its little voice, "and then I shall have the honour to drag you."

"I am quite ashamed that you should have that trouble," Fred said, with a graceful bow, but, seating himself, was dragged off to the wedding.

The first part of their way lay through a passage running downwards under the floor, which was so narrow that there was scarcely room for the thimble to glide through, and this ingenious tunnel was illuminated by the phosphoric light of dried herrings' heads, instead of torches.

"Does it not smell delightful here?" the little Mouse that dragged him squeaked. "The whole passage has been rubbed in with hog's lard from top to bottom. What can be more delicious?"

They stopped at the entrance to the tastefully-decorated room, for taste is the first consideration with Mice, as well as with many human beings, though their tastes differ. To the right, inside the room, stood the most lovely little lady-mice, giggling and whispering in each other's ears, as if they were making game of each other, and to the left stood the gentlemen-mice, most perseveringly stroking their chins; whilst in the middle, seated side by side, in a piece of transparent rind of cheese, were the bride and bridegroom, kissing each other, quite unabashed by all the company.

Fresh guests were constantly arriving, till the crowd grew so great that they almost squeezed each other to death; and now no one could get either in or out, for the bride and bridegroom thought proper to take their place right in the centre of the only door. The whole room was well smeared with the fat of bacon, and that was all the refreshment they got; but ought they not to be satisfied with smelling that? For dessert, however, a pea was shown them, on which an ingenious Mouse had nibbled the names, that is, the first letter of the names, of the newly-married couple. That was something quite extraordinary.

All the Mice protested that they had never experienced the pleasure of being present at so splendid and interesting a wedding; and that the conversation, in particular, had been so witty, varied, and rich in material for thought.

Fred then drove home again. There was no denying that he had been in very grand company; but then he had had to make himself very small, besides putting on a Tin-soldier's uniform. Truly, no small sacrifice!

FRIDAY

"It is incredible how many there are among the elder people who would often gladly seize me in my flight," the good-natured Sandman said, "more particularly those who have committed any wicked actions. 'Good Old Sandman!' they say to me, 'our eyes will not close at all, and thus we lie the whole night sleepless and see all our bad deeds, which, in the form of frightful little imps, sit at the edge of our beds, sprinkling boiling water over us, and sometimes boiling oil. If you would but come and drive them away, that we might have a little quiet sleep' – and then they sigh so deeply – 'we will gladly pay; the money lies there at the window; take as much as you like; take it all.' But I do nothing for money; money is of no use to me," the Sandman said.

"How are we to pass this night?" Fred asked, for he was no longer afraid of his old friend and amusing companion of every night.

"Well, I scarcely know whether you are inclined to come to another wedding, though it will be quite a different fête to that of last night," the Sandman said, with the most serious face in the world. "Your sister's big doll, which looks like a man, and is called Hermann, is going to marry the doll Bertha, and, as it is her brithday, there will be no lack of presents."

"Yes, I know that," Fred said, "for when the dolls want new clothes, my sister makes them keep their birthday, or marries them. That has happened at least a hundred times."

"Yes, but tonight will be the hundred-and-first time," the Sandman broke in, "and when the hundred-and-first time is over, all is over, and therefore this fête will be so particularly splendid. Just look."

Fred did look, and with the greatest curiosity, towards the table to which the Sandman pointed. There stood the pretty little cardboard house, with all the windows lighted up, and in front of the house the Tin-soldiers presented arms. The betrothed sat on the floor, leaning against one of the legs of the table, half cheerfully and half sadly, or, at any rate, thoughtfully, looking down upon the ground, for which, perhaps, in their present position, they mght have more reasons than one. But the Sandman, to whom Fred's Grandmother's black apron served as canonicals, married them, or joined them together, giving them a perfectly illegible, but otherwise legal, certificate. After the ceremony, all the Furniture joined in the following pretty song, written by the Pencil:-

"To them, ye breezes, waft our song,
To them, of kid so soft and strong,
Press forward with the eager throng,
Our homage does to them belong.
Hurrah, for kid that's soft and strong!
Echo, loudly repeat our song!"

Now appeared all the presents, but eatables the bride and bridegroom had wisely forbidden, as their love would be all-sufficient.

"Shall we take lodgings somewhere in the country here, my dear Bertha?" the bridegroom asked; "or shall we take post and travel on to the Continent?"

The inexperienced Bertha did not know which she would prefer, and it was a long time before they could come to any decision. The difficulty of a choice really became painful, when it was at length determined to consult the Swallow, which had travelled far, and the old Hen in the yard, which had five times reared a brood of chicks. The Swallow told of the warm countries, where the grapes are so beautiful and large, where the air is so soft, and where the mountains appear in colours unknown in colder climates.

"But they have not got our green cabbage, which is not good till there has been a sharp frost," the Hen said. "I was in the country one summer with all my little chicks, where there was a sand-pit, in which we could scratch to our hearts' content, and we had the undisputed right of entrance into a garden of green cabbages – oh, how green they were! I cannot imagine anything more delightful."

"But one cabbage is always exactly like the other," the Swallow objected; "and then there is very bad weather here sometimes."

"But to that we are used," the Hen said.

"And it is, besides, cold here; it snows, it freezes."

"Oh, just that, as I have said, does the cabbage good," the Hen insisted; "and, besides, we have it sometimes warm enough. Had we not a summer four years ago which lasted quite five weeks, and it was so hot, so hot, that one could scarcely breathe? And then, too, we are free from all the venomous creatures which abound in warmer countries, and we have no robbers. Whoever does not acknowledge our favoured country to be the most beautiful of all is, in my opinion, and the opinion of all sensible people, nothing but an order-disturbing rogue, and should not be allowed here at all." And the good, honest Hen cried as she added, "I have travelled, too, and have something to say about it. Shut up in a coop with my dear little ones, I was carried above thirty miles, and I can honestly say that travelling is anything but pleasant."

"Oh, the Hen is a sensible woman," the doll Bertha said; "neither am I much in favour of mountainous country, for it is all up and then down again. No, after due consideration, I decidedly vote for the sand-pit and the cabbage-garden, where we can wander about undisturbed."

And thus matters remained.

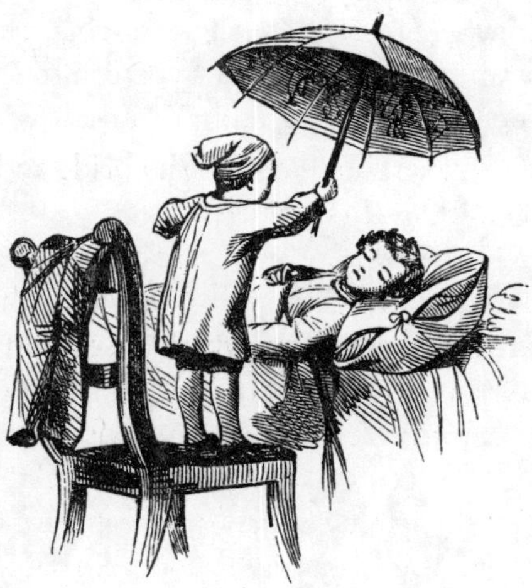

SATURDAY

"Am I now to hear stories?" little Fred said, as soon as the Sandman had put him quietly to sleep.

"Tonight we have no time for that," he answered, and opened his most beautiful umbrella over the boy. "Look at these Chinese"; and the umbrella seemed to be a large Chinese plate, with blue trees, pointed bridges, and Chinese men and women, who stood there nodding their heads. "Before tomorrow the whole world must be put in order," the Sandman said, "for tomorrow is a holy day. First, I must go into the church-steeples, to see whether the little church-spirtes have polished the bells properly, that their sound may be clear; I must go out into the fields to see whether the winds have blown the dust off the grass and leaves; and, the most important of all, I must quickly fetch down all the stars, in order to polish them. I carry them in my coat-tail, but they have all to be numbered first, as well as the holes in which they are fixed up there, so that they may be put back in their proper places, or they might not fit tightly, and we should have too many falling stars."

"Listen to me, I pray, Mr. Sandman," said an old Portrait which hung in the room. "I am Fred's Great-grandfather – do you know that? Now, I am certainly very much obliged to you for telling the boy stories, but you must not fill his head with such gross falsehoods. The stars cannot be taken down and polished, for they are regular and perfect heavenly bodies, like our earth."

"Many thanks, old Great-grandfather, many thanks!" the Sandman answered, who, in spite of his being so busy, took pleasure in the fun. "You are the venerable head of the family – the real old one, but, for all that, I am older than you. I am, in fact, a real classic heathen, whom the Romans and Greeks used to call the god of dreams. From times immemorial I have been a visitor in the first houses, and still continue so, for I am everywhere received with open arms. I know how to manage big and small – indeed, I am suited to all. But now you can relieve me for once in a way, and amuse the little sleeper with merry tales." And away went the Sandman, not forgetting to take his umbrella with him.

"One has no right, I suppose, to express an opinion," the old Portrait grumbled.

And Fred awoke out of his sweet sleep.

SUNDAY

"Good evening!" the Sandman said, and Fred nodded, but then he jumped up, and quickly turned the portrait of his Great-grandfather, with the face to the wall, so that it might not join in the talk, as it did the night before.

"Now you are going to tell me stories, my dear Sandman," the little boy said, coaxingly; "but wait, I will tell you what about. Of the five green peas that lived in the same pod, or of my Lord Cocksleg who made love to Lady Chickenleg, or of the Darning-needle that was so fine that it thought itself a sewing-needle."

"There may be too much of a good thing even," the Sandman answered. "You know, my dearest Fred, that I prefer showing you things; and now I will show you my brother, who is likewise called the Sandman, but he only comes once to all creatures that have life, and then he takes them with him on his horse, and tells them stories. Unfortunately he only knows two, one of which is so wonderful, that no one in the world can imagine it, and the other so horrible that it cannot be described." The Sandman then helped Fred to climb up into the window, and said, "Now you shall see my brother, the other Sandman, who is also called Death, but, believe me, he does not look as bad as he is drawn in picture-books – all bones. That which you see looking so bright on his dress is all silver embroidery. He wears the most beautiful hussar's uniform. A short cloak of black velvet hangs behind him, on to the fiery horse. See, how he gallops past!"

And Fred saw how, as he rode along, he took up both old and young people upon his horse. Some he took before, whilst others he seated behind him, but he always asked them first, "What character does your book show you to bear?"

"Good!" they invariably answered.

"I must see it myself," he then said, and they were obliged to show him their books. All those who bore the characters of "very good", and "exceedingly good", had their places in front of him, to listen to the heavenly story, but those who were marked "pretty good", "middling", or "bad", were seated behind him, and had to hear the horrible story. They trembled and cried, and would have thrown themselves, head first, off the horse, but they could not, for it was as if they had grown to it.

"Why, Death is the more beautiful Sandman of the two!" Fred exclaimed; "I am not in the least afraid of him."

"And you need never fear him," the Sandman said, "if you take care that you have a good character."

"Now that is instructive," the Great-grandfather's Portrait mumbled. "It was of some use speaking my mind," and the good man was quite pleased.

Well, that is the story of the Sandman; and now, my children, may he tell you something himself tonight.

The Ugly Little Duck

It was so delightful in the country, for summer was at the height of its splendour. The corn was yellow, the oats green, the hay, heaped into cocks in the meadow below, looked like little grass hillocks, and the stork strutted about on its long, red legs, chattering Egyptian, for that was the language it had learnt from its mother.

The fields and meadows were surrounded by more or less thickly-wooded forests, which also enclosed deep lakes, the smooth waters of which were sometimes ruffled by a gentle breeze. It was, indeed, delightful in the country. In the bright sunshine stood an old mansion surrounded by a moat and wall, strong and proud almost as in the feudal times. From the wall all the way down to the water grew a complete forest of burdock-leaves, which were so high, that a little child could stand upright under them; it was a real wilderness, so quiet and sombre, and here sat a Duck upon her nest, hatching a quantity of eggs; but she was almost tired of her tedious, though important, occupation, for it lasted so very long, and she seldom had any visitors. The other ducks preferred swimming about on the moat and the canals that ran through the garden, to visiting her in her solitude.

At length, however, there was a cracking in one of the eggs, then in a second,

The ugly little duck.

third, fourth, fifth, and sixth. "Piep! Piep!" sounded from here; "Piep! Piep!" sounded from there, at least a dozen times. There was, all of a sudden, life in the eggs, and the little half-naked creatures, their dwellings having become too confined for them, thrust out their heads as out of a window, looking quite confused.

"Quick! Quick!" their mother cried, so the little ones made as much haste as they possibly could. They stared about them, as if examining the green leaves, and their mother let them look as long as they liked, for green is good for the eyes.

"How large the world is!" they said; and certainly there lay before them a much more extensive space than in their eggs.

"Do you imagine this is the whole world?" their mother answered. "Oh, no, it stretches far beyond the garden, and on the other side the meadow, where the parson's cows are grazing, though I have never been there. But you are all here, I suppose?" she added, with true maternal solicitude, and she stood up, whereby, in spite of all her care, there was a great overthrow and confusion amongst the little ones. "No, I have not them all yet," she said, sighing. "The largest of the eggs lies there still. How much longer is it to last? It is becoming really too wearing." She mustered, however, all her patience, and sat down again.

"How are you getting on?" an old Duck inquired, coming to pay her friend a formal visit.

"With one of the eggs there seems no end of the trouble," the over-tired mother complained. "The shell must be too thick, so that the poor little thing cannot break through; but you must see the others, which are the prettiest little creatures that a mother could ever wish for. And what an extraordinary resemblance they bear to their father, who is certainly the handsomest drake in the whole yard, but he is giddy and faithless, as, indeed, all men are! He has not visited me once here in my solitude."

"Show me the egg which will not burst," the old Duck said, interrupting her. "Take my word for it, it is a turkey's egg. I was once played the same trick, and precious trouble I had with the little ones, for they were afraid of the water. How I coaxed, scolded, and fumed, but all of no use, they would not be induced to go in. Now let me examine the obstinate egg. Yes, it is just as I suspected; it is a turkey's egg. Take my advice, leave the nest and go and exercise the other little ones in swimming, for you are not bound by any duties towards this cheat."

"I would rather sit a little longer on it," the other said, shaking her head. "I have already had so much trouble, that it does not matter whether I am kept to it a day or two longer or not."

"Oh, if you like it, I have no objection," the old one answered, and with a stiff curtsey took her leave, philosophising on her way, "she'll have trouble enough with it."

At length the large egg burst. "Piep, piep!" cried the tardy comer, and he fell head-foremost out of the shell. He was so big and ugly, that his mother scarcely dared look at him, and the more she did so, the less she knew what to say. At last she exclaimed, involuntarily, "That is certainly the most frightfully curious young drake;

can it possibly be a turkey? But wait, we will soon see, for into the water he shall go. I will push him in myself, without further to-do; and then, if he cannot dive and swim, he may drown, and serve him right too!"

The following day it was splendid weather, the sun shining brightly upon the burdock-leaves, and the duck mamma with her whole family waddled down to the moat. "Splash!" and she was in the water. "Quick, quick!" she cried, and one duckling after another followed her example; not one would remain behind. The water closed over their heads, but they immediately came to the top again and swam most beautifully. Their legs moved of their own accord, and even the ugly, grey late, comer swam merrily with them.

"He is no turkey," the old Duck said; "only see how quickly he moves his legs, and how straight he holds himself! Yes, he is my own flesh and blood; and, after all, on more careful examination, he is a good-looking fellow enough. Now follow me quickly, and I will introduce you into the world, and present you in the poultry-yard. But mind you keep close to me, that no one may tread on you, and, of all things, take care of the cat."

They reached the yard, where there was a dreadfully noisy commotion, for two worthy families were disputing about the head of an eel, which the cat took from both of them.

"So it is in the world," the Mother-duck said, and her mouth watered, as she, too, would have gladly had the eel's head, for which she had a particular weakness. "Now move your legs," she said, "and bow prettily, slightly bending your necks, before the old duck you see there, for she is considered the highest of all. She is of pure Spanish blood, and therefore she is so solemn and proud. Do you see she has a piece of red cloth round her left leg, which is something extraordinarily splendid, and the greatest mark of distinction that can be conferred upon a duck? It means, that she shall be known to all beasts and men, and that she is to enjoy the most unusual piece of good fortune – to end her days in peace. Make haste, my children, but, for goodness' sake, don't turn your legs in so, for a well-bred young duck must keep its legs far apart, just like papa and mamma. Imitate me in all things, and pay attention to the word of command. When you bow, do not neglect to bend your neck gracefully, and then boldly say, 'Quack, quack!' Nothing more!"

So they did, but the other Ducks round about looked upon them with contempt, and said, out quite loud, "Well, well, now all this stupid pack is to be foisted upon us, as if we were not numerous enough without them; indeed, we do not require any increase of that sort – and, oh, dear! – just look at that one big thing! Such a deformity, at least, we will not allow amongst us!" Herupon an upstart Drake made a rush at the poor, green-grey youngster, and bit him in the neck.

"Leave him alone!" cried the highly-incensed mother, "for he is not doing anything to offend you; and I will not allow him to be ill-used."

"That may be; but for his age he is much too big and peculiar," the snappish Drake answered; "and naturally, therefore, he must be put down."

"They are very pretty children, indeed, that mamma has there," the old Duck with the red cloth round her leg said, "all of them, with the exception of one only, and he has certainly not succeeded."

"I am very sorry, gracious madam!" the mother answered, with difficulty swallowing her mortification. "He is certainly not a pattern of beauty, but he has a charming disposition, and swims as well as any of them; indeed, I may say a little better; and I am of opinion that he will grow up handsome enough, when, instead of growing taller, he spreads out, and gains roundness of form. He lay too long in the egg, and therefore has not his proper shape." Whilst she spoke thus in the youngster's favour, she did her best to smooth down his grey-green uniform where it had been ruffled. "Besides," the good mother continued, warmly, "the same fulness and elegance of form is not expected from a drake as from a duck. I have an idea that he will make his way.

"The other little ones are charming," the old Spanish Duck repeated. "Now make yourselves at home, and if you should happen to find an eel's head, you may bring it me without hesitation. You understand me!"

And now they were at home.

But the poor, ugly green-grey youngster, who had come last out of the egg, was bitten, jostled, and made game of by the Ducks as well as by the Chickens. "He is much too big!" they all said, with one accord. And the stuck-up Turkey, because he was born with spurs, fancied himself almost an emperor, gave himself airs, and strutted about like a ship in full sail, whilst his fiery head grew redder and redder. The poor, persecuted young thing neither knew where to stand nor where to go to, and his heart was saddened by all that he had to suffer on account of his ugliness.

Thus it was the first day, and day after day it only grew worse. The ugly, green-grey youngster was worried and hunted by all; even his own brothers and sisters were against him, and were constantly saying, "If the cat would but take you, you horror!" His mother, weighed down by sorrow, sighed, "Oh, I wish I had never born you, or were you but far away from here!" The ducks bit him, the chickens pecked him, and the girl that brought them their food kicked him.

Driven by fear and despair, he now ran and flew as far as his tired legs and weak wings would carry him, till, with a great effort, he got over the hedge, which, no doubt, was not very low. The little singing birds in the bushes flew up in a fright, and the young fugitive thought, "That is because I am so ugly." He, however, hurried forward, led by instinct, towards an unknown goal. This was a swamp, surrounded by wood, and was the dwelling-place of shoals of wild ducks. Sad and tired to death, he remained here the whole night, almost in a state of unconsciousness, whilst the full moon above bore such a friendly countenance, as if laughing at the foolish frogs, which kept jumping from the water on to the grass, and back again into the water, as if imitating the dance of merry elves. Early the next morning, aroused by the first glimmer of the sun, the wild ducks rose from their watery beds to take a turn in the warm summer air, when with surprise they saw the stranger. "What funny Guy is this?" they exclaimed. "Where can he have come from?" they inquired of each other; whilst the stranger, with all possible politeness, turned from side to side, first bowing to the right and then to the left, as no ballet-mistress, much less a ballet-master, could do.

"You are right-down ugly," the wild Ducks said; "but that does not make much difference to us, as long as you do not marry into our family."

The poor outcast thought of nothing less than marrying. All he wished for was to remain undisturbed among the rushes, and drink a little of the water of the swamp. Here he lay two whole days, when two wild Geese arrived, or rather Goslings, for they had not long come out of the egg, and therefore were they so merry.

"Well met, comrade!" one of them said, "you are so ugly, that I like you. Come with us, for close by there is another swamp, where there are some wonderfully beautiful geese, the sweetest of young damsels, who did not get married last autumn. You are just the fellow to make your fortune with them, you are so exemplarily ugly."

"Bang, bang!" it sounded at that very moment, and the two wild Goslings fell down dead, the water being discoloured with their blood. "Bang, bang!" it went again, and a quantity of geese flew up from the rushes. There was more firing, for the sportsmen lay all around the marsh, some of them sitting even in the branches of the trees that overhung the mass of rushes. The blue smoke from the powder rose like clouds amongst the dark foliage, and "splash" – the dogs sprang into the water, little heeding the fresh breeze which whistled among the waving reeds. A nice fright the poor green-grey youngster had, and he was about to hide his head under one of his wings, so that, at least, he might see no more of the horrors, when, close by him, appeared an enormous dog, its tongue hanging far out of its throat, and bloodthirsty rage sparkling in its eyes. With wide-open jaws, showing two formidable rows of murderous teeth, the water-spaniel advanced towards the poor bird, that now gave itself up as utterly lost, but, generously disdaining to seize upon its easy prey, the noble creature went on.

"Heaven be praised!" the poor outcast said. "I am so ugly that the dog does not like to touch me"; and he lay perfectly quiet, whilst the shot whizzed over his head amongst the rushes.

Not till late in the afternoon did the firing cease, but even then the poor youngster, whose life had been saved as if by a miracle, did not venture to move. He waited several hours before he drew his head from under his wing, and cautiously looked about him; but then he hastened, with all possible speed, to get away from the scene of horror. As before he had flown from the poultry-yard, so now, but with redoubled exertion, he fled, he knew not whither. A boisterous wind, which followed upon the setting of the sun, was ungracious enough to have no consideration for the scantily-covered traveller, and considerably impeded his progress, exhausting his strength.

Late in the evening our fugitive reached a miserable cottage, which was in such a wretched state that it did not know on which side to fall, and on that account it remained standing for the time being. The wind blew around him, and shook the poor bird so violently, that he had to seat himself upon his tail to be able to offer the necessary resistance. He then, with no small delight, discovered that the rickety door of the cottage, which, though it did not promise much comfort, yet offered a shelter against the now doubly-raging storm, had broken loose from the lower hinge, and that there was thus a slanting opening, through which he could slip into the room; and this he did without loss of time.

Here lived an old woman with her Tom-cat and her Hen.

The Cat was a perfect master in "purring" and in "washing", and he could turn head over heels, that no one in the neighbourhood could equal him, and one only needed to rub his hair repeatedly the contrary way to bring bright sparks from his back. The old woman called him her little son. The Hen, for her part, had very thin, short legs, on which account she was called "Gluck Small-leg". She most industriously laid the very best eggs, and her mistress loved her as if she were her own child.

Peace, concord, and happiness evidently reigned in this miserable hut, as they do in many others of a like sort.

In the morning the strange, unbidden guest was immediately discovered, when the Cat began to purr, and the Hen to gluck.

"What is this?" the old woman said, and began a close examination; but, as she could not see well, she took the young, meagre bird for a fat duck, which had got into her room by mistake. "Here is an unusual piece of good fortune!" she exclaimed, in joyous surprise. "Now I shall have duck's eggs – that is, if the stupid thing should not at last prove to be drake," she added, thoughtfully. "We will give it a trial."

So the green-grey youngster remained there three weeks on trial, but no egg made its appearance. Now, the Cat was master in the house, and the Hen mistress, and they used to say, "We, and the world," for they thought they constituted the half, and by far the better half, of the world. It appeared to the young stranger that others might have another opinion, which the Hen would by no means allow.

"Can you lay eggs?" she asked.

"No."

"Then please to hold your tongue."

And the Cat asked, "Can you purr, or arch your back?"

"No."

"Then you have no right to offer an opinion when sensible people talk."

And the poor, ugly outcast sat in the corner quite melancholy, in vain fighting against the low spirits which his self-satisfied companions certainly did not share. Involuntarily he thought of the fresh air and the bright sunshine out of doors, and felt himself agitated by so violent a desire once more to be swimming on the clear water, and to sport about in the liquid element, that he could not resist one morning, after a sleepless night, opening his heart to the Hen.

"What mad fancies are turning that poor, shallow brain of yours again?" the Hen cried, almost in a rage, in spite of her natural quiet indifference. "You have nothing to do, and it is sheer idleness that torments you and puts such foolish fancies into your head. Lay eggs, or purr, and you will be all right."

"But it is so pleasant to swim," the poor child answered; "so delightful to dive to the bottom and look up at the moon through the clear water!"

"Yes, that must be a great treat," the Hen said, contemptuously. "You must have gone stark staring mad. Ask the Cat, and I know no one more sensible, whether he likes swimming about in the water and diving to the bottom. I will not speak of myself, but just ask our mistress; and there is no one wiser than she in the whole world. Do you think she has a fancy for diving and swimming?"

"You do not understand me," the poor Duckling sighed.

"And if we do not understand you, pray who can, you conceited, impertinent creature?" the Hen replied, warmly. "You will not, surely, set yourself up as cleverer than the Cat and our mistress, not to mention myself. Pray think a little less of yourself, and thank your stars for all the kindness that has been shown you. Have you not got into a warm room here, and amongst company from whom you may learn some good? But you are a shallow prattler and a long-necked dreamer, whose society is anything but amusing. You may believe me, for I mean really well with you, and therefore tell you things you do not like to hear, which is a proof that I am your true friend. Now, of all things, mind that you lay eggs and learn how to purr."

"I think I shall wander out into the world," the young Duck said, mustering up courage.

"Do so, by all means," the Hen answered, with contempt. "One comfort, we shall lose nothing by your absence."

And now the green-grey youngster, without many parting civilities, began his wanderings again, leaving the inhospitable hut without regret, and he hurried towards the so-much-longed-for water. He swam about joyously, and boldly dived down right to the bottom, from whence he saw the pale moon like a rolling ball; but at length the loneliness and death-like silence became oppressive, and when another creature did appear, it was sure to be with the same greeting as of old, namely, "Oh, how frightful you are!"

It was now late in autumn, with frequent storms of snow and hail, and the brown and yellow leaves from the forest danced about, whipped by the wind, whilst above all was a cold leaden colour. The crows sat in the hedge and cried, "Caw! Caw!" with sheer cold. It makes one shiver to think of it. The poor outcast was anything but happy.

One frosty evening, when the sun was setting, like a fiery wheel in the gigantic triumphal car of the creation, a quantity of magnificent birds swept past, and the ugly, green-grey youngster thought he had never seen anything so beautiful, and at the same time imposing. Their spotless plumage shone like driven snow, and they uttered a cry, half singing half whistling, as they rose higher and higher in their flight towards more extensive lakes. A strange sensation came over the poor young

Duck, and he turned round and round like a top, and stretching out his neck after the departing birds, gave a cry, for the first time in his life, so loud and shrill that he was frightened at it himself. When they quite disappeared from his sight, he suddenly dived down to the bottom of the water, and when he rose again was as if beside himself. From that moment, never could he forget those beautiful, happy birds; he did not know that they were called swans, nor where they were flying to, but he loved them as he had never loved anything before. He did not envy them in the least, for how could it ever enter his head to wish himself so splendid and beautiful? He would have been contented to live among the stupid ducks, if they would but have left him in peace, a neglected, ugly thing.

The winter grew so bitterly cold, that the poor young creature had to swim about incessantly to prevent the water freezing quite over. Night after night the hole became less, till at last, exhausted by constant exertions, he got frozen tight into the ice.

Early in the morning a peasant came that way, and seeing the poor bird in so wretched a plight, he had compassion on it, and ventured boldly on to the ice, for he was a good Christian, and not one of those who first see that no inconvenience will attend an act of kindness. With his wooden shoes he broke the ice, extricated the to-all-appearance dead bird, and carried him home to his wife, where, in a warm room, the green-grey youngster soon recovered animation and strength.

The children wished to play with him, but the young Drake thought they were bent on ill-using him, so in his fright he flew into an earthenware milk-pan, which he turned over, and the milk ran about the floor. The woman uttered a loud cry and raised her hands in consternation, which thoroughly bewildered the poor bird, and he flew into the freshly-made butter, and then into the flour-tub, and out again. Oh, what a figure he was now! Bewailing her losses, the woman pursued him with the tongs, and the children, laughing and shouting, rolled over each other as they tried to catch him.

Fortunately for our youngster, who was now no longer green-grey, but of a delicate paste colour, the door was open, and, taking advantage of the general confusion, he rushed out into the open air, and with difficulty fluttered to some bushes, not far off, where he sank down, exhausted, into the deep snow. Here he lay unconscious, as in a torpor.

But it would be too painful to follow the poor outcast through all his misfortunes, and to witness the misery and privation he suffered during that severe winter; we will therefore only say that he lay in a dreamy state amongst the rushes in the marsh, when the sun again began to shine warmly upon the earth, and the larks began to sing, for it was early spring.

Then the young Drake spread out his wings, which had grown much stronger, and with ease they carried him away, so that almost before he knew it, he found himself in a large garden, where the fruit-trees were in all the splendour of full blossom, and the lilac scented the air, whilst the green branches hung down to the stream which wound picturesquely through the soft lawn. Oh, it was so springlike and enchanting! And a short distance before him three beautiful white swans came sailing along the water from behind some bushes. The poor, hitherto-despised outcast knew the magnficient birds, and suddenly a feeling of deep sadness came over him.

"I will fly to them, the beautiful birds! And they will take my life, because I, ugly as I am, have ventured to go near them. But it does not matter, for it will be better to be killed by them than being bitten by the ducks, pecked by the chickens, and kicked by the girl in the poultry-yard, or suffering all the hardships of this winter." Agitated by these feelings, without further consideration, but with assumed confidence, he swam towards the three swans, which, as soon as they perceived the stranger, shot through the water with rounded wings and ruffled feathers to meet him.

"Kill me!" the poor thing said, and with bent-down head awaited his death in quiet resignation. But what did he now see in the clear water? He saw his own reflection; but it was no longer the ugly, dirty, green-grey bird – no, it was a proud, princely swan!

True, he was hatched by a duck, but why should that not happen to a swan's egg?

The now snow-white youngster, with the lovely form, heartily rejoiced in the misery and hardships of his early youth, for he could the better appreciate all his happiness, and the heavenly beauty by which he was surrounded. And the large swans surrounded him with a friendly welcome, and lovingly stroked his neck with their bills.

Just then two young children appeared in the garden, running merrily down to the water, into which they threw bread for the swans.

"Look, look!" the youngest cried, "here is a new one!" And they clapped their hands and danced about, shouting with delight, and then ran off to call papa and mamma. Now fresh bread and cake were thrown into the water, and all said, "The new one is the most beautiful of all, so young and so graceful!" And the old swans showed no envy, but treated him as friendly as before.

But the young stranger felt quite ashamed, and hid his head under his wing. He scarcely understood his own feelings; he was too happy, but not at all proud, for a good heart is never proud. He thought, without bitterness, of how he was formerly persecuted and mocked, whereas now all said that he was the most beautiful of these magnificent birds; and the lilac, with its long green branches and sweetly-smelling blossom, bent down to him in the water. The sun shone brightly, and from the depth of his heart he said, "Such great happiness I never dreamed of when I was the Ugly Little Duck."

The old street-lamp.

The Old Street-lamp

Have you heard the story of the old Street-lamp? It is nothing so wonderfully amusing, but it will very well bear to be heard once. It was a good old Lamp, which had served for many, many years, but was about to be replaced by a new one. The last night had come that it was to sit on its post and give light in the street, and it felt exactly like an old ballet-dancer who dances for the last time, knowing that on the morrow she will be forgotten. The Lamp had great fear of the following day, as it knew that it would then be carried for the first time to the Town-hall, there to be judged by the honourable council, whether fit for further service or not. Then would be settled whether it was to be sent to one of the bridges, to give light there, or to a manufactory in the country, or perhaps an iron-foundry. True, there was no knowing what might not be made of it there, but it grieved that it did not know whether it would then retain consciousness that it had been a Street-lamp. Whatever might happen, it would anyhow be separated from the lamplighter and his wife, whom it looked upon as its family. It had become a Lamp when he was appointed lighter. His wife was then young and pretty, and only at night, when she passed the Lamp, did she look at it, but never in the daytime; but now that all three, the lamplighter, his wife, and the Lamp, had grown old, she would occasionally trim it. They were a thoroughly honest couple, and had never cheated the Lamp out of one drop of oil. This was the last night, and on the following day it was to go to the Town-hall. These were two sombre thoughts, so one can imagine how the Lamp burned. But other thoughts occupied it as well: it had seen so much, and had diffused so much light, perhaps as much as the "honourable town-council" itself; but that it did not say, for it was a worthy old Lamp, and would not hurt any one's feelings, more particularly those of its masters. So many recollections crowded upon it, and the flame burned up as an inward feeling said, "I shall be remembered too. There was that handsome young man – well, that is a good many years ago – he came with a letter, written on such pretty pink, gilt-edged paper; it was a lady's handwriting. He read it twice, kissed it, and, looking up to me, said, 'I am the happiest of men!' Only he and I knew what his love's first letter contained. I remember two other eyes as well. It is extraordinary how thoughts can travel. There was a splendid funeral procession here in the street; a young and beautiful woman lay in her coffin, covered with rich velvet and strewed over with wreaths and flowers. The whole street was filled with people, and there were so many torches burning, that I was quite eclipsed, but when the procession had passed and the torches disappeared, I saw a man who stood here at my post crying – oh, I shall never forget his sorrowing look!" Thoughts crowded one upon another on the old Street-lamp this last night of its duty. The sentinel who is relieved knows who follows, and can exchange a word with him, but the Lamp did not know its successor; when, too, there was many a hint it could have given about the rain and snow, of how far the moon shone into the street, and which way the wind mostly blew.

Close by stood three candidates for the office about to become vacant, for they thought the appointment was in the gift of the Lamp. One of these was a herring's head, for that shines in the dark, and it pleaded the saving of oil ther would be if it were placed on the lamp-post. The second was a piece of rotten wood, which also gives out light, and more, as it itself said, than a fish's head; besides which, that it was the last piece of a once-mighty tree in the forest. The third was a glow-worm – the Lamp could not imagine where it came from; however, there the worm was, and gave light too, but the rotten wood and the herring's head asserted that it only shone at certain times, and could, therefore, not be taken into consideration.

The old Lamp said that neither of them gave light enough, which, however, they would not believe; and when they heard that the appointment was not in the gift of the Lamp, they said that was very fortunate, as it was evidently too old and feeble to be able to choose at all.

Just then the Wind came round the corner of the street, and, blowing down the old Lamp's chimney, said, "What is this I hear – that you go to-morrow? Is this really the last night that I shall find you here? If that is the case, I must make you a present. I will brighten your understanding, so that you shall not only clearly and distinctly recollect what you have seen and heard, but, when anything is said or read in your presence, you shall actually see as well as hear it."

"My best thanks," the Lamp said, "for your great kindness. If only I am not melted down."

"That will not happen yet," the Wind said; "but now I must sharpen your memory, and if you receive many more such presents, yours will be a pleasant old age."

"But I hope I shall not be melted down; or can you perhaps then, too, secure me my memory?" the Lamp asked.

"Old Lamp," the Wind answered, "be reasonable"; and as the Moon just then appeared, it continued, "And what will you give?"

"I shall not give anything," the Moon answered. "I am on the decrease; and, besides, the lamps have never helped me to give light, but I have helped them." The Moon then disappeared behind a cloud again, so that it might not be asked any more. Then a Drop of Water fell upon the Lamp's chimney, as if it had come from the roof, but it said it came straight from the grey clouds as a present, and perhaps the best of all. "I will penetrate through you, so that you will have the power, whenever you wish it, to turn into rust in one night, and crumble into dust." But the Lamp thought that a bad present, and so thought the Wind too. "Is there nothing better? Is there nothing better?" he blew as loud as he could, and just then a Star fell, leaving a long streak of light behind it.

"What was that?" the Herring's head exclaimed; "did not a Star fall? And I think it went straight into the Lamp. Well, if the office is sought by such high people, we may retire!" Which it did, and the others as well; but the old Lamp gave a brighter light than ever. "That was a splendid gift!" it said. "The bright Stars, which have always been my delight, and which shine so brightly, that I have never been able to equal them, though it has been my constant aim, have honoured me by sending me a present, which consists in the power of making those whom I love see all that I see and remember. That is a delightful present! For there is only half pleasure in that which cannot be shared with others."

"That sentiment does you honour!" the Wind said, "but you do not know that a wax-candle is necessary to render the gift of any use; for unless a wax-candle is burning in you, no one will be able to see anything. The Stars did not think of that, for they imagine that everything that shines has, at least, one wax-candle within it. But now I am tired, so I will rest a little."

The next day – well, the next day we will pass over – but the next night the Lamp lay in an arm-chair; and where? – at the old lamp-lighter's. As a reward for his long and faithful services, he had begged to be allowed to keep the old Lamp. The honourable council had laughed at him, but had given him the Lamp, and now it lay in an arm-chair by the side of the warm stove. The old couple were sitting at their supper, and would gladly have made room at the table for the old Lamp, at which they cast friendly glances. They lived in a cellar, it is true, two yards under ground, but it was warm there, for they had the door well listed; it was neat and clean in their room, with curtains round the bed and at the small window, where, on the high window-ledge, stood two most peculiar flower-pots. The sailor, Christian, had brought them home with him from the East or West Indies; they were two elephants of earthenware with hollow backs, filled up with mould, and out of the one grew the finest garlic, that being the old people's kitchen-garden; whilst out of the other, which was their flower-garden, grew a beautiful geranium. On the wall hung a large coloured print of the Congress of Vienna; so they had at once all the emperors and kings. A wooden clock, with its heavy leaden weights, went "Tick! Tick!" and always too fast; but that was better, the old couple thought, than going too slow. They were eating their supper, and the old Lamp lay, as already stated, in the arm-chair, close by the side of the warm stove. It appeared to the Lamp as if the whole world were turned upside down, but when the lamplighter looked at it and spoke of all that they had experienced together, in rain and snow, in the short summer nights, and in the cold nights of winter, when it was a treat to get back into his cellar, then all seemed restored to proper order, and it was as if the past were present again. The Wind had, indeed, refreshed its memory.

The old couple were so active and industrious, not a single hour was entirely dreamed away. On Sunday afternoons one book or another was brought forth, generally a book of travels, and the old man read out loud about Africa, of the vast forests, and the elephants which ran about wild, and the old woman would give a side-glance at the earthenware elephants, which were flower-pots. "I can almost imagine it all," she said; and then the Lamp wished most anxiously that it had a lighted wax-candle inside, so that the old woman might see all as clearly as it then did – the lofty trees with the closely-intertwined branches, the naked men on horseback, and whole herds of elephants crushing the reeds and bushes beneath their broad feet.

"Of what use are all my capabilities without a wax-candle?" the Lamp sighed; "they have only oil and tallow-candles, which are of no use."

One day the old man brought a whole quantity of wax-candle ends into the cellar, the largest pieces of which were burned, and the smaller were used by the old woman to wax her thread when she sewed. Now there were wax-candles, but it never entered their heads to put a piece in the Lamp.

"Here I stand with my extraordinary talents," the Lamp said. "I have so much within me, but cannot share it with them. They do not know that I can change the white walls into the most beautiful tapestry, into dark forests, or anything that they could wish to see. Oh, they do not know it!"

The Lamp stood, well scoured, in a corner, where it could not fail to be seen, for though every one said it was only an old piece of lumber, the old people did not care, as they loved it.

One day – it was the old man's birthday – the old woman went up to the Lamp, and smilingly said, "There shall be an illumination for him"; and the old Lamp trembled with delight, for it thought, "They shall see what they little expect!" But only oil was put in; and though it burned the whole evening, the old Lamp was now convinced that the gift of the Stars would remain a useless treasure for this life. Then it dreamed – and with such talents any one might dream – that it was taken to a foundry, in order to be melted down, and it was as much frightened as when about to be judged by the town-council; but, although it had the power of turning itself into rust and dust, yet it did not do so, but was melted down; and a beautiful candlestick was made of it, in which a wax-candle was stuck. It was cast in the form of an angel, carrying a large nosegay, in the middle of which the candle was put; and the candlestick was placed upon a green writing-table in a poet's study. The room was so comfortable; there were many books and beautiful pictures, and all that the poet thought and wrote curled up the walls like smoke, and the room was turned into vast, gloomy forests, into smiling meadows, where the stork strutted about, and into the deck of a vessel on the swelling sea.

"What talents I have!" the old Lamp said, when it awoke; "I could almost wish to be melted down – but no, that must not be as long as the old people live. They love me, for my own sake; I am as a child to them, and they have scoured me, and given me oil. I am as well off as the 'Congress', and that is something very grand!"

From that time the old Lamp enjoyed greater peace of mind, and that it deserved – the honest old thing!

The Darning-needle

There was once a Darning-needle which thought itself so fine, that it imagined it was a Sewing-needle.

"Mind how you hold me!" the Darning-needle said to the Fingers as they took it up, "or you may lose me, and, if I fall, it is a great question whether I shall be found again, for I am so fine!"

"That can be managed," the Fingers said, and they laid hold of it tight round the body.

"See, I have a train!" the Darning-needle said, and it drew a long thread after it, in which there was no knot.

The Fingers applied the Needle to the cook's slipper, the upper-leather of which had burst and required mending.

"That is coarse work!" the Needle said. "I shall never get through it. I shall break! I am breaking!" and it did break. "Did I not say so?" the Needle sighed; "I am too fine!"

"Now, it is of no use," the Fingers thought, but they still had to hold it, and the cook dropped some melted sealing-wax upon it and stuck it in her neck-handkerchief.

The darning-needle.

"Now I am a breast-pin!" the Needle said. "I knew that I should come to honours, for when one is something, one is sure to rise." Then it laughed inwardly, for there is no outward appearance in a Needle, whether it laughs or not; and there it sat as proudly as if it were driving in its own carriage, and it looked about it on all sides.

"May I take the liberty to ask whether you are of gold?" it inquired of a Pin that was its neighbour. "Your outward appearance is splendid! And I see that you have a head, too, but it is very small. You must see whether you cannot get it to grow, for all cannot have sealing-wax dropped upon them!" Hereupon the Needle raised itself up so proudly, that it fell out of the handkerchief into the sink, just as the cook was washing a dish.

"Now I am going to travel!" the Needle said. "I hope I may not get lost." But lost it was.

"I am too fine for this world!" the Darning-needle said, as it lay in the gutter. "But I know my own worth, and there is always a satisfaction in that!" And the Needle did not lose its presence of mind nor its good humour.

All sorts of things floated past over its head – chips of wood, straw, and pieces of newspaper. "How they sail along!" the Needle said, "and they little think what is lying beneath them. There goes a Chip, thinking of nothing in the world but of a chip, and that is itself. Now a Piece of Straw floats past. Oh, how it twists and twirls about! But do not think too much of yourself; take care, or you may knock against a stone. There swims a Piece of Newspaper! What is in it is long forgotten, and yet see how it spreads itself out! Here I sit patient and quiet. I know what I am, and that I shall remain!"

One day, something glittering lay close by its side, and the Needle thought it was a Diamond, though it was nothing but a little Piece of Glass; but because it glittered the Needle addressed it, and introduced itself as a Breast-pin. "You are a Diamond, I suppose?" "Yes, I am something of that sort!" So each thought the other something very valuable, and they complained of the arrogance of the world.

"I lived in a box with a young lady," the Needle said. "She was a cook, and on each hand she had five Fingers, and never have I seen anything as conceited as these Fingers, though they were only made on purpose to lay hold of me, to take me out of the box, and to put me in again."

"Did they shine?" the Piece of Glass asked.

"Shine!" the Needle said, "not they; and yet they were as conceited and arrogant as possible. They were five brothers, all born Fingers, and held themselves so proudly, one by the side of the other, though they were of different lengths. The outer one, Mr. Thumb, was short and thick, and had but one joint in his back, so that he could only make one bow; but he said that if he were cut off from a man's hand, that man would be unfit for military service. Foreman, the second, dived into sweets and sours, pointed at sun and moon, and pressed upon the pen in writing; Middleman looked right over the others' heads; Ringman wore a gold ring round his body, and Littleman did nothing at all, which he was particularly proud of. It was all bragging and boasting, and that's why I went into the sink."

"And now we lie here and shine!" the Piece of Glass said. Just then there was an increase of water in the gutter, so that it overflowed, and the Piece of Glass was carried away.

"Now she has a rise," the Needle said, "and I remain; I am too fine; but that is my pride, which is to be honoured." So there it lay in its pride and ruminated deeply.

"I could almost believe that I am born of a Sunbeam, I am so very fine! Indeed, it seems as if the Sun were looking for me under the water; but I am so fine, that my own mother cannot find me. If I had my eye which broke off, I think I should cry; but no, I would not, for that would be beneath me."

One day some boys were rummaging about in the gutter, hunting for halfpence, nails, and such like. That was a dirty trick, but such as it was, it was their amusement.

"Ah!" one of them cried out, as he pricked himself with the Needle, "this is a pretty fellow!"

"I am no fellow at all, but a young lady!" the Needle said, but no one heard it. The sealing-wax had got worn off, and it had grown quite black, but that only made it look thinner, and it thought itself finer than ever.

"Here comes an egg-shell sailing along!" the boys cried, and they stuck the Needle into it.

"White walls, and I myself black," the Needle said; "that looks well, and people cannot help seeing me now. I only hope I shall not be sea-sick, for then I should break!" It was not sea-sick, nor did it break.

"There is no protection against sea-sickness like having a steel stomach, and the constant thought that one is something more than man. It has passed now. The finer one is, the more one can bear."

"Crash!" went the egg-shell, as a wagon passed over it.

"Ah! how heavy it is!" the Darning-needle said, "I shall be sea-sick after all. I am breaking, I am breaking!" But it did not break, for all the waggon passed over it. There it lay its full length, and there let it lie!

The Shadow.

The Shadow

In hot countries the sun burns fiercely, so that the inhabitants become a mahogany colour, and in the very hottest they are burnt quite black; but it was only to a hot country that the learned man of our story had gone from a cold one. He thought that he could go about there just as he had done at home, but he very soon found out his mistake, and, like all sensible people, had to remain in the house with doors and shutters closed. The houses looked as if all the people were asleep or from home. The narrow street with the high houses, in which he lived, was so situated that the sun shone into it from morning till night, and it was really unbearable. The learned man from the cold country, who was a young man, felt as if he were sitting in a red-hot oven, which had such an effect upon him, that he grew quite thin, and his Shadow even shrunk up, so that it was much smaller than it had been at home. It was only at night, after the sun had gone down, that they began to live.

It was quite a treat, when lights were brought into the room, to see how the Shadow stretched itself up the wall, for it had to stretch itself in order to regain strength. The learned man went out onto the balcony to stretch himself too, and when the stars appeared in the beautiful clear air, he began to revive. On all the balconies in the street – and in warm countries every window has a balcony – people made their appearance; for one must have air, even when one is accustomed to the mahogany colour. Above and below now all was life. Shoemakers and tailors, as well as all other people, crowded into the streets; tables and chairs were brought out, thousands of lights burned, and the people began to talk and sing. Some walked, whilst others rode; and "klingelingeling" it sounded as the mules passed along, for all had bells on their harness. The boys let off squibs and crackers, the dead were carried to their last homes, and the church-bells rang; yes, all was bustle in the street below. Only in one house, exactly opposite that in which the learned man lived, all was quiet; and yet some one lived there, for flowers stood in the balcony, growing so luxuriantly in the hot sun, which they could not do unless they were watered; and that must be done by some one; so it was evident some people lived there. The window, also, in the opposite house was opened towards evening, though it was dark within – at least in the front room, but from the back came the sounds of music. The learned man thought it wonderfully beautiful; but that may have been only in his fancy, for he thought everything wonderful in the warm country, if there had but been no sun. The stranger's landlord said he did not know who inhabited the opposite house, for no one was ever seen; and as for the music, that he thought most tedious. It seemed to him exactly as if some one were practising one piece over and over again – always the same piece, and still could not succeed with it.

One night the learned stranger awoke, and as he slept with his window open, the curtain was blown aside a little by the wind, and it seemed to him as if a wonderful brightness filled the opposite room; all the flowers shone like flames of the most beautiful colours, and in the midst of the flowers stood a tall, lovely girl, and it seemed as if she shone also. It quite dazzled his eyes, and with one jump he was out of bed. Quietly he stole behind the curtain, but the girl had gone and the brightness had disappeared; the flowers stood there, as usual, without shining in the least, but from the open window sounded the most delightful music, which sunk into the soul and roused the sweetest feelings and thoughts. It was like magic! Who could be living there? Where was the entrance even? For the ground-floor was entirely taken up with shops, and the people could not go backwards and forwards through those.

One evening the stranger was sitting on his balcony, and as a light was burning behind him in the room, it was quite natural that his Shadow should fall upon the opposite wall. Yes, there it sat on the balcony among the flowers; and when the stranger moved it moved too, for that is the habit of Shadows.

"I firmly believe my Shadow is the only living thing opposite there!" the learned man said. "Just see how nicely it sits amongst the flowers; and now, if it had sense, as the window is open, it would just slip in, look about it, and when it came back tell me what it had seen. You should make yourself useful," he said, jokingly. "Pray have the kindness to go in there. Well, are you going?" He nodded to his Shadow, and the Shadow nodded also. "Go then, but do not stop away altogether." The stranger then got up, and the Shadow on the opposite balcony did the same; the stranger turned round, and the Shadow turned round also; and if any one had paid particular attention he would have seen clearly that the Shadow went into the half-open window of the opposite house just as the stranger stepped into his room, and drew the curtain after him.

The next morning the learned man went out to drink his coffee and read the newspaper. "How is this?" he exclaimed, when he got into the sunshine. "I have no Shadow! So it really did go away last night, and has not returned! That is exceedingly unpleasant!"

He was considerably annoyed, not so much that his Shadow was gone, but because there was a story of a man who had lost his shadow, which every one in his own country knew; so that if, on his return, he told his story, people would say he was only copying, whereas there was but too much truth in it. He, therefore, made up his mind not to say a word about it, which was a very sensible determination.

At night he went onto the balcony again, having placed the light so that it would be exactly behind him, for he knew that every Shadow wants its master to be between it and the light; but he could not entice it out. He made himself small, he made himself big, but no Shadow came. "Hem! Hem!" he said, but that was of no use.

Vexatious it certainly was, but in warm countries everything grows very fast, so that after a week's time he noticed, to his great joy, that a new Shadow was sprouting out from his feet when he got into the sunshine, the roots of the old one having no doubt remained. In the course of three weeks he had a very respectable-sized Shadow, which increased more and more on his way to the northern countries, so that at last it grew so long and so big, that half of it would have been quite enough.

Well, the learned man reached home, and he wrote books about truth, goodness, and beauty, and thus many years passed by.

He was sitting one evening in his room when there was a gentle knock at the door.

"Come in!" he said, but no one came, so he opened the door himself, and there stood such a wonderfully thin man, that quite a strange feeling crept over him.

"Whom have I the honour of addressing?" he asked.

"Ah, that is just what I expected!" the thin man said, "that you would not know me. I have become so thoroughly flesh and blood, and covered with clothes too, and, no doubt, you never expected to see me so well off. Do you not know your old Shadow? You never thought that I should come back. Everything has prospered wonderfully with me since I was with you, and in every way I have become rich, so that if it is necessary I should purchase my freedom, I can do it." As he said this he jingled a bunch of valuable seals, which hung from his watch, and his fingers played with the massive gold chain he wore round his neck. How all his fingers glittered with diamond rings, all of the purest water!

"What does all this mean?" the learned man cried. "I cannot get over my surprise!"

"Well, it is not commonplace," the Shadow said; "but then you are something out of the common yourself, and you know that from your childhood up I have always trodden in your footsteps. As soon as I found that I could make my way alone in the world, I started for myself, and a brilliant position I have gained; but then an irresistible longing came over me to see you once more before you die, for you know that die you must. I wanted to see this country again as well, for one always must love the land of one's birth. I know that you have another Shadow; and if I have to pay it or you anything, pray have the goodness to tell me so."

"And is it really you?" the learned man said. "It is most extraordinary! And never would I have believed that an old Shadow could return as a man!"

"Tell me what I have to pay," the Shadow repeated, "for I do not like being any one's debtor."

"How can you talk that way?" the learned man said, "for there can be no question of any debt. You are as free as any one living, and I heartily rejoice at your good fortune. Take a seat, my old friend, and tell me how it all happened, and what you saw out there in the opposite house."

"Yes, I will tell you everything," the Shadow said, seating himself; "but then you must promise me that you will never tell any one here in the town that I have been your Shadow. I intend getting married, for I have plenty to support several families!"

"Make yourself quite easy," the learned man said; "I will not tell any one who you really are."

It was quite extraordinary how thoroughly human the Shadow was; he was dressed all in black, of the very finest cloth, had patent leather boots and a crush-hat; and then there were the seals, the chain, and the diamond rings which we know of already. He was remarkably well dressed.

"I will now begin my story," the Shadow said, placing his foot, with the patent leather boot, as firmly as he possibly could on the arm of the learned man's new Shadow. This was done either out of pride and bravado, or perhaps in the hope that the Shadow would stick to his foot; but the Shadow remained perfectly quiet and all attention, for, no doubt, it wished to know the way to get off and make itself its own master.

"Do you know who lived in the opposite house?" the Shadow said. "It was Poetry! There I remained three weeks, which is about as efficacious as living three thousand years, and reading everything that is written. That I maintain, and I am right. I have seen everything, and I know everything!"

"Poetry!" the learned man exclaimed. "Yes, yes, she is often a recluse in large cities! Poetry! Ah, I saw her for a moment, but I was half asleep! She stood on the balcony, and shone as brightly as the northern lights! But go on! Go on! You were on the balcony, and went in at the window, and then – "

"Then I found myself in the ante-room," the Shadow answered. "You could not see in there, because it was in darkness; but in a long row of rooms the opposite doors were open, and each room was lighted up. I should have been killed by the light, if I had penetrated as far as the goddess herself; but I was prudent and took my time, as every one should do!"

"And what did you see then?" the learned man asked.

"Everything," the Shadow answered. "I saw everything, and knew everything."

"And how did it look in the rooms?" the learned man asked. "Was it as in a green wood? Was it as in a solemn church? Were the rooms like the sky, studded with stars?"

"All was there!" the Shadow said, "but I did not go right in; I remained in the ante-room, in the dark; but I was very well there, I saw everything, and I knew everything; I have been at the court and in the ante-room of the goddess of Poetry!"

"But what did you see? Were all the gods of antiquity assembled? Did the old heroes fight there? Were lovely children playing there, and telling their dreams?"

"I tell you that I was there, and you can imagine that I saw everything that was to be seen. If you had come over, you would possibly not have remained a man, whereas I became one, and at the same time I learned to know my nature and my relationship to Poetry. At the time when I was with you, I did not think about it; but, you know, that always at the rising and setting of the sun I became so wonderfully big, and that by moonlight I was plainer even than you yourself. I did not then understand my nature, but in the ante-room all became clear to me. I became a man! I left it thoroughly formed, but you were no longer in the warm country. I was ashamed of my appearance, for I wanted boots and clothes; all that makes the man. I sought shelter – yes, I may tell you, for you will not set it down in a book – I sought shelter under the cake-woman's petticoats. There I hid myself, and she little thought how much she concealed. Not till night did I venture forth, when I ran about the streets in the moonshine; I stretched myself along the wall, which tickles one's back so nicely; I ran up and down, and looked through the highest windows even; I saw what no one else could see, and what no one was intended to see. It is a bad world, and I would not be a man were it not that it is a position of accepted importance. I saw the most incredible things in women and in men, in parents and in children. I saw," the Shadow said, "what no one was to know, but what every one wished to know: the neighbours' faults. If I had written a book, it would have been read eagerly; but I wrote to the people themselves, and there was consternation in every town to which I came. All were so afraid of me, but they loved me so dearly. The professors made me a professor, and the tailors gave me new clothes, so that I am well provided. I was overwhelmed with presents, and the women discovered that I was handsome. Thus I became the man that I am; and now I must say farewell. Here is my card, I live on the sunny side, and in rainy weather I am always at home." And herewith the Shadow went away.

"That is most remarkable!" the learned man said.

A year passed by and the Shadow returned.

"How does the world treat you?" he asked.

"Oh!" the learned man said, "I write about truth, goodness, and beauty, but no one cares to hear about them, and I am in despair; I take it so to heart."

"I do not take anything to heart!" the Shadow said, "and I am growing fat, as one ought to be. You are not fit for the world. You will get quite ill. You must travel. This summer I am going on a journey; will you go with me? I should like a travelling companion; will you go as my shadow? I shall be very happy to take you with me, and will pay your expenses."

"That is madness!" the learned man said.

"That depends entirely upon how one looks upon it!" the Shadow said. "Such is the world, and such it will remain!" and he went away.

The learned man was unfortunate. Cares and troubles came upon him, and what he wrote about truth, goodness, and beauty was, to most people, what a rose would be to a cow. At last he grew quite ill.

"You look exactly like a shadow!" people said to him, and as he heard the words a shudder came over the learned man.

"You must go to the warm baths!" the Shadow said, when he called; "nothing else wil do you any good. For old acquaintanceship, I will take you. I pay the expenses, and you can write the description of our journey, and can amuse me a little on the way. I want to go to the baths, for my beard does not grow as it should, which is an illness too, and one must have a beard. Now be sensible, and accept my offer; we shall travel as friends."

So they started, the Shadow as master, and the master as shadow. They drove together, they rode together, and they walked together, side by side; before and after one another, according to the position of the sun. The Shadow chose his place and acted as master in everything; the learned man making no difficulty about it, for he was an easy, good-natured man.

Thus they reached the baths, where there were many strangers, and amongst these the beautiful daughter of a king, whose malady was that she saw too clearly, which was highly distressing.

She saw at once that the new arrival was quite a different man to others. "It is said that he is here for the growth of his beard, but I know the real reason – he cannot cast a shadow."

Her curiosity was excited, and she therefore at once entered into conversation with the stranger. Being a king's daughter, she had not to stand upon much ceremony, so she said, "Your illness is, that you cannot cast a shadow."

"Your Royal Highness must have improved considerably in your health!" the Shadow said. "I know that your illness was seeing too clearly, but that defect has evidently left you, and you are cured. I have not only a shadow, but a most extraordinary one. Other people have only a common shadow, but I do not like what is common. People give their servants finer clothes than they wear themselves, and I have made my shadow human. Do you not see the person who always accompanies me? He is my shadow; and you may observe that I have even given him a shadow of his own. I like what is out of the common way."

"Can it be," the Princess said, "that I am really cured? This is the most wonderful of all baths. Water certainly has, now-a-days, most extraordinary power; but I shall not leave here, for now it is becoming interesting. The stranger pleases me, and I only hope his beard may not grow, or he will go away."

At night the Princess danced with the Shadow. She was light, but he was still lighter; such a partner she had never yet had. She told him what country she came from, and he knew it, for he had been there when she was from home. He had looked in at the upper as well as the lower windows, and had seen everything that went on there, so that he could refer to circumstances which quite astonished her. He must certainly be the wisest man living. She was inspired with great respect for him, and when they danced together again she fell in love with him. Again they danced together, and she was near telling him her passion; but she was prudent. She thought of her country, and of the many beings over whom she had to rule, and she said to herself, "He is a wise man, which is good, and he dances well, which is also good, but has he solid information? That is quite as important, and he must be examined." She therefore asked him a most difficult question, which she could not have answered herself, and the Shadow looked puzzled.

"You cannot answer that!" the Princess said.

"Oh, that is nothing but school learning!" the Shadow answered, "and I have no doubt even my shadow there at the door can answer it."

"Your shadow!" the Princess exclaimed; "that would be remarkable!"

"I do not positively say that he can do so," the Shadow said, "but I fully expect he can; indeed, he has followed me so long and listened to me, that I have little doubt of it. But I must warn your Royal Highness that he is so proud of passing for a man, that he must in every way be treated as such, if he is to be in a good humour, as he must be, in order to answer well."

"That will amuse me!" the Princess said.

And she went up to the learned man, and spoke with him about the sun and moon, and about man physically and morally, and he answered everything with great learning.

"What an extraordinary man that must be, to have so learned a shadow!" she thought. "It would be a real blessing for my subjects if I chose him as a husband. I will do so!"

All was soon arranged between them, but no one was to know anything about it till she got back to her own country.

"No one, not even my shadow!" the Shadow said, and he formed projects of his own.

Then they went to the country where the Princess ruled, when she was at home.

"Now attend to me, my good friend!" the Shadow said to the learned man. "I am now very happy, and have become as powerful as any one can be, so that now I intend to do something extraordinary for you. You shall always live with me in the palace, and drive with me in my state-carriage, and have ten thousand pounds a year; but then you must allow yourself to be called shadow by every one, and not say that you have ever been a man; besides which, once a year, when I sit on the balcony and show myself to the people, you must lie at my feet, as it becomes a shadow to do. I will now tell you that I am going to marry the Princess. This evening the wedding takes place!"

"That is too great a piece of madness!" the learned man cried; "I cannot, and will not, do it; that would be deceiving the whole country, as well as the Princess. I will tell all! That I am a man, and that you are only a Shadow dressed up!"

"No one will believe you!" the Shadow said. "Be sensible, or I call the guard."

"I will go straight to the Princess!" the learned man said. "But I will go first!" the Shadow said, "and you shall be placed under arrest!" and so it was, for the guards obeyed him, knowing he was to marry the Princess.

"You are trembling!" the Princess said, when the Shadow appeared before her: "What has happened? You must not be taken ill just when we are going to be married!"

"Oh, the most dreadful occurrence has taken place!" the Shadow said. "Only imagine! – oh, that poor shadow's brain cannot bear much! just imagine – my shadow has gone mad! He fancies he is a man, and that I – just imagine – that I am his shadow!"

"That is dreadful!" the Princess said; "I hope he is in confinement?"

"Yes, he is! And I fear he will never recover!"

"Poor Shadow!" the Princess said. "He is very unhappy, and it would be a real blessing to release him from his sufferings, and I think it will be necessary to get rid of him privately!"

"That is really hard," the Shadow said, "for he has been a faithful servant!" And he pretended to sigh.

"You are a noble character!" the Princess cried.

That night the whole town was illuminated, and the cannon were fired, "Boom!" and the soldiers presented arms. That was a wedding! The Princess and the Shadow went onto the balcony to show themselves to the people and to receive one more hurrah.

The learned man heard nothing of all that, for he had been put to death.

Grimm's Folk Tales

Grimm's Folk Tales

The Brothers Grimm

Illustrated by

E.H. Wehnert

REDWOOD EDITIONS

Contents

Colour Illustrations

"Oh, I will promise you all," said the Princess, "if you will only get my ball." *(The Frog Prince.)*

"I am looking at my little dove," said Hansel, "nodding a good-bye to me." *(Hansel and Grethel.)*

The Prince took Cinderella upon his horse, and the two little white doves sang. *(Cinderella.)*

Just as he was about to raise his axe, he perceived a pack of wolves, who howled dreadfully as they came nearer. *(Misfortune.)*

Hans now drove his cow off steadily before him, thinking of his lucky bargain. *(Hans in Luck.)*

The Soldier turned and saw a huge bear, which eyed him very ferociously. *(Bearskin.)*

When the Beast was tired, the little Tailor produced a fiddle and played a tune on it. *(The Valiant Tailor.)*

"I am drumming to show the way to the many thousands who follow me." *(The Drummer.)*

PREFACE

The "Kinder und Hausmärchen" of the Brothers Grimm is a world-renowned book. Every collector of stories has borrowed from its treasures, – hundreds of artists have illustrated it, – plays have been founded on many of the tales, – and learned essays of deep research have been written upon it by men of literary eminence.

The Brothers Grimm themselves thus speak of their work: "We may see, not seldom, when some heaven-directed storm has beaten to the earth a whole field of ripening corn, one little spot unscathed, where yet a few ears of corn stand upright, protected by the hedge or bushes which grow beside them. The warm sun shines on them day by day, and unnoticed and forgotten they ripen and are fit for the sickle, which comes not to reap them that they may be stored in some huge granary. They remain till they are full ripe, and then the hand of some poor woman plucks and binds them together and carries them home to store them up more carefully than a whole sheaf, for perchance they will have to serve for all the winter, and she cannot tell how long beyond.

"Thus does it appear to us when we consider how little is left of all that bloomed in earlier days, – how even that little is well-nigh lost, save for the popular ballads, a few legends and traditions, and these innocent household stories. The fire-side hearth and chimney-corner; the observance of high-days and holy-days; the solitude of the still forest-glade; above all, untroubled fancy; these have been the hedges which have kept intact the field of legendary lore and handed it down from age to age."

The Frog Prince

In the olden time, when wishing was having, there lived a King, whose daughters were all beautiful; but the youngest was so exceedingly beautiful that the Sun himself, although he saw her very often, was enchanted every time she came out into the sunshine.

Near the castle of this King was a large and gloomy forest, and in the midst stood an old lime-tree, beneath whose branches splashed a little fountain; so, whenever it was very hot, the King's youngest daughter ran off into this wood, and sat down by the side of this fountain; and, when she felt dull, would often divert herself by throwing a golden ball up in the air and catching it. And this was her favourite amusement.

Now, one day it happened, that this golden ball, when the King's daughter threw it into the air, did not fall down into her hand, but on the grass; and then it rolled past her into the fountain. The King's daughter followed the ball with her eyes, but it disappeared beneath the water, which was so deep that no one could see to the bottom. Then she began to lament, and to cry louder and louder; and, as she cried, a voice called out, "Why weepest thou, O King's daughter? thy tears would melt even a stone to pity." And she looked around to the spot whence the voice came, and saw a Frog stretching his thick ugly head out of the water. "Ah! you old water-paddler," said she, "was it you that spoke? I am weeping for my golden ball which has slipped away from me into the water."

"Be quiet, and do not cry," answered the Frog; "I can give thee good advice. But what wilt thou give me if I fetch thy plaything up again?"

"What will you have, dear Frog?" said she. "My dresses, my pearls and jewels, or the golden crown which I wear?"

The Frog answered, "Dresses, or jewels, or golden crowns are not for me; but if thou wilt love me, and let me by thy companion and playfellow, and sit at thy table, and eat from thy little golden plate, and drink out of thy cup, and sleep in thy little bed, – if thou wilt promise me all these, then will I dive down and fetch up thy golden ball."

"Oh, I will promise you all," said she, "if you will only get me my ball." But she thought to herself, "What is the silly Frog chattering about? Let him remain in the water with his equals; he cannot mix in society." But the Frog, as soon as he had received her promise, drew his head under the water and dived down. Presently he swam up again with the ball in his mouth, and threw it on the grass. The King's daughter was full of joy when she again saw her beautiful plaything; and, taking it up, she ran off immediately. "Stop! stop!" cried the Frog; "take me with thee. I cannot run as thou canst." But all his croaking was useless; although it was loud enough, the King's daughter did not hear it, but, hastening home, soon forgot the poor Frog, who was obliged to leap back into the fountain.

The next day, when the King's daughter was sitting at table with her father and all his courtiers, and was eating from her own little golden plate, something was heard coming up the marble stairs, splish-splash, splish-splash; and when it arrived at the top, it knocked at the door, and a voice said, "Open the door, thou youngest daughter of the King!" So she rose and went to see who it was that called her; but when she opened the door and caught sight of the Frog, she shut it again with great vehemence, and sat down at the table, looking very pale. But the king perceived that her heart was beating violently, and asked her whether it were a giant who had come to fetch her away who stood at the door. "Oh, no!" answered she; "it is no giant, but an ugly Frog."

"What does the Frog want with you?" said the King.

"Oh, dear father, when I was sitting yesterday playing by the fountain, my golden ball fell into the water, and this Frog fetched it up again because I cried so much: but first, I must tell you, he pressed me so much, that I promised him he should be my companion. I never thought that he could come out of the water, but somehow he has jumped out, and now he wants to come in here."

At that moment there was another knock, and a voice said, –

"King's daughter, youngest,
Open the door.

Hast thou forgotten
Thy promises made
At the fountain so clear
'Neath the lime-tree's shadow.
King's daughter, youngest,
Open the door."

Then the King said, "What you have promised, that you must perform; go and let him in." So the King's daughter went and opened the door, and the Frog hopped in after her right up to her chair: and as soon as she was seated, the Frog said, "Take me up;" but she hesitated so long that at last the King ordered her to obey. And as soon as the Frog sat on the chair he jumped on to the table and said, "Now push thy plate near me, that we may eat together." And she did so, but as every one saw, very unwillingly. The Frog seemed to relish his dinner much, but every bit that the King's daughter ate nearly choked her, till at last the Frog said, "I have satisfied my hunger and feel very tired; wilt thou carry me upstairs now into thy chamber, and make thy bed ready that we may sleep together?" At this speech the King's daughter began to cry, for she was afraid of the cold Frog, and dared not touch him; and besides, he actually wanted to sleep in her own beautiful, clean bed.

But her tears only made the King very angry, and he said, "He who helped you in the time of your trouble, must not now be despised!" So she took the Frog up with two fingers, and put him in a corner of her chamber. But as she lay in her bed, he crept up to it, and said, "I am so very tired that I shall sleep well; do take me up or I will tell thy father." This speech put the King's daughter in a terrible passion, and catching the Frog up, she threw him with all her strength against the wall, saying, "Now, will you be quiet, you ugly Frog!"

But as he fell he was changed from a frog into a handsome Prince with beautiful eyes, who after a little while became, with her father's consent, her dear companion and betrothed. Then he told her how he had been transformed by an evil witch, and that no one but herself could have had the power to take him out of the fountain; and that on the morrow they would go together into his own kingdom.

The next morning, as soon as the sun rose, a carriage drawn by eight white horses, with ostrich feathers on their heads, and golden bridles, drove up to the door of the palace, and behind the carriage stood the trusty Henry, the servant of the young Prince. When his master was changed into a frog, trusty Henry had grieved so much that he had bound three iron bands round his heart, for fear it should break with grief and sorrow. But now that the carriage was ready to carry the young Prince to his own country, the faithful Henry helped in the bride and bridegroom, and placed himself in the seat behind, full of joy at his master's release. They had not proceeded far when the Prince heard a crack as if something had broken behind the carriage; so he put his head out of the window and asked Henry what was broken, and Henry answered, "It was not the carriage, my master, but a band which I bound round my heart when it was in such grief because you were changed into a frog."

Twice afterwards on the journey there was the same noise, and each time the Prince thought that it was some part of the carriage that had given way; but it was only the breaking of the bands which bound the heart of the trusty Henry, who was thenceforward free and happy.

The Cat and the Mouse in Partnership

A Cat having made the acquaintance of a Mouse, told her so much of the great love and affection that he had for her, that the Mouse at last consented to live in the same house with the Cat, and to have their domestic affairs in common. "But we must provide for the winter," said the Cat, "or we shall be starved: you little Mouse cannot go anywhere, or you will meet with an accident." This advice was followed, and a pot was brought with some grease in it. However, when they had got it, they could not imagine where it should be put; at last, after a long consideration, the Cat said, "I know no better place to put it than in the church, for there no one dares to steal anything: we will set it beneath the organ, and not touch it till we really want it." So the pot was put away in safety; but not a long while afterwards the Cat began to wish for it again, so he spoke to the Mouse and said, "I have to tell you that I am asked by my aunt to stand godfather to a little son, white with brown marks, whom she has just brought into the world, and so I must go to the christening. Let me go out to-day, and do you stop at home and keep house." "Certainly," answered the Mouse; "pray, go; and if you eat anything nice, think of me: I would also willingly drink a little of the sweet red christening-wine." But it was all a story; for the Cat had no aunt, and had not been asked to stand godfather.

He went straight to the church, crept up to the grease-pot, and licked it till he had eaten off the top; then he took a walk on the roofs of the houses in the town, thinking over his situation, and now and then stretching himself in the sun and stroking his whiskers as often as he thought of the pot of fat. When it was evening he went home again, and the Mouse said, "So you have come at last: what a charming day you must have had!"

"Yes," answered the Cat; "it went off very well!"

"What have you named the kitten?" asked the Mouse.

"*Top-off!*" said the Cat, very quickly.

"*Top-off!*" replied the Mouse; "that is a curious and remarkable name: is it common in your family?"

"What does that matter?" said the Cat; "it is not worse than Crumb-stealer, as your children are called."

Not long afterwards the Cat felt the same longing as before, and said to the Mouse, "You must oblige me by taking care of the house once more by yourself; I am again asked to stand godfather, and, since the youngster has a white ring round his neck, I cannot get off the invitation." So the good little Mouse consented, and the Cat crept away behind the wall to the church again, and ate half the contents of the grease-pot. "Nothing tastes better than what one eats by oneself," said he, quite contented with his day's work; and when he came home the Mouse asked how this child was named.

"*Half-out!*" answered the Cat.

"*Half-out!* What do you mean? I never heard such a name before in my life: I will wager anything it is not in the calendar."

The Cat's mouth now began to water again at the recollection of the feasting. "All good things come in threes," said he to the Mouse. "I am again required to be godfather; this child is quite black, and has little white claws, but not a single white hair on his body; such a thing only happens once in two years, so pray excuse me this time."

"*Top-off! Half-out!*" answered the Mouse; "these are such curious names, they make me a bit suspicious."

"Ah!" replied the Cat, "there you sit in your grey coat and long tail, thinking nonsense. That comes of never going out."

The Mouse busied herself during the Cat's absence in putting the house in order, but meanwhile greedy Puss licked the grease-pot clean out. "When it is all done one will rest in peace," thought he to himself, and as soon as night came he went home fat and tired. The Mouse, however, again asked what name the third child had received. "It will not please you any better," answered the Cat, "for he is called *All-out.*"

"*All-out!*" exclaimed the Mouse; "well, that is certainly the most curious name by far. I have never yet seen it in print. *All-out!* What can that mean?" and, shaking her head, she rolled herself up and went to sleep.

After that nobody else asked the Cat to stand godfather; but the winter had arrived, and nothing more was to be picked up out-of-doors; so the Mouse bethought herself of their store of provision, and said, "Come, friend Cat, we will go to our grease-pot which we laid by; it will taste well now."

"Yes, indeed," replied the Cat; "it will taste as well as if you stroked your tongue against the window."

So they set out on their journey, and when they arrived at the church the pot stood in its old place – but it was empty! "Ah," said the Mouse, "I see what has happened; now I know you are indeed a faithful friend. You have eaten the whole as you stood godfather; first *Top-off*, then *Half-out*, then – "

"Will you be quiet?" cried the Cat. "Not a word, or I'll eat you." But the poor Mouse had "*All-out*" at her tongue's end, and had scarcely uttered it when the Cat made a spring, seized her in his mouth, and swallowed her.

This happens every day in the world.

THE WOODCUTTER'S CHILD

Once upon a time, near a large forest, there dwelt a woodcutter and his wife, who had only one child, a little girl three years old; but they were so poor that they had scarcely food sufficient for every day in the week, and often they were puzzled to know what they should get to eat. One morning the woodcutter, his heart full of care, went into the wood to work; and, as he chopped the trees, there stood before him a tall and beautiful woman, having a crown of shining stars upon her head, who thus addressed him: "I am the Guardian Angel of every Christian child; thou art poor and needy; bring me thy child, and I will take her with me. I will be her mother, and henceforth she shall be under my care." The woodcutter consented, and calling his child, gave her to the Angel, who carried her to the land of Happiness. There everything went happily; she ate sweet bread, and drank pure milk; her clothes were gold, and her playfellows were beautiful children. When she attained her fourteenth year, the Guardian Angel called her to her side, and said, "My dear child, I have a long journey for thee. Take these keys of the thirteen doors of the land of Happiness: twelve of them thou mayest open, and behold the glories therein; but the thirteenth, to which this little key belongs, thou art forbidden to open. Beware! if thou dost disobey, harm will befall thee."

The maiden promised to be obedient, and, when the Guardian Angel was gone, began her visits to the mansions of Happiness. Every day one door was unclosed, until she had seen all the twelve. In each mansion there sat an angel, surrounded by a bright light. The maiden rejoiced at the glory, and the child who accompanied her rejoiced with her. Now the forbidden door alone remained. A great desire possessed the maiden to know what was hidden there; and she said to the child, "I will not quite open it, nor will I go in, but I will only unlock the door, so that we may peep through the chink." "No, no," said the child; "that will be a sin. The Guardian Angel has forbidden it, and misfortune would soon fall upon us."

At this the maiden was silent, but the desire still remained in her heart, and tormented her continually, so that she had no peace. One day, however, all the children were away, and she thought, "Now I am alone and can peep in, no one will know what I do;" so she found the keys, and, taking them in her hand, placed the right one in the lock and turned it around. Then the door sprang open, and she saw three angels sitting on a throne, surrounded by a great light. The maiden remained a little while standing in astonishment; and then, putting her finger in the light, she drew it back, and found it covered with gold. Then great alarm seized her, and, shutting the door hastily, she ran away. But her fear only increased more and more, and her heart beat so violently that she thought it would burst; the gold also on her finger would not come off, although she washed it and rubbed it with all her strength.

Not long afterwards the Guardian Angel came back from her journey, and, calling the maiden to her, demanded the keys of the mansion. As she delivered them up, the Angel looked in her face, and asked, "Hast thou opened the thirteenth door?" "No," answered the maiden.

Then the Angel laid her hand upon the maiden's heart, and felt how violently it was beating; and she knew that her command had been disregarded, and that the child had opened the door. Then she asked again, "Hast thou opened the thirteenth door?" "No," said the maiden, for the second time.

Then the Angel perceived that the child's finger had become golden from touching the light, and she knew that the child was guilty; and she asked her for the third time, "Hast thou opened the thirteenth door?" "No," said the maiden again.

Then the Guardian Angel replied, "Thou has not obeyed me, nor done my bidding; therefore thou art no longer worthy to remain among good children."

And the maiden sank down into a deep sleep, and when she awoke she found herself in the midst of a wilderness. She wished to call out, but she had lost her voice. Then she sprang up, and tried to run away; but wherever she turned thick bushes held her back, so that she could not escape. In the deserted spot in which she was now inclosed, there stood an old hollow tree; this was her dwelling-place. In this place she slept by night; and when it rained and blew she found shelter within it. Roots and wild berries were her food, and she sought for them as far as she could reach. In the autumn she collected the leaves of the trees, and laid them in her hole; and when the frost and snow of the winter came, she clothed herself with them, for her clothes had dropped into rags. But during the sunshine she sat outside the tree, and her long hair fell down on all sides and covered her like a mantle. Thus she remained a long time, experiencing the misery and poverty of the world.

But, once, when the trees had become green again, the King of the country was hunting in the forest, and, as a bird flew into the bushes which surrounded the wood, he dismounted, and, tearing the brushwood aside, cut a path for himself with his sword. When he had at last made his way through, he saw a beautiful maiden, who was clothed from head to foot with her own golden locks, sitting under the tree. He stood in silence, and looked at her for some time in astonishment; at last he said, "Child, how came you into this wilderness?" But the maiden answered not, for she had become dumb. Then the King asked, "Will you go with me to my castle?" At that she nodded her head, and the King, taking her in his arms, put her on his horse and rode away home. Then he gave her beautiful clothing, and everything in abundance. Still she could not speak; but her beauty was so great and so won upon the King's heart, that after a little while he married her.

When about a year had passed away the Queen brought a son into the world, and the same night, while lying alone in her bed, the Guardian Angel appeared to her, and said –

"Wilt thou tell the truth and confess that thou didst unlock the forbidden door? For then will I open thy mouth, and give thee again the power of speech; but if thou remainest obstinate in thy sin, then will I take from thee thy new-born babe."

And the power to answer was given to her, but her heart was hardened, and she said, "No, I did not open the door;" and at these words the Guardian Angel took the child out of her arms and disappeared with him.

The next morning, when the child was not to be seen, a murmur arose among the people that their Queen was a murderess, who had destroyed her only son; but, although she heard everything, she could say nothing. But the King did not believe the ill report, because of his great love for her.

About a year afterwards another son was born, and on the night of his birth the Guardian Angel again appeared, and asked, "Wilt thou confess that thou didst open the forbidden door? Then will I restore to thee thy son, and give thee the power of speech; but if thou hardenest thyself in thy sin, then will I take this new-born babe also with me."

Then the Queen answered again, "No, I did not open the door;" so the Angel took the second child out of her arms and bore him away. On the morrow, when the infant could not be found, the people said openly that the Queen had slain him, and the King's councillors advised that she should be brought to trial. But the King's affection was still so great that he would not believe it, and he commanded his councillors never again to mention the report on pain of death.

The next year a beautiful little girl was born, and for the third time the Guardian Angel appeared and said to the Queen, "Follow me;" and taking her by the hand, she led her to the kingdom of Happiness, and showed to her the two other children, who were playing merrily. The Queen rejoiced at the sight, and the Angel said, "Is thy heart not yet softened? If thou wilt confess that thou didst unlock the forbidden door, then will I restore to thee both thy sons." But the Queen again answered, "No, I did not open it;" and at these words she sank upon the earth, and her third child was taken from her.

When this was rumoured abroad the next day, all the people exclaimed, "The Queen is a murderess! she must be condemned!" and the King could not this time repulse his councillors. Thereupon a trial was held, and since the Queen could make no good answer or defence, she was condemned to die upon a funeral pile. The wood was collected, she was bound to the stake, and the fire was lighted all around her. Then the iron pride of her heart began to soften,and she was moved to repentance, and she thought, "Could I but now, before my death, confess that I opened the door!" And her tongue was loosened, and she cried aloud, "Thou good Angel, I confess." At these words the rain descended from heaven and extinguished the fire; then a great light shone above, and the Angel appeared and descended upon the earth, and by her side were the Queen's two sons, one on her right hand and the other on her left, and in her arms she bore the new-born babe. Then the Angel restored to the Queen her three children, and loosening her tongue, promised her a happy future, and said, "Whoever will repent and confess their sins, they shall be forgiven."

The Wolf and the Seven Little Goats

Once upon a time there lived an old Goat who had seven young ones whom she loved as every mother loves her children. One day she wanted to go into the forest to fetch some food, so, calling her seven young ones together, she said, "Dear children, I am going away into the wood; be on your guard against the Wolf, for if he comes here, he will eat you all up – skin, hair and all. He often disguises himself, but you may know him by his rough voice and his black feet." The little Goats replied, "Dear mother, we will pay great attention to what you say; you may go away without any anxiety." So the old one bleated and ran off, quite contented, upon her road.

Not long afterwards, somebody knocked at the hut-door, and called out, "Open, dear children; your mother is here and has brought you each something." But the little Goats perceived from the rough voice that it was a Wolf, and so they said, "We will not undo the door; you are not our mother; she has a gentle and loving voice; but yours is gruff; you are a Wolf." So the Wolf went to a shop and bought a great piece of chalk, which he ate, and by that means rendered his voice more gentle. Then he came back, knocked at the hut-door, and called out, "Open, my dear children; your mother has come home, and has brought you each something." But the Wolf had placed his black paws upon the window-sill, so the Goats saw them, and replied, "No, we will not open the door; our mother has not black feet: you are a Wolf." So the Wolf went to a baker and said, "I have hurt my foot, put some dough on it." And when the baker had done so, he ran to the miller, saying, "Strew some white flour upon my feet." But the miller, thinking he was going to deceive somebody, hesitated, till the Wolf said, "If you do not do it at once, I will eat you." This made the miller afraid, so he powdered his feet with flour. Such is mankind!

Now, the villain went for the third time to the hut, and, knocking at the door, called out, "Open to me, my children; your dear mother is come, and has brought with her something for each of you out of the forest." The little Goats exclaimed, "Show us first your feet, that we may see whether you are our mother." So the Wolf put his feet up on the window-sill, and when they saw that they were white, they thought it was all right, and undid the door. But who should come in? The Wolf. They were terribly frightened, and tried to hide themselves. One ran under the table, the second got into the bed, the third into the cupboard, the fourth into the kitchen, the fifth into the oven, the sixth into the wash-tub, and the seventh into the clock-case. But the Wolf found them all out, and did not delay, but swallowed them all up one after another; only the youngest one, hid in the clock-case, he did not discover. When the Wolf had satisfied his appetite, he dragged himself out, and lying down upon the green meadow under a tree, went fast asleep.

Soon after the old Goat came home out of the forest. Ah, what a sight she saw! The hut-door stood wide open; the table, stools, and benches were overturned; the wash-tub was broken to pieces, and the sheets and pillows pulled off the bed. She sought her children, but could find them nowhere. She called them by name, one after the other, but no one answered. At last, when she came to the name of the youngest, a little voice replied, "Here I am, dear mother, in the clock-case." She took her out, and heard how the Wolf had come and swallowed all the others. You cannot think how she wept for her poor little ones.

At last she went out all in her misery, and the young Goat ran by her side; and when they came to the meadow, there lay the Wolf under the tree, snoring so that the boughs quivered. She viewed him on all sides, and perceived that something moved and stirred about in his body. "Ah, mercy!" thought she, "should my poor children, whom he has swallowed for his dinner, be yet alive!" So saying, she ran home and fetched a pair of scissors and a needle and thread. Then she cut open the monster's hairy coat, and had scarcely made one slit, before one little Goat put his head out, and, as she cut further, out jumped one after another, all six, still alive, and without any injury; for the monster, in his eagerness, had gulped them down quite whole. There was a joy! They hugged their dear mother, and jumped about like tailors keeping their wedding day. But the old mother said, "Go and pick up at once some large stones, that we may fill the monster's stomach, while he lies fast asleep." So the seven little Goats dragged up in great haste a pile of stones and put them in the Wolf's stomach, as many as they could bring; and then the old mother went, and, looking at him in a great hurry, saw that he was still insensible, and did not stir, and so she sewed up the slit.

When the Wolf at last woke up, he raised himself upon his legs, and because the stones which were lying in his stomach made him feel thirsty, he went to a brook in order to drink. But as he went along, rolling from side to side, the stones began to tumble about in his body, and he called out, –

"What rattles, what rattles
Against my poor bones?
Not little goats, I think,
But only big stones!"

And when the Wolf came to the brook he stooped down to drink, and the heavy stones made him lose his balance, so that he fell, and sank beneath the water.

As soon as the seven little Goats saw this, they came running up, singing aloud, "The Wolf is dead! the Wolf is dead!" and they danced for joy around their mother by the side of the brook.

FAITHFUL JOHN

Once upon a time there lived an old King, who fell very sick, and thought he was lying upon his death-bed; so he said, "Let faithful John come to me." This faithful John was his affectionate servant, and was so called because he had been true to him all his lifetime. As soon as John came to the bedside, the King said, "My faithful John, I feel that my end approaches, and I have no other care than about my son, who is still so young that he cannot always guide himself aright. If you do not promise to instruct him in everything he ought to know, and to be his guardian, I cannot close my eyes in peace." Then John answered, "I will never leave him; I will always serve him truly, even if it cost me my life." So the old King was comforted, and said, "Now I can die in peace. After my death you must show him all the chambers, halls, and vaults in the castle, and all the treasures which are in them; but the last room in the long corridor you must not show him, for in it hangs the portrait of the daughter of the King of the Golden Palace; if he sees her picture, he will conceive a great love for her, and will fall down in a swoon, and on her account undergo great perils, therefore you must keep him away." The faithful John pressed his master's hand again in token of assent, and soon after the King laid his head upon the pillow and expired.

After the old King had been borne to his grave, the faithful John related to the young King all that his father had said upon his deathbed, and declared, "All this I will certainly fulfil; I will be as true to you as I was to him, if it costs me my life." When the time of mourning was passed, John said to the young King, "It is now time for you to see your inheritance; I will show you your paternal castle." So he led the King all over it, up stairs and down stairs, and showed him all the riches, and all the splendid chambers; only one room he did not open, containing the perilous portrait, which was so placed that one saw it directly the door was opened, and, moreover, it was so beautifully painted, that one thought it breathed and moved; nothing in all the world could be more lifelike or more beautiful. The young King remarked, however, that the faithful John always passed by one door, so he asked, "Why do you not open that one?" "There is something in it," he replied, "which will frighten you."

But the King said, "I have seen all the rest of the castle, and I will know what is in there;" and he went and tried to open the door by force. The faithful John pulled him back, and said, "I promised your father before he died that you should not see the contents of that room, it would bring great misfortunes both upon you and me."

"Oh, no," replied the young King, "if I do not go in, it will be my certain ruin; I should have no peace night nor day until I had seen it with my own eyes. Now I will not stir from the place till you unlock the door."

Then the faithful John saw that it was of no use talking; so, with a heavy heart and many sighs, he picked the key out of the great bunch. When he had opened the door, he went in first, and thought he would cover up the picture, that the King should not see it; but it was of no use, for the King stepped upon tiptoes and looked over his shoulder; and as soon as he saw the portrait of the maiden, which was so beautiful and glittered with precious stones, he fell down on the ground insensible. The faithful John lifted him up and carried him to his bed, and thought with great concern, "Mercy on us! the misfortune has happened; what will come of it?" and he gave the young King wine until he came to himself. The first words he spoke were, "Who does that beautiful picture represent?" "That is the daughter of the King of the Golden Palace," was the reply.

"Then," said the King, "my love for her is so great, that if all the leaves on the trees had tongues, they should not gainsay it; my life is set upon the search for her. You are my faithful John, you must accompany me."

The trusty servant deliberated for a long while how to set about this business, for it was very difficult to get into the presence of the King's daughter. At last he bethought himself of a way, and said to the King, "Everything which she has around her is of gold, – chairs, tables, dishes, bowls, and all the household utensils. Among your treasures are five tons of gold; let one of the goldsmiths of your kingdom manufacture vessels and utensils of all kinds therefrom – all kind of birds, and wild and wonderful beasts, such as will please her; then we will travel with these, and try our luck." Then the King summoned all his goldsmiths, who worked day and night until many very beautiful things were ready. When all had been placed on board a ship, the faithful John put on merchant's clothes, and the King likewise, so that they might travel quite unknown. Then they sailed over the wide sea, and sailed away until they came to the city where dwelt the daughter of the King of the Golden Palace.

The faithful John told the King to remain in the ship, and wait for him. "Perhaps," said he, "I shall bring the King's daughter with me, therefore take care that all is in order, and set out the golden vessels and adorn the whole ship." Thereupon John placed in a napkin some of the golden cups, stepped upon land, and went straight to the King's palace. When he came into the castle-yard, a beautiful maid stood by the brook, who had two golden pails in her hand, drawing water; and when she had filled them and had turned round, she saw a strange man, and asked who he was. Then John answered, "I am a merchant," and opening his napkin, he showed her its contents. Then she exclaimed, "Oh, what beautiful golden things!" and, setting the pails down, she looked at the cups one after another, and said, "The King's daughter must see these; she is so pleased with anything made of gold that she will buy all these." And taking him by the hand, she led him in; for she was the lady's maid. When the King's daughter saw the golden cups, she was much pleased, and said, "They are so finely worked, that I will purchase them all." But the faithful John replied, "I am only the servant of a rich merchant; what I have here is nothing in comparison to those which my master has in his ship, than which nothing more delicate or costly has ever been worked in gold." Then the King's daughter wished to have them all brought; but he said, "It would take many days, and so great is the quantity, that your palace has not halls enough in it to place them around." Then her curiosity and desire were still more excited, and at last she said, "Take me to the ship; I will go myself and look at your master's treasure."

The faithful John conducted her to the ship with great joy, and the King, when he beheld her, saw that her beauty was still greater than the picture had represented, and thought nothing else but that his heart would jump out of his mouth. Presently she stepped on board, and the King conducted her below; but the faithful John remained on deck by the steersman, and told him to unmoor the ship and put on all the sail he could, that it might fly as a bird through the air. Meanwhile the King showed the Princess all the golden treasures, - the dishes, cups, bowls, the birds, the wild and wonderful beasts. Many hours passed away while she looked at everything, and in her joy she did not remark that the ship sailed on and on. As soon as she had looked at the last, and thanked the merchant, she wished to depart. But when she came on deck, she perceived that they were upon the high sea, far from the shore, and were hastening on with all sail. "Ah," she exclaimed in affright, "I am betrayed; I am carried off and taken away in the power of a strange merchant. I would rather die!"

But the King, taking her by the hand, said, "I am not a merchant, but a king, thine equal in birth. It is true that I have carried thee off; but that is because of my overwhelming love for thee. Dost thou know that when I first saw the portrait of thy beauteous face, that I fell down in a swoon before it?" When the King's daughter heard these words, she was reassured, and her heart was inclined towards him, so that she willingly became his bride. While they thus went on their voyage on the high sea, it happened that the faithful John, as he sat on the deck of the ship, playing music, saw three crows in the air, who came flying towards them. He stopped playing, and listened to what they were saying to each other, for he understood them perfectly. The first one exclaimed, "There he is, carrying home the daughter of the King of the Golden Palace." "But he is not home yet," replied the second. "But he has her," said the third; "she is sitting by him in the ship." Then the first began again, and exclaimed, "What matters that? When they go on shore, a fox-coloured horse will spring towards them, on which he will mount; and as soon as he is on it, it will jump up with him into the air, so that he will never again see his bride." The second one asked, "Is there no escape?" "Oh yes, if another mounts behind quickly, and takes out the firearms which are in the holster, and with them shoots the horse dead, then the young King will be saved. But who knows that? And if any one does know it, and tells him, such a one will be turned to stone from the toe to the knee." Then the second spoke again, "I know still more: if the horse should be killed, the young King will not then retain his bride; for when they come into the castle, a beautiful bridal shirt will lie there upon a dish, and seem to be woven of gold and silver, but it is nothing but sulphur and pitch; and if he puts it on, it will burn him to his marrow and bones." Then the third Crow asked, "Is there no escape?" "Oh yes," answered the second; "if some one takes up the shirt with his gloves on, and throws it into the fire, so that it is burnt, the young King will be saved. But what does that signify? Whoever knows it, and tells him, will be turned to stone from his knee to his heart." Then the third Crow spoke: "I know still more: even if the bridal shirt be consumed, still the young King will not retain his bride. For if, after the wedding, a dance is held, while the young Queen dances, she will suddenly turn pale, and fall down as if dead; and if some one does not raise her up, and take three drops of blood from her right breast and throw them away, she will die. But whoever knows that, and tells it, will have his whole body turned to stone, from the crown of his head to the toes of his feet."

After the Crows had thus talked with one another, they flew away, and the trusty John, who had perfectly understood all they had said, was from that time very quiet and sad; for if he concealed from his master what he had heard, misfortune would happen to him, and if he told him all he must give up his own life. But at last he thought, "I will save my master, even if I destroy myself."

As soon as they came on shore, it happened just as the Crow had foretold, and an immense fox-red horse sprang up. "Capital!" said the King; "this shall carry me to my castle," and he tried to mount; but the faithful John came straight up, and swinging himself quickly on, drew the firearms out of the holster and shot the horse dead. Then the other servants of the King, who were not on good terms with the faithful John, exclaimed, "How shameful to kill the beautiful creature, which might have borne the King to the castle!" But the King replied, "Be silent, and let him go; he is my very faithful John – who knows the good he may have done?" Now they went into the castle, and there stood a dish in the hall, and the splendid bridal shirt lay in it, and seemed nothing else than gold and silver. The young King went up to it and wished to take it up, but the faithful John pushed him away, and taking it up with his gloves on, bore it quickly to the fire and let it burn. The other servants thereupon began to murmur, saying, "See, now he is burning the King's bridal shirt!" But the young King replied, "Who knows what good he has done? Let him alone – he is my faithful John."

Soon after, the wedding was celebrated, and a grand ball was given, and the bride began to dance. So the faithful John paid great attention, and watched her countenance; all at once she grew pale, and fell as if dead to the ground. Then he sprang up hastily, raised her up and bore her to a chamber, where he laid her down, kneeled beside her, and drawing the three drops of blood out of her right breast, threw them away. As soon as she breathed again, she raised herself up; but the young King had witnessed everything, and not knowing why the faithful John had done this, was very angry, and called out, "Throw him into prison!" The next morning the trusty John was brought up for trial, and led to the gallows; and as he stood upon them, and was about to be executed, he said, "Every one condemned to die may once before his death speak. Shall I also have that privilege?" "Yes," answered the King, "it shall be granted you." Then the faithful John replied, "I have been unrighteously judged, and have always been true to you;" and he narrated the conversation of the Crows which he heard at sea; and how, in order to save his master, he was obliged to do all he had done. Then the King cried out, "Oh, my most trusty John, pardon, pardon; lead him away!" But the trusty John had fallen down at the last word and was turned into stone.

At this event both the King and the Queen were in great grief, and the King thought, "Ah, how wickedly have I rewarded his great fidelity!" and he had the stone statue raised up and placed in his sleeping-chamber, near his bed; and as often as he looked at it, he wept and said, "Ah, could I bring you back to life again, my faithful John!"

After some time had passed, the Queen bore twins, two little sons, who were her great joy. Once when the Queen was in church, and the two children at home playing by their father's side, he looked up at the stone statue full of sorrow, and exclaimed with a sigh, "Ah, could I restore you to life, my faithful John!" At these words the statue began to speak, saying, "Yes, you can make me alive again, if you will bestow on me that which is dearest to you." The King replied, "All that I have in the world I will give up for you." The statue spake again: "If you, with your own hand, cut off the heads of both your children and sprinkle me with their blood, I shall be brought to life again." The King was terrified when he heard that he must himself kill his two dear children; but he remembered his servant's great fidelity, and how the faithful John had died for him, and drawing his sword he cut off the heads of both his children with his own hand. And as soon as he had sprinkled the statues with blood, life came back to it, and the trusty John stood again alive and well before him, and said, "Your faith shall not go unrewarded;" and taking the heads of the two children, he set them on again, and anointed their wounds with their blood, and thereupon they healed again in a moment, and the children sprang away and played as if nothing had happened.

Now the King was full of happiness, and as soon as he saw the Queen coming, he hid the faithful John and both the children in a great closet. As soon as she came in he said to her, "Have you prayed in the church?" "Yes," she answered; "but I thought continually of the faithful John, who has come to such misfortune through us." Then he replied, "My dear wife, we can restore his life again to him, but it will cost us both our little sons, whom he must sacrifice." The Queen became pale and was terrified at heart, but she said, "We are guilty of his life on account of his great fidelity." Then he was very glad that she thought as he did, and going up to the closet, he unlocked it, brought out the children and the faithful John, saying, "God be praised! he is saved, and we have still our little sons:" and then he told her all that happened. Afterwards they lived happily together to the end of their days.

The Three Little Men in the Wood

Once upon a time there lived a man, whose wife had died; and a woman, also, who had lost her husband: and this man and this woman had each a daughter. These two maidens were friendly with each other, and used to walk together, and one day they came by the widow's house. Then the widow said to the man's daughter, "Do you hear, tell your father I wish to marry him, and you shall every morning wash in milk and drink wine, but my daughter shall wash in water and drink water." So the girl went home and told her father what the woman had said, and he replied, "What shall I do? marriage is a comfort, but it is also a torment." At last, as he could come to no conclusion, he drew off his boot and said: "Take this boot, which has a hole in the sole, and go with it out-of-doors and hang it on the great nail, and then pour water into it. If it holds water, I will again take a wife; but if it runs through, I will not have her." The girl did as he bid her but the water drew the hole together and the boot became full to overflowing. So she told her father how it had happened, and he, getting up, saw it was quite true; and going to the widow he settled the matter, and the wedding was celebrated.

The next morning, when the two girls arose, milk to wash in and wine to drink were set for the man's daughter, but only water, both for washing and drinking, for the woman's daughter. The second morning, water for washing and drinking stood before both the man's daughter and the woman's; and on the third morning, water to wash in and water to drink were set before the man's daughter, and milk to wash in and wine to drink before the woman's daughter, and so it continued.

Soon the woman conceived a deadly hatred for her step-daughter and knew not how to behave badly enough to her, from day to day. She was envious too, because her step-daughter was beautiful and lovely, and her own daughter was ugly and hateful.

Once, in the winter time, when the river was frozen as hard as a stone, and hill and valley were covered with snow, the woman made a cloak of paper, and called the maiden to her and said, "Put on this cloak, and go away into the wood to fetch me a little basketful of strawberries, for I have a wish for some."

"Mercy on us!" said the maiden, "in winter there are no strawberries growing; the ground is frozen, and the snow, too, has covered everything. And why must I go in that paper cloak? It is so cold out-of-doors that it freezes one's breath even, and if the wind does not blow off this cloak, the thorns will tear it from my body."

"Will you dare to contradict me?" said the stepmother. "Make haste off, and let me not see you again until you have found me a basket of strawberries." Then she gave her a small piece of dry bread, saying, "On that you must subsist the whole day." But she thought – out-of-doors she will be frozen and starved, so that my eyes will never see her again!

So the girl did as she was told, and put on the paper cloak, and went away with the basket. Far and near there was nothing but snow, and not a green blade was to be seen. When she came to the forest she discovered a little cottage, out of which three little Dwarfs were peeping. The girl wished them good morning, and knocked gently at the door. They called her in, and entering the room, she sat down on a bench by the fire to warm herself, and eat her breakfast. The Dwarfs called out. "Give us some of it!" "Willingly," she replied, and, dividing her bread in two, she gave them half. They asked, "What do you here in the forest, in the winter time, in this thin cloak?"

"Ah!" she answered, "I must seek a basketful of strawberries, and I dare not return home until I can take them with me." When she had eaten her bread, they gave her a broom, saying, "Sweep away the snow with this from the back door." But when she was gone out-of-doors the three Dwarfs said one to another, "What shall we give her, because she is so gentle and good, and has shared her bread with us?" Then said the first, "I grant to her that she shall become more beautiful every day." The second said, "I grant that a piece of gold shall fall out of her mouth for every word she speaks." The third said, "I grant that a King shall come and make her his bride."

Meanwhile, the girl had done as the Dwarfs had bidden her, and had swept away the snow from behind the house. And what do you think she found there? Actually, ripe strawberries! which came quite red and sweet up under the snow. So, filling her basket in great glee, she thanked the little men and gave them each her hand, and then ran home to take her stepmother what she wished for. As she went in and said,

"Good evening," a piece of gold fell from her mouth. Thereupon she related what had happened to her in the forest; but at every word she spoke a piece of gold fell, so that the whole floor was covered.

"Just see her arrogance," said the step-sister, "to throw away money in that way!" but in her heart she was jealous, and wished to go into the forest too, to seek strawberries. Her mother said, "No, my dear daughter; it is too cold, you will be frozen!" but as her girl let her have no peace, she at last consented, and made her a beautiful fur cloak to put on; she also gave her buttered bread and cooked meat to eat on her way.

The girl went into the forest and came straight to the little cottage. The three Dwarfs were peeping out again, but she did not greet them; and, stumbling on without looking at them or speaking, she entered the room, and seating herself by the fire, began to eat the bread and butter and meat. "Give us some of that," exclaimed the Dwarfs; but she answered, "I have not got enough for myself, so how can I give any away?" When she had finished they said, "You have a broom there, go and sweep the back door clean." "Oh, sweep it yourself," she replied; "I am not your servant." When she saw that they would not give her anything she went out at the door, and the three Dwarfs said to each other, "What shall we give her? she is so ill-behaved, and has such a bad and envious disposition, that nobody can wish well to her." The first said, "I grant that she becomes more ugly every day." The second said, "I grant that at every word she speaks a toad shall spring out of her mouth." The third said, "I grant that she shall die a miserable death." Meanwhile the girl had been looking for strawberries out-of-doors, but as she could find none she went home very peevish. When she opened her mouth to tell her mother what had happened to her in the forest, a toad jumped out of her mouth at each word, so that every one fled away from her in horror.

The stepmother was now still more vexed, and was always thinking how she could do the most harm to her husband's daughter, who every day became more beautiful. At last she took a kettle, set it on the fire, and boiled a net therein. When it was sodden she hung it on the shoulder of the poor girl, and gave her an axe, that she might go upon the frozen pond and cut a hole in the ice to drag the net. She obeyed, and went away and cut an ice-hole; and while she was cutting, an elegant carriage came by, in which the King sat. The carriage stopped, and the King asked, "My child, who are you? and what do you here?" "I am a poor girl, and am dragging a net," said she. Then the King pitied her, and saw how beautiful she was, and said, "Will you go with me?" "Yes, indeed, with all my heart," she replied, for she was glad to get out of the sight of her mother and sister.

So she was handed into the carriage, and driven away with the King; and as soon as they arrived at his castle the wedding was celebrated with great splendour, as the Dwarfs had granted to the maiden. After a year the young Queen bore a son; and when the stepmother heard of her great good fortune, she came to the castle with her daughter, and behaved as if she had come on a visit. But one day, when the King had gone out, and no one was present, this bad woman seized the Queen by the head, and her daughter caught hold of her feet, and raising her out of the bed, they threw her out of the window into the river which ran past. Then, laying her ugly daughter in the bed, the old woman covered her up, even over her head; and when the King came back he wished to speak to his wife, but the old woman exclaimed, "Softly! softly! do not go near her; she is lying in a beautiful sleep, and must be kept quiet to-day." The King, not thinking of any evil design, came again the next morning the first thing; and when he spoke to his wife, and she answered, a toad sprang out of her mouth at every word, as a piece of gold had done before. So he asked what had happened, and the old woman said, "That is produced by her weakness, she will soon lose it again."

But in the night the kitchen-boy saw a Duck swimming through the brook, and the Duck asked,

"King, King what are you doing?
Are you sleeping, or are you waking?"

And as he gave no answer, the Duck said,

"What are my guests a-doing?"

Then the boy answered,

"They all sleep sound."

And she asked him,

"How fares my child?"

And he replied,

"In his cradle he sleeps."

Then she came up in the form of the Queen to the cradle, and gave the child drink, shook up his bed, and covered him up, and then swam again away as a duck through the brook. The second night she came again; and on the third she said to the kitchen-boy, "Go and tell the King to take his sword, and swing it thrice over me, on the threshold." Then the boy ran and told the King, who came with his sword, and swung it thrice over the Duck; and at the third time his bride stood before him, bright, living, and healthful, as she had been before.

Now the King was in great happiness, but he hid the Queen in a chamber until the Sunday when the child was to be christened; and when all was finished he asked, "What ought to be done to one who takes another out of a bed and throws her into the river?" "Nothing could be more proper," said the old woman, "than to put such a one into a cask, stuck round with nails, and to roll it down the hill into the water." Then the King said, "You have spoken your own sentence;" and ordering a cask to be fetched, he caused the old woman and her daughter to be put into it, and the bottom being nailed up, the cask was rolled down the hill until it fell into the water.

"Oh, I will promise you all," said the Princess, "if you will only get my ball." (The Frog Prince.)

"I am looking at my little dove," said Hansel,
"nodding a good-bye to me." (Hansel and Grethel.)

The little brother and sister.

THE LITTLE BROTHER AND SISTER

There was once a little Brother who took his Sister by the hand, and said, "Since our own dear mother's death we have not had one happy hour; our stepmother beats us every day, and, if we come near her, kicks us away with her foot. Our food is the hard crusts of bread which are left, and even the dog under the table fares better than we, for he often gets a nice morsel. Come, let us wander forth into the wide world." So the whole day long they travelled over meadows, fields, and stony roads, and when it rained the Sister said, "It is heaven crying in sympathy." By evening they came into a large forest, and were so wearied with grief, hunger, and their long walk, that they laid themselves down in a hollow tree, and went to sleep. When they awoke the next morning, the sun had already risen high in the heavens, and its beams made the tree so hot, that the little boy said to his Sister, "I am so thirsty, if I knew where there was a brook I would go and drink. Ah! I think I hear one running;" and so saying, he got up, and taking his Sister's hand, they went in search of the brook.

The wicked stepmother, however, was a witch, and had witnessed the departure of the two children; so, sneaking after them secretly, as is the habit of witches, she had enchanted all the springs in the forest.

Presently they found a brook which ran trippingly over the pebbles, and the Brother would have drunk out of it, but the Sister heard how it said as it ran along, "Who drinks of me will become a tiger!" So the Sister exclaimed, "I pray you, Brother, drink not, or you will become a tiger, and tear me to pieces!" So the Brother did not drink, although his thirst was so great, and he said, "I will wait till the next brook." As they came to the second, the Sister heard it say, "Who drinks of me becomes a wolf!" The Sister ran up crying, "Brother, do not, pray do not, drink, or you will become a wolf and eat me up!" Then the Brother did not drink, saying, "I will wait until we come to the next spring, but then I must drink, you may say what you will; my thirst is much too great." Just as they reached the third brook, the Sister heard the voice saying, "Who drinks of me will become a fawn, – who drinks of me will become a fawn!" So the Sister said, "O, my Brother! do not drink, or you will be changed to a fawn, and run away from me!" But he had already kneeled down, and drunk of the water, and, as the first drops passed his lips, his shape became that of a fawn.

At first the sister cried over her little changed Brother, and he wept too, and knelt by her very sorrowful; but at last the maiden said, "Be still, dear little Fawn, and I will never forsake you;" and, undoing her golden garter, she put it round his neck, and weaving rushes made a white girdle to lead him with. This she tied to him, and, taking the other end in her hand, she led him away, and they travelled deeper and deeper into the forest. After they had walked a long distance they came to a little hut, and the Maiden, peeping in, found it empty, and thought, "Here we can stay and dwell." Then she looked for leaves and moss to make a soft couch for the Fawn, and every morning she went out and collected roots and berries and nuts for herself, and tender grass for the Fawn, which he ate out of her hand, and played happily around her. In the evening, when the Sister was tired, and had said her prayers, she laid her head upon the back of the Fawn, which served for a pillow, on which she slept soundly. Had but the Brother regained his own proper form, their life would have been happy indeed.

Thus they dwelt in this wilderness, and some time had elapsed, when it happened that the King of the country held a great hunt in the forest; and now resounded through the trees the blowing of horns, the barking of dogs, and the lusty cries of the hunters, so that the little Fawn heard them, and wanted very much to join. "Ah!" said he to his Sister, "let me go to the hunt, I cannot restrain myself any longer;" and he begged so hard that at last she consented. "But," said she to him, "return again in the evening, for I shall shut my door against the wild huntsmen, and, that I may know you, do you knock, and say, 'Sister, let me in,' and if you do not speak I shall not open the door." As soon as she had said this, the little Fawn sprang off, quite glad and merry in the fresh breeze. The King and his huntsmen perceived the beautiful animal, and pursued him; but they could not catch him, and when they thought they had him for certain, he sprang away over the bushes, and got out of sight. Just as it was getting dark, he ran up to the hut, and, knocking, said, "Sister mine, let me in."

Then she undid the little door, and he went in, and rested all night long upon his soft couch. The next morning the hunt was commenced again, and as soon as the little Fawn heard the horns and the tally-ho of the sportsmen he could not rest, and said, "Sister dear, open the door, I must be off." The Sister opened it, saying, "Return at evening, mind, and say the words as before." When the King and his huntsmen saw again the Fawn with the golden necklace, they followed him close, but he was too nimble and quick for them. The whole day long they kept up with him, but towards evening the huntsmen made a circle round him, and one wounded him slightly in the foot behind, so that he could only run slowly. Then one of them slipped after him to the little hut, and heard him say, "Sister dear, open the door," and saw that the door was opened and immediately shut behind. The huntsman, having observed all this, went and told the King what he had seen and heard, and he said, "On the morrow I will once more pursue him."

The Sister, however, was terribly frightened when she saw that her Fawn was wounded, and, washing off the blood, she put herbs upon the foot, and said, "Go and rest upon your bed, dear Fawn, that the wound may heal." It was so slight, that the next morning he felt nothing of it, and when he heard the hunting cries outside, he exclaimed, "I cannot stop away – I must be there, and none shall catch me so easily again!" The Sister wept very much, and told him, "Soon they will kill you, and I shall be here all alone in this forest, forsaken by all the world: I cannot let you go."

"I shall die here in vexation," answered the Fawn, "if you do not: for when I hear the horn, I think I shall jump out of my skin." The Sister, finding she could not prevent him, opened the door with a heavy heart, and the Fawn jumped out, quite delighted, into the forest. As soon as the King perceived him, he said to his huntsmen, "Follow him all day long till the evening, but let no one do him an injury." When the sun had set, the King asked his huntsmen to show him the hut; and as they came to it, he knocked at the door, and said, "Let me in, dear Sister." Then the door was opened, and, stepping in, the King saw a maiden more beautiful than he had ever before seen. She was frightened when she saw not her Fawn, but a man step in, who had a golden crown upon his head. But the King, looking at her with a friendly glance, reached her his hand, saying, "Will you go with me to my castle, and be my dear wife?" "Oh, yes," replied the maiden; "but the Fawn must go too: him I will never forsake." The King replied, "He shall remain with you as long as you live, and shall want for nothing." In the meantime the Fawn had come in, and the Sister, binding the girdle to him, again took it in her hand, and led him away with her out of the hut.

The King took the beautiful maiden upon his horse, and rode to his castle, where the wedding was celebrated with great splendour, and she became Queen, and they lived together a long time; while the Fawn was taken care of and lived well, playing about the castle-garden. The wicked stepmother, however, on whose account the children had wandered forth into the world, supposed that long ago the Sister had been torn to pieces by the wild beasts, and the little Brother hunted to death in his

Fawn's shape by the hunters. As soon, therefore, as she heard how happy they had become, and how everything prospered with them, envy and jealousy were roused in her heart, and left her no peace; and she was always thinking in what way she could work misfortune to them. Her own daughter, who was as ugly as night, and had but one eye, for which she was continually reproached, said, "The luck of being a Queen has never yet happened to me." "Be quiet now," said the old woman, "and make yourself contented: when the time comes, I shall be at hand." As soon, then, as the time came when the Queen brought into the world a beautiful little boy, which happened when the King was out hunting, the old witch took the form of a chambermaid, and got into the room where the Queen was lying, and said to her, "The bath is ready, which will restore you, and give you fresh strength; be quick, before it gets cold." Her daughter being at hand, they carried the weak Queen between them into the room, and laid her in the bath, and then, shutting the door to, they ran off; but first they had made up an immense fire in the stove, which must soon suffocate the young Queen.

When this was done, the old woman took her daughter, and, putting a cap on her, laid her in the bed in the Queen's place. She gave her, too, the form and appearance of the real Queen, as far as she could; but she could not restore the lost eye, and, so that the King might not notice it, she turned upon that side where there was no eye. When he came home at evening, and heard that a son was born to him, he was much delighted, and prepared to go to his wife's bedside, to see how she did. So the old woman called out in a great hurry, "For your life, do not undraw the curtains; the Queen must not yet see the light, and must be kept quiet." So the King went away, and did not discover that a false Queen was laid in the bed.

When midnight came, and every one was asleep, the nurse, who sat by herself, wide awake, near the cradle, in the nursery, saw the door open and the true Queen come in. She took the child in her arms, and rocked it a while, and then, shaking up its pillow, laid it down in its cradle, and covered it over again. She did not forget the Fawn either, but, going to the corner where he was, stroked his back, and then went silently out at the door. The nurse asked in the morning of the guards, if any one had passed into the castle during the night; but they answered, "No, we have seen nobody." For many nights afterwards she came constantly, and never spoke a word; and the nurse saw her always, but she would not trust herself to speak about it to any one.

When some time had passed away, the Queen one night began to speak, and said, –

"How fares my child, how fares my fawn?
Twice more will I come, but never again."

The nurse made no reply; but, when she had disappeared, went to the King, and told him all. The King exclaimed, "Oh, heavens! what does this mean? – the next night I will watch myself by the child." In the evening he went into the nursery, and about midnight the Queen appeared, and said, –

"How fares my child, how fares my fawn?
Once more I will come, but never again."

And she nursed the child, as she was used to do, and then disappeared. The King dared not speak; but he watched the following night, and this time she said, –

"How fares my child, how fares my fawn?
This time have I come, but never again."

At these words, the King could hold back no longer, but sprang up and said, "You can be no other than my dear wife!" Then she answered, "Yes, I am your dear wife;" and at that moment her life was restored by God's mercy, and she was again as beautiful and charming as ever. She told the King the fraud which the witch and her daughter had practised upon him, and he had them both tried and sentence pronounced against them. The daughter was taken into the forest, where the wild beasts tore her in pieces, but the old witch was led to the fire and miserably burnt. And as soon as she was reduced to ashes, the little Fawn was unbewitched, and received again his human form; and the Brother and Sister lived happily together to the end of their days.

HANSEL AND GRETHEL

Once upon a time there dwelt near a large wood a poor woodcutter, with his wife and two children by his former marriage, a little boy called Hansel, and a girl named Grethel. He had little enough to break or bite; and once, when there was a great famine in the land, he could not procure even his daily bread; and as he lay thinking in his bed one evening, rolling about for trouble, he sighed, and said to his wife, "What will become of us? How can we feed our children, when we have no more than we can eat ourselves?"

"Know, then, my husband," answered she, "we will lead them away, quite early in the morning, into the thickest part of the wood, and there make them a fire, and give them each a little piece of bread; then we will go to our work, and leave them alone, so they will not find the way home again, and we shall be freed from them." "No, wife," replied he, "that I can never do; how can you bring your heart to leave my children all alone in the wood; for the wild beasts will soon come and tear them to pieces?"

"Oh, you simpleton!" said she, "then we must all four die of hunger; you had better plane the coffins for us." But she left him no peace till he consented, saying, "Ah, but I shall regret the poor children."

The two children, however, had not gone to sleep for very hunger, and so they overheard what the stepmother said to their father. Grethel wept bitterly, and said to Hansel, "What will become of us?" "Be quiet, Grethel," said he; "do not cry – I will soon help you." And as soon as their parents had fallen asleep, he got up, put on his coat, and, unbarring the back door, slipped out. The moon shone brightly, and the white pebbles which lay before the door seemed like silver pieces, they glittered so brightly. Hansel stooped down, and put as many into his pocket as it would hold; and then going back, he said to Grethel, "Be comforted, dear sister, and sleep in peace; God will not forsake us." And so saying, he went to bed again.

The next morning, before the sun arose, the wife went and awoke the two children. "Get up, you lazy things; we are going into the forest to chop wood." Then she gave them each a piece of bread, saying, "There is something for your dinner; do not eat it before the time, for you will get nothing else." Grethel took the bread in her apron, for Hansel's pocket was full of pebbles; and so they all set out upon their way. When they had gone a little distance, Hansel stood still, and peeped back at the house; and this he repeated several times, till his father said, "Hansel, what are you peeping at, and why do you lag behind? Take care, and remember your legs."

"Ah, father," said Hansel, "I am looking at my white cat sitting upon the roof of the house, and trying to say good-bye." "You simpleton!" said the wife, "that is not a cat; it is only the sun shining on the white chimney." But in reality Hansel was not looking at a cat; but every time he stopped, he dropped a pebble out of his pocket upon the path.

When they came to the middle of the wood, the father told the children to collect wood, and he would make them a fire, so that they should not be cold. So Hansel and Grethel gathered together quite a little mountain of twigs. Then they set fire to them; and as the flame burnt up high, the wife said, "Now, you children, lie down near the fire, and rest yourselves, whilst we go into the forest and chop wood; when we are ready, I will come and call you."

Hansel and Grethel sat down by the fire, and when it was noon, each ate the piece of bread; and because they could hear the blows of an axe, they thought their father was near: but it was not an axe, but a branch which he had bound to a withered tree, so as to be blown to and fro by the wind. They waited so long, that at last their eyes closed from weariness, and they fell fast asleep. When they awoke, it was quite dark, and Grethel began to cry, "How shall we get out of the wood?" But Hansel tried to comfort her by saying, "Wait a little while till the moon rises, and then we will quickly find the way." The moon soon shone forth, and Hansel, taking his sister's hand, followed the pebbles, which glittered like new-coined silver pieces, and showed them the path. All night long they walked on, and as day broke they came to their father's house. They knocked at the door, and when the wife opened it, and saw Hansel and Grethel, she exclaimed, "You wicked children! why did you sleep so long in the wood? We thought you were never coming home again." But their father was very glad, for it had grieved his heart to leave them all alone.

Not long afterwards there was again great scarcity in every corner of the land; and one night the children overheard their mother saying to their father, "Everything is again consumed; we have only half a loaf left, and then the song is ended: the children must be sent away. We will take them deeper into the wood, so that they may not find the way out again; it is the only means of escape for us."

But her husband felt heavy at heart, and thought, "It were better to share the last crust with the children." His wife, however, would listen to nothing that he said, and scolded and reproached him without end.

He who says A must say B too; and he who consents the first time must also the second.

The children, however, had heard the conversation as they lay awake, and as soon as the old people went to sleep Hansel got up, intending to pick up some pebbles as before; but the wife had locked the door so that he could not get out. Nevertheless he comforted Grethel, saying, "Do not cry; sleep in quiet; the good God will not forsake us."

Early in the morning the stepmother came and pulled them out of bed, and gave them each a slice of bread, which was still smaller than the former piece. On the way, Hansel broke his in his pocket, and, stooping every now and then, dropped a crumb upon the path. "Hansel, why do you stop and look about?" said his father, "keep in the path." "I am looking at my little dove," answered Hansel, "nodding a good-bye to me." "Simpleton!" said the wife, "that is no dove, but only the sun shining on the chimney." But Hansel kept still dropping crumbs as he went along.

The mother led the children deep into the wood, where they had never been before, and there making an immense fire, she said to them. "Sit down here and rest, and when you feel tired you can sleep for a little while. We are going into the forest to hew wood, and in the evening, when we are ready, we will come and fetch you."

When noon came Grethel shared her bread with Hansel, who had strewn his on the path. Then they went to sleep; but the evening arrived and no one came to visit the poor children, and in the dark night they awoke, and Hansel comforted his sister by saying, "Only wait, Grethel, till the moon comes out, then we shall see the crumbs of bread which I have dropped, and they will show us the way home." The moon shone and they got up, but they could not see any crumbs, for the thousands of birds which had been flying in the woods and fields had picked them all up. Hansel kept saying to Grethel, "We will soon find the way;" but they did not, and they walked the whole night long and the next day, but still they did not come out of the wood; and they got so hungry, for they had nothing to eat but the berries which they found upon the bushes. Soon they got so tired that they could not drag themselves along, so they lay down under a tree and went to sleep.

It was now the third morning since they had left their father's house, and they still walked on; but they only got deeper and deeper into the wood, and Hansel saw that if help did not come very soon they would die of hunger. As soon as it was noon they saw a beautiful snow-white bird sitting upon a bough, which sang so sweetly that they stood still and listened to it. It soon left off, and spreading its wings flew off; and they followed it until it arrived at a cottage, upon the roof of which it perched; and when they went close up to it they saw that the cottage was made of bread and cakes, and the window-panes were of clear sugar.

"We will go in there," said Hansel, "and have a glorious feast. I will eat a piece of the roof, and you can eat the window. Will they not be sweet?" So Hansel reached up and broke a piece off the roof, in order to see how it tasted; while Grethel stepped up to the window and began to bite it. Then a sweet voice called out in the room, "Tip-tap, tip-tap, who raps at my door?" and the children answered, "The wind, the wind, the child of heaven;" and they went on eating without interruption. Hansel thought the roof tasted very nice, and so he tore off a great piece; while Grethel broke a large round pane out of the window, and sat down quite contentedly. Just then the door opened, and a very old woman, walking upon crutches, came out. Hansel and Grethel were so frightened that they let fall what they had in their hands; but the old woman, nodding her head, said, "Ah, you dear children, what has brought you here? Come in and stop with me, and no harm shall befall you;" and so saying she took them both by the hand, and led them into her cottage. A good meal of milk and pancakes, with sugar, apples, and nuts, was spread on the table, and in the back room were two nice little beds, covered with white, where Hansel and Grethel laid themselves down, and thought themselves in heaven. The old woman behaved very kindly to them, but in reality she was a wicked witch who waylaid children, and built the bread-house in order to entice them in; but as soon as they were in her power she killed them, cooked and ate them, and made a great festival of the day. Witches have red eyes, and cannot see very far, but they have a fine sense of smelling, like wild beasts, so that they know when children approach them. When Hansel and Grethel came near the witch's house she laughed wickedly, saying, "Here comes two who shall not escape me." And early in the morning, before they awoke, she went up to them, and saw how lovingly they lay sleeping, with their chubby red cheeks; and she mumbled to herself, "That will be a good bite." Then she took up Hansel with her rough hand, and shut him up in a little cage with a lattice-door; and although he screamed loudly it was of no use. Grethel came next, and shaking her till she awoke, she said, "Get up, you lazy thing, and fetch some water to cook something good for your brother who must remain in that stall and get fat; when he is fat enough I shall eat him." Grethel began to cry, but it was all useless, for the old witch made her do as she wished. So a nice meal was cooked for Hansel, but Grethel got nothing else but a crab's claw.

Every morning the old witch came to the cage and said, "Hansel, stretch out your finger that I may feel whether you are getting fat." But Hansel used to stretch out a bone, and the old woman, having very bad sight, thought it was his finger, and wondered very much that he did not get more fat. When four weeks had passed, and Hansel still kept quite lean, she lost all her patience, and would not wait any longer. "Grethel," she called out in a passion, "get some water quickly; be Hansel fat or lean, this morning I will kill and cook him." Oh, how the poor little sister grieved, as she was forced to fetch the water, and fast the tears ran down her cheeks! "Dear good God, help us now!" she exclaimed. "Had we only been eaten by the wild beasts in the wood, then we should have died together." But the old witch called out, "Leave off that noise; it will not help you a bit."

So early in the morning Grethel was forced to go out and fill the kettle, and make a fire. "First, we will bake, however," said the old woman; "I have already heated the oven and kneaded the dough;" and so saying, she pushed poor Grethel up to the oven, out of which the flames were burning fiercely. "Creep in," said the witch, "and see if it is hot enough, and then we will put in the bread;" but she intended when Grethel got in to shut up the oven and let her bake, so that she might eat her as well as Hansel. Grethel perceived what her thoughts were, and said, "I do not know how to do it; how shall I get in?" "You stupid goose," said she, "the opening is big enough. See, I could even get in myself!" and she got up, and put her head into the oven. Then Grethel gave her a push, so that she fell right in, and then shutting the iron door she bolted it. Oh! how horribly she howled; but Grethel ran away, and left the ungodly witch to burn to ashes.

Now she ran to Hansel, and, opening his door, called out, "Hansel, we are saved; the old witch is dead!" So he sprang out, like a bird out of his cage when the door is opened; and they were so glad that they fell upon each other's necks, and kissed each other over and over again. And now, as there was nothing to fear, they went into the witch's house, where in every corner were caskets full of pearls and precious stones. "These are better than pebbles," said Hansel, putting as many into his pocket as it would hold; while Grethel thought, "I will take some home too," and filled her apron full. "We must be off now," said Hansel, "and get out of this enchanted forest;" but when they had walked for two hours they came to a large piece of water. "We cannot get over," said Hansel; "I can see no bridge at all." "And there is no boat either," said Grethel, "but there swims a white duck, I will ask her to help us over;" and she sang,

Little Duck, good little Duck,
Grethel and Hansel, here we stand,
There is neither stile nor bridge,
Take us on your back to land."

So the Duck came to them, and Hansel sat himself on, and bade his sister to sit behind. "No," answered Grethel, "that will be too much for the Duck, she shall take us over one at a time." This the good little bird did, and when both were happily arrived on the other side, and had gone a little way, they came to a well-known wood, which they knew the better every step they went, and at last they perceived their father's house. Then they began to run, and, bursting into the house, they fell on their father's neck. He had not had one happy hour since he had left the children in the forest: and his wife was dead. Grethel shook her apron, and the pearls and precious stones rolled out upon the floor, and Hansel threw down one handful after the other out of his pocket. Then all their sorrows were ended, and they lived together in great happiness.

My tale is done. There runs a mouse; whoever catches her may make a great, great cap out of her fur.

Rapunzel.

RAPUNZEL

Once upon a time there lived a man and his wife, who much wished to have a child, but for a long time in vain. These people had a little window in the back part of their house, out of which one could see into a beautiful garden which was full of fine flowers and vegetables; but it was surrounded by a high wall, and no one dared to go in, because it belonged to a Witch, who possessed great power, and who was feared by the whole world. One day the woman stood at this window looking into the garden, and there she saw a bed which was filled with the most beautiful radishes, and which seemed so fresh and green that she felt quite glad, and a great desire seized her to eat of these radishes. This wish tormented her daily, and as she knew that she could not have them she fell ill, and looked very pale and miserable. This frightened her husband, who asked her, "What ails you, my dear wife?"

"Ah!" she replied, "if I cannot get any of those radishes to eat out of the garden behind the house I shall die!" The husband, loving her very much, thought, "Rather than let my wife die, I must fetch her some radishes, cost what they may." So, in the gloom of the evening, he climbed the wall of the Witch's garden, and, snatching a handful of radishes in great haste, brought them to his wife, who made herself a salad with them, which she relished extremely. However, they were so nice and so well-flavoured, that the next day after she felt the same desire for the third time, and could not get any rest, so that her husband was obliged to promise her some more. So, in the evening, he made himself ready, and began clambering up the wall; but, oh! how terribly frightened he was, for there he saw the old Witch, standing before him. "How dare you," – she began, looking at him with a frightful scowl, – "how dare you climb over into my garden to take away my radishes like a thief? Evil shall happen to you for this."

"Ah!" replied he, "let pardon be granted before justice; I have only done this from a great necessity; my wife saw your radishes from her window, and took such a fancy to them that she would have died if she had not eaten of them." Then the Witch ran after him in a passion, saying, "If she behave as you say, I will let you take away all the radishes you please, but I make one condition; you must give me the child which your wife will bring into the world. All shall go well with it, and I will care for it like a mother." In his anxiety the man consented, and when the child was born the Witch appeared at the same time, gave the child the name "Rapunzel," and took it away with her.

Rapunzel grew to be the most beautiful child under the sun, and when she was twelve years old the Witch shut her up in a tower, which stood in a forest, and had neither stairs nor door, and only one little window just at the top. When the Witch wished to enter, she stood beneath, and called out, –

"Rapunzel! Rapunzel!
Let down your hair."

For Rapunzel had long and beautiful hair, as fine as spun gold; and as soon as she heard the Witch's voice she unbound her tresses, opened the window, and then the hair fell down twenty ells, and the Witch mounted up by it.

After a couple of years had passed away it happened that the King's son was riding through the wood, and came by the tower. There he heard a song so beautiful that he stood still and listened. It was Rapunzel, who, to pass the time of her loneliness away, was exercising her sweet voice. The King's son wished to ascend to her, and looked for a door in the tower, but he could not find one. So he rode home, but the song had touched his heart so much that he went every day to the forest and listened to it; and as he thus stood one day behind a tree, he saw the Witch come up and heard her call out, –

"Rapunzel! Rapunzel!
Let down your hair."

Then Rapunzel let down her tresses, and the Witch mounted up. "Is that the ladder on which one must climb? Then I will try my luck too," said the Prince; and the following day, as he felt quite lonely, he went to the tower, and said, –

"Rapunzel! Rapunzel!
Let down your hair."

Then the tresses fell down, and he climbed up. Rapunzel was much frightened at first when a man came in, for she had never seen one before; but the King's son talked in a loving way to her, and told how his heart had been so moved by her singing that he had no peace until he had seen her himself. So Rapunzel lost her terror, and when he asked her if she would have him for a husband, and she saw that he was young and handsome, she thought, "Any one may have me rather than the old woman:" so, saying "Yes," she put her hand within his: "I will willingly go with you, but I know not how to descend. When you come, bring with you a skein of silk each time, out of which I will weave a ladder, and when it is ready I will come down by it, and you must take me upon your horse." Then they agreed that they should never meet till the evening, as the Witch came in the day time. The old woman remarked nothing about it, until one day Rapunzel innocently said, "Tell me, mother, how it happens you find it more difficult to come up to me than the young King's son, who is with me in a moment!"

"Oh, you wicked child!" exclaimed the Witch; "what do I hear? I thought I had separated you from all the world, and yet you have deceived me." And, seizing Rapunzel's beautiful hair in a fury, she gave her a couple of blows with her left hand, and, taking a pair of scissors in her right, snip, snap, she cut off all her beautiful tresses, and they fell upon the ground. Then she was so hard-hearted that she took the poor maiden into a great desert, and left her to die in great misery and grief.

But the same day when the old Witch had carried Rapunzel off, in the evening she made the tresses fast above the window-latch, and when the King's son came, and called out, –

"Rapunzel! Rapunzel!
Let down your hair."

she let them down. The Prince mounted; but when he got to the top he found, not his dear Rapunzel, but the Witch, who looked at him with furious and wicked eyes. "Aha!" she exclaimed, scornfully, "you would fetch your dear wife; but the beautiful bird sits no longer in her nest, singing; the cat has taken her away, and will now scratch out your eyes. To you Rapunzel is lost; you will never see her again."

The Prince lost his senses with grief at these words, and sprang out of the window of the tower in his bewilderment. His life he escaped with, but the thorns into which he fell put out his eyes. so he wandered blind, in the forest, eating nothing but roots and berries, and doing nothing but weep and lament for the loss of his dear wife. He wandered about thus, in great misery, for some years, and at last arrived at the desert where Rapunzel, with her twins, a boy and a girl which had been born, lived in great sorrow. Hearing a voice which he thought he knew he followed in its direction; and, as he approached, Rapunzel recognised him, and fell upon his neck and wept. Two of her tears moistened his eyes, and they became clear again, so that he could see as well as formerly.

Then he led her away to his kingdom, where he was received with great demonstrations of joy, and where they lived long, contented and happy.

What became of the old Witch no one ever knew.

The Valiant Little Tailor

One summer's morning a Tailor was sitting on his bench by the window in very good spirits, sewing away with all his might, and presently up the street came a peasant woman, crying, "Good preserves for sale! Good preserves for sale!" This cry sounded nice in the Tailor's ears, and, sticking his diminutive head out of the window, he called out, "Here, my good woman, just bring your wares here!" The woman mounted the three steps up to the Tailor's house with her heavy basket, and began to unpack all the pots together before him. He looked at them all, held them up to the light, put his nose to them, and at last said, "These preserves appear to me to be very nice, so you may weigh me out four half-ounces, my good woman; I don't mind even if you make it a quarter of a pound." The woman, who expected to have met with a good customer, gave him what he wished, and went away grumbling, very much dissatisfied.

"Now!" exclaimed the Tailor, "Heaven will send me a blessing on this preserve, and give me fresh strength and vigour;" and, taking the bread out of the cupboard, he cut himself a slice the size of the whole loaf, and spread the preserve upon it. "That will taste by no means badly," said he; "but, before I have a bite, I will just get this waistcoat finished." So he laid the bread down near him and stitched away, making larger and larger stitches every time for joy. Meanwhile the smell of the preserve mounted to the ceiling, where flies were sitting in great numbers, and enticed them down, so that soon a regular swarm of them had settled on the bread. "Holloa! who invited you?" exclaimed the Tailor, hunting away the unbidden guests; but the flies, not understanding his language, would not be driven off, and came again in greater numbers than before. This put the little man in a boiling passion, and, snatching up in his rage a bag of cloth, he brought it down with an unmerciful swoop upon them. When he raised it again he counted no less than seven lying dead before him with outstretched legs. "What a fellow you are!" said he to himself, wondering at his own bravery. "The whole town shall know of this." In great haste he cut himself out a band, hemmed it, and then put on it in large characters, "SEVEN AT ONE BLOW!" "Ah," said he, "not one city alone, the whole world shall know it!" and his heart fluttered with joy, like a lambkin's tail.

The little Tailor bound the belt round his body, and prepared to travel forth into the wide world, thinking the workshop too small for his valiant deeds. Before he set out, however, he looked round his house to see if there was anything he could take with him; but he found only an old cheese, which he pocketed, and remarking a bird before the door which was entangled in the bushes, he caught it, and put that in his pocket also. Directly after he set out bravely on his travels; and, as he was light and active, he felt no weariness. His road led him up a hill, and when he reached the highest point of it he found a great Giant sitting there, who was looking about him very composedly.

The little Tailor, however, went boldly up, and said, "Good day, comrade; in faith you sit there and see the whole world stretched below you. I am also on my road thither to try my luck. Have you a mind to go with me?"

The Giant looked contemptuously at the little Tailor, and said, "You vagabond! you miserable fellow!"

"That may be," replied the Tailor; "but here you may read what sort of a man I am;" and, unbuttoning his coat, he showed the Giant his belt. The Giant read, "Seven at one blow;" and thinking they were men whom the Tailor had slain, he conceived a little respect for him. Still he wished to prove him first; so taking up a stone, he squeezed it in his hand, so that water dropped out of it. "Do that after me," said he to the other, "if you have any strength."

"If it be nothing worse than that," said the Tailor, "that's play to me." And, diving into his pocket, he brought out the cheese, and squeezed it till the whey ran out of it, and said, "Now, I think, that's a little better."

The Giant did not know what to say, and could not believe it of the little man; so, taking up another stone, he threw it so high that one could scarcely see it with the eye, saying, "There, you mannikin, do that after me."

"Well done," said the Tailor; "but your stone must fall down again to the ground. I will throw one up which shall not come back:" and, dipping into his pocket, he took out the bird and threw it into the air. The bird, rejoicing in its freedom, flew straight up, and then far away, and did not return. "How does that little affair please you, comrade?" asked the Tailor.

"You can throw well, certainly," replied the Giant; "now let us see if you are in trim to carry something out of the common." So saying he led him to a huge oak-tree, which lay upon the ground, and said, "If you are strong enough, just help me to carry this tree out of the forest."

"With all my heart," replied the Tailor; "do you take the trunk upon your shoulder, and I will raise the boughs and branches, which are the heaviest, and carry them."

The Giant took the trunk upon his shoulder, but the Tailor placed himself on the branch, so that the Giant, who was not able to look round, was forced to carry the whole tree and the Tailor besides. He, being behind, was very merry, and chuckled at the trick, and presently began to whistle the song, "There rode three tailors out at the gate," as if the carrying of trees were child's play. The Giant, after he had staggered along a short distance with his heavy burden, could go no further, and shouted out, "Do you hear? I must let the tree fall." The Tailor, springing down, quickly embraced the tree with both arms, as if he had been carrying it, and said to the Giant, "Are you such a big fellow, and yet cannot you carry this tree by yourself?"

Then they journeyed on further, and as they came to a cherry-tree, the Giant seized the top of the tree where the ripest fruits hung, and, bending it down, gave it to the Tailor to hold, bidding him eat. But the Tailor was much too weak to hold the tree down, and when the Giant let go the tree flew up into the air, and the Tailor was carried with it. He came down on the other side, however, without injury, and the Giant said, "What does that mean? Have you not strength enough to hold that twig?" "My strength did not fail me," replied the Tailor; "do you suppose that that was any hard thing for one who has killed seven at one blow? I have sprung over the tree because the hunters were shooting below there in the thicket. Spring after me if you can." The Giant made the attempt, but could not clear the tree, and stuck fast in the branches; so that in this affair, too, the Tailor was the better man.

After this the Giant said, "Since you are such a valiant fellow, come with me to our house, and stop a night with us." The Tailor consented, and followed him; and when they entered the cave, there sat by the fire two other Giants, each having a roast sheep in his hand, of which he was eating. The Tailor sat down, thinking, "Ah, this is much more like the world than is my workshop." And soon the Giant showed him a bed where he might lie down and go to sleep. The bed, however, was too big for him, so he slipt out of it, and crept into a corner. When midnight came, and the Giant thought the Tailor would be in a deep sleep, he got up, and, taking a great iron bar, beat the bed right through at one stroke, and supposed he had thereby given the Tailor his death-blow. At the earliest dawn of morning the Giants went forth into the forest, quite forgetting the Tailor, when presently up he came, quite merry, and showed himself before them. The Giants were terrified, and, fearing he would kill them all, they ran away in great haste.

The Tailor journeyed on, always following his nose, and after he had wandered some long distance, he came into the courtyard of a royal palace; and as he felt rather tired he laid himself down on the grass and went to sleep. Whilst he lay there the people came and viewed him on all sides, and read upon his belt, "Seven at one blow." "Ah," said they, "what does this great warrior here in time of peace? This must be some mighty hero." So they went and told the King, thinking that, should war break out, here was an important and useful man, whom one ought not to part with at any price. The King took counsel, and sent one of his courtiers to the Tailor to ask for his fighting services, if he should be awake. The messenger stopped at the sleeper's side, and waited till he stretched out his limbs and opened his eyes, and then he laid before him his message. "Solely on that account did I come here," was the reply; "I am quite ready to enter into the King's service." Then he was conducted away with great honour, and a fine house was appointed him to dwell in.

The courtiers, however, became jealous of the Tailor, and wished he were a thousand miles away. "What will happen?" said they to one another. "If we go to battle with him, when he strikes out seven will fall at one blow, and nothing will be left for us to do." In their rage they came to the resolution to resign, and they went all together to the King, and asked his permission, saying, "We are not prepared to keep company with a man who kills seven at one blow." The King was grieved to lose all his faithful servants for the sake of one, and wished that he had never seen the Tailor, and would willingly have now been rid of him. He dared not, however, dismiss him, because he feared the Tailor would kill him and all his subjects, and place himself upon the throne. For a long time he deliberated, till at last he came to a decision; and, sending for the Tailor, he told him that, seeing he was so great a hero, he wished to ask a favour of him. "In a certain forest in my kingdom," said the King, "there live two Giants, who, by murder, rapine, fire, and robbery, have committed great havoc, and no one dares to approach them without perilling his own life. If you overcome and kill both these Giants, I will give you my only daughter in marriage, and the half of my kingdom for a dowry: a hundred knights shall accompany you, too, in order to render you assistance."

"Ah, that is something for such a man as I," thought the Tailor to himself; "a beautiful Princess and half a kingdom are not offered to one every day." "Oh, yes," he replied, "I will soon manage these two Giants, and a hundred horsemen are not necessary for that purpose; he who kills seven at one blow need not fear two."

Thus talking the little Tailor set out, followed by the hundred knights, to whom he said, as soon as they came to the borders of the forest, "Do you stay here; I would rather meet these Giants alone." Then he sprang off into the forest, peering about him right and left; and after a while he saw the two Giants lying asleep under a tree, snoring so loudly, that the branches above them shook violently. The Tailor, full of courage, filled both his pockets with stones and clambered up the tree. When he got to the middle of it he crept along a bough, so that he sat just above the sleepers, and then he let fall one stone after another upon the breast of one of them. For some time the Giant did not stir, until, at last awaking, he pushed his companion, and said, "Why are you beating me?"

"You are dreaming," he replied; "I never hit you." They laid themselves down again to sleep, and presently the Tailor threw a stone down upon the other. "What is that?" he exclaimed. "What are you knocking me for?"

"I did not touch you; you must dream," replied the first. So they wrangled for a few minutes; but, being both very tired with their day's work, they soon fell asleep again. Then the Tailor began his sport again, and, picking out the biggest stone, threw it with all his force upon the breast of the first Giant. "That is too bad!" he exclaimed; and, springing up like a madman, he fell upon his companion, who, feeling himself equally aggrieved, they set to in such good earnest, that they rooted up trees and beat one another about until they both fell dead upon the ground. Now the Tailor jumped down, saying, "What a piece of luck they did not uproot the tree on which I sat, or else I must have jumped on another like a squirrel, for I am not given to flying." Then he drew his sword, and cutting a deep wound in the breast of each, he went to the horsemen and said, "The deed is done; I have given each his death-stroke; but it was a hard job, for in their necessity they uprooted trees to defend themselves with; still, all that is of no use when such an one as I come, who killed seven at one stroke."

"Are you not wounded, then?" asked they.

"That is not to be expected: they have not touched a hair of my head," replied the little man. The knights could scarcely believe him, till, riding away into the forest, they found the Giants lying in their blood and the uprooted trees around them.

Now the Tailor demanded his promised reward of the King; but he repented of his promise, and began to think of some new scheme to get rid of the hero. "Before you receive my daughter and the half of my kingdom," said he to him, "you must perform one other heroic deed. In the forest there runs wild a unicorn, which commits great havoc, and which you must first of all catch."

"I fear still less for a unicorn than I do for two Giants! Seven at one blow! that is my motto," said the Tailor. Then he took with him a rope and an axe and went away to the forest, bidding those who were ordered to accompany him to wait on the outskirts. He had not to search long, for presently the unicorn came near and prepared to rush at him as if it would pierce him on the spot. "Softly, softly!" he exclaimed; "that is not done so easily;" and, waiting till the animal was close upon him, he sprang nimbly behind a tree. The unicorn, rushing with all its force against the tree, fixed its horn so fast in the trunk, that it could not draw it out again, and so it was made prisoner. "Now I have got my bird," said the Tailor; and, coming from behind the tree, he first bound the rope around its neck, and then, cutting the horn out of the tree with his axe, he put all in order, and, leading the animal, brought it before the King.

The King, however, would not yet deliver up the promised reward, and made a third request, that, before the wedding, the Tailor should catch a wild boar which did much injury, and he should have the huntsmen to help him. "With pleasure," was the reply; "it is mere child's play." The huntsmen, however, he left behind, to their entire content, for this wild boar had already so often hunted them, that they had no pleasure in hunting it. As soon as the boar perceived the Tailor, it ran at him with gaping mouth and glistening teeth, and tried to throw him on the ground; but our flying hero sprang into a little chapel which was near, and out again at a window on the other side in a trice. The boar ran after him, but he, skipping round, shut the door behind it, and there the raging beast was caught, for it was much too unwieldy and heavy to jump out of the window. The Tailor now called the huntsmen up, that they might see his prisoner with their own eyes; but our hero presented himself before the King, who was compelled now, whether he would or no, to keep his promise, and surrender his daughter and the half of his kingdom.

Had he known that it was no warrior, but only a Tailor, who stood before him, it would have gone to his heart still more!

So the wedding was celebrated with great splendour, though with little rejoicing, and out of a Tailor was made a King.

Some little while afterwards the young Queen heard her husband talking in his sleep, and saying, "Boy, make me a waistcoat, and stitch up these trowsers, or I will lay the yard-measure over your ears!" Then she remarked of what condition her lord was, and complained in the morning to her father, and begged he would deliver her from her husband, who was nothing else than a tailor. The King comforted her by saying, "This night leave your chamber door open; my servants shall stand without, and when he is asleep they shall enter, bind him, and bear him away to a ship, which shall carry him forth into the wide world." The wife was contented with his proposal; but the King's armour-bearer, who had overheard all, went to the young King and disclosed the whole plot. "I will shoot a bolt upon this affair," said the brave Tailor. In the evening at their usual time they went to bed, and when his wife believed he slept she got up, opened the door, and laid herself down again. The Tailor, however, only feigned to be asleep, and began to exclaim in a loud voice, "Boy, make me this waistcoat, and stitch up these trowsers, or I will beat the yard-measure about your ears! Seven have I killed with one blow, two Giants have I slain, a unicorn have I led captive, and a wild boar have I caught, and shall I be afraid of those who stand without my chamber?" When the men heard these words spoken by the Tailor, a great fear overcame them, and they ran away as if the wild huntsmen were behind them; neither afterwards durst any man venture to oppose him. Thus became the Tailor a King, and so he remained the rest of his days.

Little Red-Cap

Once upon a time there lived a sweet little girl, who was beloved by every one who saw her; but her grandmother was so excessively fond of her that she never knew when she had thought and done enough for her.

One day the grandmother presented the little girl with a red velvet cap; and as it fitted her very well, she would never wear anything else; and so she was called Little Red-Cap. One day her mother said to her, "Come, Red-Cap, here is a piece of nice meat, and a bottle of wine: take these to your grandmother; she is ill and weak, and will relish them. Make haste before she gets up; go quietly and carefully; and do not run, lest you should fall and break the bottle, and then your grandmother will get nothing. When you go into her room, do not forget to say 'Good-morning;' and do not look about in all the corners." "I will do everything as you wish," replied Red-Cap, taking her mother's hand.

The grandmother dwelt far away in the wood, half an hour's walk from the village, and as Little Red-Cap entered among the trees, she met a wolf; but she did not know what a malicious beast it was, and so she was not at all afraid. "Good day, Little Red-Cap," he said.

"Many thanks, Wolf," said she.

"Whither away so early, Little Red-Cap?"

"To my grandmother's," she replied.

"What are you carrying under your apron?"

"Meat and wine," she answered. "Yesterday we baked the meat, that grandmother, who is ill and weak, might have something nice and strengthening."

"Where does your grandmother live?" asked the Wolf.

"A good quarter of an hour's walk further in the forest. The cottage stands under three great oak-trees; near it are some nut bushes, by which you will easily know it."

But the Wolf thought to himself, "She is a nice tender thing, and will taste better than the old woman: I must act craftily, that I may snap them both up."

Presently he came up again to Little Red-Cap, and said, "Just look at the beautiful flowers which grow around you; why do you not look about you? I believe you don't hear how beautifully the birds sing. You walk on as if you were going to school; see how merry everything is around you in the forest."

So Little Red-Cap opened her eyes; and when she saw how the sunbeams glanced and danced through the trees, and what splendid flowers were blooming in her path, she thought, "If I take my grandmother a fresh nosegay she will be very pleased; and it is so very early that I can, even then, get there in good time;" and running into the forest she looked about for flowers. But when she had once begun she did not know how to leave off, and kept going deeper and deeper among the trees in search of some more beautiful flower. The Wolf, however, ran straight to the house of the old grandmother, and knocked at the door.

"Who's there?" asked the old lady.

"Only Little Red-Cap, bringing you some meat and wine: please open the door," replied the Wolf.

"Lift up the latch," cried the grandmother; "I am too weak to get up."

So the Wolf lifted the latch, and the door flew open; and jumping without a word on the bed, he gobbled up the poor old lady. Then he put on her clothes, and tied her cap over his head; got into the bed, and drew the blankets over him. All this time Red-Cap was still gathering flowers; and when she had plucked as many as she could carry, she remembered her grandmother, and made haste to the cottage. She wondered very much to see the door wide open; and when she got into the room, she began to feel very ill, and exclaimed, "How sad I feel! I wish I had not come to-day." Then she said, "Good morning," but received no answer; so she went up to the bed, and drew back the curtains, and there lay her grandmother, as she thought, with the cap drawn half over her eyes, looking very fierce.

"Oh, grandmother, what great ears you have!"

"The better to hear with," was the reply.

"And what great eyes you have!"

"The better to see with."

"And what great hands you have!"

"The better to touch you with."

"But, grandmother, what great teeth you have!"

"The better to eat you with;" and scarcely were the words out of his mouth, when the Wolf made a spring out of bed, and swallowed up poor Little Red-Cap.

As soon as the Wolf had thus satisfied his appetite, he laid himself down again in the bed, and began to snore very loudly. A huntsman passing by overheard him, and thought, "How oddly the old woman snores! I must see if she wants anything."

So he stepped into the cottage; and when he came to the bed, he saw the Wolf lying in it. "What! do I find you here, you old sinner? I have long sought you," exclaimed he; and taking aim with his gun, he shot the old Wolf dead.

Some folks say that the last story is not the true one, but that one day, when Red-Cap was taking some baked meats to her grandmother's, a Wolf met her, and wanted to mislead her; but she went straight on, and told her grandmother that she had met a Wolf, who wished her good-day; but he looked so wickedly out of his great eyes, as if he would have eaten her had she not been on the highroad.

So the grandmother said, "Let us shut the door, that he may not enter."

Soon afterwards came the Wolf, who knocked, and exclaimed, "I am Red-Cap, grandmother; I bring you some roast meat." But they kept quite still, and did not open the door; so the Wolf, creeping several times round the house, at last jumped on the roof, intending to wait till Red-Cap went home in the evening, and then to sneak after her and devour her in the darkness. The old woman, however, saw all that the rascal intended; and as there stood before the door a great stone trough, she said to Little Red-Cap, "Take this pail, child: yesterday I boiled some sausages in this water, so pour it into that stone trough." Red-Cap poured many times, until the huge trough was quite full. Then the Wolf sniffed the smell of sausages, and smacked his lips, and wished very much to taste; and at last he stretched his neck too far over, so that he lost his balance, and slipped quite off the roof, right into the great trough beneath, wherein he was drowned; and Little Red-Cap ran home in high glee, but no one sorrowed for Mr. Wolf!

Old Mother Frost

There was once a widow who had two daughters, one of whom was beautiful and industrious, and the other ugly and lazy. She behaved most kindly, however, to the ugly one, because she was her own daughter; and made the other do all the hard work, and live like a kitchen maid. The poor maiden was forced out daily on the highroad, and had to sit by a well and spin so much that the blood ran from her fingers. Once it happened that her spindle became quite covered with blood, so, kneeling down by the well, she tried to wash it off, but, unhappily, it fell out of her hands into the water. She ran crying to her stepmother, and told her misfortune: but she scolded her terribly, and behaved most cruelly, and at last said, "Since you have let your spindle fall in, you must yourself fetch it out again!" Then the maiden went back to the well, not knowing what to do, and, in her distress of mind, she jumped into the well to fetch the spindle out. As she fell she lost all consciousness, and when she came to herself again she found herself in a beautiful meadow, where the sun was shining, and many thousands of flowers blooming around her. She got up and walked along till she came to a baker's, where the oven was full of bread, which cried out, "Draw me, draw me, or I shall be burnt. I have been baked long enough." So she went up, and, taking the bread-peel, drew out one loaf after the other. Then she walked on further, and came to an apple tree, whose fruit hung very thick, and which exclaimed, "Shake us, shake us; we apples are all ripe!" So she shook the tree till the apples fell down like rain, and, when none were left on, she gathered them all together in a heap, and went further. At last she came to a cottage, out of which an old woman was peeping, who had such very large teeth that the maiden was frightened and ran away. The old woman, however, called her back, saying, "What are you afraid of, my child? Stop with me: if you will put all things in order in my house, then shall all go well with you; only you must take care that you make my bed well, and shake it tremendously, so that the feathers fly; then it snows upon earth. I am 'Old Mother Frost.'" As the old woman spoke so kindly, the maiden took courage, and consented to engage in her service. Now, everything made her very contented, and she always shook the bed so industriously that the feathers blew down like flakes of snow; therefore her life was a happy one, and there were no evil words; and she had roast and baked meat every day.

For some time she remained with the old woman; but, all at once, she became very sad, and did not herself know what was the matter. At last she found she was home-sick; and, although she fared a thousand times better than when she was at home, still she longed to go. So she told her mistress, "I wish to go home, and if it does not go so well with me below as up here, I must return." The mistress replied, "It appeared to me that you wanted to go home, and, since you have served me so truly, I will fetch you up again myself." So saying, she took her by the hand and led her before a great door, which she undid; and, when the maiden was just beneath it, a great shower of gold fell, and a great deal stuck to her, so that she was covered over and over with gold. "That you must have for your industry," said the old woman, giving her the spindle which had fallen into the well. Thereupon the door was closed, and the maiden found herself upon the earth, not far from her mother's house; and, as she came into the court, the cock sat upon the house, and called, –

"Cock-a-doodle-doo!
Our golden maid's come home again."

Then she went in to her mother, and, because she was so covered with gold, she was well received.

The maiden related all that had happened; and, when the mother heard how she had come by these great riches, she wished her ugly, lazy daughter to try her luck. So she was forced to sit down by the well and spin; and, in order that her spindle might become bloody, she pricked her finger by running a thorn into it; and then, throwing the spindle into the well, she jumped in after it. Then, like the other, she came upon the beautiful meadow, and travelled on the same path. When she arrived at the baker's, the bread called out, "Draw me, draw me out, or I shall be burnt. I have been baked long enough." But she answered, "I have no wish to make myself dirty about you," and so went on. Soon she came to the apple tree, which called out, "Shake me, shake me; my apples are all quite ripe." But she answered, "You do well to come to me; perhaps one will fall on my head;" and so she went on further. When she came to "Old Mother Frost's" house she was not afraid of the teeth, for she had been warned; and so she engaged herself to her. The first day she set to work in earnest, was very industrious, and obeyed her mistress in all she said to her, for she thought about the gold which she would present to her. On the second day however, she began to idle; on the third, still more so; and then she would not get up of a morning. She did not make the beds, either, as she ought, and the feathers did not fly. So the old woman got tired, and dismissed her from her service, which pleased the lazy one very well, for she thought, "Now the gold-shower will come." Her mistress led her to the door; but, when she was beneath it, instead of gold, a tubful of pitch was poured down upon her. "That is the reward of your service," said "Old Mother Frost," and shut the door to. Then came Lazy-bones home, but she was quite covered with pitch; and the cock upon the house when he saw her, cried –

"Cock-a-doodle doo!
Our dirty maid's come home again."

But the pitch stuck to her, and, as long as she lived, would never come off again.

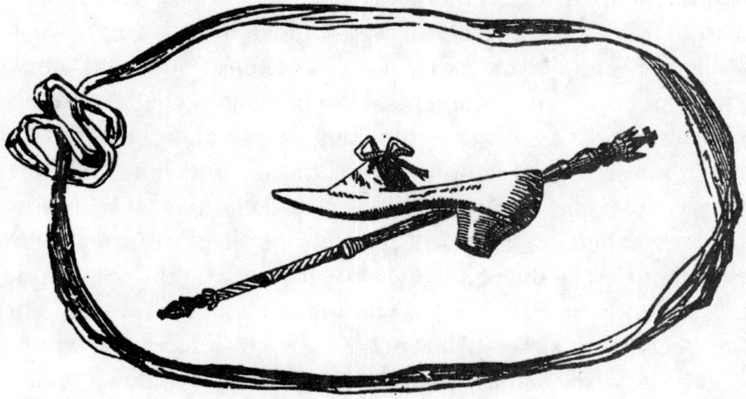

CINDERELLA

Once upon a time the wife of a certain rich man fell very ill, and as she felt her end drawing nigh she called her only daughter to her bedside, and said, "My dear child, be pious and good, and then the good God will always protect you, and I will look down upon you from heaven and think of you." Soon afterwards she closed her eyes and died. Every day the maiden went to her mother's grave and wept over it, and she continued to be good and pious; but when the winter came, the snow made a white covering over the grave, and in the spring-time, when the sun had withdrawn this covering, the father took to himself another wife.

The wife brought home with her two daughters, who were beautiful and fair in the face, but treacherous and wicked at heart. Then an unfortunate era began in the poor step-child's life. "Shall the stupid goose sit in the parlour with us?" said the two daughters. "They who would eat bread must earn it; out with the kitchen-maid!" So they took off her fine clothes, and put upon her an old grey cloak, and gave her wooden shoes for her feet. "See how the once proud princess is decked out now," said they, and they led her mockingly into the kitchen. Then she was obliged to work hard from morning to night, and to go out early to fetch water, to make the fire, and cook and scour. The sisters treated her besides with every possible insult, derided her, and shook the peas and beans into the ashes, so that she had to pick them out again. At night, when she was tired, she had no bed to lie on, but was forced to sit in the ashes on the hearth; and because she looked dirty through this, they named her CINDERELLA.

One day it happened that the father wanted to go to the fair, so he asked his two daughters what he should bring them. "Some beautiful dresses," said one; "Pearls and precious stones," replied the other, "But you, Cinderella," said he, "what will you have?" "The first bough, father, that knocks against your hat on your way homewards, break it off for me," she replied. So he bought the fine dresses, and the pearls and precious stones, for his two step-daughters; and on his return, as he rode through a green thicket, a hazel-bough touched his hat, which he broke off and took with him. As soon as he got home, he gave his step-daughters what they had wished for, and to Cinderella he gave the hazel-branch. She thanked him very much, and going to her mother's grave she planted the branch on it, and wept so long that her tears fell and watered it, so that it grew and became a beautiful tree. Thrice a-day Cinderella went beneath it to weep and pray; and each time a little white Bird flew on the tree, and if she wished aloud, then the little Bird threw down to her whatever she wished for.

After a time it fell out that the King appointed a festival, which was to last three days, and to which all the beautiful maidens in the country were invited, from whom his son was to choose a bride. When the two step-daughters heard that they might also appear, they were very glad, and calling Cinderella, they said, "Comb our hair, brush our shoes, and fasten our buckles, for we are going to the festival at the King's palace." Cinderella obeyed, crying, because she wished to go with them to the dance; so she asked her stepmother whether she would allow her.

"You, Cinderella!" said she; "you are covered with dust and dirt – will you go to the festival? You have no clothes or shoes, and how can you dance?" But, as she urged her request, the mother said at last, "I have now shaken into the ashes a tubful of beans; if you have picked them up again in two hours, you shall go."

Then the maiden left the room, and went out at the back-door into the garden, and called out, "You tame pigeons, and doves, and all you birds of heaven, come and help me to gather the good beans into the tub, and the bad ones you may eat." Presently, in at the kitchen-window came two white pigeons, and after them the doves, and soon all the birds under heaven flew chirping in down upon the ashes. They then began, pick, pick, pick, and gathered all the good seeds into the tub; and scarcely an hour had passed when all was completed, and the birds flew away again. Then the maiden took the tub to the stepmother, rejoicing at the thought that she might now go to the festival; but the stepmother said, "No Cinderella, you have no clothes, and cannot dance; you will only be laughed at." As she began to cry, the stepmother said, "If you can pick up quite clean two tubs of beans which I throw amongst the ashes in one hour, you shall accompany them;" and she thought to herself, "She will never manage it." As soon as the two tubs had been shot into the

The Prince took Cinderella upon his horse, and the two little white doves sang. (Cinderella.)

Just as he was about to raise his axe, he perceived a pack of wolves, who howled dreadfully as they came nearer. (Misfortune.)

ashes, Cinderella went out at the back door into the garden, and called out as before, "You tame pigeons, and doves, and all you birds under heaven, come and help me to gather the good ones into the tubs, and the bad ones you may eat." Presently, in at the kitchen-window came two white pigeons, and soon after them the doves, and soon all the birds under heaven flew chirping in down upon the ashes. They then began, pick, pick, pick, and gathered all the seeds into the tub; and scarcely had half-an-hour passed before all was picked up, and off they flew again. The maiden now took the tubs to the stepmother, rejoicing at the thought that she could go to the festival. But the mother said, "It does not help you a bit; you cannot go with us, for you have no clothes, and cannot dance; we should be ashamed of you." Thereupon she turned her back upon the maiden, and hastened away with her two proud daughters.

As there was no one at home, Cinderella went to her mother's grave, under the hazel-tree, and said, –

"Rustle and shake yourself, dear tree,
And silver and gold throw down to me."

Then the Bird threw down a dress of gold and silver, and silken slippers ornamented with silver. These Cinderella put on in great haste, and then she went to the ball. Her sisters and stepmother did not know her at all, and took her for some foreign princess, as she looked so beautiful in her golden dress; for of Cinderella they thought not but that she was sitting at home picking the beans out of the ashes. Presently the Prince came up to her, and, taking her by the hand, led her to the dance. He would not dance with any one else, and even would not let go her hand; so that when any one else asked her to dance, he said, "She is my partner." They danced till evening, when she wished to go home; but the Prince said, "I will go with you, and see you safe," for he wanted to see to whom the maiden belonged. She flew away from him, however, and sprang into the pigeon-house; so the Prince waited till the father came, whom he told that the strange maiden had run into the pigeon-house. Then the stepmother thought, "Could it be Cinderella?" And they brought an axe wherewith the Prince might cut open the door, but no one was found within. And when they came into the house, there lay Cinderella in her dirty clothes among the ashes, and an oil-lamp was burning in the chimney; for she had jumped quickly out on the other side of the pigeon-house, and had run to the hazel-tree, where she had taken off her fine clothes, and laid them on the grave, and the Bird had taken them again, and afterwards she had put on her little grey cloak, and seated herself among the ashes in the kitchen.

The next day, when the festival was renewed, and her stepmother and her sisters had set out again, Cinderella went to the hazel-tree and sang as before: –

"Rustle and shake yourself, dear tree,
And silver and gold throw down to me."

Then the Bird threw down a much more splendid dress than the former, and when the maiden appeared at the ball every one was astonished at her beauty. The Prince, however, who had waited till she came, took her hand, and would dance with no one else; and if others came and asked, he replied as before, "She is my partner." As soon as evening came she wished to depart, and the Prince followed her, wanting to see into whose house she went; but she sprang away from him, and ran into the garden behind the house. Therein stood a fine large tree, on which hung the most beautiful pears, and the boughs rustled as though a squirrel was among them; but the Prince could not see whence the noise proceeded. He waited, however, till the father came, and told him, "The strange maiden has escaped from me, and I think she has climbed up into this tree." The father thought to himself, "Can it be Cinderella?" and taking an axe he chopped down the tree, but there was no one on it. When they went into the kitchen, there lay Cinderella among the ashes, as before, for she had sprung down on the other side of the tree, and, having taken her beautiful clothes again to the Bird upon the hazel-tree, she had put on once more her old grey cloak.

The third day, when her stepmother and her sisters had set out, Cinderella went again to her mother's grave, and said, –

"Rustle and shake yourself, dear tree,
And silver and gold throw down to me."

Then the Bird threw down to her a dress which was more splendid and glittering than she had ever had before, and the slippers were of pure gold. When she arrived at the ball they knew not what to say for wonderment, and the Prince danced with her alone as at first, and replied to every one who asked her hand, "She is my partner." As soon as evening came she wished to go, and as the Prince followed her she ran away so quickly that he could not overtake her. But he had contrived a stratagem, and spread the whole way with pitch, so that it happened as the maiden ran that her left slipper came off. The Prince took it up, and saw it was small and graceful, and of pure gold; so the following morning he went with it to the father, and said, "My bride shall be no other than she whose foot this golden slipper fits." The two sisters were glad of this, for they had beautiful feet, and the elder went with it to her chamber to try it on, while her mother stood by. She could not, however, get her great toe into it, and the shoe was much too small; but the mother, reaching a knife, said, "Cut off your toe, for if you are queen, you need not go any longer on foot." The maiden cut it off, and squeezed her foot into the shoe, and, concealing the pain she felt, went down to the Prince. Then he placed her as his bride upon his horse, and rode off; and as they passed by the grave, there sat two little doves upon the hazel-tree, singing, –

"Backwards peep, backwards peep,
There's blood upon the shoe;
The shoe's too small, and she behind
Is not the bride for you."

Then the Prince looked behind, and saw the blood flowing; so he turned his horse back, and took the false bride home again, saying, she was not the right one. Then the other sister must needs fit on the shoe, so she went to the chamber and got her toes nicely into the shoe, but the heel was too large. The mother, reaching a knife, said, "Cut a piece off your heel, for when you become queen you need not go any longer on foot." She cut a piece off her heel, squeezed her foot into the shoe, and, concealing the pain she felt, went down to the Prince. Then he put her upon his horse as his bride, and rode off; and as they passed the hazel-tree, there sat two little doves, who sang, –

"Backwards peep, backwards peep,
There's blood upon the shoe;
The shoe's too small, and she behind
Is not the bride for you."

Then he looked behind, and saw the blood trickling from her shoe, and that the stocking was dyed quite red; so he turned his horse back, and took the false bride home again, saying, "Neither is this one the right maiden; have you no other daughter?" "No," replied the father, "except little Cinderella, daughter of my deceased wife, who cannot possibly be the bride." The Prince asked that she might be fetched; but the stepmother said, "Oh, no! she is much too dirty; I dare not let her be seen." But the Prince would have his way; so Cinderella was called, and she, first washing her hands and face, went in and curtseyed to the Prince, who gave her the golden shoe. Cinderella sat down on a stool, and taking off her heavy wooden shoes, put on the slipper, which fitted her to a shade; and as she stood up, the Prince looked in her face, and recognising the beautiful maiden with whom he had danced, exclaimed, "This is my true bride." The stepmother and the two sisters were amazed and white with rage, but the Prince took Cinderella upon his horse, and rode away; and as they came up to the hazel-tree the two little white doves sang, –

"Backwards peep, backwards peep,
There's no blood on the shoe;
It fits so nice, and she behind
Is the true bride for you."

And as they finished they flew down and lighted upon Cinderella's shoulders, and there they remained; and the wedding was celebrated with great festivities, and the two sisters were smitten with blindness as a punishment for their wickedness.

The Riddle

Once upon a time there was a King's son, who had a mind to see the world; so he set forth, and took no one with him but a faithful servant. One day he came into a great forest, and when evening drew on he could find no shelter, and did not know where to pass the night. Just then he perceived a maiden who was going towards a little cottage, and as he approached he saw that she was young and beautiful, so he asked her whether he and his servant could find a welcome in the cottage for the night. "Yes, certainly," replied the maiden in a sorrowful voice, "you can; but I advise you not to enter." "Why not?" asked the Prince. The maiden sighed, and answered, "My stepmother practises wicked arts; she acts not hospitably to strangers." He perceived now that he was come to a Witch's cottage; but because it was very dark, and he could go no further, he went in, for he was not at all afraid. The old woman was sitting in an arm-chair by the fire, and looked at the strangers out of her red eyes. "Good evening," she muttered, appearing very friendly; "sit yourselves down and rest." Then she poked up the fire on which a little pot was boiling. The daughter warned them both to be cautious, and neither to eat nor drink anything, for the old woman brewed bad drinks; so they slept quietly till morning. As they made ready for their departure, and the Prince was already mounted on horseback, the old

Witch said, "Wait a bit, I will bring you a parting draught." While she went for it the Prince rode away; but the servant, who had to buckle his saddle, was left alone when she came with the draught. "Take that to thy master," she said, but at the same moment the glass cracked, and the poison spurted on the horse, and so strong was it that the poor animal fell backwards dead. The servant ran after his master, and told him what had occurred; but as he would not leave the saddle behind, he went back to fetch it. As he came to the dead horse he saw a crow perched upon it feeding himself. "Who knows whether we shall meet with anything better to-day?" said the servant, and killing the crow he took it with him. The whole day long they journeyed on in the forest, but could not get out of it; and at the approach of night, finding an inn, they entered it. The servant gave the crow to the host, that he might cook it for their supper; but they had fallen into a den of thieves, and in the gloom of night twelve ruffians came, intending to rob and murder the strangers. Before they began, however, they sat down to table, and the host and the Witch joined them, and then they all partook of a dish of pottage, in which the flesh of the crow was boiled. Scarcely had they eaten two morsels apiece when they all fell down dead; for the poison which had killed the horse had impregnated the flesh of the crow. There was now no one left in the house but the daughter of the host, who seemed to be honest, and had had no share in the wicked deeds. She opened all the doors to the Prince, and showed him the heaped-up treasure; but the Prince said she might keep it all, for he would have none of it, and so rode on further with his servant.

After they had wandered a long way in the world, they came to a city where dwelt a beautiful but haughty Princess, who had declared that whoever propounded to her a riddle which she could not solve should be her husband; but if she solved it he must have his head cut off. Three days was the time given to consider, but she was always so sharp that she discovered the proposed riddle before the appointed time. Nine suitors had been sacrificed in this way, when the Prince arrived, and being blinded with her great beauty, resolved to stake his life upon her. So he went before her and proposed his riddle; namely, "What is this? One killed no one, and yet killed twelve." She knew not what it was, and thought and thought, but she could not make it out; and, although she searched through all her riddle books she could find nothing to help her; in short, her wisdom was quite at fault. At last at her wits' ends how to help herself, she bade her maid slip into the sleeping-room of the Prince, and there listen to his dreams, thinking perhaps he might talk in his sleep and unfold the riddle. The bold servant, however, had put himself instead of his master into the bed; and when the servant came into the room he tore off the cloak in which she had wrapped herself, and hunted her out with a rod. The second night the Princess sent her chambermaid to see if she could be more fortunate in listening; but the servant snatched her mantle away, and hunted her away with a rod. The third night the Prince himself thought he should be safe, and so he lay in his own bed; and the Princess herself came, having on a dark grey cloak, and sat herself down by him. When she thought he was asleep and dreaming she spoke to him, hoping he would answer, as many do; but he was awake, and heard and understood everything very well. First she asked, "One kills none; what is that?" He answered, "A crow which ate of a dead and poisoned horse, and died of it." Further she asked, "And yet killed twelve; what is that?" "Twelve robbers who partook of the crow, and died from eating it."

As soon as she knew the riddle she tried to slip away, but he held her mantle so fast that she left it behind. The following morning the Princess announced that she had discovered the riddle, and bade the twelve judges come and she would solve it before them. The Prince, however, requested a hearing for himself, and said, "She has stolen in upon me by night and asked me, or she would never have found it out." The judges said, "Bring us a witness." Then the servant brought up the three mantles; and when the judges saw the dark grey cloak which the Princess used to wear, they said, "Let the cloak be adorned with gold and silver, that it may be a wedding garment."

The musicians of Bremen.

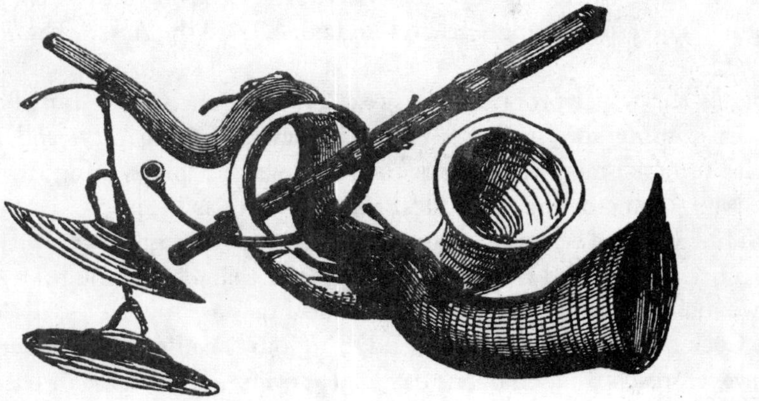

The Musicians of Bremen

A certain man had a Donkey, which had served him faithfully for many long years, but whose strength was so far gone that at last it was quite unfit for work. So his master was thinking how much he could make of the skin, but the Donkey perceiving that no good wind was blowing, ran away along the road to Bremen. "There," thought he, "I can be town musician." When he had run some way, he found a Hound lying by the road-side, yawning like one who was very tired. "What are you yawning for now, you big fellow?" asked the Ass.

"Ah," replied the Hound, "because every day I grow older and weaker; I cannot go any more to the hunt, and my master has well-nigh beaten me to death, so that I took to flight; and now I do not know how to earn my bread."

"Well! do you know," said the Ass, "I am going to Bremen, to be town-musician there; suppose you go with me and take a share in the music. I will play on the lute, and you shall beat the kettle-drums." The Dog was satisfied, and off they set.

Presently they came to a Cat, sitting in the middle of the path, with a face like three rainy days! "Now then, old shaver, what has crossed you?" asked the Ass.

"How can one be merry when one's neck has been pinched like mine?" answered the Cat. "Because I am growing old, and my teeth are all worn to stumps, and because

I would rather sit by the fire and spin, than run after mice, my mistress wanted to drown me; and so I ran away. But now good advice is dear, and I do not know what to do."

"Go with us to Bremen. You understand nocturnal music, so you can be town musician." The Cat consented, and went with them. The three vagabonds soon came near a Farm-yard, where, upon the barn-door, the Cock was sitting crowing with all his might. "You crow through marrow and bone," said the Ass, "what do you do that for?"

"That is the way I prophesy fine weather," said the Cock; "but, because grand guests are coming for the Sunday, the housewife has no pity, and has told the cookmaid to make me into soup for the morrow; and this evening my head will be cut off. Now I am crowing with a full throat as long as I can."

"Ah, but you, Red-comb," replied the Ass, "rather come away with us. We are going to Bremen, to find there something better than death; you have a good voice, and if we make music together it will have full play."

The Cock consented to this plan, and so all four travelled on together. They could not, however, reach Bremen in one day, and at evening they came into a forest, where they meant to pass the night. The Ass and the Dog laid themselves down under a large tree, the Cat and the Cock climbed up into the branches, but the latter flew right to the top, where he was most safe. Before he went to sleep he looked all round the four quarters, and soon thought he saw a little spark in the distance; so, calling his companions, he said they were not far from a house, for he saw a light. The Ass said, "If it is so, we had better get up and go further, for the pasturage here is very bad;" and the Dog continued, "Yes, indeed! a couple of bones with some meat on would also be very acceptable!" So they made haste towards the spot where the light was, and which shone now brighter and brighter, until they came to a well-lighted robber's cottage. The Ass, as the biggest, went to the window and peeped in. "What do you see, Gray-horse?" asked the Cock. "What do I see?" replied the Ass; "a table laid out with savoury meats and drinks, with robbers sitting around enjoying themselves."

"That were the right sort of thing for us," said the Cock.

"Yes, yes, I wish we were there," replied the Ass. Then these animals took counsel together how they should contrive to drive away the robbers, and at last they thought of a way. The Ass placed his fore feet upon the window ledge, the Hound got on his back, the Cat climbed up upon the Dog, and lastly the Cock flew up and perched upon the head of the Cat. When this was accomplished, at a given signal they commenced together to perform their music: the Ass brayed, the Dog barked, the Cat mewed, and the Cock crew; and they made such a tremendous noise, and so loud, that the panes of the window were shivered. Terrified at these unearthly sounds, the robbers got up with great precipitation, thinking nothing less than that some spirits had come, and fled off into the forest. The four companions immediately sat down at the table, and quickly ate up all that was left, as if they had been fasting for six weeks.

As soon as the four players had finished, they extinguished the light, and each sought for himself a sleeping place, according to his nature and custom. The Ass laid himself down upon some straw, the Hound behind the door, the Cat upon the hearth, near the warm ashes, and the Cock flew up upon a beam which ran across the room. Weary with their long walk, they soon went to sleep.

At midnight, the robbers perceived from their retreat that no light was burning in their house, and all appeared quiet; so the captain said, "We need not to have been frightened into fits;" and, calling one of the band, he sent him forward to reconnoitre. The messenger, finding all still, went into the kitchen to strike a light, and, taking the glistening fiery eyes of the Cat for live coals, he held a lucifer-match to them, expecting it to take fire. But the Cat, not understanding the joke, flew in his face, spitting and scratching, which dreadfully frightened him, so that he made for the back door; but the Dog, who laid there, sprang up and bit his leg; and as he limped upon the straw where the Ass was stretched out, it gave him a powerful kick with its hind foot. This was not all, for the Cock, awaking at the noise, clapped his wings, and cried from the beam, "Cock-a-doodle-doo, cock-a-doodle-doo!"

Then the robber ran back as well as he could to his captain, and said, "Ah, my master, there dwells a horrible witch in the house, who spat on me and scratched my face with her long nails; and then before the door stands a man with a knife, who chopped at my leg; and in the yard there lies a black monster, who beat me with a great wooden club; and besides all, upon the roof sits a judge, who called out, 'Bring the knave up, do!' so I ran away as fast as I could."

After this the robbers dared not again go near their house; but everything prospered so well with the four town musicians of Bremen, that they did not forsake their situation! And there they are to this day, for anything I know.

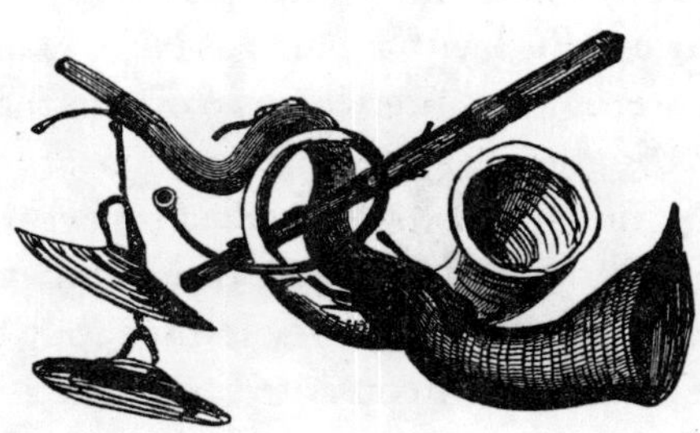

The Giant with the Three Golden Hairs

There was once upon a time a poor woman whose son was born with a caul, and so it was foretold of him that in his fourteenth year he should marry the King's daughter. As it happened the King soon after came into the village, quite unknown to any one, and when he asked the people what news there was, they answered, "A few days since a child with a caul was born, which is a sure sign that he will be very lucky; and, indeed, it has been foretold of him that in his fourteenth year he will marry the King's daughter."

The King had a wicked heart, and was disturbed concerning this prophecy, so he went to the parents, and said to them in a most friendly manner, "Give me up your child and I will take care of him." At first they refused, but the stranger begged for it with much gold, and so at last they consented and gave him the child, thinking, "It is a luck-child, and, therefore, everything must go on well with it."

The King laid the child in a box and rode away till he came to a deep water, into which he threw the box, saying to himself, "From this unsought-for bridegroom have I now freed my daughter."

The box, however, did not sink, but floated along like a boat, and not one drop of water penetrated it. It floated at last down to a mill two miles from the King's palace, and in the mill-dam it stuck fast. The miller's boy, who was fortunately standing there, observed it, and drew it ashore with a hook, expecting to find a great treasure. When, however, he opened the box, he saw a beautiful child alive and merry. He took it to the people at the mill, who, having no children, adopted it for their own, saying, "God has sent it to us." They took good care of the child, and it grew up a steady, good lad.

It happened one day that the King went into the mill for shelter during a thunderstorm, and asked the people whether the boy was their child. "No," they answered; "he is a foundling, who, fourteen years ago, floated into our dam in a box, which the miller's boy drew out of the water." The King observed at once, that it was no other than the luck-child whom he had thrown into the water, and so said to them, "Good people, could not the youth carry a letter to my wife the Queen? If so I will give him two pieces of gold for a reward."

"As my lord the King commands," they replied, and bade the youth get ready.

Then the King wrote a letter to the Queen, wherein he said, "So soon as this boy arrives with this letter, let him be killed and buried, and let all be done before I return."

The youth set out on his journey with the letter, but he lost himself, and at evening came into a great forest. In the gloom he saw a little light, and going up to it he found a cottage, into which he went, and perceived an old woman sitting by the fire. As soon as she saw the lad she was terrified, and exclaimed, "Why do you come here; and what would you do?"

"I am come from the mill," he answered, "and am going to my lady the Queen to carry a letter; but because I have lost my way in this forest, I wish to pass the night here."

"Poor boy!" said the woman, "you have come a den of robbers, who, when they return, will murder you."

"Let who will come," he replied, "I am not afraid; I am so weary that I can go no further;" and, stretching himself upon a bench, he went to sleep. Presently the robbers entered, and asked in a rage what strange lad was lying there. "Ah," said the old woman, "it is an innocent youth, who has lost himself in the forest, and whom I have taken in out of compassion. He carries with him a letter to the Queen."

The robbers seized the letter and read it, and understood that as soon as the youth arrived he was to be put to death. Then the robbers also took compassion on him, and the captain tore up the letter and wrote another, wherein he declared that the youth upon his arrival was to be married to the Princess. They let him sleep quietly on his bench till morning, and as soon as he awoke they gave him the letter and showed him the right road.

When the Queen received the letter she did as it commanded, and caused a splendid marriage feast to be prepared, and the Princess was given in marriage to the luck-child, who, since he was both young and handsome, pleased her well, and they were all very happy. Some little time afterwards the King returned to his palace and found the prophecy fulfilled, and his daughter married to the luck-child. "How did this happen?" he asked. "In my letter I gave quite another command."

Then the Queen handed him the letter, that he might read for himself what it stated. The King perceived directly that it had been forged by another person, and he asked the youth what he had done with the original letter that had been entrusted to him. "I know nothing about it," he replied; "it must have been changed in the forest where I passed the night."

Inflamed with rage the King answered, "Thou shalt not escape so easily; he who would have my daughter must fetch for me three golden hairs from the head of the Giant; bring thou to me what I desire, then shalt thou receive my daughter."

The King hoped by this means to get rid of him, but he answered, "The three Golden hairs I will fetch, for I fear not the Giant;" and so he took leave and began his wanderings.

The road led him by a large town, where the watchman at the gate asked him what trade he understood, and what he knew. "I know everything," replied the youth.

"Then you can do us a kindness," said the watch, "if you tell us the reason why the fountain in our market-place, out of which wine used to flow, now, all at once, does not even give water."

"That you shall know," was the answer; "but you must wait till I return."

Then he went on further and came to a rather large city; where the watchman asked him, as before, what trade he understood, and what he knew. "I know everything," he replied.

"Then you can do us a kindness, if you tell us the reason why a tree, growing in our town, which used to bear golden apples, does not now even have any leaves."

"That you shall know," replied the youth, "if you wait till I return;" and so saying he went further till he came to a great lake, over which it was necessary that he should pass. The ferryman asked him what trade he understood, and what he knew. "I know everything," he replied.

"Then," said the ferryman, "you can do me a kindness, if you tell me why, for ever and ever, I am obliged to row backwards and forwards, and am never to be released." "You shall learn the reason why," replied the youth; "but wait till I return."

As soon as he got over the water he found the entrance into the Giant's kingdom. It was black and gloomy, and the Giant was not at home; but his old grandmother was sitting there in an immense armchair. "What do you want?" said she, looking at him fixedly. "I want three Golden hairs from the head of the King of these regions," replied the youth, "else I cannot obtain my bride." "That is a bold request," said the woman; "for if he comes home and finds you here it will be a bad thing for you; but still you can remain, and I will see if I can help you."

Then she changed him into an ant, and told him to creep within the fold of her gown, where he wold be quite safe.

"Yes," he said, "that is all very well; but there are three things I am desirous of knowing: – Why a fountain, which used to spout wine, is now dry, and does not even give water. – Why a tree, which used to bear golden apples, does not now have leaves. – And why a ferryman is always rowing backwards and forwards and never gets released."

"Those are difficult questions," replied the old woman; "but do you keep quiet, and pay attention to what the King says when I pluck each of the three golden hairs."

As soon as evening came the Giant returned, and scarcely had he entered, when he remarked that the air was not quite pure. "I smell! I smell the flesh of man!" he exclaimed; "all is not right." Then he peeped into every corner and looked about, but could find nothing. Presently his old grandmother began to scold, screaming, "There now, just as I have dusted and put everything in order, you are pulling them all about again: you are for ever having man's flesh in your nose! Sit down and eat your supper."

When he had finished he felt tired, and the old woman took his head in her lap, and said she would comb his hair a bit. Presently he yawned, then winked, and at last snored. Then she plucked out a golden hair and laid it down beside her.

"Bah!" cried the King, "what are you about?"

"I have had a bad dream," answered the old woman, "and so I plucked one of your hairs."

"What did you dream, then?" asked he.

"I dreamt that a market-fountain, which used to spout wine, is dried up, and does not even give water: what is the matter with it, pray?"

"Why, if you must know," answered he, "there sits a toad under a stone in the spring, which, if any one kills, the wine will gush out as before."

Then the old woman went on combing till he went to sleep again, and snored so that the windows shook. Presently she pulled out a second hair.

"Confound it! what are you about?" exclaimed the King in a passion.

"Don't be angry," said she; "I did it in a dream."

"What did you dream about this time?" he asked.

"I dreamt that in a certain royal city there grew a fruit-tree, which formerly bore golden apples, but now has not a leaf upon it: what is the cause of it?"

"Why," replied the King, "at the root a mouse is gnawing. But if they kill it golden apples will grow again; if not, the mouse will gnaw till the tree dies altogether. However, let me go to sleep in peace now; for it you disturb me again you will catch a box on the ears."

Nevertheless the old woman, when she had rocked him again to sleep, plucked out a third golden hair. Up jumped the King in a fury and would have ill-treated her, but she pacified him and said, "Who can help bad dreams?"

"What did you dream this time?" he asked, still curious to know.

"I dreamt of a ferryman, who is for ever compelled to row backwards and forwards, and will never be released. What is the reason thereof?"

"Oh, you simpleton!" answered the Giant. "When one comes who wants to cross over, he must give the oar into his hand; then will the other be obliged to go to and fro, and he will be free."

Now, since the old woman had plucked the three golden hairs, and had received answers to the three questions, she let the Giant lie in peace, and he slept on till daybreak.

As soon as he went out in the morning the old woman took the ant out of the fold of her gown, and restored him again to his human form.

"There you have the three golden hairs from the King's head, and what he replied to the three questions you have just heard."

"Yes, I have heard, and will well remember," said the luck-child; and, thanking the old woman for her assistance in his trouble, he left those regions, well pleased that he had been so lucky in everything. When he came to the ferryman he had to give him the promised answer. But he said, "First row me over, and then I will tell you how you may be freed;" and as soon as they reached the opposite side he gave him the advice, "When another comes this way, and wants to pass over, give him the oar in his hand."

Then he went on to the first city, where stood the barren tree, and where the watchman waited for the answer. So he said to him, "Kill the mouse which gnaws at the root of the tree, and then it will again bear golden apples." The watchman thanked him, and gave him for a reward two asses laden with gold, which followed him. Next he came to the other city, where the dry fountain was, and he told the watchman as the Giant had said, – "Under a stone in the spring there sits a toad, which you must uncover and kill, and then wine will flow again as before."

The watchman thanked him, and gave to him, as the other had done, two asses laden with gold.

Now the lucky youth soon reached home, and his dear bride was very glad when she saw him return, and heard how capitally everything had gone with him. He brought the King what he had desired – the three golden hairs from the head of the Giant; and when his Majesty saw the four asses laden with gold he was quite pleased, and said, "Now are the conditions fulfilled, and you may have my daughter: but tell me, dear son-in-law, whence comes all this gold? This is, indeed, bountiful treasure."

"I was ferried over a river," he replied, "and there I picked it up, for it lies upon the shore like sand."

"Can I not fetch some as well?" asked the King, feeling quite covetous.

"As much as you like; there is a ferryman who will row you across, and then you can fill your sacks on the other side."

The covetous King set out in great haste upon his journey, and as soon as he came to the river beckoned to the ferryman to take him over. The man came and bade him step into his boat; and as soon as they reached the opposite shore, the ferryman put the oar into his hand and sprang on shore himself.

So the King was obliged to take his place, and there he is obliged to row to and fro for ever for his sins.

And there he still rows, for no one has yet come to take the oar from him.

The Three Languages

In Switzerland there lived an old Count, who had an only son, who was quite stupid and never learned anything. One day the father said, "My son, listen to what I have to say; do all I may, I can knock nothing into your head. Now you shall go away, and an eminent master shall try his hand with you."

So the youth was sent to a foreign city, and remained a whole year with his master, and at the end of that time he returned home. His father asked him at once what he had learned, and he replied, "My father, I have learned what the dogs bark."

"Mercy on us!" exclaimed the father, "is that all you have learned? I will send you to some other city, to another master." So the youth went away a second time, and after he had remained a year with his master, came home again. His father asked him, as before, what he had learned, and he replied, "I have learned what the birds sing." This answer put the father in a passion, and he exclaimed, "Oh, you prodigal! has all this precious time passed, and have you learned nothing? Are you not ashamed to come into my presence? Once more, I will send you to a third master; but if you learn nothing this time I will no longer be a father to you."

With this third master the boy remained, as before, a twelvemonth; and when he came back to his father, he told him that he had learned the language that the frogs croak. At this the father flew into a great rage, and, calling his people together, said, "This youth is no longer my son; I cast him off, and command that you lead him into the forest and take away his life."

The servants led him away into the forest, but they had not the heart to kill him, and so they let him go. They cut out, however, the eyes and the tongue of a fawn, and took them for a token to the old Count.

The young man wandered along, and after some time came to a castle, where he asked for a night's lodging. The Lord of the castle said, "Yes, if you will sleep down below. There is the tower; you may go, but I warn you it is very perilous, for it is full of wild dogs, which bark and howl at every one, and, at certain hours, a man must be thrown to them, whom they devour."

Now, on account of these dogs the whole country round was in terror and sorrow, for no one could prevent their ravages; but the youth, being afraid of nothing, said, "Only let me in to these barking hounds, and give me something to throw to them; they will not harm me."

Since he himself wished it, they gave him some meat for the wild hounds, and let him into the tower. As soon as he entered, the dogs ran about him quite in a friendly way, wagging their tails, and never once barking; they ate, also, the meat he brought, and did not attempt to do him the least injury. The next morning, to the astonishment of every one, he came forth unharmed, and told the Lord of the castle, "The hounds have informed me, in their language, why they thus waste and bring destruction upon the land. They have the guardianship of a large treasure beneath the tower, and till that is raised, they have no rest. In what way and manner this is to be done I have also understood from them."

At these words every one began rejoicing, and the Lord promised him his daughter in marriage, if he could raise the treasure. This task he happily accomplished, and the wild hounds thereupon disappeared, and the country was freed from that plague. Then the beautiful maiden was married to him, and they lived happily together.

After some time, he one day got into a carriage with his wife and set out on the road to Rome. On their way thither, they passed a swamp, where the frogs sat croaking. The young Count listened, and when he heard what they said, he became quite thoughtful and sad, but he did not tell his wife the reason. At last they arrived at Rome, and found the Pope was just dead, and there was a great contention among the Cardinals as to who should be his successor. They at length resolved, that he on whom some miraculous sign should be shown should be elected. Just as they had thus resolved, at the same moment the young Count stepped into the church, and suddenly two snow-white doves flew down, one on each of his shoulders, and remained perched there. The clergy recognised in this circumstance the sign they required, and asked him on the spot whether he would be Pope. The young Count was undecided, and knew not whether he were worthy; but the Doves whispered to him that he might take the honour, and so he consented. Then he was anointed and consecrated, and so was fulfilled what the Frogs had prophesied – and which had so disturbed him, – that he should become the Pope. Upon his election he had to sing a mass, of which he knew nothing; but the two Doves sitting upon his shoulder told him all that he required.

The Handless Maiden

A certain Miller had fallen by degrees into great poverty, until he had nothing left but his mill and a large apple-tree. One day, when he was going into the forest to cut wood, an old man, whom he had never seen before, stepped up to him, and said, "Why do you trouble yourself with chopping wood? I will make you rich, if you will promise me what stands behind your mill."

The Miller thought to himself that it could be nothing but his apple-tree, so he said "Yes," and concluded the bargain with the strange man. The other, however, laughed derisively, and said, "After three years I will come and fetch what belongs to me;" and then he went away.

As soon as the Miller reached home, his wife came to him, and said, "Tell me, husband, whence comes this sudden flow of gold into our house? All at once every chest and cupboard is filled, and yet no man has brought any in; I cannot tell how it has happened."

The Miller, in reply, told her, "It comes from a strange lord, whom I met in the forest, who offered me great treasure, and I promised him, in return, what stands behind the mill, for we can very well spare the great apple-tree."

"Ah, my husband," exclaimed his wife, "it is the Evil Spirit whom you have seen;

he did not mean the apple-tree, but our daughter, who was behind the mill sweeping the yard."

This Miller's daughter was a beautiful and pious maiden, and during all the three years lived in the fear of God without sin. When the time was up, and the day came when the Evil One was to fetch her, she washed herself quite clean and made a circle around herself with chalk. Quite early came the Evil One, but he could not approach her; so, in a rage, he said to the Miller, "Take away from her all water, that she may not be able to wash herself, else have I no power over her." The Miller did so, for he was afraid. The next morning came the Evil One again, but she had wept upon her hands so that they were quite clean. Then he was baffled again, and in his anger said to the Miller, "Cut off both her hands, or else I cannot now obtain her." The Miller was horrified, and said, "How can I cut off the hands of my own child?" But the Evil One pressed him, saying, "If you do not not, you are mine, and I will take you yourself away!" At last the Miller promised, and he went to the maiden, and said, "My child, if I do not cut off both your hands, the Evil One will carry me away, and in my terror I have promised him. Now help me in my trouble, and forgive me for the wickedness I am about to do you."

She replied, "Dear father, do with me what you will; I am your daughter."

Thereupon she laid down both her hands, and her father cut them off. For the third time now the Evil One came, but the maiden had let fall so many tears upon her arms, that they were both quite clean. So he was obliged to give her up, and after this lost all power over her.

The Miller now said to her, "I have received so much good through you, my daughter, that I will care for you most dearly all your life long."

But she answered, "Here I cannot remain; I will wander forth into the world, where compassionate men will give me as much as I require."

Then she had her arms bound behind her back, and at sunrise departed on her journey, and walked the whole day long till night fell. At that time she arrived at a royal garden, and by the light of the moon she saw a tree standing there bearing the most beautiful fruits, but she could not enter, for there was water all round. Since, however, she had walked the whole day without tasting a morsel, she was tormented by hunger, and said to herself, "Ah, would I were there, that I might eat of the fruit, else shall I perish with hunger." So she kneeled and prayed to God, and all at once an angel came down, who made a passage through the water, so that the ground was dry for her to pass over. Then she went into the garden, and the angel with her. There she saw a tree full of beautiful pears, but they were all numbered; so she stepped up and ate one to appease her hunger, but no more. The gardener perceived her do it, but because the angel stood by he was afraid, and thought the maiden was a spirit; so he remained quiet and did not address her. As soon as she had eaten the pear she was satisfied, and went and hid herself under the bushes.

The next morning the King to whom the garden belonged came down, and counting the pears found that one was missing; and he asked the gardener whither it was gone. The gardener replied, "Last night a spirit came, who had no hands, and ate the pear with her mouth." The King then asked, "How did the spirit come through the water? and whither did it go after it had eaten the pear?"

The gardener answered, "One clothed in snow-white garments came down from heaven and made a passage through the waters, so that the spirit could walk through on dry land. And because it must have been an angel, I was afraid, and neither called out nor questioned it; and as soon as the spirit had finished the fruit, she returned as she came."

The King said, "If it be as you say, I will this night watch with you."

As soon as it was dark the King came into the garden, bringing with him a priest, who was to address the spirit, and all three sat down under the tree. About midnight the maiden crept out from under the bushes and again ate with her mouth a pear off the tree, whilst the angel clothed in white stood by her. Then the priest went towards her, and said, "Art thou come from God or from earth? Art thou a spirit or a human being?" She replied, "I am no spirit, but a poor maiden, deserted by all, save God alone."

The King said, "If you are forsaken by all the world, yet will I not forsake you;" and he took her with him to his royal palace, and, because she was so beautiful and pious, he loved her with all his heart, and ordered silver hands to be made for her, and made her his bride.

After a year had passed by, the King was obliged to go to war, so he commended the young Queen to the care of his mother, and told her to write him word if she had a child born, and to pay her especial attention. Soon afterwards the Queen bore a fine boy; so the old mother wrote a letter to her son, containing the joyful news. The messenger, however, rested on his way by a brook, and, being weary with his long journey, fell asleep. Then came the Evil One, who had always been trying to do some evil to the Queen, and changed the letter for another, wherein it was said that the Queen had brought a changeling into the world. As soon as the King had read this letter, he was frightened and much troubled; nevertheless, he wrote an answer to his mother, that she should take great care of the Queen until his arrival. The messenger went back with this letter, but on his way rested at the same spot, and went to sleep. Then the Evil One came a second time, and put another letter in his pocket, wherein it was said the Queen and her child should be killed. When the old mother received this letter, she was struck with horror, and could not believe it; so she wrote another letter to the King; but she received no answer, for the Evil One again placed a false letter in the messenger's pocket; and in this last it said that she should preserve the tongue and eyes of the Queen for a sign that she had fulfilled the order.

The old mother was sorely grieved to shed innocent blood, so she caused a calf to be fetched by night, and cut out its tongue and eyes. Then she said to the queen, "I cannot let you be killed, as the King commands; but you must remain here no longer. Go forth with your child, into the wide world, and never return here again."

Thus saying, she bound the child upon the young Queen's back, and the poor wife went away weeping bitterly. Soon she entered a large wild forest, and there she fell upon her knees and prayed to God; and the angel appeared, and led her to a little cottage, and over the door was a shield inscribed with the words, "Here may every one live freely." Out of the house came a snow-white maiden, who said, "Welcome, Lady Queen!" and led her in. Then she took the little child from the Queen's back, and gave it some nourishment, and laid it on a beautifully covered bed. Presently the Queen asked, "How do you know that I am a queen?" and the maiden answered, "I am an angel sent from God to tend your child;" and in this cottage she lived seven years, and was well cared for, and through God's mercy to her, on account of her piety, her hands grew again as before.

Meanwhile the King had come home again, and his first thought was to see his wife and child. Then his mother began to weep, and said, "You wicked husband, why did you write to me that I should put to death two innocent souls!" and, showing him the two letters which the Evil One had forged, she continued, "I have done as you commanded;" and she brought him the tokens, the two eyes and the tongue. Then the King began to weep so bitterly for his dear wife and son that the old mother pitied him, and said, "Be comforted, she lives yet! I caused a calf to be slain, from whom I took these tokens; but the child I bound on your wife's back, and I bade them go forth into the wide world; and she promised never to return here, because you were so wrathful against her."

"So far as heaven is blue," exclaimed the King, "I will go; and neither will I eat nor drink until I have found again my dear wife and child, if they have not perished of hunger by this time."

Thereupon the King set out, and for seven long years sought his wife in every stony cleft and rocky cave, but found her not; and he began to think she must have perished. And all this time he neither ate nor drank, but God sustained him.

At last he came into a large forest, and found there the little cottage whereon the shield was with the words, "Here may every one live freely." Out of the house came the white maiden, and she took him by the hand; and, leading him in, said, "Be welcome, Great King! Whence comest thou?"

He replied, "For seven long years I have sought everywhere for my wife and child; but I have not succeeded."

Then the angel offered him meat and drink, but he refused both, and would only rest a little while. So he lay down to sleep, and covered his face with a napkin.

Now went the angel into the chamber where sat the Queen, with her son, whom she usually called "SORROWFUL," and said to her, "Come down, with your child: your husband is here." So she went to where he lay, and the napkin fell from off his face; so the Queen said, "SORROWFUL, pick up the napkin, and cover again your father's face." The child did as he was bid; and the King, who heard in his slumber what passed, let the napkin again fall from off his face. At this boy became impatient, and said, "Dear mother, how can I cover my father's face? Have I indeed a father on the earth? I have learnt the prayer, 'Our Father which art in heaven;' and you have told me my father was in heaven, – the good God: how can I talk to this wild man; he is not my father."

As the King heard this he raised himself up, and asked the Queen who she was. The Queen replied: "I am your wife, and this is your son, SORROWFUL." But when he saw her human hands, he said, "Mu wife had silver hands." "The merciful God," said the Queen, "has caused my hands to grow again;" and the angel, going into the chamber, brought out the silver hands, and showed them to him.

Now he perceived that they were certainly his dear wife and child; and he kissed them gladly, saying, "A heavy stone is taken from my heart;" and, after eating a meal together with the angel, they went home to the King's mother.

Their arrival caused great rejoicings everywhere: and the King and Queen celebrated their marriage again, and ever afterwards lived happily together to the end of their lives.

Clever Alice.

Clever Alice

~

Once upon a time there was a man who had a daughter, who was called "Clever Alice;" and when she was grown up, her father said, "We must see about her marrying." "Yes," replied her mother, "when one comes who shall be worthy of her."

At last a certain youth, by name Hans, came from a distance to make a proposal for her, but he put in one condition, that the Clever Alice should also be very prudent. "Oh," said her father, "she has got a head full of brains;" and the mother added, "Ah, she can see the wind blow up the street, and hear the flies cough!"

"Very well," replied Hans, "but if she is not very prudent, I will not have her." Soon afterwards they sat down to dinner, and her mother said, "Alice, go down into the cellar and draw some beer."

So Clever Alice took the jug down from the wall, and went into the cellar, jerking the lid up and down on her way to pass away the time. As soon as she got downstairs, she drew a stool and placed it before the cask, in order that she might not have to stoop, whereby she might do some injury to her back, and give it an undesirable bend. then she placed the can before her and turned the tap, and while the beer was running, as she did not wish her eyes to be idle, she looked upon the wall above and below, and presently perceived, after much peeping into this and that corner, a hatchet, which the bricklayers had left behind, sticking out of the ceiling right above her. At the sight of this the Clever Alice began to cry, saying, "Oh, if I marry Hans, and we have a child, and he grows up, and we send him into the cellar to draw beer, the hatchet will fall upon his head and kill him;" and so saying, she sat there weeping with all her might over the impending misfortune.

Meanwhile the good folks upstairs were waiting for the beer, but as Clever Alice did not come, her mother told the maid to go and see what she was stopping for. The maid went down into the cellar,and found Alice sitting before the cask crying heartily, and she asked, "Alice, what are you weeping about?" "Ah," she replied, "have I not cause? If I marry Hans, and we have a child, and he grow up, and we send him here to draw beer, the hatchet will fall upon his head and kill him."

"Oh," said the maid, "what a clever Alice we have!" And, sitting down, she began to weep, too, for the misfortune that was to happen.

After a while, and the maid did not return, the good folks above began to feel very thirsty; so the husband told the boy to go down into the cellar, and see what had become of Alice and the maid. The boy went down, and there sat Clever Alice and the maid both crying, so he asked the reason; and Alice told him the same tale of the hatchet that was to fall on her child, as she had told the maid. When she had finished, the boy exclaimed, "What a clever Alice we have!" and fell weeping and howling with the others.

Upstairs they were still waiting, and the husband said, when the boy did not return, "Do you go down, wife, into the cellar, and see why Alice stops." So she went down, and finding all three sitting there crying, asked the reason, and Alice told her about the hatchet which must inevitably fall upon the head of her son. Then the mother likewise exclaimed, "Oh, what a clever Alice we have!" and, sitting down, began to weep with the others. Meanwhile the husband waited for his wife's return; but at last he felt so very thirsty that he said, "I must go myself down into the cellar and see what Alice stops for." As soon as he entered the cellar, there he found the four sitting and crying together, and when he heard the reason, he also exclaimed, "Oh, what a clever Alice we have!" and sat down to cry with the others. All this time the bridegroom above sat waiting, but when nobody returned, he thought they must be waiting for him, and so he went down to see what was the matter. When he entered, there sat the five crying and groaning, each one in a louder key than his neighbour. "What misfortune has happened?" he asked. "Ah, dear Hans!" cried Alice, "if we should marry one another, and have a child, and he grow up, and we, perhaps, send him down here to tap the beer, the hatchet which has been left sticking there may fall on his head, and so kill him; and do you not think that enough to weep about?"

"Now," said Hans, "more prudence than this is not necessary for my housekeeping; because you are such a clever Alice I will have you for my wife." And, taking her hand, he led her home, and celebrated the wedding directly.

After they had been married a little while, Hans said one morning, "Wife, I will go out to work and earn some money; do you go into the field and gather some corn wherewith to make bread."

"Yes," she answered, "I will do so, dear Hans." And when he was gone, she cooked herself a nice mess of pottage to take with her. As she came to the field, she said to herself, "What shall I do? Shall I cut first, or eat first? Ay, I will eat first!" Then she ate up the contents of her pot, and when it was finished, she thought to herself, "Now, shall I reap first or sleep first? Well, I think I will have a nap!" and so she laid herself down amongst the corn, and went to sleep. Meanwhile Hans returned home, but Alice did not come, and so he said, "Oh, what a prudent Alice I have! she is so industrious that she does not even come home to eat anything." By-and-by, however, evening came on, and still she did not return; so Hans went out to see how much she had reaped; but, behold, nothing at all, and there lay Alice fast asleep among the corn! So home he ran very fast, and brought a net with little bells hanging on it, which he threw over her head while she slept on. When he had done this, he went back again and shut to the house door, and, seating himself on his stool, began working very industriously.

At last, when it was quite dark, the Clever Alice awoke, and as soon as she stood up, the net fell over her hair, and the bells jingled at every step she took. This quite frightened her, and she began to doubt whether she were really Clever Alice, and said to herself, "Am I she, or am I not?" This question she could not answer, and she stood still a while longer considering. At last she thought she would go home and ask whether she were really herself – supposing they would be able to tell. When she came to the house-door it was shut; so she tapped at the window, and asked, "Hans, is Alice within?" "Yes," he replied, "she is." Now she was really terrified, and exclaiming, "Ah, heaven, then I am not Alice!" she ran up to another house; but as soon as the folks within heard the jingling of the bells they would not open their doors, and so nobody would receive her. Then she ran straight away from the village, and no one has ever seen her since.

The wedding of Mrs. Fox.

The Wedding of Mrs. Fox

First Tale

There was once upon a time a Fox with nine tails, who thought his wife was not faithful to him, and determined to put it to the proof. So he stretched himself along under a bench, and keeping his legs perfectly still, he appeared as if quite dead. Mrs. Fox, meanwhile, had ascended to her room, and shut herself in; and her maid, the young Cat, stood near the hearth cooking. As soon as it was known that Mr. Fox was dead, several suitors came to pay their respects to his widow. The maid, hearing some one knocking at the front door, went and looked out, and saw a young Fox, who asked,

"How do you do, Miss Kitten?
Is she asleep or awake?"

The maid replied –

"I neither sleep nor wake;
Would you know my business?
Beer and butter both I make;
Come and be my guest."

"I am obliged, Miss Kitten," said the young Fox; "but how is Mrs. Fox?"

"She sits in her chamber,
Weeping so sore;
Her eyes red with crying –
Mr. Fox is no more."

"Tell her then, my maiden, that a young Fox is here, who wishes to marry her," said he. So the Cat went pit-pat, pit-a-pat up the stairs, and tapped gently at the door, saying, "Are you there, Madam Fox?" "Yes, my good little Cat," was the reply. "There is a suitor below." "What does he look like?" asked her mistress. "Has he nine as beautiful tails as my late husband?" "Oh, no," answered the maid, "he has only one." "Then I will not have him," said the mistress. The young Cat went down and sent away the suitor; and soon after there came a second knock at the door from another Fox, with *two* tails, who wished to marry the widow; he fared, however, no better than the former one. Afterwards came six more, one after the other, each having one tail more than he who preceded him; but these were all turned away. At last there arrived a Fox with nine tails, like the deceased husband; and when the widow heard of it, she said, full of joy, to the Cat, "Now you may open all the windows and doors, and turn the old Fox out of the house." But just as the wedding was about to be celebrated, the old Fox roused himself from his sleep beneath the bench, and drubbed the whole rabble, together with his wife, out of the house, and hunted them far away.

Second Tale

Narrates that when the old Fox appeared dead, the Wolf came as a suitor, and knocked at the door; and the Cat, who served as a servant to the Widow, got up to see who was there.

"Good day, Miss Cat; how does it happen that you are sitting all alone? What good are you about?"

The Cat answered, "I have been making some bread and milk. Will my lord be my guest?"

"Thanks, many thanks!" replied the Wolf; "is Madam Fox not at home?"

The Cat sang,

"She sits in her chamber,
Weeping so sore;
Her eyes red with crying –
Mr. Fox is no more."

Then the Wolf said, "If she wishes for another husband she had better come down to me."

So the Cat ran up the stairs, her tail trailing behind, and when she got to the chamber door, she knocked five times, and asked, "Is Madam Fox at home? If so, and she wishes to have another husband, she must come downstairs."

Mrs. Fox asked, "Does the gentleman wear red stockings, and has he a pointed mouth?" "No," replied the Cat. "Then he will not do for me," said Mrs. Fox, and shut the door.

After the Wolf had been turned away, there came a Dog, a Stag, a Hare, a Bear, a Lion, and all the beasts of the forest, one after another. But each one was deficient of the particular qualities which the old Fox had possessed, and the Cat was obliged therefore to turn away every suitor. At last came a young Fox; and when the question was asked whether he had red stockings and a pointed mouth, the Cat replied, "Yes;" and she was bid to call him up and prepare for the wedding. Then they threw the old Fox out of the window, and the Cat caught and ate as many mice as she could, in celebration of the happy event.

And after the marriage they had a grand ball, and, as I have never heard to the contrary, perhaps they are dancing still.

THUMBLING

Once upon a time there lived a poor peasant, who used to sit every evening by the hearth, poking the fire, while his wife spun. One night, he said, "How sad it is that we have no children! everything is so quiet here, while in other houses it is so noisy and merry."

"Ah!" sighed his wife, "if we had but only one, and were he no bigger than my thumb, I should still be content, and love him with all my heart." A little while after the wife fell ill; and after seven months a child was born, who, although he was perfectly formed in all his limbs, was not actually bigger than one's thumb. So they said to one another that it had happened just as they wished; and they called the child "Thumbling." Every day they gave him all the food he could eat; still he did not grow a bit, but remained exactly the height he was when first born; he looked about him, however, very knowingly, and showed himself to be a bold and clever fellow, who would prosper in everything he undertook.

One morning the peasant was making ready to go into the forest to fell wood, and said, "Now I wish I had some one who could follow me with the cart."

"Oh father!" exclaimed Thumbling, "I will bring the cart; don't you trouble yourself; it shall be there at the right time."

The father laughed at this speech, and said, "How shall that be? You are much too small to lead the horse by the bridle."

"That matters not, father. If mother will harness the horse, I can sit in his ear, and tell him which way to take."

"Well, we will try for once," said the father; and so, when the hour came, the mother harnessed the horse, and placed Thumbling in its hear, and told him how to guide it. Then he set out quite like a man, and the cart went on the right road to the forest; and just as it turned a corner, and Thumbling called out, "Steady, steady!" two strange men met it; and one said to the other, "My goodness! what is this? Here comes a cart, and the driver keeps calling to the horse, but I can see no one." "That cannot be all right," said the other: "let us follow and see where the cart stops."

The cart went on safely deep into the forest, and straight to the place where the wood was cut. As soon as Thumbling saw his father, he called to him, "Here, father; here I am, you see, with the cart: just take me down." The peasant caught the bridle of the horse with his left hand, and with his right took his little son out of its ear, and he sat himself down merrily on a straw. When the two strangers saw the little fellow, they knew not what to say for astonishment; and one of them took his companion aside, and said, "This little fellow might make our fortune, if we could exhibit him in the towns. Let us buy him." They went up to the peasant, and asked, "Will you sell us your son? We will treat him well." "No," replied the man; "he is my heart's delight, and not to be bought for all the money in the world!" But, Thumbling, when he heard what was said, climbed up by his father's skirt, and sat himself on his shoulder, and whispered in his ear, "Let me go now, and I will soon come back again." So his father gave him to the two men for a fine piece of gold, and they asked him where he would sit. "Oh," replied he, "put me on the rim of your hat, and then I can walk round and survey the country. I will not fall off." They did as he wished; and when he had taken leave of his father, they set out. Just as it was getting dark he asked to be lifted down; and, after some demur, the man on whose hat he was took him off and placed him on the ground. In an instant Thumbling ran off, and crept into a mousehole, where they could not see him. "Good evening, masters," said he, "you can go home without me;" and with a quiet laugh, he crept into his hole still further. The two men poked their sticks into the hole, but all in vain, for Thumbling only went down further; and when it had grown quite dark, they were obliged to return home full of vexation and with empty pockets.

As soon as Thumbling perceived that they were off, he crawled out of his hiding-place, and said, "How dangerous it is to walk in this field in the dark: one might soon break one's head or legs!" and so saying he looked round, and by great good luck he saw an empty snail-shell. "God be praised!" he exclaimed, "here I can sleep securely;" and in he went. Just as he was about to fall asleep he heard two men coming by, one of whom said to the other, "How shall we manage to get at the parson's gold and silver?"

"That I can tell you," interrupted Thumbling.

"What was that?" exclaimed the thief, frightened. "I heard some one speak." They stood still and listened; and then Thumbling said, "Take me with you, and I will help you."

"Where are you?" asked the thieves.

"Search on the ground, and mark where my voice comes from," replied he. The thief looked about, and at last found him; and lifted him up in the air, "What! will you help us, you little wight?" said they.

"Do you see, I can creep between the iron bars into the chamber of the parson, and reach out to you whatever you require."

"Very well; we will see what you can do," said the thief.

When they came to the house, Thumbling crept into the chamber, and cried out, with all his might, "Will you have all that is here?" The thieves were terrified, and said, "Speak gently, or some one will awake."

But Thumbling feigned not to understand, and exclaimed, louder still, "Will you have all that is here?"

This awoke the cook, who slept in the room, and sitting up in her bed she listened. The thieves, however, had run back a little way, quite frightened; but, taking courage again, and thinking the little fellow wished to tease them, they came and whispered to him to make haste and hand them out something. At this, Thumbling cried out still more loudly, "I will give you it all, only put your hands in." The listening maid heard this clearly, and, springing out of bed, hurried out at the door. The thieves ran off as if they were pursued by the wild huntsman, but the maid, as she could see nothing, went to strike a light. When she returned, Thumbling escaped without being seen into the barn, and the maid, after she had looked round, and searched in every corner, without finding anything, went to bed again, believing she had been dreaming with her eyes open. Meanwhile Thumbling had crept in amongst the hay, and found a beautiful place to sleep, where he intended to rest till daybreak, and then to go home to his parents.

Other things, however, was he to experience, for there is much tribulation and trouble going on in this world.

The maid got up at dawn of day to feed the cow. Her first walk was to the barn, where she took an armful of hay, and just the bundle where poor Thumbling lay asleep. He slept so soundly, however, that he was not conscious, and only awoke when he was in the cow's mouth. "Ah, goodness!" exclaimed he, "how ever came I into this mill!" but soon he saw where he really was. Then he took care not to come between the teeth, but presently slipped quite down the cow's throat. "There are no windows in this room," said he to himself, "and no sunshine, and I brought no light with me." Overhead his quarters seemed still worse, and, more than all, he felt his room growing narrower, as the cow swallowed more hay. So he began to call out in terror, as loudly as he could, "Bring me no more food! I do not want any more food!" Just then the maid was milking the cow, and when she heard the voice without seeing anything, and knew it was the same she had listened to in the night, she was so frightened that she slipped off her stool and overturned the milk. In great haste she ran to her master, saying, "Oh, Mr. Parson, the cow has been speaking."

"You are crazy," he replied; but still he went himself into the stable to see what was the matter, and scarcely had he stepped in when Thumbling began to shout out again, "Bring me no more food, bring me no more food." This terrified the parson himself, and he thought an evil spirit had entered into his cow, and so ordered her to be killed. As soon as that was done, and they were dividing the carcass, a fresh accident befell Thumbling, for a wolf, who was passing at the time, made a snatch at the cow, and tore away the part where he was stuck fast. However, he did not lose courage, but as soon as the wolf had swallowed him, he called out from inside, "Oh, Mr. Wolf, I know of a capital meal for you." "Where is it to be found?" asked the Wolf. "In the house by the meadow; you must creep through the gutter, and there you will find cakes, and bacon, and sausages, as many as you can eat," replied Thumbling, describing exactly his father's house.

The wolf did not wait to be told twice, but in the night crept in, and ate away in the larder to his heart's content. When he had finished he tried to escape by the way he entered, but the hole was not large enough. Thereupon Thumbling, who had reckoned on this, began to make a tremendous noise inside the poor wolf, screaming and shouting as loud as he could. "Will you be quiet?" said the Wolf; "you will awake the people." "Eh, what?" cried the little man, "since you have satisfied yourself, it is my turn now to make merry;" and he set up a louder howling than before. At last his father and mother awoke, and came to the room and looked through the chinks of the door; and as soon as they perceived the ravages the wolf had committed, they ran and brought, the man his axe, and the woman the scythe. "Stop you behind," said the man, as they entered the room; "if my blow does not kill him, you must give him a cut with your weapon, and chop off his head if you can."

When Thumbling heard his father's voice, he called out, "Father dear, I am here, in the wolf's body." "Heaven be praised!" said the man, full of joy, "our dear child is found again;" and he bade his wife take away the scythe, lest it should do any harm to his son. Then he raised his axe, and gave the wolf such a blow on its head that it fell dead, and, taking a knife, he cut it open, and released the little fellow his son. "Ah," said his father, "what troubled we have had about you!" "Yes, father," replied Thumbling, "I have been travelling a great deal about the world. Heaven be praised! I breathe fresh air again."

"Where have you been, my son?" he inquired.

"Once I was in a mouse's hole, once inside a cow, and lastly inside that wolf; and now I will stop here with you," said Thumbling.

"Yes," said the old people, "we will not sell you again for all the riches of the world;" and they embraced and kissed him with great affection. Then they gave him plenty to eat and drink, and had new clothes made for him, for his old ones were worn out with travelling.

The Golden Bird.

THE GOLDEN BIRD

A long, long while ago there was a King who had, adjoining his palace, a fine pleasure-garden, in which stood a tree, which bore golden apples, and as soon as the apples were ripe they were counted, but the next day one was missing. This vexed the King very much, and he ordered that watch should be kept every night beneath the tree; and having three sons he sent the eldest, when evening set in, into the garden; but about midnight the youth fell into a deep sleep, and in the morning another apple was missing. The next night the second son had to watch, but he also fared no better; for about midnight he fell fast asleep, and another apple was wanting in the morning. The turn came now to the third son, who was eager to go; but the King hesitated for a long time, thinking he would be even less wakeful than his brothers, but at last he consented. The youth lay down under the tree and watched steadily, without letting sleep be his master; and just as twelve o'clock struck something rustled in the air, and, looking up, he saw a bird flying by, whose feathers were of bright gold. The bird lighted upon the tree, and had just picked off one of the apples, when the youth shot a bolt at it, which did not prevent its flying away, but one of its golden feathers dropped off. The youth took the feather up, and, showing it the next morning to the King, told him what he had seen during the night. Thereupon the King assembled his council, and everyone declared that a single feather like this was worth a kingdom. "Well, then," said the King, "if this feather is so costly, I must and will have the whole bird, for one feather is of no use to me." The eldest son was now sent out on his travels, and, relying on his own prudence, he doubted not that he should find the Golden Bird. When he had walked about a mile he saw sitting at the edge of a forest a Fox, at which he levelled his gun; but it cried out, "Do not shoot me, and I will give you a piece of good advice! You are now on the road to the Golden Bird, and this evening you will come into a village where two inns stand opposite to each other: one will be brightly lit up and much merriment will be going on inside, but turn not in there; enter rather into the other, though it seem a poor place to you."

The young man, however, thought to himself, "How can such a silly beast give me rational advice?" and, going nearer, he shot at the Fox; but he missed, and the Fox ran away with its tail in the air. After this adventure he walked on, and towards evening he came to the village where stood the two public-houses, in one of which singing and dancing were going on; while the other looked a very ill-conditioned house. "I should be a simpleton," said he to himself, "if I were to go into this dirty inn while that capital one stood opposite." So he entered the dancing-room, and there, living in feasting and rioting, he forgot the Golden Bird, his father, and all good manners.

As time passed by and the eldest son did not return home, the second son set out also on his travels to seek the Golden Bird. The Fox met him as it had its brother, and gave him good counsel, which he did not follow. He likewise arrived at the two inns, and out of the window of the riotous house his brother leaned, and invited him in. He could not resist, and entered, and lived there only to gratify his pleasures.

Again a long time elapsed with no news of either brother, and the youngest wished to go and try his luck; but his father would not consent. "It is useless," said he; "you are still less likely than your brothers to find the Golden Bird, and, if a misfortune should happen to you, you cannot help yourself, for you are not very quick." The King at last, however, was forced to consent, for he had no rest while he refused.

On the edge of the forest the Fox was again sitting, and again it offered in return for its life the same piece of good advice. The youth was good-hearted, and said, "Be not afraid, little Fox; I will do you no harm."

"You shall not repent of your goodness," replied the Fox; "but, that you may travel quicker, get up behind on my tail."

Scarcely had he seated himself when away they went, over hedged and ditches, uphill and downhill, so fast that their hair whistled in the wind.

As soon as they arrived at the village the youth dismounted, and, following the advice he had received, turned, without looking round, into the mean-looking house, where he passed the night comfortably. The next morning, when he went into the fields, he found the Fox already there, who said, "I will tell you what further you must do. Go straight forwards, and you will come to a castle, before which a whole troop of soldiers will be sleeping and snoring; be not frightened at them, but go right through the middle of the troop into the castle, and through all the rooms, till you come into a chamber where a Golden Bird hangs in a wood cage. Near by stands an empty golden cage for show, but take care you do not take the bird out of its ugly cage to place it in the golden one, or you will fare badly." With these words the Fox again stretched out its tail, and the King's son mounting as before, away they went over hill and valley, while their hair whistled in the wind from the pace they travelled at. When they arrived at the castle the youth found everything as the Fox had said. He soon discovered the room where the Golden Bird sat in its wooden cage, and by it stood the golden one, and three golden apples were lying around. The youth though it would be a pity to take the bird in such an ugly and dirty cage, and, opening the door, he put it in the splendid one. At the moment he did this the bird set up a piercing shriek, which woke the soldiers, who started up and made him a prisoner. The next morning he was brought to trial, and when he confessed all he was condemned to death. Still the King said he would spare his life under one condition; namely, if he brought to him the Golden Horse, which travelled faster than the wind, and then for a reward he should also receive the Golden Bird.

The young Prince walked out, sighing and sorrowful, for where was he to find the Golden Horse? All at once he saw his old friend the Fox, who said, "There, you see what has happened, because you did not mind what I said. But be of good courage; I will protect you, and tell you where you may find the horse. You must follow this road straight till you come to a castle: in the stable there this horse stands. Before the door a boy will lie fast asleep and snoring, so you must lead away the horse quietly; but there is one thing you must mind: put on his back the old saddle of wood and leather, and not the golden one which hangs close by, for if you do it will be very unlucky." So saying the Fox stretched out its tail, and again they went as fast as the wind. Everything was as the Fox had said, and the youth went into the stall where the Golden Horse was; but, as he was about to put on the dirty saddle, he thought it would be a shame if he did not put on such a fine animal the saddle which appeared to belong to him, and so he took up the golden saddle. Scarcely had it touched the back of the horse when it set up a loud neigh, which awoke the stable-boys, who put our hero into confinement. The next morning he was condemned to death; but the King promised to give him his life and the horse, if he would bring the Beautiful Daughter of the King of the Golden Castle.

With a heavy heart the youth set out, and by great good fortune soon met the Fox. "I should have left you in your misfortune," it said; "but I felt compassion for you, and am willing once more to help you out of your trouble. Your road to the palace lies straight before you, and when you arrive there, about evening, wait till night, when the Princess goes to take a bath. As soon as she enters the bath-house, do you spring up and give her a kiss, and she will follow you wheresoever you will; only take care that she does not take leave of her parents first, or all will be lost.

With these words the Fox again stretched out its tail, and the King's son seating himself thereon, away they went over hill and valley and like the wind. When they arrived at the Golden Palace, the youth found everything as the Fox had foretold, and he waited till midnight when everybody was in a deep sleep, and at that hour the beautiful Princess went to her bath, and he sprang up instantly and kissed her. The Princess said she was willing to go with him, but begged him earnestly, with tears in her eyes, to permit her first to take leave of her parents. At first he withstood her prayers; but, when she wept still more, and even fell at his feet, he at last consented. Scarcely had the maiden stepped up to her father's bedside, when he awoke, and all the others who were asleep awakening too, the poor youth was captured and put in prison.

The next morning the King said to him, "Thy life is forfeited, and thou canst only find mercy if thou clearest away the mountain which lies before my window, and over which I cannot see; but thou must remove it within eight days. If thou accomplish this, then thou shalt have my daughter as a reward."

The King's son at once began digging and shovelling away; but when, after seven days, he saw how little was effected and that all his work went for nothing, he fell into great grief and gave up all hope. But on the evening of the seventh day the Fox appeared and said, "You do not deserve that I should notice you again, but go away and sleep while I work for you."

When he awoke the next morning, and looked out of the window, the hill had disappeared, and he hastened to the King full of joy, and told him the conditions were fulfilled; and now, whether he liked it or not, the King was obliged to keep his word, and give up his daughter.

Away then went these two together, and no long time passed before they met the faithful Fox. "You have the best certainly," said he, "but to the Maid of the Golden Castle belongs also the Golden Horse."

"How shall I obtain it?" inquired the youth.

"That I will tell you," answered the Fox; "first take to the King who sent you to the Golden Castle the beautiful Princess. Then there will be unheard-of joy, and they will readily show you the Golden Horse and give it to you. Do you mount it, and then give your hand to each for a parting shake, and last of all to the Princess, whom you must keep tight hold of, and pull her up behind you, and as soon as that is done ride off, and no one can pursue you, for the horse goes as fast as the wind." All this was happily accomplished, and the King's son led away the beautiful Princess in triumph on the Golden Horse. The Fox did not remain behind, and said to the Prince, "Now I will help you to the Golden Bird. When you come near the castle where it is, let the maiden get down, and I will take her into my cave. Then do you ride into the castle-yard, and at the sight of you there will be such joy that they will readily give you the bird; and as soon as you hold the cage in your hand ride back to us, and fetch again the maiden.

As soon as this deed was done, and the Prince had ridden back with his treasure, the Fox said, "Now you must reward me for my services."

"What do you desire?" asked the youth.

"When we come into yonder wood, shoot me dead and cut off my head and feet."

"That were a curious gratitude," said the Prince; "I cannot possibly do that."

"If you will not do it, I must leave you," replied the Fox; "but before I depart I will give you one piece of counsel. Beware of these two points: buy no gallows-flesh, and sit not on the brink of a spring!" With these words it ran into the forest.

The young Prince thought, "Ah, that is a wonderful animal, with some curious fancies! Who would buy gallows-flesh? and I don't see the pleasure of sitting on the brink of a spring!" Onwards he rode with his beautiful companion, and by chance the way led him through the village where his two brothers had stopped. There he found a great uproar and lamentation; and when he asked the reason, he was told that two persons were about to be hanged. When he came nearer, he saw that they were his two brothers, who had done some villainous deeds, besides spending all their money. He inquired if they could not be freed, and was told by the people that he might buy them off if he would, but they were not worth his gold, and deserved nothing but hanging. Nevertheless, he did not hesitate, but paid down the money, and his two brothers were released.

After this they all four set out in company, and soon came to the forest where they had first met the Fox; and as it was cool and pleasant beneath the trees, for the sun was very hot, and the two brothers said, "Come, let us rest awhile here by this spring, and eat and drink." The youngest consented, forgetting in the heat of conversation the warning he had received, and feeling no anxiety; but all at once the brothers threw him backwards into the water, and taking the maiden, the horse, and the bird, went home to their father. "We bring you," said they to him, "not only the Golden Bird, but also the Golden Horse and the Princess of the Golden Castle." At their arrival there was great joy; but the Horse would not eat, the Bird would not sing, and the Maiden would not speak, but wept bitterly from morning to night.

The youngest brother, however, was not dead. The spring, by great good luck, was dry, and he fell upon soft moss without any injury; but he could not get out again. Even in this necessity the faithful Fox did not leave him, but soon came up, and scolded him for not following its advice. "Still I cannot forsake you," it said; "but I will again help you to escape. Hold fast upon my tail, and I will draw you up to the top." When this was done, the Fox said, "You are not yet out of danger, for your brothers are not confident of your death, and have set spies all round the forest, who are to kill you if they should see you."

The youth thereupon changed clothes with a poor man who was sitting near, and in that guise went to the King's palace. Nobody knew him; but instantly the Bird began to sing, the Horse began to eat, and the beautiful Maiden ceased weeping. Bewildered at this change, the King asked what it meant. "I know not," replied the Maiden; "but I who was sad am now gay, for I feel as if my true husband were returned." Then she told him all that had happened; although the other brothers had threatened her with death if she disclosed anything. The King summoned before him all the people who were in the castle, and among them came the poor youth, dressed as a beggar, in his rags; but the Maiden knew him, and fell upon his neck. The wicked brothers were seized and tried; but the youngest married the Princess, and succeeded to the King's inheritance.

But what happened to the poor Fox? Long after, the Prince went once again to the wood, and there met the Fox, who said, "You have now everything you can desire, but to my misfortunes there is no end, although it lies in your power to release me." And, with tears, it begged the Prince to cut off its head and feet. At last he did so; and scarcely was it accomplished when the Fox became a man, who was no other than the brother of the Princess, delivered at length from the charm which bound him. From that day nothing was ever wanting to the happiness of the Hero of the Golden Bird.

The Travels of Thumbling

A certain Tailor had a son who was so very diminutive in stature that he went by the nickname of Thumbling; but the little fellow had a great deal of courage in his soul, and one day he said to his father, "I must and will travel a little." "You are very right, my son," replied his father; "take a long darning-needle with you, and stick a lump of sealing-wax on the end of it, and then you will have a sword to travel with."

Now, the Tailor would eat once more with his son, and so he skipped into the kitchen to see what his wife had cooked for their last meal. It was just ready, however, and the dish stood upon the hearth, and he asked his wife what it was.

"You can see for yourself," replied she.

Just then Thumbling jumped on the fender and peeped into the pot; but, happening to stretch his neck too far over the edge of it, the smoke of the hot meat carried him up the chimney. For a little distance he rode on the smoke in the air; but at last he sank down on the earth. The little tailor was now embarked in the wide world, and went and engaged with a master in his trade; but with him the eating was not good, so Thumbling said to the mistress, "If you do not give us better food, I shall leave you, and early to-morrow morning write on your door with chalk. "Too many potatoes, too little meat; adieu, my lord potato-king.' " "What do you think you will do, grasshopper?" replied the mistress, and in a passion she snatched up a piece of cloth, and would have given him a thrashing; but the little fellow crept nimbly under a thimble and peeped out beneath at the mistress, and made faces at her. So she took up the thimble and tried to catch him; but Thumbling skipped into the cloth, and as she threw it away to look for him he slipped into the crevice of the table. "He, he, he, old mistress!" laughed he, putting his head up; and when she would have hit him, he dropped down into the drawer beneath. At last, however, she did catch him, and hunted him out of the house.

The little tailor wandered about till he came to a great forest, where he met a band of robbers who were going to steal the King's treasure. As soon as they saw the tailor, they thought to themselves, "Ah, such a little fellow as that can creep through the keyhole and serve us as a picklock!" "Hilloa!" cried one, "you Goliath, will you go with us to the treasure chamber? You can easily slip in, and hand us out the gold and silver."

Thumbling considered for a while, and at last consented and went with them to the place. Then he looked all over the doors to see if there were any chinks, and presently discovered one which was just wide enough for him to get through. Just as he was about to creep in one of the watchmen at the door saw him, and said to the other, "What ugly spider is that crawling there? I will crush it."

"Oh, let the poor thing be," said the other; "he has done nothing to you." So Thumbling got luckily through the chink into the chamber, and, opening the window beneath which the robbers stood, threw out, one by one, the silver dollars. Just as the tailor was in the heat of his work, he heard the King coming to visit his treasure-chamber, and in a great hurry he hid himself. The King observed that many dollars were gone; but he could not imagine who could have stolen them, for the locks and bolts were all fast, and everything appeared quite safe. So he went away again, and said to the watchmen, "Have a care! there is some one at my gold." Presently Thumbling began his work again, and the watchmen heard the gold moving, chinking, and falling down with a ring; so they sprang in, and would have seized the thief. But the tailor, when he heard them coming, was still quicker, and ran into a corner and covered himself over with a dollar, so that nothing of him could be seen. Then he called to the watchmen, "Here I am!" and they went up to the place; but before they could search he was in another corner, crying, "Ha, ha! here I am!" The watchmen turned there, but he was off again in a third corner, crying, "He, he, he! here I am!" So it went on, Thumbling making fools of them each time; and they ran here and there so often about the chamber, that at last they were wearied out and went away. Then he threw the dollars out as before; and, when he came to the last, he gave it a tremendous jerk, and, jumping out after it, flew down upon it to the ground. The robbers praised him very highly, saying, "You are a mighty hero; will you be our captain?" Thumbling refused, as he wished first to see the world. So they shared the booty among them; but the little tailor only took a farthing, because he could not carry any more.

After this deed he buckled his sword again round his body, and, bidding the robbers good day, set out further on his travels. He went to several masters seeking work; but none of them would have him, and at last he engaged himself as waiter at an inn. The maids, however, could not bear him, for he could see them without their seeing him, and he gave information to the master of what they took secretly from the larder, and how they helped themselves out of the cellar. So the servants determined among themselves to serve him out by playing him some trick. Not long afterwards one of them was mowing grass in the garden, and saw Thumbling skipping about from daisy to daisy, so she mowed down in a great hurry the grass where he was, and tying it in a bundle together threw it slily into the cows's tall. A great black cow instantly swallowed it up, and Thumbling, too, without injuring him; but he was not at all pleased, for it was a very dark place, and no light to be seen at all! While the cow was being milked, Thumbling called out, "Holloa! when will that pail be full?" but the noise of the running milk prevented his being heard. By-and-bye the master came into the stable and said, "This cow must be killed to-morrow!" This speech made Thumbling tremble, and he shouted out in a shrill tone, "Let me out first, I say; let me out!"

The master heard him but could not tell where the voice came from, and he asked, "Where are you?"

"In the dark," replied Thumbling; but this the master could not understand, so he went away.

The next morning the cow was killed. Happily Thumbling escaped without a wound from all the cutting and carving, and was sent away in the sausage-meat. As soon as the butcher began his work, he cried with all his might, "Don't chop too deep! don't chop too deep!" But the whirring of the cleaver again prevented his being heard. Necessity is the mother of invention, and so Thumbling set his wits to work, and jumped so cleverly out between the cuts, that he came off with a whole skin. He was not able to get away very far, but fell into the basin where the fragments were, and presently he was rolled up in a skin for a sausage. He found his quarters here very narrow, but soon afterwards, when he was hung up in the chimney to be smoked, the time appeared dreadfully long to him. At last, one day he was taken down, for a guest was to be entertained with a sausage. When the good wife cut the sausage in half, he took care not to stretch out his neck too far, lest it should be cut through. Then, seizing his opportunity, he made a jump, and sprang quite out.

In this house however, where things had gone so badly, the little tailor would not stop any longer; so he set out again on his travels. His liberty did not last very long. In the open fields he met a Fox, who snapped him up in a twinkling. "Ah, Mr. Fox," called Thumbling, "I don't want to stick here in your throat; let me out again."

"You are right," replied the Fox, "You are no use there; but if you will promise me all the hens in your father's farmyard, I will let you off scot-free."

"With all my heart," said Thumbling; "you shall have all the fowls, I promise you."

Then the Fox let him out, and carried him home; and as soon as the farmer saw his dear son again, he gave all the hens instantly to the Fox as his promised reward. Thereupon Thumbling pulled out the farthing which he had earned upon his wanderings, and said, "See I have brought home with me a beautiful piece of gold."

"But why did they give the Fox the poor little hens to gobble up?"

"Why, you simpleton, don't you think your father would rather have his dear child than all the fowls in his farmyard!"

THE GODFATHER DEATH

A certain poor man had twelve children, and was obliged to work day and night to find them bread to eat; but when the thirteenth child was born, he ran out in despair on the highroad to ask the first person he should meet to stand godfather to it.

Presently he met Death striding along on his withered legs, who said, "Take me for godfather." The man asked him who he was, and received for reply, "I am Death, who makes all things equal." "Then," answered the man, "you are the right person – you make no difference between the rich and the poor; you shall be godfather to my boy."

Death replied, "I will make your child rich and famous; he who has me for a friend can need nought." Then the man told him the christening was fixed for the following Sunday, and invited him to come; and at the right time he did appear, and acted very becomingly on the occasion.

When the boy arrived at years of discretion, the godfather came and took him away with him, and leading him into a forest showed him an herb which grew there. "Now," said Death, "you shall receive your christening gift. I make you a famous physician. Every time you are called to a sick person I will appear to you. If I stand at the head of your patient, you may speak confidently that you can restore him, and if you give him a morsel of that vegetable, he will speedily get well, but if I stand at the feet of the sick he is mine, and you may say all medicine is in vain, for the best physician in the world could not cure him. Dare not, however, use the herb against my will, for then it will go ill with you."

In a very short space of time the youth became the most renowned physician in the world. "He only wants just to see the sick person, and he knows instantly whether he will live or die," said every one to his neighbour; and so it came to pass, that from far and near people came to him, bringing him the sick, and giving him so much money that he soon became a very rich man. Once it happened that the King fell sick, and our Physician was called in to say if recovery were possible. When he came to the bedside, he saw that Death stood at the feet of the King. "Ah," thought he, "if I might this once cheat Death; he will certainly take offence; but then I am his godchild, and perhaps he will shut his eyes to it, – I will venture."

So saying he took up the sick man, and turned him round, so that Death stood at the head of the King; then he gave the King some of the herb, and he instantly rose up quite refreshed.

Soon afterwards Death, with an angry and gloomy face, came to the Physician, and pressed him on the arm, saying, "You have put my light out, but this time I will excuse you, because you are my godchild; however, do not dare to act so again, for it will cost you your life, and I shall come and take you away."

Soon after this event the daughter of the King fell into a serious illness, and, as she was his only child, he wept day and night until his eyes were almost blinded. He also caused to be made known, that whoever saved her life should receive her for a bride, and inherit his crown. When the Physician came to the bedside of the sick, he perceived Death at her feet, and he remembered the warning of his godfather; but the great beauty of the Princess, and the fortune which her husband would receive, so influenced him that he cast all other thoughts to the wind. He would not see that Death cast angry looks at him, and threatened him with his fist; but he raised up his patient, and laid her head where her feet had been. Then he gave her a portion of the wonderful herb, and soon her cheeks regained their colour, and her blood circulated freely.

When Death thus saw his kingdom a second time invaded, and his power mocked, he strode swiftly to the side of the Physician and said, "Now is your turn come;" and he struck him with his icy-cold hand so hard, that the Physician was unable to resist, and was obliged to follow Death to his underground abode. There the Physician saw thousands upon thousands of lamps burning in immeasurable rows, some large, others small, and others yet smaller. Every moment some were extinguished, but others in the same instant blazed out, so that the flames appeared to dance up here and there in continual variation.

"Do you see?" said Death. "These are the lamps of men's lives. The larger ones belong to children, the next to those in the flower of their age, and the smallest to the aged and grey-headed. Yet some of the children and youth in the world have but the smallest lamps."

The Physician begged to be shown his own lamp, and Death pointed to one almost expiring, saying, "There, that is thine."

"Ah, my dear godfather," exclaimed the Physician, frightened, "kindle a new one for me; for your love of me do it; that I may enjoy some years of life, marry the Princess, and come to the crown."

"I cannot," answered Death; "one lamp must be extinguished before another can be lighted."

"Then place the old one over a new lamp, that its dying fire may kindle a fresh blaze," said the Physician, entreatingly.

Death made as if he would perform his wish, and prepared a large and fresh lamp; but he did it very slowly, in order to revenge himself, and the little flame died before he finished. Then the Physician sank to the earth, and fell for ever into the hands of Death!

The Robber Bridegroom

There was once a Miller who had a beautiful daughter, whom he wished to see well married. Not long after there came a man who appeared very rich, and the Miller, not knowing anything to his disadvantage, promised his daughter to him. The maiden, however, did not take a fancy to the suitor, nor could she love him as a bride should; and, moreover, she had no confidence in him, but as often as she looked at him, or thought about him, her heart sank within her. Once he said to her, "You are my bride, yet you never visit me." The maiden answered "I do not know where your house is." "It is deep in the shades of the forest," said the man. Then the maiden tried to excuse herself by saying she should not be able to find it; but the Bridegroom said, "Next Sunday you must come and visit me; I have already invited guests, and, in order that you may find your way through the forest, I will strew the path with ashes."

When Sunday came, the maiden prepared to set out; but she felt very anxious and knew not why, and, in order that she might know her way back, she filled her pockets with beans and peas. These she threw to the right and left of the path of ashes, which she followed till it led her into the thickest part of the forest; there she came to a solitary house, which looked so gloomy and desolate that she felt quite miserable. She went in, but no one was there, and the most profound quiet reigned throughout. Suddenly a voice sang –

"Return, fair maid, return to your home;
'Tis to a murderer's den you've come."

The maiden looked round, and perceived that it was a bird in a cage against the wall which sang the words. Once more it uttered them –

"Return, fair maid, return to your home;
'Tis to a murderer's den you've come."

The maiden went from one room to the other, through the whole house, but all were empty, and not a human being was to be seen anywhere. At last she went into the cellar, and there sat a withered old woman, shaking her head. "Can you tell me," asked the maiden, "whether my bridegroom lives in this house?"

"Ah, poor girl," said the old woman, "when are you to be married? You are in a murderer's den. You think to be a bride, and to celebrate your wedding, but you will only wed with Death! See here, I have a great cauldron filled with water, and if you fall into their power they will kill you without mercy, cook, and eat you, for they are cannibals. If I do not have compassion and save you, you are lost."

So saying, the old woman led her behind a great cask, where no one could see her. "Be as still as a mouse," said she, "and don't move hand or foot, or all is lost. At night, when the robbers are asleep, we will escape; I have long sought an opportunity." She had scarcely finished speaking when the wicked band returned, dragging with them a poor girl, to whose shrieks and cries they paid no attention. They gave her some wine to drink, three glasses, one white, one red, and one yellow, and at the last she fell down in a swoon. Meanwhile the poor Bride behind the cask trembled and shuddered to see what a fate would have been hers. Presently one of the robbers remarked a gold ring on the finger of the girl, and, as he could not draw it off easily, he took a hatchet and chopped off the finger. But the finger, with the force of the blow, flew up and fell behind the cask, right into the lap of the Bride; and the robber, taking a light, went to seek it, but could not find it. Then one of the others asked, "Have you looked behind the cask?"

"Oh! do come and eat," cried the old woman in a fright; "come and eat, and leave your search till the morning: the finger will not run away."

"The old woman is right," said the robbers, and, desisting from their search, they sat down to their meal; and the old woman mixed with their drink a sleeping draught, so that presently they lay down to sleep on the floor and snored away. As soon as the Bride heard them, she came from behind the cask and stepped carefully over the sleepers, who lay side by side, fearing to awake any of them. Heaven helped her in her trouble, and she got over this difficulty well; and the old woman started up too and opened the door, and then they made as much haste as they could out of the murderers' den. The wind had blow away the ashes, but the beans and peas the Bride had scattered in the morning had sprouted up, and now showed the path in the moonlight. All night long they walked on, and by sunrise they came to the mill, and the poor girl narrated her adventures to her father the Miller.

Now, when the day came that the wedding was to be celebrated, the Bridegroom appeared, and the Miller gathered together all his relations and friends. While they sat at table each kept telling some tale, but the Bride sat silent, listening. Presently the Bridegroom said, "Can you not tell us something, my heart; do not you know of anything to tell?"

"Yes," she replied. "I will tell you a dream of mine. I thought I went through a wood, and by-and-bye I arrived at a house wherein there was not a human being, but on the wall there hung a bird in a cage which sang –

'Return, fair maid, return to your home;
'Tis to a murderer's den you've come.'

And it sang this twice. – My treasure, thus dreamed I. – Then I went through all the rooms, and every one was empty and desolate, and at last I stepped down into the cellar, and there sat a very old woman, shaking her head from side to side. I asked her, 'Does my Bridegroom dwell in this house?' and she replied, 'Ah, dear child, you have fallen into a murderer's den; thy lover does dwell here, but he will kill you.' – My treasure, thus dreamed I. – Then, I thought that the old woman hid me behind a great cask, and scarcely had she done so when the robbers came home, dragging a maiden with them, to whom they gave three glasses of wine, one red, one white, and one yellow; and at the third her heart snapped. – My treasure, thus dreamed I. – Then one of the robbers saw a gold ring on her finger, and because he could not draw it off he took up a hatchet and hewed at it, and the finger flew up, and fell behind the cask into my lap. And there is the finger with the ring!"

With these words she threw it down before him, and showed it to all present.

The Robber, who during her narration had become pale as death, now sprang up, and would have escaped; but the guests held him, and delivered him up to the judges.

And soon afterwards he and his whole band were condemned to death for their wicked deeds.

The Six Swans

A King was once hunting in a large wood, and pursued his game so hotly, that none of his courtiers could follow him. But when evening approached he stopped, and looking around him perceived that he had lost himself. He sought a path out of the forest, but could not find one, and presently he saw an old woman with a nodding head, who came up to him. "My good woman," said he to her, "can you not show me the way out of the forest?" "Oh, yes, my Lord King," she replied; "I can do that very well, but upon one condition, which, if you do not fulfil, you will never again get out of the wood, but will die of hunger."

"What, then, is this condition?" asked the King.

"I have a daughter," said the old woman, "who is as beautiful as any one you can find in the whole world, and well deserves to be your bride. Now, if you will make her your Queen, I will show you your way out of the wood." In the anxiety of his heart, the King consented, and the old woman led him to her cottage, where the daughter was sitting by the fire. She received the King as if she had expected him, and he saw at once that she was very beautiful, but yet she did not quite please him, for he could not look at her without a secret shuddering. However, after all he took the maiden up on his horse, and the old woman showed him the way, and the King arrived safely at his palace, where the wedding was to be celebrated.

The King had been married once before, and had seven children by his first wife, six boys and a girl, whom he loved above everything else in the world. He became afraid, soon, that the stepmother might not treat them very well, and might even do them some great injury, so he took them away to a lonely castle which stood in the midst of a forest. This castle was so hidden, and the way to it so difficult to discover, that he himself could not have found it if a wise woman had not given him a ball of cotton which had the wonderful property, when he threw it before him, of unrolling itself and showing him the right path. The King went, however, so often to see his dear children, that the Queen noticed his absence, became inquisitive, and wished to know what he went to fetch out of the forest. So she gave his servants a great quantity of money, and they disclosed to her the secret, and also told her of the ball of cotton which alone could show her the way. She had now no peace until she discovered where this ball was concealed, and then she made some fine silken shirts, and, as she had learnt of her mother, she sewed within each one a charm. One day soon after, when the King was gone out hunting, she took the little shirts and went into the forest, and the cotton showed her the path. The children, seeing some one coming in the distance, thought it was their dear father, and ran out towards her full of joy. Then she threw over each of them a shirt, which, as it touched their bodies, changed them into Swans, which flew away over the forest. The Queen then went home quite contented, and thought she was free of her stepchildren; but the little girl had not met her with the brothers, and the Queen did not know of her.

The following day the King went to visit his children, but he found only the maiden. "Where are your brothers?" asked he. "Ah, dear father," she replied, "they are gone away and have left me alone;" and she told him how she had looked out of the window and seen them changed into Swans, which had flown over the forest; and then she showed him the feathers which they had dropped in the courtyard, and which she had collected together. The King was much grieved, but he did not think that his wife could have done this wicked deed, and, as he feared the girl might also be stolen away, he took her with him. She was, however, so much afraid of the stepmother, that she begged him not to stop more than one night in the castle.

The poor Maiden thought to herself, "This is no longer my place, I will go and seek my brothers;" and when night came she escaped and went quite deep into the wood. She walked all night long and great part of the next day, until she could go no further from weariness. Just then she saw a rude hut, and walking in she found a room with six little beds, but she dared not get into one, but crept under, and, laying herself upon the hard earth, prepared to pass the night there. Just as the sun was setting, she heard a rustling, and saw six white Swans come flying in at the window. They settled on the ground and began blowing one another until they had blown all their feathers off, and their swan's down stripped off like a shirt. Then the maiden knew them at once for her brothers, and gladly crept out from under the bed, and the brothers were not less glad to see their sister, but their joy was of short duration.

"Here you must not stay," said they to her; "this is a robbers' hiding-place; if they should return and find you here, they will murder you." "Can you not protect me, then?" inquired the sister.

"No," they replied; "for we can only lay aside our swan's feathers for a quarter of an hour each evening, and for that time we remain our human form, but afterwards we resume our changed appearance."

Their sister then asked them with tears, "Can you not be restored again?"

"Oh no," replied they; "the conditions are too difficult. For six long years you must neither speak nor laugh, and during that time you must sew together for us six little shirts of star-flowers, and should there fall a single word from your lips, then all your labour will be in vain." Just as the brother finished speaking, the quarter of an hour elapsed, and they all flew out of the window again like Swans.

The little sister, however, made a solemn resolution to rescue her brothers, or die in the attempt; and she left the cottage, and, penetrating deep into the forest, passed the night amid the branches of a tree. The next morning she went out and collected the star-flowers to sew together. She had no one to converse with, and for laughing she had no spirits, so there up in the tree she sat, intent upon her work. After she had passed some there there, it happened that the King of that country was hunting in the forest, and his huntsmen came beneath the tree on which the Maiden sat. They called to her and asked, "Who art thou?" But she gave no answer. "Come down to us," continued they; "we will do thee no harm." She simply shook her head, and, when they pressed her further with questions, she threw down to them her gold necklace, hoping therewith to satisfy them. They did not, however, leave her, and she threw down her girdle, but in vain; and even her rich dress did not make them desist. At last the hunter himself climbed the tree and brought down the maiden, and took her before the King. The King asked her, "Who art thou? What dost thou upon that tree?" But she did not answer; and then he asked her in all the languages that he knew, but she remained dumb to all, as a fish. Since, however, she was so beautiful, the King's heart was touched, and he conceived for her a strong affection. Then he put around her his cloak, and, placing her before him on his horse, took her to his castle. There he ordered rich clothing to be made for her, and, although her beauty shone as the sunbeams, not a word escaped her. The King placed her by his side at table, and there her dignified mien and manners so won upon him, that he said, "This Maiden will I marry, and no other in the world;" and after some days he was united to her.

Now, the King had a wicked stepmother who was discontented with his marriage, and spoke evil of the young Queen. "Who knows whence the wench comes?" said she. "She who cannot speak is not worthy of a King." A year after, when the Queen brought her first-born into the world, the old woman took him away. Then she went to the King and complained that the Queen was a murderess. The King, however, would not believe it, and suffered no one to do any injury to his wife, who sat composedly sewing at her shirts and paying attention to nothing else. When a second child was born, the false stepmother used the same deceit, but the King again would not listen to her words, but said, "She is too pious and good to act so: could she but speak and defend herself, her innocence would come to light." But when again, the third time, the old woman stole away the child, and then accused the Queen, who answered not a word to the accusation, the King was obliged to give her up to be tried, and she was condemned to suffer death by fire.

When the time had elapsed, and the sentence was to be carried out, it happened that the very day had come round when her dear brothers should be made free; the six shirts were also ready, all but the last, which yet wanted the left sleeve. As she was led to the scaffold, she placed the shirts upon her arm, and just as she had mounted it, and the fire was about to be kindled, she looked round, and saw six Swans come flying through the air. Her heart leapt for joy as she perceived her deliverers approaching, and soon the Swans, flying towards her, alighted so near that she was enabled to throw over them the shirts, and as soon as she had done so their feathers fell off and the brothers stood up alive and well; but the youngest wanted his left arm, instead of which he had a swan's wing. They embraced and kissed each other, and the Queen, going to the King, who was thunderstruck, began to say, "Now may I speak, my dear husband, and prove to you that I am innocent and falsely accused;" and then she told him how the wicked woman had stolen away and hidden her three children. When she had concluded, the King was overcome with joy, and the wicked stepmother was led to the scaffold and bound to the stake and burnt to ashes.

The King and the Queen for ever after lived in peace and prosperity with their six brothers.

Old Sultan

A certain Peasant had a trusty dog called Sultan, who had grown quite old in his service, and had lost all his teeth, so that he could not hold anything fast. One day the Peasant stood with his wife at the house-door, and said, "This morning I shall shoot old Sultan, for he is no longer of any use." His Wife, however, compassionating the poor animal, replied, "Well, since he has served us so long and so faithfully, I think we may very well afford him food for the rest of his life." "Eh, what?" replied her husband; "you are not clever; he has not a tooth in his head, and never a thief is afraid of him, so he must trot off. If he has served us, he has also received every day his dinner."

The poor Dog, lying stretched out in the sun not far from his master, heard all he said, and was much troubled at learning that the morrow would be his last day. He had one good friend, the Wolf in the forest, to whom he slipt at evening, and complained of the sad fate which awaited him. "Be of good courage, my father," said the Wolf; "I will help you out of your trouble. I have just thought of something. Early to-morrow morning your master goes haymaking with his wife, and they will take with them their child, because no one will be left in the house. And while they are at work they will put him behind the hedge in the shade, and set you by to watch him. I will then spring out of the wood and steal away the child, and you must run after me hotly as if you were pursuing me. I will let it fall, and you shall take it back to its parents, who will then believe you have saved it, and they will be too thankful to do you any injury; and so you will come into great favour, and they will never let you want again."

This plan pleased the Dog, and it was carried out exactly as proposed. The father cried when he saw the Wolf running off with the child, but as old Sultan brought it back he was highly pleased, and stroked him, and said, "Not a hair of your head shall be touched; you shall eat your meals in comfort to the end of your days." He then told his wife to go home and cook old Sultan some bread and broth, which would not need biting, and also to bring the pillow out of his bed, that he might give it to him for a resting-place. Henceforth old Sultan had as much as he could wish for himself; and soon afterwards the Wolf visited him and congratulated him on his prosperous circumstances. "But, my father," said he slily, "you will close your eyes if I by accident steal away a fat sheep from your master." "Reckon not on that," replied the Dog; "my master believes me faithful; I dare not give you what you ask." The Wolf, however, thought he was not in earnest, and by night came slinking into the yard to fetch away the sheep. But the Peasant, to whom the Dog had communicated the design of the Wolf, caught him and gave him a sound thrashing with the flail. The Wolf was obliged to scamper off, but he cried out to the Dog, "Wait a bit, you rascal, you shall pay for this!

The next morning the wolf sent the Boar to challenge the Dog, that they might settle their affair in the forest. Old Sultan, however, could find no other second than a Cat, who had only three legs, and, as they went out together, the poor Cat limped along, holding her tail high in the air from pain. The Wolf and his second were already on the spot selected,but as they saw their opponent coming they thought he was bringing a great sabre with him, because they saw in front the erect tail of the Cat; and, whenever the poor animal hopped on its three legs, they thought nothing else than he was going to take up a great stone to throw at them. Both of them, thereupon, became very nervous, and the Boar crept into a heap of dead leaves, and the Wolf climbed up a tree. As soon as the Dog and Cat arrived on the spot they wondered what had become of their adversary. The wild Boar, however, had not quite concealed himself, for his ears were sticking out; and, while the Cat was considering them attentively, the Boar twitched one of his ears, and the Cat took it for a mouse, and, making a spring, gave it a good bite. At this the Boar shook himself with a great cry, and ran away, calling out, "There sits the guilty one, up in the tree!" The Dog and the Cat looked up and saw the Wolf, who was ashamed at himself for being so fearful, and, begging the Dog's pardon, entered into treaty with him.

The Almond-tree

Long, long ago, perhaps two thousand years, there was a rich man who had a beautiful and pious wife; and they were very fond of one another, but had no children. Still they wished for some very much, and the wife prayed for them day and night; still they had none.

Before their house was a yard; in it stood an almond-tree, under which the woman stood once in the winter peeling an apple; and as she peeled the apple she cut her finger, and the blood dropped on to the snow. "Ah," said the woman, with a deep sigh, and she looked at the blood before her, and was very sad; "had I but a child as red as blood and as white as snow!" and as she said that, her heart grew light; and it seemed to her as if something would come of her wish. Then she went into the house; and a month passed, the snow disappeared; and two months, then all was green; and three months, then came the flowers out of the ground; and four months, then all the trees in the wood squeezed up against one another, and the green boughs all grew twisted together, and the little birds sang, so that the whole wood resounded, and the blossoms fell from the trees. When the fifth month had gone, and she stood under the almond-tree, it smelt so sweet, that her heart leaped for joy, and she could not help falling down on her knees; and when the sixth month had passed, the fruits were

The almond-tree.

large, and she felt very happy; at the end of the seventh month, she snatched the almonds and ate them so greedily, that she was dreadfully ill; then the eighth month passed away, and she called her husband and cried, and said, "If I die, bury me under the almond-tree;" then she was quite easy, and was glad, till the next month was gone; then she had a child as white as snow, and as red as blood; and when she saw it, she was so delighted that she died.

Then her husband buried her under the almond-tree and began to grieve most violently: a little time and he was easier; and when he had sorrowed a little longer he left off; and a little time longer and he took another wife.

With the second wife he had a daughter; but the child by the first wife was a little son, and was as red as blood, and as white as snow. When the woman looked at her daughter, she loved her so much; but then she looked at the little boy, and it seemed to go right through her heart; and it seemed as if he always stood in her way, and then she was always thinking how she could get all the fortune for her daughter; and it was the Evil One who suggested it to her, so that she couldn't bear the sight of the little boy, and poked him about from one corner to another, and buffeted him here, and cuffed him there, so that the poor child was always in fear; and when he came home from school he had no peace.

Once the woman had gone into the store-room, and the little daughter came up and said, "Mother, give me an apple." "Yes, my child," said the woman, and gave her a beautiful apple out of the box: the box had a great heavy lid, with a great, sharp iron lock. "Mother," said the little daughter, "shall not brother have one too?" That annoyed the woman; but she said, "Yes, when he comes from school." And as she saw out of the window that he was coming, it was just as if the Evil One came over her, and she snatched the apple away from her daughter again, and said, "You shall not have one before your brother!" She threw the apple into the box and shut it. Then the little boy came in at the door; and the Evil One made her say, in a friendly manner, "My son, will you have an apple?" and she looked at him wickedly. "Mother," said the little boy, "how horribly you look! yes, give me an apple." Then she thought she must pacify him. "Come with me," she said, and opened the lid; "reach out an apple;" and as the little boy bent into the box, the Evil One whispered to her – bang! she slammed the lid to, so that his head flew off and fell amongst the red apples. Then in the fright she thought, "Could I get that off my mind!" Then she went up into her room to the chest of drawers, and got out a white cloth from the top drawer, and she set the head on the throat again and tied the handkerchief round, so that nothing could be seen; and placed him outside the door on a chair, and gave him the apple in his hand. After a while little Marline came in the kitchen to her mother, who stood by the fire and had a kettle with hot water before her, which she kept stirring round. "Mother," said little Marline, "brother is sitting outside the door, and looks quite white, and has got an apple in his hand. I asked him to give me the apple, but he didn't answer me; then I was quite frightened." "Go again," said the Mother, "and if he will not answer you, give him a box on the ear." Then Marline went to her brother, and said, "Give me the apple;" but he was silent. Then she gave him a box on the ear, and the head tumbled off, at which she was frightened, and began to cry and sob. Then she ran to her mother, and said, "Oh, mother, I have knocked my brother's head off!" and she cried and cried, and would not be pacified. "Marline," said the Mother, "what have you done? But be quiet, so that nobody may notice it; it can't be helped now; we'll bury him under the almond-tree."

Then the mother took the little boy and put him into a box, and put it under the almond-tree; but little Marline stood by, and cried and cried, and the tears all fell into the box.

Soon the father came home and sat down to table, and said, "Where is my son?" Then the mother brought in a great big dish of stew; and little Marline cried, and could not leave off. Then said the father again, "Where is my son?" "Oh," said the mother, "he has gone across the country to Mütten; he is going to stop there a bit!"

"What is he doing there? and why did he not say good-bye to me?" "Oh, he wanted to go, and asked me if he might stop there six weeks, he will be taken care of there!" "Ah," said the man, "I feel very sorry; that was not right; he ought to have wished me good-bye." With that he began to eat, and said to Marline, "What are you crying for? your brother will soon come back." "Oh, wife," said he then, "how delicious this tastes; give me some more!" And he ate till all the broth was done.

Little Marline went to her box and took from the bottom drawer her best silk handkerchief, and carried it outside the door, and cried bitter tears. Then she laid herself under the almond-tree on the green grass; and when she had laid herself there, all at once she felt quite light and happy, and cried no more. Then the almond-tree began to move, and when the boughs spread out quite wide, and then went back again; just as when one is very much pleased and claps with the hands. At the same time a sort of mist rose from the tree; in the middle of the mist it burned like a fire; and out of the fire there flew a beautiful bird that sang very sweetly, and flew high up in the air: and when it had flown away, the almond-tree was as it had been before. The little Marline was as light and happy as if her brother were alive still and went into the house to dinner.

The bird flew away and perched upon a Goldsmith's house, and began to sing, –

"My mother killed me;
My father grieved for me;
My sister, little Marline,
Wept under the almond-tree:
Kywitt, kywitt, what a beautiful bird am I!"

The Goldsmith sat in his workshop and was making a gold chain when he heard the bird that sat upon his roof and sang, and it seemed to him so beautiful. Then he got up, and as he stepped over the sill of the door he lost one of his slippers; but he went straight up the middle of the street with one slipper and one sock on. He had his leather apron on, and in the one hand he had the gold chain, and in the other the pincers, and the sun shone brightly up the street. He went and stood and looked at the bird. "Bird," said he then, "how beautifully you can sing! Sing me that song again." "Nay," said the Bird," I don't sing twice for nothing. Give me the gold chain and I will sing it you again." "There," said the Goldsmith, "take the gold chain; now sing me that again." Then the bird came and took the gold chain in the right claw, and sat before the Goldsmith, and sang, –

"My mother killed me;
My father grieved for me;
My sister, little Marline,
Wept under the almond-tree:
Kywitt, kywitt, what a beautiful bird am I!"

Then the bird flew off to a Shoemaker, and perched upon the roof of his house, and sang, –

"My mother killed me;
My father grieved for me;
My sister, little Marline,
Wept under the almond-tree:
Kywitt, kywitt, what a beautiful bird am I!"

The Shoemaker heard it, and ran outside the door in his shirt-sleeves and looked up at the roof, and was obliged to hold his hand before his eyes to prevent the sun from blinding him. "Bird," said he, "how beautifully you can sing!" Then he called in at the door, "wife, come out, here's a bird; look at the bird; he just can sing beautifully." Then he called his daughter, and children, and apprentices, servant-boy, and maid, and they all came up the street and looked at the bird: oh, how beautiful he was, and he had such red and green feathers, and round about the throat was all like gold, and the eyes sparkled in his head like stars! "Bird," said the Shoemaker, "now sing me that piece again." "Nay," said the Bird, "I don't sing twice for nothing, you must make me a present of something." "Wife," said the man, "go into the shop; on the top shelf there stands a pair of red shoes, fetch them down." The wife went and fetched the shoes. "There, Bird," said the man; "now sing me that song again." Then the bird came and took the shoes in the left claw, and flew up on to the roof again, and sang, –

"My mother killed me;
My father grieved for me;
My sister, little Marline,
Wept under the almond-tree:

Kywitt, kywitt, what a beautiful bird am I!"

And when he had done singing he flew away. The chain he had in the right claw, and the shoes in his left claw; and he flew far away to a mill; and the mill went clipp-clapp, clipp-clapp, clipp-clapp. And in the mill there sat twenty miller's men; they were shaping a stone, and chipped away, hick-hack, hick-hack, hick-hack; and the mill went clipp-clapp, clipp-clapp, clipp-clapp. Then the bird flew and sat on a lime-tree that stood before the mill, and sang, –

"My mother killed me;"

then one left off;

"My father grieved for me;"

then two more left off and heard it;

"My sister,"

then again four left off;

"little Marline,"

now there were only eight chipping away;

"Wept under"

now only five;

"the almond-tree:"

now only one:

"Kywitt, kywitt, what a beautiful bird am I!"

Then the last left off, when he heard the last word. "Bird," said he, "how beautifully you sing! let me, too, hear that; sing me that again." "Nay," said the Bird, "I don't sing twice for nothing. Give me the millstone and I will sing it again." "Ay," said he, "if it belonged to me alone, you should have it." "Yes," said the others, "if he sings again he shall have it." Then the bird came down, and all the twenty millers caught hold of a pole, and raised the stone up, hu, uh, upp! hu, uh, upp! And the bird stuck his head through the hole, and took it round his neck like a collar, and flew back to the tree, and sang, –

"My mother killed me;
My father grieved for me;
My sister, little Marline,
Wept under the almond-tree:
Kywitt, kywitt, what a beautiful bird am I!"

And when he had done singing he spread his wings, and had in his right claw the gold chain, in his left the shoes, and round his neck the millstone, and he flew far away to his father's house.

In the room sat the father, the mother, and little Marline, at dinner; and the father said, "Oh, dear, how light and happy I feel!" "Nay," said the mother, "I am all of a tremble, just as if there were going to be a heavy thunderstorm." But little Marline sat and cried and cried, and the bird came flying, and as he perched on the roof the father said, "I feel so cheerful, and the sun shines so deliciously outside, it's exactly as if I were going to see some old acquaintance again." "Nay," said the wife, "I am so frightened, my teeth chatter, and it's like fire in my veins;" and she tore open her stays; but little Marline sat in a corner and cried, and held her plate before her eyes and cried it quite wet. Then the bird perched on the almond-tree, and sang, –

"My mother killed me;"

Then the mother held her ears and shut her eyes, and would neither see nor hear; but it rumbled in her ears like the most terrible storm, and her eyes burned and twittered like lightning.

"My father grieved for me;"

"Oh, mother," said the man, "there is a beautiful bird that sings so splendidly; the sun shines so warm, and everything smells all like cinnamon!"

"My sister, little Marline,"

Then Marline laid her head on her knees and cried away; but the man said, "I shall go out, I must see the bird close." "Oh, do not go," said the woman; "it seems as if the whole house shook and were on fire!" But the man went out and looked at the bird.

"Wept under the almond-tree:
Kywitt, kywitt, what a beautiful bird am I!"

And the bird let the gold chain fall, and it fell just round the man's neck, and fitted beautifully. Then he went in and said, "See what an excellent bird it is; it has given me such a beautiful gold chain, and it looks so splendid." But the woman was so frightened that she fell her whole length on the floor, and her cap tumbled off her head. Then the bird sang again, –

"My mother killed me;"

"Oh, that I were a thousand fathoms under the earth, not to hear that!"

"My father grieved for me;"

Then the woman fainted.

"My sister, little Marline,"

"Ah," said Marline, "I will go out too, and see if the bird will give me something!" and she went out. Then the bird threw the shoes down.

"Wept under the almond-tree:
Kywitt, kywitt, what a beautiful bird am I!"

Then, she was so happy and lively, she put the new red shoes on, and danced and jumped back again. "Oh," said she, "I was so dull when I went out, and now I am so happy. That is a splendid bird; he has given me a pair of red shoes."

"Well," said the woman, and jumped up, and her hair stood on end like flames of fire, "I feel as if the whole world were coming to an end; I will go out too, and see if it will make me easier." And as she stepped outside the door – bang! the bird threw the millstone on to her head, so that she was completely overwhelmed. The father and little Marline heard it and went out. Then a smoke, and flames, and fire rose from the place, and when that had passed there stood the little brother; and he took his father and little Marline by the hand, and all three embraced one another heartily, and went into the house to dinner.

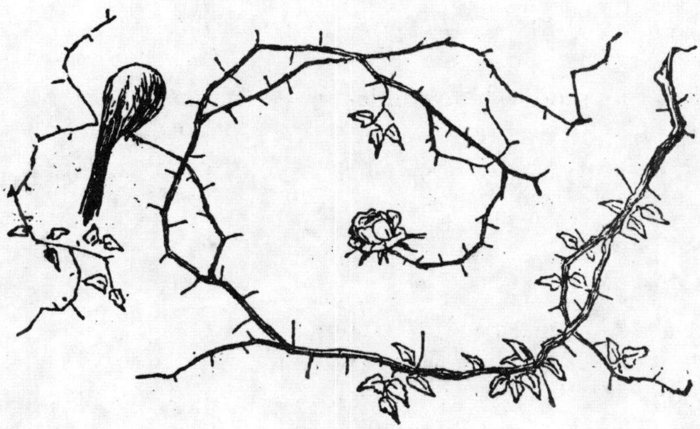

Briar Rose

~

In olden times there lived a King and Queen, who lamented day by day that they had no children, and yet never a one was born. One day, as the Queen was bathing and thinking of her wishes, a Frog skipped out of the water, and said to her,"Your wish shall be fulfilled, – before a year passes you shall have a daughter."

As the Frog had said, so it happened, and a little girl was born who was so beautiful that the King almost lost his senses, but he ordered a great feast to be held, and invited to it not only his relatives, friends, and acquaintances, but also all the wise women who are kind and affectionate to children. There happened to be thirteen in his dominions, but, since he had only twelve golden plates out of which they could eat, one had to stop at home. The fête was celebrated with all the magnificence possible, and, as soon as it was over, the wise women presented the infant with their wonderful gifts: one with virtue, another with beauty, a third with riches, and so on, so that the child had everything that is to be desired in the world. Just as eleven had given their presents, the thirteenth old lady stepped in suddenly. She was in a tremendous passion because she had not been invited, and, without greeting or looking at any one, she exclaimed loudly, "The Princess shall prick herself with a spindle on her fifteenth birthday and die!" and without a word further she turned her

Briar Rose.

back and left the hall. All were terrified, but the twelfth fairy, who had not yet given her wish, then stepped up, but because she could not take away the evil wish, but only soften it, she said, "She shall not die, but shall fall into a sleep of a hundred years' duration."

Then the King, who naturally wished to protect his child from this misfortune, issued a decree commanding that every spindle in the kingdom should be burnt. Meanwhile all the gifts of the wise women were fulfilled, and the maiden became so beautiful, gentle, virtuous, and clever, that every one who saw her fell in love with her. It happened on the day when she was just fifteen years old that the Queen and the King were not at home, and so she was left alone in the castle. The maiden looked about in every place, going through all the rooms and chambers just as she pleased, until she came at last to an old tower. Up the narrow winding staircase she tripped until she arrived at a door, in the lock of which was a rusty key. This she turned, and the door sprang open, and there in the little room sat an old woman with a spindle spinning flax. "Good day, my good old lady," said the Princess, "what are you doing here?"

"I am spinning," said the old woman, nodding her head.

"What thing is that which twists round so merrily?" inquired the maiden, and she took the spindle to try her hand at spinning. Scarcely had she done so when the prophecy was fulfilled, for she pricked her finger; and at the very same moment she fell back upon a bed which stood near in a deep sleep. This sleep extended over the whole palace. The King and Queen, who had just come in, fell asleep in the hall, and all their courtiers with them – the horses in the stable, the doves upon the eaves, the flies upon the walls, and even the fire upon the hearth, all ceased to stir – the meat which was cooking ceased to frizzle, and the cook at the instant of pulling the hair of the kitchen-boy lost his hold and began to snore too. The wind also fell entirely, and not a leaf rustled on the trees round the castle.

Now around the palace a thick hedge of briars began growing, which every year grew higher and higher, till the castle was quite hid from view, so that one could not even see the flag upon the tower. Then there went a legend through the land of the beautiful maiden Briar Rose, for so was the sleeping Princess named, and from time to time Princes came endeavouring to penetrate through the hedge into the castle; but it was not possible, for the thorns held them, as if by hands, and the youths were unable to release themselves, and so perished miserably.

After the lapse of many years, there came another King's son into the country, and heard an old man tell the legend of the hedge of briars; how that behind it stood a castle where slept a wondrously beauteous Princess called Briar Rose, who had slumbered nearly a hundred years, and with her the Queen and King and all their court. The old man further related what he had heard from his grandfather, that many Princes had come and tried to penetrate the hedge, and had died a miserable death. But the youth was not to be daunted, and however much the old man tried to dissuade him, he would not listen, but cried out, "I fear not, I will see this hedge of briars!"

Just at that time came the last day of the hundred years when Briar Rose was to awake again. As the young Prince approached the hedge, the thorns turned to fine large flowers, which of their own accord made a way for him to pass through, and again closed up behind him. In the courtyard he saw the horses and dogs lying fast asleep, and on the eaves were the doves with their heads beneath their wings. As soon as he went into the house, there were the flies asleep upon the wall, the cook still stood with his hand on the hair of the kitchen-boy, the maid at the board with the unplucked fowl in her hand. He went on, and in the hall he found the courtiers lying asleep, and above, by the throne, were the King and Queen. He went on further, and all was so quiet that he could hear himself breathe, and at last he came to the tower and opened the door of the little room where slept Briar Rose. There she lay, looking so beautiful that he could not turn away his eyes, and he bent over her and kissed her. Just as he did so she opened her eyes, awoke, and greeted him with smiles. Then they went down together, and immediately the King and Queen awoke, and the whole court, and all stared at each other wondrously. Now the horses in the stable got up and shook themselves, – the dogs wagged their tails, – the doves upon the eaves drew their heads from under their wings, looked around, and flew away, – the flies upon the walls began to crawl, the fire to burn brightly and to cook the meat, – the meat began again to frizzle, – the cook gave his lad a box upon the ear which made him call out, – and the maid began to pluck the fowl furiously. The whole palace was once more in motion as if nothing had occurred, for the hundred years' sleep had made no change in any one.

By-and-by the wedding of the Prince with Briar Rose was celebrated with great splendour, and to the end of their lives they lived happy and contented.

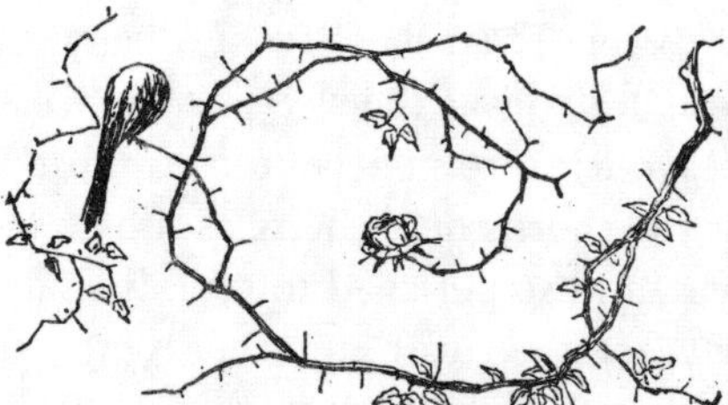

MISFORTUNE

When misfortune pursues any one, it will find him out into whatever corner he may creep, or however far he may flee over the world.

Now, once upon a time, a certain many became so poor, that he had not a single faggot of wood left wherewith to light his fire. So, he went into the forest to fell a tree, but they were all too large and too strong; and he penetrated deeper among them till he found one which he thought would do. Just as he was about to raise his axe he perceived a pack of wolves, coming out of the brushwood, who howled dreadfully as they came nearer. The man threw away his axe, and ran till he came to a bridge. The deep water, however, had rotted the bridge; and so, just as he was about to run over it, it cracked and fell into the water. What was he to do now? If he stopped still, the wolves would overtake him and tear him to pieces; so, in his perplexity, he jumped into the water, but there, because he could not swim, he soon began to sink. By chance a couple of fishermen, who sat on the other bank, saw him; and one of them swam after him and brought him to shore. Then they laid him down beneath an old wall, to dry in the sunshine and regain his strength a bit. But, just as he recovered his senses, and tried to thank the fishermen for their help and to tell his tale, the wall fell upon him and crushed him!

KING THRUSH-BEARD

A certain King had a daughter who was beautiful above all belief, but withal so proud and haughty, that no suitor was good enough for her, and she not only turned back every one who came but also made game of them all. Once the King proclaimed a great festival, and invited thereto from far and near all the marriageable young men. When they arrived they were all set in a row, according to their rank and standing: first the Kings, then the Princes, the Dukes, the Marquesses, the Earls, and last of all the Barons. Then the King's daughter was led down the rows, but she found something to make game of in all. One was too fat. "The wine-tub!" said she. Another was too tall. "Long and lanky has no grace," she remarked. A third was too short and fat. "To stout to have any wits," said she. A fourth was too pale. "Like death himself," was her remark; and a fifth who had a great deal of colour she called "a cockatoo." The sixth was not straight enough, and him she called "a green log scorched in the oven!" And so she went on, nicknaming every one of the suitors, but she made particularly merry with a good young King whose chin had grown rather crooked. "Ha, ha!" laughed she, "he has a chin like a thrush's beak;" and after that day he went by the name of Thrush-beard.

The old King, however, when he saw that his daughter did nothing but mock at and make sport of all the suitors who were collected, became very angry, and swore that she should take the first decent beggar for a husband who came to the gate.

A couple of days after this a player came beneath the windows to sing and earn some bounty if he could. As soon as the King saw him he ordered him to be called up, and presently he came into the room in all his dirty ragged clothes, and sang before the King and Princess, and when he had finished he begged for a slight recompense. The King said, "Thy song has pleased so much that I will give thee my daughter for a wife."

The Princess was terribly frightened, but the King said, "I have taken an oath, and mean to perform it, that I will give you to the first beggar." All her remonstrances were in vain, the priest was called, and the Princess was married in earnest to the player. When the ceremony was performed, the King said, "Now it cannot be suffered that you should stop here with your husband, in my house, no! you must travel about the country with him."

So the beggarman led her away with him, and she was forced to trudge along with him on foot. As they came to a large forest she asked –

"To whom belongs this beautiful wood?"

The echo replied –

"King Thrush-beard the good!
Had you taken him, so was it thine."

"Ah, silly," said she,

"What a lot had been mine
Had I happily married King Thrush-beard!"

Next they came to a meadow, and she asked,

"To whom belongs this meadow so green?"

"To King Thrush-beard," was again the reply.

Then they came to a great city, and she asked,

"To whom does this beautiful town belong?"

"To King Thrush-beard," said one.

"Ah, what a simpleton was I that I did not marry him when I had the chance!" exclaimed the poor Princess.

"Come," broke in the Player, "it does not please me, I can tell you, that you are always wishing for another husband: am I not good enough for you?"

By-and-by they came to a very small hut, and she said, "Ah, heavens, to whom can this miserable, wretched hovel belong?"

The Player replied, "That is my house, where she shall live together."

The Princess was obliged to stoop to get in at the door, and when she was inside, she asked, "Where are the servants?" "What servants?" exclaimed her husband, "you must yourself do all that you want done. Now make a fire and put on some water, that you may cook my dinner, for I am quite tired."

The Princess, however, understood nothing about making fires or cooking, and the beggar had to set to work himself, and as soon as they had finished their scanty meal they went to bed. In the morning the husband woke up his wife very early, that she might set the house to rights, and for a couple of days they lived on in this way, and made an end of their store. Then the husband said, "Wife, we must not go on in this way any longer, stopping here, doing nothing; you must weave some baskets." So he went out and cut some osiers and brought them home, but when his wife attempted to bend them the hard twigs wounded her hands and made them bleed. "I see that won't suit," said her husband; "you had better spin, perhaps that will do better."

So she sat down to spin, but the harsh thread cut her tender fingers very badly, so that the blood flowed freely. "Do you see," said the husband, "how you are spoiling your work? I made a bad bargain in taking you! Now I must try and make a business in pots and earthen vessels: you shall sit in the market and sell them."

"Oh, if anybody out of my father's dominions should come and see me in the market selling pots," thought the Princess to herself, "how they will laugh at me!"

However, all her excuses were in vain: she must either do that or die of hunger.

The first time all went well, for the people bought of the Princess, because she was so pretty-looking, and not only gave her what she asked, but some even laid down their money and left the pots behind. On her earnings this day they lived for some time as long as they lasted; and then the husband purchased a fresh stock of pots. With these she placed her stall at a corner of the market, offering them for sale. All at once a drunken hussar came plunging down the street on his horse, and rode right into the midst of her earthenware, and shattered it into a thousand pieces. The accident, as well it might, set her a-weeping, and in her trouble, not knowing what to do, she ran home crying, "Ah, what will become of me, what will my good man say?" When she had told her husband he cried out. "Who ever would have thought of sitting at the corner of the market to sell earthenware? but well, I see you are not accustomed to any ordinary work. There, leave off crying; I have been to the King's palace, and asked if they were not in want of a kitchen-maid, and they have agreed to take you, and there you will live free of cost."

Now the Princess became a kitchenmaid, and was obliged to do as the cook bade her, and wash up the dirty things. Then she put a jar into each of her pockets, and in them she took home what was left of what fell to her share of the good things, and of these she and husband made their meals. Not many days afterwards it happened that the wedding of the King's eldest son was to be celebrated, and the poor wife placed herself near the door of the saloon to look on. As the lamps were lit and guests more and more beautiful entered the room, and all dressed most sumptuously, she reflected on her fate with a saddened heart, and repented of the pride and haughtiness which had so humiliated and impoverished her. Every now and then the servants threw her out of the dishes morsels of rich delicacies which they carried in, and whose fragrant smells increased her regrets, and these pieces she put into her pockets to carry home. Presently the King entered, clothed in silk and velvet, and having a golden chain round his neck. As soon as he saw the beautiful maiden standing at the door, he seized her by the hand and would dance with her, but she, terribly frightened, refused; for she saw it was King Thrush-beard, who had wooed her, and whom she had laughed at. Her struggles were of no avail, he drew her into the ballroom, and there tore off the band to which the pots were attached, so that they fell down and the soup ran over the floor, while the pieces of meat, &c. skipped about in all directions. When the fine folks saw this sight they burst into one universal shout of laughter and derision, and the poor girl was so ashamed that she wished herself a thousand fathoms below the earth. She ran out at the back door and would have escaped; but on the steps she met a man, who took her back, and when she looked at him, lo! it was King Thrush-beard again. He spake kindly to her, and said, "Be not afraid; I and the musician, who dwelt with you in the wretched hut, are one; for love of you I have acted thus; and the hussar who rode in among the pots was also myself. All this has taken place in order to humble your haughty disposition, and to punish you for your pride, which led you to mock me."

At these words she wept bitterly, and said, "I am not worthy to be your wife, I have done you so great a wrong." But he replied, "Those evil days are passed: we will now celebrate our marriage."

Immediately after came the bridesmaids, and put on her the most magnificent dresses: and then her father and his whole court arrived, and wished her happiness on her wedding-day; and now commenced her true joy as Queen of the country of King Thrush-beard.

Rumpelstiltskin

There was once a poor Miller who had a beautiful daughter; and one day, having to go to speak with the King, he said, in order to make himself appear of consequence, that he had a daughter who could spin straw into gold. The King was very fond of gold, and thought of himself, "That is an art which would please me very well;" and so he said to the Miller, "If your daughter is so very clever, bring her to the castle in the morning, and I will put her to the proof."

As soon as she arrived the King led her into a chamber which was full of straw; and, giving her a wheel and a reel, he said, "Now set yourself to work, and if you have not spun this straw into gold by an early hour to-morrow, you must die." With these words he shut the room door, and left the maiden alone.

There she sat for a long time, thinking how to save her life; for she understood nothing of the art whereby straw might be spun into gold; and her perplexity increased more and more, till at last she began to weep. All at once the door opened and in stepped a little Man, who said, "God evening, fair maiden; why do you weep so sore?" "Ah," she replied, "I must spin this straw into gold, and I am sure I do not know how."

The little Man asked, "What will you give me if I spin it for you?"

"My necklace," said the maiden.

The Dwarf took it, placed himself in front of the wheel, and whirr, whirr, whirr, three times round, and the bobbin was full. Then he set up another, and whirr, whirr, whirr, thrice round again, and a second bobbin was full; and so he went all night long, until all the straw was spun, and the bobbins were full of gold. At sunrise the King came, very much astonished to see the gold; the sight of which gladdened him, but did not make his heart less covetous. He caused the maiden to be led into another room, still larger, full of straw; and then he bade her spin it into gold during the night if she valued her life. The maiden was again quite at a loss what to do; but while she cried the door opened suddenly, as before, and the Dwarf appeared and asked her what she would give him in return for his assistance. "The ring off my finger," she replied. The little Man took the ring and began to spin at once, and by the morning all the straw was changed to glistening gold. The King was rejoiced above measure at the sight of this, but still he was not satisfied; but, leading the maiden into another still larger room, full of straw as the others, he said, "This your must spin during the night; but if you accomplish it you shall be my bride." "For," thought he to himself, "a richer wife thou canst not have in all the world."

When the maiden was left alone, the Dwarf again appeared, and asked, for the third time, "What will you give me to do this for you?"

"I have nothing left that I can give you," replied the maiden.

"Then promise me your first-born child if you become Queen," said he.

The Miller's daughter thought, "Who can tell if that will ever happen?" and, ignorant how else to help herself out of her trouble, she promised the Dwarf what he desired; and he immediately set about and finished the spinning. When morning came, and the King found all he had wished for done, he celebrated his wedding, and the fair Miller's daughter became Queen.

About a year after the marriage, when she had ceased to think about the little Dwarf, she brought a fine child into the world; and, suddenly, soon after its birth, the very man appeared and demanded what she had promised. The frightened Queen offered him all the riches of the kingdom if he would leave her her child; but the Dwarf answered, "No; something human is dearer to me than all the wealth of the world."

The Queen began to weep and groan so much, that the Dwarf compassionated her, and said, "I will leave you three days to consider; if you in that time discover my name you shall keep your child."

All night long the Queen racked her brains for all the names she could think of, and sent a messenger through the country to collect far and wide any new names. The following morning came the Dwarf, and she began with "Caspar," "Melchior," "Balthassar," and all the odd names she knew; but at each the little Man exclaimed, "That is not my name." The second day the Queen inquired of all her people for uncommon and curious names, and called the Dwarf "Ribs-of-Beef," "Sheep-shank," "Whalebone;" but at each he said, "This is not my name." The third day the messenger came back and said, "I have not found a single name; but as I came to a high mountain near the edge of the forest, where foxes and hares say goodnight to each other, I saw there a little house, and before the door a fire was burning, and round this fire a very curious little Man was dancing on one leg, and shouting, –

" 'To-day I stew, and then I'll bake,
To-morrow I shall the Queen's child take;
Ah! how famous it is that nobody knows
That my name is Rumpelstiltskin.' "

When the queen heard this she was very glad, for now she knew his name; and soon after came the Dwarf, and asked, "Now, my lady Queen, what is my name?"

First she said, "Are you called Conrade?" "No."

"Are you called Hal?" "No."

"Are you called Rumpelstiltskin?"

"A witch has told you! a witch has told you!" shrieked the little Man, and stamped his right foot so hard in the ground with rage that he could not draw it out again. Then he took hold of his left leg with both hands, and pulled away so hard that his right came off in the struggle, and he hopped away howling terribly. And from that day to his the Queen has heard no more of her troublesome visitor.

Little Snow-White

Once upon a time in the depth of winter, when the flakes of snow were falling like feathers from the clouds, a Queen sat at her palace window, which had an ebony black frame, stitching her husband's shirts. While she was thus engaged and looking out at the snow she pricked her finger, and three drops of blood fell upon the snow. Because the red looked so well upon the white, she thought to herself, "Had I now but a child as white as this snow, as red as this blood, and as black as the wood of this frame!" Soon afterwards a little daughter was born to her, who was as white as snow, and red as blood, and with hair as black as ebony, and thence she was named "Snow-White," and when the child was born the mother died.

About a year afterwards the King married another wife, who was very beautiful, but so proud and haughty that she could not bear any one to be better-looking than herself. She possessed a wonderful mirror, and when she stepped before it and said, –

"Oh, mirror, mirror on the wall,
Who is the fairest of us all?"

it replied, –

"Thou art the fairest, lady Queen."

Then she was pleased, for she knew that the mirror spoke truly.

Little Snow-White, however, grew up, and became pretty and prettier, and when she was seven years old her complexion was as clear as the noon-day, and more beautiful than the Queen herself. When the Queen now asked her mirror, –

"Oh, mirror, mirror on the wall,
Who is the fairest of us all?"

it replied, –

"Thou wert the fairest, lady Queen;
Snow-White is fairest now, I ween."

This answer so frightened the Queen that she became quite yellow with envy. From that hour, whenever she perceived Snow-White, her heart was hardened against her, and she hated the maiden. Her envy and jealousy increased so that she had no rest day nor night, and she said to a Huntsman, "Take the child away into the forest, I will never look upon her again. You must kill her, and bring me her heart and tongue for a token."

The Huntsman listened and took the maiden away, but when he drew out the knife to kill her, she began to cry, saying, "Ah, dear Huntsman, give me my life! I will run into the wild forest, and never come home again."

This speech softened the Hunter's heart, and her beauty so touched him that he had pity on her and said, "Well, run away then, poor child;" but he thought to himself, "The wild beasts will soon devour you." Still he felt as if a stone had been taken from his heart, because her death was not by his hand. Just at that moment a young boar came roaring along to the spot, and as soon as he clapt eyes upon it the Huntsman caught it, and, killing it, took its tongue and heart, and carried them to the queen for a token of his deed.

But now the poor little Snow-White was left motherless and alone, and overcome with grief, she was bewildered at the sight of so many trees, and knew not which way to turn. Presently she set off running, and ran over stones and through thorns, and wild beasts sprang up as she passed them, but they did her no harm. She ran on till her feet refused to go farther, and as it was getting dark, and she saw a little house near, she entered in to rest. In this cottage everything was very small, but more neat and elegant than I can tell you. In the middle stood a little table with a white cover over it, and seven little plates upon it, each plate having a spoon and a knife and a fork, and there were also seven little mugs. Against the wall were seven little beds ranged in a row, each covered with snow-white sheets. Little Snow-White, being both hungry and thirsty, ate a little morsel of porridge out of each plate, and drank a drop or two of wine out of each glass, for she did not wish to take away the whole share of any one. After that, because she was so tired, she laid herself down on one bed, but it did not suit; she tried another, but that was too long; a fourth was too short, a fifth too hard, but the seventh was just the thing, and tucking herself up in it she went to sleep, first commending herself to God.

When it became quite dark the lords of the cottage came home, seven Dwarfs, who dug and delved for ore in the mountains. They first lighted seven little lamps, and perceived at once – for they illumined the whole apartment – that somebody had been in, for everything was not in the order in which they had left it. The first asked, "Who has been sitting on my chair?" The second, "Who has been eating off my plate?" The third said, "Who has been nibbling at my bread?" The fourth, "Who has been at my porridge?" The fifth, "Who has been meddling with my fork?" The sixth grumbled out, "Who has been cutting with my knife?" The seventh said, "Who has been drinking out of my glass?" Then the first looking round began again. "Who has been lying on my bed?" he asked, for she saw that the sheets were tumbled. At these words the others came, and looking at their beds cried out too, "Some one has been lying in our beds!" But the seventh little man, running up to his, saw Snow-White sleeping in it; so he called his companions, who shouted with wonder and held up their seven torches, so that the light fell upon the maiden. "Oh heavens! oh heavens!" said they, "what a beauty she is!" and they were so much delighted that they would not awaken her, but left her to repose, and the seventh Dwarf, in whose bed she was, slept with each of fellows one hour, and so passed the night.

As soon as morning dawned Snow-White awoke, and was quite frightened when she saw the seven little men; but they were very friendly, and asked her what she was called. "My name is Snow-White," was her reply. "Why have you entered our cottage?" they asked. Then she told them how her stepmother would have had her killed, but the Huntsman had spared her life, and how she had wandered about the whole day until at last she had found their house. When her tale was finished the Dwarfs said, "Will you see after our household; be our cook, make the beds, wash, sew, and knit for us, and keep everything in neat order? if so, we will keep you here, and you shall want for nothing."

And Snow-White answered, "Yes, with all my heart and will;" and so she remained with them, and kept their house in order. In the mornings the Dwarfs went into the mountains and searched for ore and gold, and in the evenings they came home and found their meals ready for them. During the day the maiden was left alone, and therefore the good Dwarfs warned her and said, "Be careful of your stepmother, who will soon know of your being here; therefore let nobody enter the cottage."

The Queen meanwhile, supposing that she had eaten the heart and tongue of her daughter-in-law, did not think but that she was above all comparison the most beautiful of every one around. One day she stepped before her mirror, and said, –

"Oh, mirror, mirror on the wall,
Who is the fairest of us all?"

and it replied, –

"Thou wert the fairest, lady Queen;
Snow-White is fairest now, I ween.
Amid the forest, darkly green,
She lives with Dwarfs – the hills between."

This reply frightened her, for she knew that the mirror spoke the truth, and she perceived that the Huntsman had deceived her, and that Snow-White was still alive. Now she thought and thought how she should accomplish her purpose, for so long as she was not the fairest in the whole country, jealousy left her no rest. At last a thought struck her, and she dyed her face and clothed herself as a pedlar woman, so that no one could recognise her. In this disguise she went over the seven hills to the seven Dwarfs, knocked at the door of the hut, and called out, "Fine goods for sale! beautiful goods for sale!" Snow-White peeped out of the window and said, "Good day, my good woman, what have you to sell?" "Fine goods, beautiful goods!" she replied, "stays of all colours;" and she held up a pair which was made of variegated silks. "I may let in this honest woman," thought Snow-White; and she unbolted the door and bargained for one pair of stays. "You can't think, my dear, how it becomes you!" exclaimed the old woman, "Come, let me lace it up for you." Snow-White suspected nothing, and let her do as she wished, but the old woman laced her up so quickly and so tightly that all her breath went, and she fell down like one dead. "Now," thought the old woman to herself, hastening away, "now am I once more the most beautiful of all!"

Not long after her departure, at eventide, the seven Dwarfs came home, and were much frightened at seeing their dear little maid lying on the ground, and neither moving nor breathing, as if she were dead. They raised her up, and when they saw she was laced too tight they cut the stays in pieces, and presently she began to breathe again, and by little and little she revived. When the Dwarfs now heard what had taken place, they said, "The old pedlar woman was no other than your wicked mother-in-law; take more care of yourself, and let no one enter when we are not with you."

Meanwhile the old Queen had reached home, and going before her mirror, she repeated her usual words, –

"Oh, mirror, mirror on the wall,
Who is the fairest of us all?"

and it replied as before, –

> *"Thou wert the fairest, lady Queen;*
> *Snow-White is fairest now, I ween.*
> *Amid the forest, darkly green,*
> *She lives with Dwarfs – the hills between."*

As soon as it had finished, all her blood rushed to her heart, for she was so frightened to hear that Snow-White was yet living. "But now," thought she to herself, "will I contrive something which shall destroy her completely." Thus saying, she made a poisoned comb, by arts which she understood, and, then disguising herself, she took the form of an old widow. She went over the seven hills to the house of the seven Dwarfs, and, knocking at the door, called out, "Good wares to sell to-day!" Snow-White peeped out and said, "You must go further, for I dare not let you in."

"But still you may look," said the old woman, drawing out her poisoned comb and holding it up. The sight of this pleased the maiden so much, that she allowed herself to be persuaded, and opened the door. As soon as she made a purchase the old woman said, "Now let me for once comb you properly," and Snow-White consented, but scarcely was the comb drawn through the hair when the poison began to work, and the maiden soon fell down senseless. "You pattern of beauty," cried the wicked old Queen, "it is now all over with you," and so saying she departed.

Fortunately, evening soon came, and the seven Dwarfs returned, and as soon as they saw Snow-White lying, like dead, upon the ground, they suspected the old Queen, and soon discovered the poisoned comb, they immediately drew it out, and the maiden very soon revived and related all that had happened. Then they warned her against the wicked stepmother, and bade her to open the door to nobody.

Meanwhile the Queen, on her arrival home, had again consulted her mirror and received the same answer as twice before. This made her tremble and foam with rage and jealousy, and she swore Snow-White should die if it cost her her own life. Thereupon she went into an inner secret chamber where no one could enter, and there made an apple of the most deep and subtle poison. Outwardly it looked nice enough, and had rosy cheeks which would make the mouth of every one who looked at it water; but whoever ate the smallest piece of it would surely die. As soon as the apple was ready, the old Queen again dyed her face, and clothed herself like a peasant's wife, and then over the seven mountains to the seven Dwarfs she made her way. She knocked at the door, and Snow-White stretched out her head and said, "I dare not let anyone enter; the seven Dwarfs have forbidden me."

"That is hard for me," said the old woman; "for I must take back my apples: but there is one which I will give you."

"No," answered Snow-White, "no, I dare not take it."

"What! are you afraid of it?" cried the old woman; "there, see, I will cut the apple in halves; do you eat the red cheeks, and I will eat core." (The apple was so artfully made that the red cheeks alone were poisoned.) Snow-White very much wished for the beautiful apple, and when she saw the woman eating the core she could no longer resist, but, stretching out her hand, took the poisoned part. Scarcely had she placed a piece in her mouth when she fell down dead upon the ground. Then the queen, looking at her with glittering eyes, and laughing bitterly, exclaimed, "White as snow, red as blood, black as ebony!" This time the Dwarfs cannot re-awaken you."

When she reached home and consulted her mirror –

"Oh, mirror, mirror on the wall,
Who is the fairest of us all?"

it answered –

"Thou art the fairest, lady Queen."

Then her envious heart was at rest, as peacefully as an envious heart can rest.

When the little Dwarfs returned home in the evening, they found Snow-White lying on the ground, and there appeared to be no life in her body; she seemed to be quite dead. They raised her up, and searched if they could find anything poisonous; unlaced her, and even uncombed her hair, and washed her with water and with wine; but nothing availed: the dear child was really and truly dead. Then they laid her upon a bier, and all seven placed themselves around it, and wept and wept for three days without ceasing. Afterwards they would bury her, but she looked still fresh and lifelike, and even her red cheeks had not deserted her, so they said to one another, "We cannot bury her in the black ground," and they ordered a case to be made of transparent glass. In this one could view the body on all sides, and the Dwarfs wrote her name with golden letters upon the glass, saying that she was a King's daughter. Now they replaced the glass-case upon the ledge of a rock, and one of them always remained by it watching. Even the beasts bewailed the loss of Snow-White; first came an owl, then a raven, and last of all a dove.

For a long time Snow-White lay peacefully in her case, and changed not, but looked as if she were only asleep, for she was still white as snow, red as blood, and black-haired as ebony. By-and-bye it happened that a King's son was travelling in the forest, and came to the Dwarfs' house to pass the night. He soon perceived the glass-case upon the rock, and the beautiful maiden lying within, and he read also the golden inscription.

When he had examined it, he said to the Dwarfs, "Let me have this case, and I will pay what you like for it."

But the Dwarfs replied, "We will not sell it for all the gold in the world."

"Then give it to me," said the Prince; "for I cannot live without Snow-White. I will honour and protect her so long as I live."

When the Dwarfs saw he was so much in earnest, they pitied him, and at last gave him the case, and the Prince ordered it to be carried away on the shoulders of one of his attendants. Presently it happened that they stumbled over a rut, and with the shock the piece of poisoned apple which lay in Snow-White's mouth fell out. Very soon she opened her eyes, and, raising the lid of the glass-case, she rose up and asked, "Where am I?"

Full of joy, the Prince answered, "You are safe with me;" and he related to her what she had suffered, and how he would rather have her than any other for his wife, and he asked her to accompany him home to the castle of the King his father. Snow-White consented, and when they arrived there the wedding between them was celebrated as speedily as possible, with all the splendour and magnificence proportionate to the happy event.

By chance the old mother-in-law of Snow-White was also invited to the wedding, and when she was dressed in all her finery to go, she first stepped in front of her mirror, and asked, –

"Oh, mirror, mirror on the wall,
Who is the fairest of us all?"

and it replied,

"Thou wert the fairest, oh lady Queen;
The Prince's bride is more fair, I ween."

At these words the old Queen was in a fury, and was so terribly mortified that she knew not what to do with herself. At first she resolved not to go to the wedding, but she could not resist the wish for a sight of the young queen, and as soon as she entered she recognised Snow-White, and was so terrified with rage and astonishment that she remained rooted to the ground. Just then a pair of red-hot iron shoes were brought in with a pair of tongs and set before her, and these she was forced to put on and to dance in them till she fell down dead.

Roland

Once upon a time there lived a real old Witch who had two daughters one ugly and wicked, whom she loved very much, because she was her own child; and the other fair and good, whom she hated, because she was her stepdaughter. One day the stepchild wore a very pretty apron, which so pleased the other that she turned jealous, and told her mother she must and would have the apron. "Be quiet, my child," said she "you shall have it; your sister has long deserved death. To-night, when she is asleep, I will come and cut off her head; but take care that you lie nearest the wall, and push her quite to the side of the bed."

Luckily the poor maiden, hid in a corner, heard this speech, or she would have been murdered; but all day long she dared not go out of doors, and when bedtime came she was forced to lie in the place fixed for her: but happily the other sister soon went to sleep, and then she contrived to change places and get quite close to the wall. At midnight the old Witch sneaked in, holding in her right hand an axe, while with her left she felt for her intended victim; and then raising the axe in both her hands, she chopped off the head of her own daughter.

As soon as she went away, the maiden got up and went to her sweetheart, who was called Roland, and knocked at his door. When he came out she said to him, "Dearest

Roland, we must flee at once; my stepmother would have killed me, but in the dark she has murdered her own child; if day comes, and she discovers what she has done, we are lost!"

"But I advise you," said Roland, "first to take away her magic wand, or we cannot save ourselves if she should follow and catch us."

So the maiden stole away the wand, and taking up the head dropped three drops of blood upon the ground: one before the bed, one in the kitchen, and one upon the step: this done, she hurried away with her lover.

When the morning came and the old Witch had dressed herself, she called to her daughter and would have given her the apron, but no one came. "Where are you?" she called. "Here upon the step," answered one of the drops of blood. The old woman went out, but seeing nobody on the step, she called a second time, "Where are you?" "Hi, hi, here in the kitchen; I am warming myself," replied the second drop of blood. She went into the kitchen, but could see nobody; and once again she cried, "Where are you?"

"Ah! here I sleep in the bed," said the third drop; and she entered the room, but what a sight met her eyes! There lay her own child covered with blood, for she herself had cut off her head.

The old Witch flew into a terrible passion, sprang out of the window, and looking far and near, presently spied out her stepdaughter, who was hurrying away with Roland. "That won't help you!" she shouted; "were you twice as far, you should not escape me." So saying, she drew on her boots, in which she went an hour's walk with every stride, and before long she overtook the fugitives. But the maiden, as soon as she saw the Witch in sight, changed her dear Roland into a lake with the magic wand, and herself into a duck, who could swim upon its surface. When the old Witch arrived at the shore, she threw in bread-crumbs, and tried all sorts of means to entice the duck; but it was all of no use, and she was obliged to go away at evening without accomplishing her ends. When she was gone the maiden took her natural form, and Roland also, and all night long till daybreak they travelled onwards. Then the maiden changed herself into a rose, which grew amid a very thorny hedge, and Roland became a fiddler. Soon after came the old Witch, and said to him, "Good player, may I, break off your flower?" "Oh! yes," he replied, "and I will accompany you with a tune." In great haste she climbed up the bank to reach the flower, and as soon as she was in the hedge he began to play, and whether she liked it or not she was obliged to dance to the music, for it was a bewitched tune. The quicker he played, the higher was she obliged to jump, till the thorns tore all the clothes off her body, and scratched and wounded her so much that at last she fell down dead.

Then Roland, when he saw they were saved, said, "Now I will go to my father, and arrange the wedding."

"Yes," said the maiden, "and meanwhile I will rest here, and wait for your return, and, that no one may know me, I will change myself into a red stone."

Roland went away and left her there, but when he reached home he fell into the snares laid for him by another maiden, and forgot his true love, who for a long time waited his coming; but at last, in sorrow and despair of ever seeing him again, she changed herself into a beautiful flower, and thought that perhaps some one might pluck her and carry her to his home.

A day or two after a shepherd who was tending his flock in the field chanced to see the enchanted flower; and because it was so very beautiful he broke it off, took it with him, and laid it by in his chest. From that day everything prospered in the shepherd's house, and marvellous things happened. When he arose in the morning he found all the work already done: the room was swept, the chairs and tables dusted, the fire lighted upon the hearth, and the water fetched; when he came home at noonday the table was laid, and a good meal prepared for him. He could not imagine how it was all done, for he could find nobody ever in his house when he returned, and there was no place for any one to conceal himself. The good arrangements certainly pleased him well enough, but he became so anxious at last to know who it was, that he went and asked the advice of a wise woman. The woman said, "There is some witchery in the business; listen one morning if you can hear anything moving in the room, and if you do and can see anything, be it what it will, throw a white napkin over it, and the charm will be dispelled."

The shepherd did as he was bid, and the next morning, just as day broke, he saw his chest open and the flower come out of it. He instantly sprang up and threw a white napkin over it, and immediately the spell was broken, and a beautiful maiden stood before him, who acknowledged that she was the handmaid who, as a flower, had put his house in order. She told him her tale, and she pleased the shepherd so much, that he asked her if she would marry him, but she said, "No," for she would still keep true to her dear Roland, although he had left her; nevertheless, she promised still to remain with the shepherd, and see after his cottage.

Meanwhile, the time had arrived for the celebration of Roland's wedding, and, according to the old custom, it was proclaimed through all the country round, that every maiden might assemble to sing in honour of the bridal pair. When the poor girl heard this, she was so grieved that it seemed as if her heart would break, and she would not have gone to the wedding if others had not come and taken her with them.

When it came to her turn to sing, she stepped back till she was quite by herself, and as soon as she began, Roland jumped up, exclaiming, "I know the voice! that is my true bride! no other will I have!" All that he had hitherto forgotten and neglected to think of was suddenly brought back to his heart's remembrance, and he would not again let her go.

And now the wedding of the faithful maiden to the dear Roland was celebrated with great magnificence; and their sorrows and troubles being over, happiness became their lot.

[illegible]

[illegible]

[illegible]

[illegible]

[illegible]

[illegible]

The knapsack, the hat, and the horn.

The Knapsack, the Hat, and the Horn

Once upon a time there were three brothers, who every day sank deeper and deeper in poverty, until at last their need was so great that they were in danger of death from starvation, having nothing to bite or break. So they said to one another, "We cannot go on in this way; we had better go forth into the wide world and seek our fortunes." With these words they got up and set out, and travelled many a long mile over green fields and meadows without happening with any luck. One day they arrived in a large forest, and in the middle of it they found a hill, which, on their nearer approach, they saw was all silver. At this sight the eldest brother said, "Now I have met with my expected good fortune, and I desire nothing better." And, so saying, he took as much of the silver as he could carry, and turned back again to his house.

The others, however, said, "We desire something better than mere silver;" and they would not touch it, but went on further. After they had travelled a couple of days longer, they came to another hill, which was all gold. There the second brother stopped, and soon became quite dazzled with the sight. "What shall I do?" said he to himself; "shall I take as much gold as I can, that I may have enough to live upon, or, shall I go further still?" At last he came to a conclusion, and, putting what he could in his pockets, he bade his brother good-bye and returned home. The third brother said, however, "Silver and gold will I not touch; I will seek my fortune yet; perhaps something better than all will happen to me."

So he travelled along for three days alone, and at the end of the third he came to a great forest, which was a great deal more extensive than the former, and so much so that he could not find the end: and, moreover, he was almost perished with hunger and thirst. He climbed up a high tree to discover if he could by chance find an outlet to the forest; but so far as his eyes could reach there was nothing but tree-tops to be seen. His hunger now began to trouble him very much, and he thought to himself, "Could I now only for this once have a good meal, I might get on." Scarcely were the words out of his mouth when he saw, to his great astonishment, a napkin under the tree, spread over with all kinds of good food, very grateful to his senses. "Ah, this time," thought he, "my wish is fulfilled at the very nick:" and, without any consideration as to who brought or who cooked the dishes, he sat himself down and ate to his heart's content. When he had finished, he thought it would be a shame to leave such a fine napkin in the wood, so he packed it up as small as he could, and carried it away in his pocket. After this he went on again, and, as he felt hungry towards evening, he wished to try his napkin; and, spreading it out, he said aloud, "I should like to see you again spread with cheer;" and scarcely had he spoke when as many dishes as there was room for stood upon the napkin. At the sight he exclaimed, "Now you are dearer to me than a mountain of silver and gold, for I perceive you are a wishing-cloth;" but, however, he was not yet satisfied, but would go farther and seek his fortune.

The next evening he came up with a Charcoal-burner, who was busy with his coals, and who was roasting some potatoes at his fire for his supper. "Good evening, my black fellow," said our hero; "how do you find yourself in your solitude?" "One day is like another," replied he, "and every night potatoes: have you a mind for some? if so, be my guest."

"Many thanks," replied the traveller; "but I will not deprive you of your meal; you did not reckon on having a guest; but, if you have no objection, you shall yourself have an invitation to supper." "Who will invite me?" asked the Charcoal-burner; "I do not see that you have got anything with you, and there is no one in the circuit of two hours' walk who could give you anything."

"And yet there shall be a meal," returned the other, "better than you have ever seen."

So saying, he took out his napkin, and, spreading it on the ground, said, "Cloth, cover thyself!" and immediately meats boiled and baked, as hot as if just out of the kitchen, were spread about. the Charcoal-burner opened his eyes wide, but did not stare long, but soon began to eat away, cramming his black mouth as full as he could. When they had finished, the man, smacking his lips, said, "Come, your cloth pleases me; it would be very convenient for me here in the wood, where I have no one to cook. I will strike a bargain with you. There hangs a soldier's knapsack, which is certainly both old and shabby; but it possesses a wonderful virtue, and, as I have no more use for it, I will give it you in exchange for your cloth."

"But first I must know in what this wonderful virtue consists," said the traveller.

"I will tell you," replied the other. "If you tap thrice with your fingers upon it, out will come a corporal and six men, armed from head to foot, who will do whatsoever you command them."

"In faith," cried our hero, "I do not think I can do better; let us change;" and, giving the man his wishing-cloth, he took the knapsack off its hook, and strode away with it on his back.

He had not gone very far before he wished to try the virtue of his bargain; so he tapped upon it, and immediately the seven warriors stepped before him, and the leader asked his commands. "What does my lord and master desire?"

"March back quickly to the Charcoal-burner, and demand my wishing-cloth again," said our hero.

The soldiers wheeled round to the left, and before very long they brought what he desired, having taken it from the Collier without so much as asking his leave. This done, he dismissed them, and travelled on again, hoping his luck might shine brighter yet. At sunset he came to another Charcoal-burner, who was also preparing his supper at the fire, and asked, "Will you sup with me? Potatoes and salt, without butter, is all I have; sit down if you choose."

"No," replied the traveller; "this time you shall be my guest;" and he unfolded his cloth, which was at once spread with the most delicate fare. They ate and drank together, and soon got very merry; and when their meal was done, the Charcoal-burner said, "Up above there on that board lies an old worn-out hat, which possesses the wonderful power, if one put it on and presses it down on his head, of causing, as it were, twelve field-pieces to go off, one after the other, and shoot down all that comes in their way. The hat is of no use to me in that way, and therefore I should like to exchange it for your cloth."

"Oh! I have no objection to that," replied the other; and, taking the hat, he left his wishing-cloth behind him; but he had not gone very far before he tapped on his knapsack, and bade the soldiers who appeared to fetch it back from his guest.

"Ah," thought he to himself, "one thing happens so soon upon another, that it seems as if my luck would have no end." And his thoughts did not deceive him; for he had scarcely gone another day's journey when he met with a third Charcoal-burner, who invited him, as the others had, to a potato-supper. However, he spread out his wishing-cloth, and the feast pleased the Charcoal-burner so well, that he offered him, in return for his cloth, a horn, which had still more wonderful properties than either the knapsack or hat; for, when one blew it, every wall and fortification fell down before its blast, and even whole villages and towns were overturned. For this horn he gladly gave his cloth, but he soon sent his soldiers back for it; and now he had not only that, but also the knapsack, the hat, and the horn.

"Now,"said he, "I am a made man, and it is high time that I should return home and see how my brothers get on."

When he arrived at the old place, he found his brothers had built a splendid palace with their gold and silver, and were living in clover. He entered their house, but because he came in with coat torn to rags, the shabby hat upon his head, and the old knapsack on his back, his brothers would not own him. They mocked him saying, "You pretend to be our brother; why, he despised silver and gold, and sought better luck for himself; he would come accompanied like a mighty king, not as a beggar!" and they hunted him out of doors.

This treatment put the poor man in such a rage, that he knocked upon the knapsack so many times till a hundred and fifty men stood before him in rank and file. He commanded them to surround his brothers' house, and two of them to take hazel-sticks and thrash them both until they knew who he was. They set up a tremendous howling, so that the people ran to the spot and tried to assist the two brothers; but they could do nothing against the soldiers. By-and-by the King himself heard the noise, and he ordered out a captain and troop to drive the disturber of the peace out of the city; but the man with his knapsack soon gathered together a greater company, who beat back the captain and his men, and sent them home with bleeding noses. At this the King said, "This vagabond fellow shall be driven away;" and the next day he sent a larger troop against him; but they fared no better than the first. The beggar, as he was called, soon ranged more men in opposition, and, in order to do the work quicker, he pressed his hat down upon his head a couple of times; and immediately the heavy guns began to play, and soon beat down all the King's people, and put the rest to flight. "Now," said our hero, "I will never make peace till the King gives me his daughter to wife, and he places me upon the throne as ruler of his whole dominion." This vow which he had taken he caused to be communicated to the King, who said to his daughter "Must is a hard nut to crack: what is there left to me but that I do as this man desires? If I wish for peace, and to keep the crown upon my head, I must yield."

So the wedding was celebrated; but the Princess was terribly vexed that her husband was such a common man, and wore not only a very shabby hat, but also carried about with him everywhere a dirty old knapsack. She determined to get rid of them; and day and night she was always thinking how to manage it. It struck her suddenly that perhaps his wonderful power lay in the knapsack; so she flattered, caressed him, saying, "I wish you would lay aside that dirty knapsack; it becomes you so ill that I am almost ashamed of you."

"Dear child," he replied, "this knapsack is my greatest treasure; as long as I possess it I do not fear the greatest power on earth;" and he further told her all its wonderful powers. When he had finished, the Princess fell on his neck as if she would kiss him; but she craftily untied the knapsack, and, loosening it from his shoulders, ran away with it. As soon as she was alone she tapped upon it, and ordered the warriors who appeared to bind fast her husband and lead him out of the royal palace. They obeyed; and the false wife caused other soldiers to march behind, who were instructed to hunt the poor man out of the kingdom. It would have been all over with him had he not still possessed the hat, which he pressed down on his head as soon as his hands were free, and immediately the cannons began to go off, and demolished all before them. The Princess herself was at last obliged to go and beg pardon of her husband. He at last consented to make peace, being moved by her supplications and promises to behave better in future; and she acted so lovingly, and treated him so well for some time after, that he entrusted her with the secret, that although he might be deprived of the knapsack, yet so long as he had the hat no one could overcome him. As soon as she knew this, she waited until he was asleep and then stole away the hat, and caused her husband to be thrown into a ditch. The horn, however, was still left to him; and in a great passion, he blew upon it such a blast that in a minute down came tumbling the walls, forts, houses, and palaces, and buried the King and his daughter in the ruins. Luckily he ceased to blow for want of breath; for had he kept it up any longer all the houses would have been overturned, and not one stone left upon another. After this feat nobody dared to oppose him, and he set himself up as King over the whole country.

The Little Farmer

~

There was a certain village, wherein several rich farmers were settled, and only one poor one, who was therefore called "The Little Farmer." He had not even a cow, nor money to buy it, though he and his wife would have been only too happy to have had one. One day he said to her, "A good thought has just struck me: our father-in-law, the carver, can make us a calf out of wood and paint it brown, so that it will look like any other; in time, perhaps, it will grow big and become a cow." This proposal pleased his wife, and the carver was instructed accordingly, and he cut out the calf, painted it as it should be, and so made it that its head was bent down as if eating.

When the next morning, the cows were driven out to pasture, the Farmer called the Shepherd in and said, "See, I have here a little calf, but it is so small that it must as yet be carried." The Shepherd said, "Very well;" and, taking it under his arm, carried it down to the meadow and set it among the grass. All day the calf stood there as if eating, and the Shepherd said, "It will soon grow big and go alone: only see how it is eating!" At evening time, when he wanted to drive his flocks home, he said to the calf, "Since you can stand there to satisfy your hunger, you must also be able to walk upon your four legs, and I shall not carry you home in my arms." The Little

Farmer stood before his house-door waiting for his calf, and as the Shepherd drove his herd through the village he asked after it. The Shepherd replied, "It is still standing there eating: it would not listen and come with me." The Farmer exclaimed, "Eh, what! I must have my calf!" and so they both went together down to the meadow, but some one had stolen the calf, and it was gone. The Shepherd said, "Perhaps it has run away itself;" but the Farmer replied, "Not so – that won't do for me;" and dragging him before the Mayor, he was condemned for his negligence to give the Little Farmer a cow in the place of the lost calf.

Now the Farmer and his wife possessed the long-desired cow, and were very glad; but having no fodder they could give her nothing to eat, so that very soon they were obliged to kill her. The flesh they salted down, and the skin the Little Farmer took to the next town to sell, to buy another calf with what he got for it. On the way he passed a mill, where a raven was sitting with a broken wing, and out of compassion he took the bird up and wrapped it in the skin he was carrying. But the weather being just then very bad, a great storm of wind and rain falling, he was unable to go further, and, turning into the mill, begged for shelter. The Miller's wife was at home alone, and said to the Farmer, 'Lie down on that straw," and gave him a piece of bread and cheese, The Farmer ate it and lay down, with his skin near him, and the Miller's wife thought he was asleep. Presently in came a man, whom she received very cordially, and invited to sup with her; but the Farmer, when he heard talk of the feast, was vexed that he should have been treated only to bread and cheese. So the woman went down into the cellar and brought up four dishes, – roast meat, salad, boiled meat, and wine. As they were sitting down to eat there was a knock outside, and the woman exclaimed, "Oh, gracious! there is my husband!" In a great hurry she stuck the roast meat in the oven, the wine under the pillow, the salad upon the bed, and the boiled meat under it, while her guest stepped into a closet where she kept the linen. This done she let in her husband, and said, "God be praised you are returned again! what weather it is, as if the world were coming to an end!"

The Miller remarked the man lying on the straw, and asked what the fellow did there. His Wife said, "Ah, the poor fellow came in the wind and rain and begged for shelter, so I gave him some bread and cheese and showed him the straw!"

The husband said he had no objection, but bade her bring him quickly something to eat. The wife said, "I have nothing but bread and cheese," and her husband told her that he should be contented, and asked the Farmer to come and share his meal. The Farmer did not let himself be twice asked, but got up and ate away. Presently the Miller remarked the skin lying upon the ground in which was the raven, and asked, "What have you there!" The Farmer replied, "I have a truth-teller therein." "Can it tell me the truth too?" inquired the Miller.

"Why not?" said the other; "but he will only say four things, and the fifth he keeps to himself." The Miller was curious, and wished to hear it speak, and the Farmer squeezed the raven's head, so that it squeaked out. The Miller then asked, "What did he say?" and the Farmer replied, "The first thing is, under the pillow lies wine." That is a rare tell-tale!" cried the Miller, and went and found the wine. "Now again," said he. The Farmer made the raven croak again, and said, "Secondly, he declares there is roast meat in the oven." "That is a good tell-tale!" again cried the Miller, and, opening the oven, he took out the roast meat. Then the Farmer made the raven croak again, and said, "For the third thing, he declares there is salad on the bed."

"That is a good tell-tale!" cried the Miller, and went and found the salad. Then the Farmer made his bird croak once more, and said, "For the fourth thing, he declares there is boiled meat under the bed."

"That is a capital tell-tale!" cried the Miller, while he went and found as it said.

The worthy pair now sat down together at the table, but the Miller's wife felt terribly anxious, and went to bed, taking all the keys with her. The Miller was very anxious to know the fifth thing, but the Man said, "First let us eat quietly these four things, for the other is somewhat dreadful."

After they had finished their meal, the Miller bargained as to how much he should give for the fifth thing, and at last he agreed for three hundred dollars. Then the Farmer once more made the raven croak, and when the Miller asked what it said, he told him, "He declares that in the cupboard where the linen is there is an evil spirit."

The Miller said, "The evil spirit must walk out!" and tried the door but it was locked, and the woman had to give up the key to the Farmer, who unlocked it. The unbidden guest at once bolted out, and ran out of the house, while the Miller said, "Ah, I saw the black fellow, that was all right!" Soon they went to sleep; but at daybreak the Farmer took his three hundred dollars and made himself scarce.

The Farmer was now quite rich at home, and built himself a fine house, so that his fellows said, "The Little Farmer has certainly found the golden snow, of which he has brought away a basketful;" and they summoned him before the Mayor, that he might be made to say whence his riches came. The man replied, "I have sold my cow's skin in the city for three hundred dollars." And as soon as the others heard this they desired also to make a similar profit. The farmers ran home, killed all their cows, and, taking their skins off, took them to the city to sell them for so good a prize. The Mayor, however, said, "My maid must go first;" and when she arrived at the city she went to the merchant, but he gave her only three dollars for her skin. And when the rest came he would not give them so much, saying, "What should I do with all these skins?"

The farmers were much vexed at being outwitted by their poor neighbour, and, bent on revenge, they complained to the Mayor of his deceit. The innocent Little Farmer was condemned to death unanimously, and was to be rolled in a cask full of holes into the sea. He was led away, and a priest sent for who should say for him the mass for the dead. Every one else was obliged to remove to a distance, and when the Farmer looked at the priest he recognised the guest whom he had met at the mill. So he said to him, "I have delivered you out of the cupboard, now deliver me from this cask." Just at that moment the Shepherd passed by with a flock of sheep, and the Farmer, knowing that for a long time the man had desired to be mayor, cried out with all his might, "No, no! I will not do it; if all the world asked me I would not be it! No, I will not!"

When the Shepherd heard this he came up and said, "What are you doing here? What will you not do?'

The Farmer replied, "They will make me mayor if I keep in this cask; but no, I will not be here!"

"Oh," said the Shepherd, "if nothing more is wanting to be mayor I am willing to put myself in the cask!"

"Yes, you will be mayor if you do that," said the Farmer; and, getting out of the cask, the other got in, and the Farmer nailed the lid down again. Now he took the Shepherd's flock and drove it away, while the parson went to the Judge and told him he had said the prayers for the dead. Then they went and rolled the cask down to the water, and while it rolled the Shepherd called out, "Yes, I should like to be mayor!" They thought it was the Little Farmer who spoke; and saying, "Yes, we mean it; only you must first go below there;" and they sent the cask right into the sea.

That done the farmers returned home; and as they came into the village, so came also the Little Farmer, driving a flock of sheep quietly and cheerfully. The sight astounded the others, and they asked, "Whence comest thou? dost thou come out of the water?" "Certainly," answered he; "I sank deeper and deeper till I got to the bottom, where I pushed up the head of the cask, and, getting out, there were beautiful meadows, upon which many lambs were pasturing, and I brought this flock of them up with me."

"Are there any more?" inquired the farmers. "Oh yes," replied he, "more than you know what to do with!"

Then the farmers agreed that they would go and each fetch up a flock for himself; but the Mayor said, "I must go first." So they went together down to the water, and there happened to be a fine blue sky with plenty of fleecy clouds over it, which were mirrored in the water and looked like little lambs. The farmers called one to another, "Look there! we can see the sheep already on the ground below the water!" and the Mayor, pressing quite forward, said, "I will go first and look about me, and see if it is a good place, and then call you."

So saying he jumped in plump, and, as he splashed the water about, the others thought he was calling "Come along!" and so one after another the whole assemblage plunged in in a grand hurry. Thus was the whole village cleared out, and the "Little Farmer," as their only heir, became a very rich man.

Jorinde and Joringel.

Jorinde and Joringel

Once upon a time, in a castle in the midst of a large thick wood, there lived an old Witch all by herself. By day she changed herself into a cat or an owl; but in the evening she resumed her right form. She was able also to allure to her the wild animals and birds, whom she killed, cooked, and ate, for whoever ventured within a hundred steps of her castle was obliged to stand still, and could not stir from the spot until she allowed it; but if a pretty maiden came into the circle the Witch changed her into a bird, and then put her into a basket, which she carried into one of the rooms in the castle; and in this room were already many thousand such baskets of rare birds.

Now there was a young maiden called Jorinde, who was exceedingly pretty, and she was betrothed to a youth named Joringel, and just at the time that the events which I am about to relate happened, they were passing the days together in a round of pleasure. One day they went into the forest for a walk, and Joringel said, "Take care that you do not go too near the castle." It was a beautiful evening; the sun shining between the stems of the trees, and brightening up the dark green leaves and the turtle doves cooing softly upon the may-bushes. Jorinde began to cry, and sat down in the sunshine with Joringel, who cried too, for they were quite frightened, and thought they should die, when they looked round and saw how far they had wandered, and that there was no house in sight. The sun was yet half above the hills and half below, and Joringel, looking through the brushwood, saw the old walls of the castle close by them, which frightened him terribly, so that he fell off his seat. Then Jorinde sang, –

> *"My little bird, with his ring so red,*
> *Sings sorrow, and sorrow and woe;*
> *For he sings that the turtle-dove soon will be dead,*
> *Oh sorrow, and sorrow – jug, jug, jug."*

Joringel lifted up his head, and saw Jorinde was changed into a nightingale, which was singing, "Jug, jug, jug," and presently an owl flew round thrice, with his eyes glistening, and crying, "Tu wit, tu woo." Joringel could not stir; there he stood like a stone, and could not weep, nor speak, nor move hand or foot. Meanwhile the sun set, and, the owl flying into a bush, out came an ugly old woman, thin and yellow, with great red eyes, and a crooked nose which reached down to her chin. She muttered and seized the nightingale, and carried it away in her hand, while Joringel remained there incapable of moving or speaking. At last the Witch returned, and said, with a hollow voice, "Greet you, Zachiel! if the moon shines on your side, release this one at once." Then Joringel became free, and fell down on his knees before the Witch, and begged her to give him back Jorinde; but she refused, and said he should never again have her, and went away. He cried, and wept, and groaned after her, but all to no purpose; and at length he rose and went into a strange village, where for some time he tended sheep. He often went round about the enchanted castle, but never too near, and one night, after so walking, he dreamt that he found a blood-red flower, in the middle of which lay a fine pearl. This flower, he thought, he broke off, and, going therewith to the castle, all he touched with it was free from enchantment, and thus he regained his Jorinde.

When he awoke next morning he began his search over hill and valley to find such a flower, but nine days had passed away. At length, early one morning he discovered it, and in its middle was a large dewdrop, like a beautiful pearl. Then he carried the flower day and night, till he came to the castle; and, although he ventured within the enchanted circle, he was not stopped, but walked on quite to the door.Joringel was now in high spirits, and touching the door with his flower, it flew open. He entered, and passed through the hall, listening for the sound of the birds, which at last he heard. He found the room, and went in, and there was the Enchantress feeding the birds in the seven thousand baskets. As soon as she saw Joringel, she became frightfully enraged, and spat out poison and gall at him, but she dared not come too close. He would not turn back for her, but looked at the baskets of birds; but, alas! there were many hundreds of nightingales, and how was he to know his Jorinde? While he was examining them he perceived the old woman secretly taking away one of the baskets, and slipping out of the door. Joringel flew after her, and touched the basket with his flower, and also the old woman, so that she could not longer bewitch; and at once Jorinde stood before him, and fell upon his neck, as beautiful as she ever was. Afterwards he disenchanted all the other birds, and then returned home with his Jorinde, and for many years they lived together happily and contentedly.

The Fox and the Cat

Once upon a time it fell out that a Cat met a Fox in a wood; and, thinking him clever and well experienced in the ways of the world, she spoke friendly to him, and said, "Good day, dear master Fox; how do you do, how do you get on, and how do you find your living in these dear times?"

The Fox considered the Cat from head to foot with all the pride in his nature, and doubted for a time whether to answer or not. At last he said, "Oh, you wretched shaver! you pied simpleton! you hungry mouse-hunter! what has put it into your head to ask me how I fare? what have you learnt? how many arts do you understand!"

"I understand but a single one." replied the Cat decisively.

"And what sort of an art is that?" inquired the Fox.

"When the dogs pursue me, to climb up a tree, and so save myself," said the Cat.

"Oh, is that all!" returned the Fox; "why, I understand a hundred arts; and have, moreover, a sackful of cunning! I pity you! Come with me, and I will show you how to escape the hounds."

Presently a Hunter came riding along with four dogs. The Cat ran nimbly up a tree, and perched herself upon its highest point, where the branches and leaves completely concealed her, and then called to the Fox, "Open your sack, my Fox! open your sack?" But the hounds had already seized poor Reynard, and held him tight. "Oh, Mr. Fox," cried the Cat, when she saw the end, "you are come to a standstill in spite of your hundred arts. Now, could you have crept up a tree like me, your life would not have been sacrificed!"

The Three Luck-Children

There was once upon a time a father, who called his three sons to him, and gave the first a cock, the second a scythe, and the third a cat, and then addressed them thus: – "I am very old, and my end draweth nigh, but I wish to show my care for you before I die. Money I have not, and what I now give you appears of little worth; but do not think that, for if each of you use his gift carefully, and seek some country where such a thing is not known, your fortunes will be made."

Soon after, the father died, and the eldest son set out on his travels with his cock, but wherever he came, such a creature was already well known. In the towns he saw it from afar, sitting upon the church-steeples, and turning itself round with the wind; and in the villages he heard more than one crow, and nobody troubled himself about another, so that it did not seem as if he would ever make his fortune by it. At last, however, it fell out that he arrived on an island where the people knew nothing about cocks, nor even how to divide their time. They knew, certainly when it was evening and morning, but at night, if they did not sleep through it, they could not comprehend the time. "See," said he to them, "what a proud creature it is, what a fine red crown it wears on its head, and it has spurs like a knight! Thrice during the night it will crow at certain hours, and the third time it calls you may know the sun will soon rise; but, if it crows by day, you may prepare then for a change of weather."

The good people were well pleased, and the whole night they laid awake and listened to the cock, which crowed loudly and clearly at two, four, and six o'clock. The next day they asked if the creature were not for sale, and how much he asked, and he replied, "As much gold as an ass can bear." "A ridiculously small sum," said they, "for such a marvellous creature!" and gave him readily what he asked.

When he returned home with his money, his brothers were astonished, and the second said he would also go out and see what luck his scythe would bring him. But at first it did not seem likely that fortune would favour him, for all the countrymen he met carried equally good scythes upon their shoulders. At last, however, he also came to an island whose people were ignorant of the use of scythes; for when a field of corn was ripe, they planted great cannons and shot it down! In this way, it was no uncommon thing that many of them shot quite over it; others hit the ears instead of the stalks, and shot them quite away, so that a great quantity was always ruined, and the most doleful lamentations ensued. But our hero, when he arrived, mowed away so silently and quickly, that the people held their breath and noses with wonder, and willingly gave him what he desired, which was a horse laden with as much gold as it could carry.

On his return the third brother set out with his cat to try his luck, and it happened to him exactly as it had done to the others: so long as he kept on the old roads he met with no place which did not already boast its cat; indeed, so many were there that the new-born kittens were usually drowned. At last he voyaged to an island where, luckily for him, cats were unknown animals; and yet, the mice were so numerous that they danced upon the tables and chairs, whether the master of the house were at home or not. These people complained continually of the plague, and the King himself knew not how to deliver them from it; for in every corner the mice were swarming, and destroyed what they could not carry away in their teeth. The cat, however, on its arrival, commenced a grand hunt; and so soon cleared a couple of rooms of the troublesome visitors, that the people begged the King to buy it for the use of his kingdom. The King gave willingly the price that was asked for the wonderful animal, and the third-brother returned home with a still larger treasure, in the shape of a mule laden with gold.

Meanwhile the cat was having capital sport in the royal palace with the mice, and bit so many that the dead were not to be numbered. At last she became very thirsty with the hot work, and stopped, and, raising its head, cried, "Miau, miau!" At the unusual sound, the King, together with all his courtiers, were much frightened, and in terror they ran out of the castle. There the King held a council what it were best to do, and at length it was resolved to send a herald to the cat, to demand that it should quit the castle, or force would be used to make it. "For," said the councillors, "we would rather be plagued by the mice, to which we are accustomed, than surrender ourselves a prey to this beast." A page was accordingly sent to the cat to ask whether it would quit the castle in peace; but the cat, whose thirst had all the while been increasing, replied nothing but "Miau, miau!" The page understood it to say, "No, no!" and brought the King word accordingly. The councillors agreed then that it should feel their power, and cannons were brought and fired, so that the castle was presently in flames. When the fire reached the room where the cat was, it sprang out of the window, but the besiegers ceased not until the whole was levelled with the ground.

[illegible]
[illegible]
[illegible]
[illegible]
[illegible]

How Six Travelled Through the World

There was once a man who understood a variety of arts; he had served in the army, where he had behaved very bravely, but when the war came to an end he received his discharge, and three dollars only for his services. "Wait a bit! this does not please me," said he; "if I find the right people, I will make the King give me the treasures of the whole kingdom." Thereupon, inflamed with anger, he went into a forest, where he found a man who had just uprooted six trees, as if they were straw, and he asked him whether he would be his servant, and travel with him. "Yes," replied the man; "but I will first take home to my mother this bundle of firewood;" and, taking up one of the trees, he wound it round the other five, and, raising the bundle upon his shoulder, bore it away. Soon he returned, and said to his master, "We two shall travel well through the world!" They had not gone far before they came up with a hunter who was kneeling upon one knee, and preparing to take aim with his gun. The master asked what he was going to shoot, and he replied, "Two miles from hence sits a fly upon the branch of an oak-tree, whose left eye I wish to shoot out."

How six travelled through the world.

"Oh, go with me!" said the man; "for, if we three are together, we must pass easily through the world."

The huntsman consented, and went with him, and soon they arrived at seven windmills, whose sails were going round at a rattling pace, although right or left there was no wind and not a leaf stirring. At this sight the man said, "I wonder what drives these mills, for there is not breeze!" and they went on: but they had not proceeded more than two miles when they saw a man sitting upon a tree, who held one nostril while he blew out of the other. "My good fellow," said our hero, "what are you driving up there?"

"Did you not see," replied the man, "two miles from hence, seven windmills? it is those which I am blowing, that the sails may go round."

"Oh, then come with me, said our hero; "for, if four people like us travel together, we shall soon get through the world."

So the blower got up and accompanied him, and in a short while they met with another man standing upon one leg, with the other leg unbuckled and lying by his side. The leader of the others said, "You have done this, no doubt, to rest yourself?" "Yes," replied the man, "I am a runner, and in order that I may not spring along too quickly I have unbuckled one of my legs, for when I wear both I go as fast as a bird can fly."

"Well, then, come with me," said our hero; "five such fellows as we are will soon get through the world."

The five heroes went on together, and soon met a man who had a hat on, which he wore quite over one ear. The captain of the others said to him, "Manners! manners! don't hang your hat on one side like that; you look like a simpleton!"

"I dare not do so," replied the other; "for, if I set my hat straight, there will come so sharp a frost that the birds in the sky will freeze and fall dead upon the ground."

"Then come with me," said our hero, "for it is odd if six fellows like us cannot travel quickly through the world."

These six new companions went into a city where the King had proclaimed, that whoever should run a race with his daughter, and bear away the prize, should become her husband; but if he lost the race he should also lose his head. This was mentioned to our hero, who said that he would have his servant run for him; but the King told him that in that case he must agree that his servant's life, as well as his own, should be sacrificed if the wager were lost. To this he agreed and swore, and then he bade his runner buckle on his other leg, and told him to be careful and to make sure of winning. The wager was, that whoever first brought water from a distant spring should be victor. Accordingly the runner and the princess both received a cup, and they both began to run at the same moment. But the princess had not proceeded many steps before the runner was quite out of sight, and it seemed as if but a puff of wind had passed. In a short time he came to the spring, and, filling his cup, he turned back again, but had not gone very far, before, feeling tired, he set his cup down again, and laid down to take a nap. He made his pillow of a horse's skull which lay upon the ground; thinking, from its being hard, that he would soon awake. Meantime, the princess, who was a better runner than many of the men at court, had arrived at the spring, and was returning with her cup of water, when she perceived her opponent lying asleep. In great joy, she exclaimed, "My enemy is given into my own hands!" and, emptying his cup, she ran on faster still. All would not have been lost, if, by good luck, the huntsman had not been standing on the castle, looking on with his sharp eyes. When he saw the princess was gaining the advantage, he loaded his gun and shot so cleverly that he carried away the horse's skull under the runner's head, without doing the man any injury. This awoke him, and, jumping up, he found his cup empty and the princess far in advance. However, he did not lose courage, but ran back again to the spring, and filling his cup returned home ten minutes earlier than his opponent. "See, you," said he, "now I have used my legs, the former was not worth called running."

The King was disgusted, and his daughter not less, that a common soldier should carry off the prize, and they consulted together how they should get rid of him and his companions. At last the King said, "Do not distress yourself, my dear: I have found a way to prevent their return." Then he called to the six travellers, and, saying to them, "You must now eat and drink and be merry," he led them into a room with a floor of iron, doors of iron, and the windows guarded with iron bars. In the room was a table set out with choice delicacies, and the King invited them to enter and refresh themselves, and as soon as they were inside he locked and bolted all the doors. That done, he summoned the cook, and commanded him to keep a fire lighted beneath till the iron was red-hot. The Cook obeyed, and the six champions, sitting at table, soon began to feel warm, and at first thought it arose from eating; but as it kept getting warmer and warmer, they rose to leave the room, and found the doors and windows all fast. Then they perceived that the King had some wicked design in hand, and wished to suffocate them. "But he shall not succeed!" cried the man with the hat; "I will summon such a frost as shall put to shame and crush this fire;" and, so, saying, he put his hat on straight, and immediately such a frost fell, that all the heat disappeared, and even the meats upon the dishes began to freeze. When two hours had passed, the King thought they would be stifled, and he caused the door to be opened, there stood all six fresh and lively, and requested to come out to warm themselves, for the cold in the room had been so intense that all the dishes were frozen! In a great passion the King went down to the Cook and scolded him, and asked why he had not obeyed his instructions. The Cook, however, pointing to the fire, said, "There is heat enough there, I should think;" and the King was obliged to own there was, and he saw clearly that he should not be able to get rid of his visitors in that way.

The King now began to think afresh how he could free himself, and he caused the master to be summoned, and said, "Will you not take money, and give up your right to my daughter? If so, you shall have as much as you wish."

"Well, my lord King," replied the man, "just give me as much as my servant can carry, and you are welcome to keep your daughter."

This answer pleased the King very much, and our hero said that he would come and fetch the sum in fourteen days. During that time he collected all the tailors in the kingdom, and made them sew him a sack, which took up all the time. As soon as it was ready, the Strong Man, who had uprooted the trees, took the sack upon his shoulder, and carried it to the King. At the sight of him, the King said, "What a powerful fellow this must be, carrying this great sack upon his shoulders!" and, sorely frightened, he wondered how much gold he would slip in. The King, first of all, caused a ton of gold to be brought, which required sixteen ordinary men to lift; but the Strong Man, taking it up with one hand, shoved it into the sack, saying, "Why do you not bring more at a time? – this scarcely covers the bottom of the sack." Then by degrees the King caused all his treasures to be brought, which the Strong Man put in, and yet they did not half fill his sack. "Bring more, more!" said he; "these are only a couple of crumbs." Then they were obliged to bring seven thousand waggons laden with gold, and all these the man pushed into his sack – gold, waggons, oxen, and all. Still it was not full, and the Strong Man offered to take whatever they brought, if they would but fill his sack. When everything that they could find was put in, the man said, "Well, I must make an end to this; and, besides, if one's sack is not quite full, why it can be tied up so much the easier!" and, so saying, he hoisted it upon his back, and went away, and his companions with him.

When the King saw this one man bearing away all of the riches of his kingdom, he got into a tremendous passion, and ordered his cavalry to pursue the six men, and at all risks to bring back the Strong Man with the sack. Two regiments accordingly pursued them quickly, and shouted out to them, "You are our prisoners! lay down the sack of gold, or you will be hewn to pieces!"

What is that you are saying?" asked the Blower; "you will make us prisoners! but first you shall have a dance in the air!" So saying, he held one nostril, and blew with the other the two regiments right away into the blue sky, so that one flew over the hills on the right side and the other on the left. One sergeant begged for mercy: he had nine wounds, and was a brave fellow undeserving of such disgrace. So the Blower went after him a gentle puff which brought him back without harming him, and then sent him back to the King with a message that, whatever number of knights he might yet send, all would be blown into the air like the first lot. When the King heard this message, he said, "Let the fellows go! they will meet with their desserts!" So the six companions took home all the wealth of that kingdom, and, sharing it with one another, lived contentedly all the rest of their days.

The gold children.

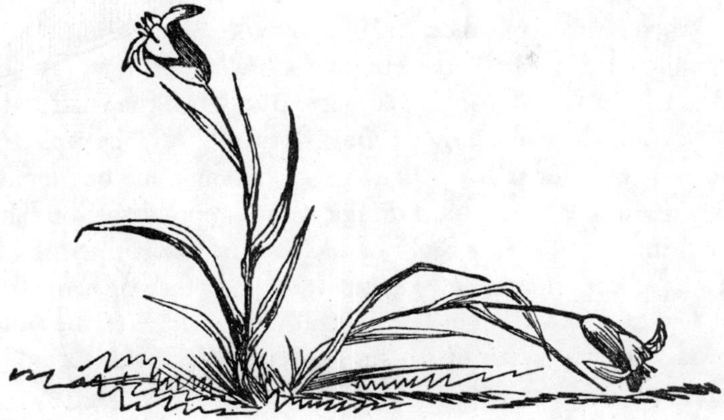

THE GOLD CHILDREN

Once upon a time there was a poor Man and his Wife, who had nothing in the world but their hut, and they lived from hand to mouth by catching fish. But once it happened that the man, sitting by the water's edge, threw in his net and drew out a Golden Fish. And while he was looking at the fish with great wonderment, it exclaimed, "Do you hear, Fisherman? throw me back into the water, and I will change your hut into a fine castle." But the Fisherman replied, "What use is a castle to me if I have nothing to eat?" "That is taken care about," rejoined the Fish, "for in the castle you will find a cupboard, which, on opening, you will see full of dishes of the most delicate food, and as much as you like."

"Well, if that be so," said the Man, "you shall soon have your wish."

"Yes," said the fish, "but there is one condition: that you disclose to nobody in the world, whoever he may be, from whence your luck comes, for if you speak a single word about it, all will be lost."

The Man threw the wonderful Fish back into the water and went home, and where formerly stood his hut was a large castle. The sight made him open his eyes, and stepping in, he found his Wife dressed out in costly clothes, sitting in a magnificent room. She appeared very pleased, and said, "Husband, how has all this happened? this is very nice!"

"Yes," replied her Husband, "it pleases me also; but now I am tremendously hungry, so give me something to eat."

His Wife said, "I have got nothing, and I am sure I do not know where to find food in this new house!"

"Oh! there is a great cupboard; open that," said the Husband; and, as soon as she did so, behold! there were cakes, meat, fruit, and wine. At the sight of these the Wife laughed exultingly, and cried, "What else can you wish for now, my dear?" and she and he commenced eating and drinking at once. But, when they had had enough, the Wife asked, "Now, my husband, when comes all this?" "Ah," he replied, "do not ask me! I dare not tell you, for if I let out the secret to any one our fortune will fly." "Well, if I may not know, I am sure I do not want," replied she; but she was not in earnest, and let him have no peace night or day, teasing and tormenting him so long, till at last, in a fit of impatience, he let out that all their fortune came from a Golden Fish which he had caught and set at liberty again. Scarcely were the words out of his mouth, when all the fine castle, with its cupboard, disappeared, and they found themselves again in their old hut.

Now was the Man obliged to take up with his old trade of fishing, and fortune so favoured him that he pulled out a second time the Golden Fish. "Alas!" said the Fish, "let me go again, and I will give you back your castle, with the cupboard of meat and wine; only keep it secret, and reveal not on any account from whence they spring, or again you will lose all."

"I will take care," replied the Fisherman, and threw the Fish into the water. At home immediately everything was in its former splendour, and the wife rejoiced at her good fortune; but her curiosity could not rest, and after a couple of days she began to plague her husband again to tell her the source of their prosperity. For a long time the man held his tongue, but at length he got into such a passion, that he broke out and told the secret. At the same moment the castle disappeared, and they found themselves in the old hut. "There, are you satisfied now?" said the Man to his Wife; "now we may feel the pangs of hunger again." "Ah," she replied, "I would rather not have wealth at all than not know whence it comes; for then I have no peace of mind."

The Man went fishing again, and in a few days he was lucky enough to pull up the Golden Fish for the third time. "Well, well," said the Fish, "I see I am fated to fall into your hands, so take me home and cut me into six pieces; two of which you must give to your wife to eat, two to your horse, and two you must put in the ground, and then you will be blessed."

The Man took home the fish, and did as it had said, and it happened that from the two pieces which he sowed in the ground two golden lilies grew up; from the eating of the two pieces by the mare, two golden foals were born; and from the wife's eating of her share, she brought forth two golden children.

The children grew up beautiful and fair, and with them the two lilies and the two foals; and one day the children said to their father, "We will mount our golden steeds and travel in the world."

But he replied sorrowfully, "How shall I manage, when you are out, to know how you are getting on?"

"The two golden lilies," said they, "will remain here, and by them you can see how we prosper; are they fresh, so are we well; do they droop, so are we ill; do they die, so are we dead."

With these words they rode away, and soon came to an inn wherein were many people, who, when they saw the two golden children, laughed at them mockingly. One of them, when he heard the jeers, was ashamed, and would not go onward, but turned round and went home to his father; while the other rode on till he came to a large forest. Just as he was about to ride into it, the people said to him, "You had better not go there, for the forest is full of robbers, who will act badly to you, and certainly when they see you are golden, and your horse too, they will kill you."

But the youth would not be frightened, and said, "I must and will go."

Then he took bears' skins, and covered with them himself and his horse, so that nothing golden could be seen, and this done, he rode confidently into the wood. When he had ridden a little way he heard a rustling among the bushes, and soon distinguished voices talking to one another. One said, "Here comes one!" but another said, "Let him alone; he's only a bear-hunter, and as poor and cold as a church-mouse. What should we do with him?"

So the Gold Child rode without danger through the forest, and came to no harm. Next it happened that he came to a village, wherein he saw a maiden so beautiful that he thought there could be no one more so in the world. He conceived a great love for her, and went to her and asked her whether she would be his wife. The maiden was very much pleased, and consented, saying, "Yes, I will become your wife, and be faithful to you all your life." Then they celebrated the wedding together, and just as they were in the middle of the festivities the father of the bride returned, and, when he saw that his daughter was married, he asked, in great astonishment, where the bridegroom was? They showed him the Golden Child, who still wore his bear-skins around him, and the father exclaimed, "Never shall a bear-hunter marry my daughter!" and he would have murdered him. The bride begged for his life, saying, "He is my husband, and I love him with all my heart;" and she begged so piteously that her father at last spared him.

The father, however, was always thinking about this man, and one morning he rose early in order to look at his daughter's husband, and see whether he were a common and ragged beggar or no. But when he looked, behold there was a magnificent Golden Man in the bed, while the thrown-off bear's skin laid upon the ground. So the father went away, thinking, "What a good thing it was I restrained my passion, or I should have made a grand mistake."

The same night the Gold Child dreamt that he hunted a fine stag, and when he awoke in the morning, he said to his bride, "I must be off to the hunt!" She was grieved, and begged him to stay, and said, "A great misfortune may easily happen to you;" but he answered, "I must and will go!" So he rode away into the forest, and soon met a proud stag, just as he had dreamed. He aimed at it, and would have shot, but the stag sprang off. Then he followed it over hedges and ditches without wearying the whole day, and at evening it disappeared from his sight. When now the Gold Child looked round, he stood before a little house, wherein dwelt a Witch. He knocked at the door, and a little old woman came, and asked, "What are you doing so late in the midst of this forest?"

"Have you not seen a stag?" he inquired.

"Yes," she replied; "I know the stag well:" and just then a little dog which was in-doors barked loudly at the stranger. "Will you be quiet, you rascally dog?" he cried; "or I will shoot you dead." At this the Witch exclaimed in a great passion, "What! will you kill my dog?" and bewitched him at once, so that he lay there like a stone. His poor wife meanwhile waited for him in vain, and soon she thought, "Ah! what I feared in the anguish of my heavy heart has fallen upon him."

But at home the other brother stood by the golden lilies, and suddenly one of them fell off. "Ah, Heaven!" said he, " some great misfortune has happened to my brother! I must be off, and see if, haply, I can save him."

But the father said, "Stop here. If I lose you too, what will become of me?"

"I must and will go," said the youth. So he mounted his golden horse, and rode away till he came to the large forest where his brother lay in the form of a stone. Out of her house came the old Witch, called to him, and would have enchanted him too, but he went not near her, but said, "I will shoot you down if you do not restore to me my brother."

She was frightened, but still she acted very unwillingly, and, touching the stone with her fingers, the Gold Child took again his human form. The two Gold Children were overjoyed when they saw one another again, and kissed and embraced, and rode together out of the forest. There they parted – the one returned to his bride, and the other to his father. When the latter arrived, his father said to him. "I knew that you had saved your brother, for the golden lily all at once revived, and now flourishes again.

After this time they lived contentedly and happily, and all went well with them till the end of their lives.

The soaring lark.

The Soaring Lark

There was once a man who had to go a very long journey, and on his departure he asked his three daughters what he should bring them. The eldest chose pearls, the second diamonds, but the third said, "Dear father, I wish for a singing, soaring lark." The father promised her she should have it if he could meet with one; and then, kissing all three, he set out.

When the time came round for his return, he had bought the pearls and the diamonds for the two elder sisters, but the lark he had sought in vain everywhere; and this grieved him very much, for the youngest daughter was his dearest child. By chance his road led through a forest, in the middle of which stood a noble castle, and near that a tree, upon whose topmost bough he saw a singing, soaring lark. "Ah! I happen with you in the very nick of time!" he exclaimed, and bade his servant climb the tree and catch the bird. But as soon as he stepped up to the tree a Lion sprang from behind, shaking his mane, and roaring so that the leaves upon the branches trembled. "Who will steal my singing, soaring lark?" cried the beast; "I will eat you up!"

"I did not know," replied the man, "that the bird belonged to you; I will repair the intended injury, and buy myself off with gold; only let me have my life."

"Nothing can save you," said the Lion, "except you promise me the first person who meets you on your return home; if you do that, I will give you not only your life, but also the bird for your daughter."

This condition the man refused, saying, "That might be my youngest daughter, who is dearest to me, and will most likely run to meet me on my return." But the servant was anxious, and said, "It does not follow that your daughter will come; it may be a cat or a dog." At length the man let himself be persuaded, and, taking the singing, soaring lark, he promised the Lion whatever should first meet him.

Soon he arrived at home, and on entering his house the first who greeted him was no other than his dearest daughter, who came running up, kissed and embraced him, and when she saw the lark in his hand was almost beside herself with joy. The poor father, however, could not rejoice, but began to weep, and said, "My dearest child, this bird I have bought very dear; I was forced to promise you for it to a wild Lion, and when he gets you he will tear you in pieces and eat you." Then he told her all that had passed, and begged her not to go away, let what might be the consequences. But his daughter consoled him and said, "My dear father, what you have promised you must perform; I will go and soften the heart of this Lion, so that I shall soon return to you."

The next morning she had the way shown to her, and taking leave, she went boldly into the forest. But this Lion was an enchanted Prince, who by day, with all his attendants, had the forms of lions, and by night they resumed their natural human figure. On her arrival, therefore, the maiden was received kindly, and led into the castle; and when night came on, and the Lion took his natural form, the wedding was celebrated with great splendour. Here they lived contented with each other, sleeping by day and watching by night. One day the Prince said to his wife, "To-morrow is a feast-day in your father's house, because your eldest sister is to be married, and if you wish to go, my lions shall accompany you."

She replied that she should like very much to see her father again, and went, accompanied by the lions. On her arrival there was much great rejoicing, for all had believed that she had been torn in pieces by the lions, and killed long ago. But she told them what a handsome husband she had, and how well she fared, and stopped with them so long as the wedding lasted; after which she went back into the forest.

Not many weeks afterwards the second daughter was to be married, and the youngest was again invited to the wedding; but she said to the Lion, "This time I will not go alone, for you must accompany me." But the Lion said it would be dangerous for him; for, should a ray from a burning light touch him, then he would instantly be changed into a pigeon, and in that form fly about for seven long years.

"Oh! do go with me!" entreated his bride; "I will protect you and ward off all light."

So at last they went away together, taking their little child with them; and the Princess caused a room to be built, strong and thick, so that no ray could pierce through, wherein her husband was to sit when the bridal lights were put up. But the door was made of green wood, which split, and left a little chink which no one perceived. Now the marriage was performed, but, as the train returned from church with its multitude of torches and lights passing by the door, a ray pierced through the chink and fell like a hair line upon the Prince, who, in the same instant that it touched him, was changed into a Dove. When, then, the Princess entered the room she found only a white Dove, who said to her, "For seven years must I fly about the world, but at every seventh mile I will let fall a drop of red blood and a white feather, which shall show you the way; and, if you follow in their track, ultimately you will save me."

With these words the Dove flew out of the doors, and she followed it; and at every seventh mile it let fall a drop of blood and a feather which showed her its path. Thus she travelled further and further over the world, without looking about or resting, so that the seven years were at length almost spent; and the prospect cheered her heart, thinking that so soon they would be saved; and yet were they far enough off it. Once while she walked on no feather fell, and not even a drop of blood, and when she cast her eyes upwards the Dove had disappeared. Then she thought to herself, "No man can help you now;" so she mounted up to the Sun, and asked, "Has thou seen a white Dove on the wing, for thou shinest into every chasm and over every peak?"

"No, I have not seen one," replied the Sun; "but I will give you this little casket; open it if you stand in need of help."

She thanked the Sun and walked on till evening, when the Moon shone out, and then she asked it, "Hast thou seen a white Dove on the wing, for thou shinest over every field and through every wood all night long?"

"No, I have not seen one," replied the Moon; but I will give you this egg; break it if ever you fall into trouble."

She thanked the Moon and walked on till the North Wind passed by, and she asked again, "Has thou not seen a white Dove, for thou passest through all the boughs, and shakest every leaf under Heaven?"

"No, I have not seen one," replied the North Wind; "but I will ask the three other Winds, who may, perhaps, have seen him you seek."

So the East and West Winds were asked, but they had seen nothing; but the South Wind said, "I have seen the white Dove; it has flown to the Red Sea, where it has again become a Lion, for the seven years are up; and the Lion stands there in combat with a caterpillar, who is really an enchanted Princess."

At these words the North Wind said to her, "I will advise you; go to the Red Sea; on the right shore thereof stands great reeds; count them, and cut off the eleventh and beat the caterpillar therewith. The Lion will then vanquish it, and both will take again their human forms. This done, look round, and you will see the griffin which sits on the Red Sea, and upon its back leap with your beloved Prince, and the bird will bear you safely to your home. There, I give you a nut to let fall when you are in the midst of the sea; for a large nut-tree will then grow out of the water, upon which the griffin will rest; and if it cannot rest there you will then know that it is not strong enough to carry you over; but if you forget to let the nut drop, you will both fall into the sea."

So the Princess set out, and found everything as the North Wind had said. She counted the reeds on the shore, and cut off the eleventh one, wherewith she beat the caterpillar till it was conquered by the lion, and immediately both took their human forms. But, as soon as the Princess who had been a caterpillar regained her nature, she seized the Prince, and leapt with him on to the back of a griffin, and so flew away. Thus the poor wanderer was again forsaken, and sat down to weep, but soon she recovered herself and said, "So far as the wind blows, and so long as the cock crows, I will travel, until I find my husband again!"

With this resolve she travelled on further and further, till she at length arrived at the place where they had lived together. Here she heard that a festival would soon be held, when the marriage of her husband and the Princess would be performed, and in her distress she opened the casket which the Sun had given her, and found a dress in it as glittering as the Sun himself. She took it out, and, putting it on, went up to the castle, and everybody, the Princess included, regarded her with wonderment. The dress pleased the intended bride so much that she thought it would make a magnificent bridal garment, and inquired if it were for sale.

"Not for gold or silver," was the reply, "but for flesh and blood!"

The Princess asked the stranger what she meant, and she replied "Let me for one night sleep in the chamber of the bridegroom?"

To this request the bride would not at first accede, but for love of the dress she consented, and ordered her servant to give the Prince a sleeping-draught. Then when night came the stranger was led into the room where the Prince was already fast asleep. There she sat herself down upon the bed, and said, "For seven long years have I followed you, the Sun and the Moon have I visited and inquired after you, and at the Red Sea I helped you against the caterpillar: will you, then, quite forget me?"

But the Prince slept so soundly that her words appeared only like the rushing of the wind through the fir-trees; and so at daybreak she was conducted out of the chamber, and had to give up the golden dress. Then thinking how little it had helped her, she became very sad, and going away to a meadow, sat down there and wept. While she did so she suddenly bethought herself of the egg which the Moon had given her, and on cracking it there came out a hen with twelve chickens, all of gold, which ran about to peck, and crept under the old hen's wing, so that nothing in the world could be prettier. She got up and drove them before her on the meadow, till the bride saw them out of her window, and they pleased her so much that she even came down and asked if they were not for sale. "Not for gold or silver, but for flesh and blood," replied the stranger: "let me sleep once more in the chamber where the bridegroom sleeps."

The bride consented, and would have deceived her as the night before, but the Prince, on going to bed, asked his servant what the rustling and murmuring he had heard the previous night had been caused by. The servant told him all that had

Hans now drove his cow off steadily before him,
thinking of his lucky bargain. (Hans in Luck.)

The Soldier turned and saw a huge bear, which eyed him very ferociously. (Bearskin.)

happened, and that he had given him a sleeping-draught, because a poor maiden had slept that night in his room, and would again do so. The Prince bade him pour out the sleeping-draught, and when the maiden came at night, and began to tell her sorrowful tale as she had done before, he recognised the voice of his true wife, and sprang up, exclaiming, "Now am I saved! all this has passed to me like a dream, for the strange Princess has bewitched me, so that I must have forgotten everything, had not you been sent at the right time to deliver me."

Then as quickly as possible they both went out of the palace, for they were afraid of the father of the Princess, who was an enchanter. They set themselves upon the griffin, who carried them over the Red Sea, and as soon as they were in the middle of it, the Princess let drop her nut. Thereupon a great nut-tree grew up, whereon the bird rested, and then it carried them straight to their home, where they found their child grown tall and handsome, and with him they ever afterwards lived happily to the end of their lives.

The Rabbit's Bride

Once there was a woman and her daughter who lived in a garden full of fine cabbages, but a Rabbit came in and ate them up. The woman said one day to her daughter "Go into the garden and hunt that Rabbit."

Mary said to the Rabbit, "There, there, little Rabbit! do not eat all the cabbages."

"Come with me, Mary," it said, "and sit upon my bushy tail, and go with me to my bushy house."

Mary would not; and the next day the Rabbit came again, and ate the cabbages, and the woman said to the daughter, "Go into the garden, and hunt the Rabbit."

Mary said to the Rabbit, "There, there, little Rabbit! do not eat all the cabbages."

"Come with me, then, Mary," said the Rabbit; "sit upon my bushy tail, and come with me to my bushy house."

Mary would not; and the third day the Rabbit came again, and ate the cabbages, and the woman said again to her daughter, "Go into the garden, and hunt the Rabbit."

Mary said to the Rabbit, "There, there, little Rabbit! eat not all our cabbages."

"Come with me, then, Mary," said the Rabbit; "sit upon my bushy tail, and come with me to my bushy house."

So Mary this time sat herself upon the Rabbit's tail, and he carried her out to his hut, and said, "Now cook me green lettuces and bran, while I will ask the wedding guests." Soon all the visitors came. (Who, then, were the wedding guests? That I cannot tell you, except as another has told me: they were all Rabbits, and the Crow was there as the parson to marry the bride and bridegroom, and the Fox as the Clerk, and the altar was under a rainbow.)

But Mary was sad, because she was alone; and the little Rabbit came and said, "Get up, get up! the wedding folks are merry and pleased."

Mary said "No," and wept; and the little Rabbit went away, but soon returned, and said, "Get up, get up! the wedding folks are hungry."

The Bride said "No!" again, and still cried. The little Rabbit went away, but soon came back, and said again, "Get up, get up! the wedding folks are waiting for you."

Mary said "No!" again, and the little Rabbit went away; but she made a doll of straw with her own clothes, and gave it a red lip, and set it on the kettle with bran, and went home to her mother. Once more came the little Rabbit, and said, "Get up, get up!" and, going towards the doll, he knocked it on the head, so that it fell over on one side.

The the little Rabbit thought his bride was dead, and went away sad and sorrowful.

Hans in Luck

Hans had served his master seven years, and at the end of that time he said to him, "Master, since my time is up, I should like to go home to my mother; so give me my wages, if you please."

His Master replied, "You have served me truly and honestly, Hans, and such as your service was, such shall be your reward;" and with these words he gave him a lump of gold as big as his head. Hans thereupon took his handkerchief out of his pocket, and, wrapping the gold up in it, threw it over his shoulder and set out on the road towards his native village. As he went along, carefully setting one foot to the ground before the other, a horseman came in sight, trotting gaily and briskly along upon a capital animal. "Ah," said Hans aloud, "what a fine thing that riding is! one is seated, as it were, upon a stool, kicks against no stones, spares one's shoes, and gets along without any trouble!"

The Rider, overhearing Hans making these reflections, stopped and said, "Why, then, do you travel on foot, my fine fellow?"

"Because I am forced," replied Hans, "for I have got a bit of a lump to carry home; it certainly is gold, but then I can't carry my head straight, and it hurts my shoulder."

If you like we will exchange," said the Rider; "I will give you my horse, and you can give me your lump of gold."

"With all my heart," cried Hans; "but I tell you fairly you undertake a very heavy burden."

The man dismounted, took the gold, and helped Hans on to the horse, and, giving him the reins into his hands, said, "Now, when you want to go faster, you must chuckle with your tongue and cry, "Gee up! gee up!"

Hans was delighted indeed when he found himself on the top of a horse, and riding along so freely and gaily. After awhile he thought he should like to go rather quicker, and so he cried , "Gee up! gee up!" as the man had told him. The horse soon set off at a hard trot, and, before Hans knew what he was about, he was thrown over head and heels into a ditch which divided the fields from the road. The horse, having accomplished this feat, would have bolted off if he had not been stopped by a Peasant who was coming that way, driving a cow before him. Hans soon picked himself up on his legs, but he was terribly put out, and said to the countryman, "That is bad sport, that riding, especially when one mounts such a beast as that, which stumbles and throws one off so as to nearly break one's neck: I will never ride on that animal again. Commend me to your cow: one may walk behind her without any discomfort, and besides one has, every day for certain, milk, butter, and cheese. Ah! what would I not give for such a cow!"

"Well," said the Peasant, "such an advantage you may soon enjoy! I will exchange my cow for your horse."

Hans now drove his cow off steadily before him, thinking of his lucky bargain in this wise: "I have a bit of bread, and I can, as often as I please, eat with it butter and cheese; and when I am thirsty I can milk my cow and have a draught: and what more can I desire?"

As soon, then, as he came to an inn he halted, and ate with great satisfaction all the bread he had brought with him for his noonday and evening meals, and washed it down with a glass of beer, to buy which he spent his two last farthings. This over, he drove his cow further, but still in the direction of his mother's village. The heat meantime became more and more oppressive as noontime approached, and just then Hans came to a common which was an hour's journey across. Here he got into such a state of heat that his tongue clave to the roof of his mouth, and he thought to himself, "This won't do; I will just milk my cow, and refresh myself." Hans, therefore, tied her up to a stump of a tree, and, having no pail, placed his leathern cap below, and set to work, but not a drop of milk could he squeeze out. He had placed himself, too, very awkwardly, and at last the impatient cow gave him such a kick on the head that he tumbled over on the ground, and for a long time knew not where he was. Fortunately, not many hours after, a Butcher passed by, trundling a young pig along upon a wheelbarrow. "What trick is this!" exclaimed he, helping up poor Hans; and Hans told him all that had passed. The Butcher then handed him his flask, and said, "There, take a drink; it will revive you. You cow might well give no milk: she is an old beast, and worth nothing at the best but for the plough or the butcher!"

"Eh, eh!" said Hans, pulling his hair over his eyes, "who would have thought it? It is all very well when one can kill a beast like that at home, and make a profit of the flesh; but for my part I have no relish for cow's flesh; it is too tough for me! Ah! a young pig like yours is the thing that tastes something like, let alone the sausages!"

"Well now, for love of you," said the Butcher, "I will make an exchange, and let you have my pig for your cow."

"Heaven reward you for your kindness!" cried Hans; and, giving up the cow, he untied the pig from the barrow, and took into his hand the string with which it was tied.

Hans walked on again, considering how everything had happened just as he wished, and how all his vexations had turned out for the best after all! Presently a Boy overtook him, carrying a fine white goose under his arm, and after they had said "Good day" to each other, Hans began to talk about his luck, and what profitable exchanges he had made. The Boy on his part told him that he was carrying the goose to a christening-feast. "Just lift it," said he to Hans, holding it up by his wings, "just feel how heavy it is; why, it has been fattened up for the last eight weeks, and whoever bites it when it is cooked will have to wipe the grease from each side of his mouth!"

"Yes," said Hans, weighing it with one hand, "it is weighty, but my pig is no trifle either."

While he was speaking the Boy kept looking about on all sides, and shaking his head suspiciously, and at length he broke out, "I am afraid it is not all right about your pig. In the village, through which I have just come, one has been stolen out of the sty of the mayor himself; and I am afraid, very much afraid, you have it now in your hand! They have sent out several people, and it would be a very bad job for you if they found you with the pig; the best thing you can do is to hide it in some dark corner!"

Honest Hans was thunderstruck, and exclaimed, "Ah, Heaven help me in this fresh trouble! you know the neighbourhood better than I; do you take my pig and let me have your goose," said he to the boy.

"I shall have to hazard something at that game," replied the Boy, "but still I do not wish to be the cause of your meeting with misfortune;" and, so saying, he took the rope into his own hand, and drove the pig off quickly by a side path, while Hans, lightened of his cares, walked on homewards with the goose under his arm. "If I judge rightly," thought he to himself, "I have gained even by this exchange: first there is the good roast; then the quantity of fat which will drip out will make goose broth for a quarter of a year; and then there are the fine white feathers, which when once I have put into my pillow I warrant I shall sleep without rocking. What pleasure my mother will have!"

As he came to the last village on his road there stood a Knife-grinder, with his barrow by the hedge, whirling his wheel round, and singing –

"Scissors and razors and such-like I grind,
And gaily my rags are flying behind."

Hans stopped and looked at him, and at last he said, "You appear to have a good business, if I may judge by your merry song?"

"Yes," answered the Grinder, "this business has a golden bottom! A true knife-grinder is a man who as often as he puts his hand into his pocket feels money in it! But what a fine goose you have got; where did you buy it?"

"I did not buy it at all," said Hans, "but took it in exchange for my pig." "And the pig?" "I exchanged for my cow." "And the cow?" "I exchanged a horse for her." "And the horse?" "For him I gave a lump of gold as big as my head." "And the gold?" "That was my wages for a seven years' servitude." "And I see you have known how to benefit yourself each time," said the Grinder; "but, could you now manage that you heard the money rattling in your pocket as you walked, your fortune would be made." "Well! how shall I manage that?" said Hans.

"You must become a grinder like me; to this trade nothing peculiar belongs but a grindstone, the other necessaries find themselves. Here is one which is a little worn, certainly, and so I will not ask anything more for it than your goose; are you agreeable?"

"How can you ask me?" said Hans; "why, I shall be the luckiest man in the world; having money as often as I dip my hand into my pocket, what have I to care about any longer?"

So saying, he handed over the goose, and received the grindstone in exchange.

"Now," said the Grinder, picking up an ordinary big flint stone which lay near, "now, there you have a capital stone, upon which only beat them long enough and you may straighten all your old nails! Take it, and use it carefully!"

Hans took the stone and walked on with a satisfied heart, his eyes glistening with joy. "I must have been born," said he, "to a heap of luck; everything happens just as I wish, as if I were a Sunday-child."

Soon, however, having been on his legs since daybreak, he began to feel very tired, and was plagued too with hunger, since he had eaten all his provision at once in his joy about the cow bargain. At last he felt quite unable to go farther, and was forced, too, to halt every minute, for the stones encumbered him very much. Just then the thought overcame him, what a good thing it were if he had no need to carry them any longer, and at the same moment he came up to a stream. Here he resolved to rest and refresh himself with a drink, and so that the stones might not hurt him in kneeling he laid them carefully down by his side on the bank. This done, he stooped down to scoop up some water in his hand, and then it happened that he pushed one stone a little too far, so that both presently went plump into the water. Hans, as soon as he saw them sinking to the bottom, jumped up for joy, and then kneeled down and returned thanks, with tears in his eyes, that so mercifully, and without any act on his part, and in so nice a way, he had been delivered from the heavy stones, which alone hindered him from getting on.

"So lucky as I am," exclaimed Hans, "is no other man under the sun!"

Then with a light heart, and free from every burden, he leaped gaily along till he reached his mother's house.

The Goose Girl.

The Goose Girl

Once upon a time there lived an old Queen, whose husband had been dead some years, and left her with one child, a beautiful daughter. When this daughter grew up she was betrothed to a King's son, who lived far away; and when the time arrived that she should be married, and as she had to travel into a strange country, the old lady packed up for her use much costly furniture, utensils of gold and silver, cups and jars; in short, all that belonged to a royal bridal treasure, for she loved her child dearly. She sent also a maid to wait upon her and to give her away to the bridegroom, and two horses for the journey; and the horse of the Princess, called Falada, could speak. As soon as the hour of departure arrived, the mother took her daughter into a chamber, and there with a knife she cut her finger with it so that it bled; then she held a napkin beneath, and let three drops of blood fall into it which she gave to her daughter, saying, "Dear child, preserve this well, and it will help you out of trouble."

Afterwards the mother and daughter took a sorrowful leave of each other, and the Princess placed the napkin in her bosom, mounted her horse, and rode away to her intended bridegroom. After she had ridden on foot for about an hour she became very thirsty, and said to her servant, "Dismount, and procure me some water from yonder stream in the cup which you carry with you, for I am very thirsty."

"If you are thirsty," replied the servant, "dismount yourself, and stoop down to drink the water, for I will not be your maid!"

The Princess, on account of her great thirst, did as she was bid, and bending over the brook she drank of its water, without daring to use her golden cup. While she did so the three Drops of Blood said, "Ah, if thy mother knew this, her heart would break." And the Princess felt humbled, but said nothing, and remounted her horse. Then she rode several miles further, but the day was so hot and the sun so scorching that she felt thirsty again; and as soon as she reached a stream she called her handmaiden again, and bade her take the golden cup and fill it with water, for she had forgotten all the saucy words which before had passed. The maiden, however, replied more haughtily than before, "If you wish to drink, help yourself! I will not be your maid!"

The Princess thereupon got off her horse, and helped herself at the stream, while she wept and cried, "Ah! woe's me!" and the three drops of Blood said again, "If your mother knew this, her heart would break." As she leaned over the water, the napkin wherein were the three drops of blood fell out of her bosom and floated down the stream without her perceiving it, because of her great anguish. But her servant had seen what happened, and she was glad, for now she had power over her mistress; because, with the loss of the drops of blood, she became weak and powerless. When, then, she would mount again upon the horse Falada, the Maid said, "No, Falada belongs to me; you must get on this horse;" and she was forced to yield. Then the servant bade her take off her royal clothes, and put on her common ones instead; and, lastly, she made the Princess promise and swear by the open sky that she would say nought of what had passed at the King's palace; for if she had not so sworn she would have been murdered. But Falada observed all that passed with great attention.

Now was the servant mounted upon Falada, and the rightful Princess upon a sorry hack; and in that way they travelled on till they came to the King's palace. On their arrival there were great rejoicings, and the young Prince, running towards them, lifted the servant off her horse, supposing that she was the true bride; and she was led up the steps in state, while the real Princess had to stop below. Just then the old King chanced to look out of his window, and saw her standing in the court, and he remarked how delicate and beautiful she was; and, going to the royal apartments, he inquired there of the bride who it was she had brought with her, and left below in the courtyard.

"Only a girl I brought with me for company," said the bride. "Give the wench some work to do, that she may not grow idle."

The old King, however, had no work for her, and knew of nothing; until at last he said, "Ah! there is a boy who keeps the geese: she can help him." This youth was called Conrad, and the true bride was set to keep geese with him.

Soon after this, the false bride said to her betrothed, "Dearest, will you grant me a favour?" "Yes," said he, "with the greatest pleasure." "Then let the knacker be summoned, that he may cut off the head of the horse on which I rode hither, for it has angered me on the way." In reality she feared lest the horse might tell how she had used the rightful Princess, and she was glad when it was decided that Falada should die. This came to the ears of the Princess, and she promised secretly to the knacker to give him a piece of gold, if he would show her a kindness, which was that he would nail the head of Falada over a certain large and gloomy arch, through which she had to pass daily with the geese, so that then she might still see, as she had been accustomed, her old steed. The knacker promised, and, after killing the horse, nailed the head in the place which was pointed out, over the door of the arch.

Early in the morning, when she and Conrad drove the geese through the arch, she said in passing, –

"Ah, Falada, that you should hang there!"

and the Head replied, –

"Ah, Princess, that you should pass here!
If thy mother knew thy fate,
Then her heart would surely break!"

Then she drove on through the town to a field; and when they arrived on the meadow, she sat down and unloosened her hair, which was of pure gold; and its shining appearance so charmed Conrad, that he endeavoured to pull out a couple of locks. So she sang, –

"Blow, blow, thou wind,
Blow Conrad's hat away;
Its rolling do not stay
Till I have combed my hair,
And tied it up behind."

Immediately there came a strong wind, which took Conrad's hat quite off his head, and led him a rare dance all over the meadows; so that when he returned, what with combing and curling, the Princess had rearranged her hair, so that he could not catch a loose lock. This made Conrad very angry, and he would not speak to her; so that all day long they tended their geese in silence, and at evening they went home.

The following morning they passed again under the gloomy arch, and the true Princess said, –

"Ah, Falada, that you should hang there!"

and Falada replied, –

"Ah, Princess, that you should pass here!
If thy mother knew thy fate,
Then her heart would surely break!"

Afterwards when they got into the meadow, Conrad tried again to snatch one of her golden locks; but she sang immediately, –

"Blow, blow, thou wind,
Blow Conrad's hat away;
Its rolling do not stay
Till I have combed my hair,
And tied it up behind."

So the wind blew, and carried the hat so far away, that by the time Conrad had caught it again, her hair was all combed out, and not a single one loose; so they tended the geese till evening as before.

After they returned home, Conrad went to the old King, and declared he would no longer keep geese with the servant.

"Why not?" asked the old King.

"Oh! she vexes me the whole day long," said Conrad; and then the King bade him relate all that had happened. So Conrad did, and told how, in the morning, when they passed through a certain archway, she spoke to a horse's head, which was nailed up over the door, and said, –

"Ah, Falada, that you should hang there!"

and it replied, –

"Ah, Princess, that you should pass here!
If thy mother knew thy fate,
Then her heart would surely break!"

and, further, when they arrived in the meadow, how she caused the wind to blow his hat off, so that he had to run after it ever so far. When he had finished his tale, the old King ordered him to drive the geese out again the next morning; and he himself, when morning came, stationed himself behind the gloomy archway, and heard the servant talk to the head of Falada. Then he followed them also into the fields, and hid himself in a thicket by the meadow; and there he saw with his own eyes the Goose Girl and boy drive in their geese; and, after awhile, she sat down, and, unloosening her hair, which shone like gold, began to sing the old rhyme, –

"Blow, blow, thou wind,

Blow Conrad's hat away;
Its rolling do not stay
Till I have combed my hair,
And tied it up behind."

Then the King felt a breeze come, which took off Conrad's hat, so that he had to run a long way after it; while the Goose Girl combed out her hair, and put it back in proper trim, before his return. All this the King observed, and then went home unremarked; and when the Goose Girl returned at evening, he called her aside, and asked her what it all meant. "That I dare not tell you, nor any other man," replied she; "for I have sworn by the free sky not to speak of my griefs, else had I lost my life."

The King pressed her to say what it was, and left her no peace about it; but still she refused. So at last he said, "If you will not tell me, tell your griefs to this fireplace;" and he went away. Then she crept into the fireplace, and began to weep and groan; and soon she relieved her heart by telling her tale. "Here sit I," she said, "forsaken by all the world and yet I am a King's daughter; and a false servant has exercised some charm over me, whereby I was compelled to lay aside my royal clothes; and she has also taken my place at the bridegroom's side, and I am forced to perform the common duties of a Goose Girl. Oh, if my mother knew this, her heart would break with grief!"

The old King, meanwhile, stood outside by the chimney, and listened to what she said; and when she had finished, he came in, and called her away from the fireplace. Then her royal clothes were put on, and it was a wonder to see how beautiful she was; and the old King, calling his son, showed him that it was a false bride whom he had taken, who was only a servant-girl; but the true bride stood there as a Goose Girl. The young King was glad indeed at heart when he saw her beauty and virtue; and a great feast was announced, to which all people and good friends were invited. On a raised platform sat the bridegroom, with the Princess on one side, and the servant-girl on the other. But the latter was dazzled, and recognised her mistress no longer in her shining dress. When they had finished their feasting, and were beginning to be gay, the old King set a riddle to the servant-girl: What such an one were worthy of who had, in such and such a manner, deceived her masters; and he related all that had happened to the true bride. The servant-girl replied, "Such an one deserves nothing better than to be put into a cask, stuck all round with sharp nails, and then by two horses to be dragged through street after street till the wretch be killed!"

"Thou art the woman, then!" exclaimed the King; "thou hast proclaimed thine own punishment, and it shall be strictly fulfilled."

The sentence was immediately carried into effect, and afterwards the young King married his rightful bride, and together they ruled their kingdom long in peace and happiness.

THE WATER OF LIFE

Once upon a time there was a King who was so ill that everybody despaired of his life, and his three sons were very sorry, and went out into the palace gardens to weep. There they met an old man, who asked the cause of their grief, and they told him their Father was so ill that he must die, for nothing could save him. The old Man said, "I know a means of saving him: if he drinks of the water of life it will restore him to health; but it is very difficult to find."

"I will soon find it," said the eldest Son, and, going to the sick King, he begged his permission to set out in search of the water of life, which alone could save him. "No; the danger is too great," said the King; "I prefer to die." Nevertheless the Son begged and entreated so long that the King consented, and the Prince went away, thinking in his own heart, "If I bring this water I am the dearest to my Father, and I shall inherit his kingdom."

After he had ridden a long way he met a Dwarf on the road, who asked him, "Whither away so quickly?"

"You stupid dandyprat," replied the Prince proudly, "why should I tell you that?" and he rode off. But the little Man was angry and he wished an evil thing, so that, soon after, the Prince came into a narrow mountain-pass, and the further he rode the

The Water of Life.

narrower it grew, till at last it was so close that he could get no further; but neither could he turn his horse round, nor dismount, and he sat there like one amazed. Meanwhile the sick King waited a long while for him, but he did not come; and the second Son asked leave to go too and seek the water, for he thought to himself, "If my Brother is dead the kingdom comes to me." At first the King refused to spare him; but he gave way, and the Prince set out on the same road as the elder one had taken, and met also the same Dwarf, who stopped him and asked him, "Whither ride you so hastily?" "Little dandyprat," replied the Prince, "what do you want to know for?" and he rode off without looking round. The Dwarf, however, enchanted him, and it happened to him as it had to his Brother: he came to a defile where he could move neither forwards nor backwards. Such is the fate of all haughty people.

Now, when the second Son did not return, the youngest begged leave to go and fetch the water, and the King was obliged at last to give his consent. When he met the Dwarf, and was asked whither he was going so hurriedly, he stopped and replied, "I seek the water of life, for my Father is sick unto death." "Do you know where to find it?" asked the Dwarf. "No," replied the Prince. "Since you have behaved yourself as you ought," said the Dwarf, "and not haughtily like your false Brothers, I will give you information and show you where you may obtain the water of life. It flows from a fountain in the court of an enchanted castle, into which you can never penetrate if I do not give you an iron rod and two loaves of bread. With the rod knock thrice at the iron door of the castle, and it will spring open. Within lie two lions with open jaws, but if you throw down to each a loaf of bread they will be quiet. Then hasten and fetch some of the water of life before it strikes twelve, for then the door will shut again, and you will be imprisoned."

The Prince thanked the Dwarf, and taking the rod and bread, he set out on his journey, and as he arrived at the castle he found it as the Dwarf had said. At the third knock the door sprang open; and, when he had stilled the Lions with the bread, he walked into a fine large hall, where sat several enchanted Princes, from whose fingers he drew off the rings, and he also took away with him a sword and some bread which lay there. A little further he came to a room wherein stood a beautiful maiden, who was so pleased to see him that she kissed him and said he had freed her, and should have her whole kingdom, and if he came in another year their wedding should be celebrated. Then she told him where the fountain of the water of life was placed, and he hastened away lest it should strike twelve ere he gained it. He came next into a room where a fine clean covered bed stood, and, being tired, he laid down to rest himself a bit. But he went to sleep, and when he awoke it struck the quarter to twelve, and the sound made him hurry to the fountain, from which he took some water in a cup which stood near. This done, he hastened to the door, and was scarcely out before it struck twelve, and the door swung to so heavily that it carried away a piece of his heel.

But he was very glad, in spite of this, that he had procured the water, and he journeyed homewards, and passed again where the Dwarf stood. When the Dwarf saw the sword and bread which he had brought away he declared he had done well, for with the sword he could destroy whole armies: but the bread was worth nothing. Now, the Prince was not willing to return home to his Father without his Brothers, and so he said to the Dwarf, "Dear Dwarf, can you tell me where my Brothers are? they went out before me in search of the water of life, and did not return." "They are stuck fast between two mountains," replied the Dwarf; "because they were so haughty, I enchanted them there."

Then the Prince begged for their release, till at last the Dwarf brought them out; but he warned the youngest to beware of them, for they had evil in their hearts.

When his Brothers came he was very glad, and he related to them all that had happened to him; how he had found the water of life and brought away a cup full of it; and how he had rescued a beautiful Princess who for a whole year was going to wait for him, and then he was to return to be married to her, and receive a rich kingdom. After this tale the three Brothers rode away together, and soon entered a province where there were war and famine raging, and the King thought he should perish, so great was his necessity. The youngest Prince went to this King and gave him the bread, with which he fed and satisfied his whole people; and then the Prince gave him the sword, wherewith he defeated and slew all his enemies, and regained peace and quiet. This effected, the Prince took back the bread and sword, and rode on further with his Brothers, and by-and-bye they came to two other provinces where also war and famine were destroying the people. To each King the Prince lent his bread and sword, and so saved three kingdoms. After this they went on board a ship to pass over the sea which separated them from home, and during the voyage the two elder Brothers said to one another, "Our Brother has found the water of life and we have not; therefore our Father will give the kingdom which belongs to us to him, and our fortune will be taken away." Indulging these thoughts they became so envious that they consulted together how they should kill him, and one day waiting till he was fast asleep, they poured the water out of his cup and took it for themselves, while they filled his up with bitter salt-water. As soon as they arrived home the youngest Brother took his cup to the sick King, that he might drink out of it and regain his health. But scarcely had he drunk a very little of the water when he became worse than before, for it was as bitter as wormwood. While the King lay in this state, the two elder Princes came, and accused their Brother of poisoning their Father; but they had brought the right water, and they handed it to the King. Scarcely had he drunk a little out of the cup when the King felt his sickness leave him, and soon he was as strong and healthy as in his young days. The two Brothers now went to the youngest Prince, mocking him, and saying, "You certainly found the water of life; but you had the trouble and we had the reward; you should have been more cautious and kept your eyes open, for we took your cup while you were asleep on the sea; and, moreover, in a year one of us intends to fetch your Princess. Beware, however, that you betray us not; the King will not believe you, and if you say a single word your life will be lost; but if you remain silent you are safe." The old King, nevertheless, was very angry with his youngest Son, who had conspired, as he believed, against his life. He caused his court to be assembled, and sentence was given to the effect that the Prince should be secretly shot; and once as he rode out hunting, unsuspicious of any evil, the Huntsman was sent with him to perform the deed. By-and-by, when they were alone in the wood, the Huntsman seemed so sad that the Prince asked him what ailed him. The Huntsman replied, "I cannot and yet must tell you." "Tell me boldly what it is," said the Prince, "I will forgive you." "Ah! it is no other than that I must shoot you, for so has the King ordered me," said the Huntsman with a deep sigh.

The Prince was frightened, and said, "Let me live, dear Huntsman, let me live! I will give you my royal coat and you shall give me yours in exchange." To this the Huntsman readily assented, for he felt unable to shoot the Prince, and after they had exchanged their clothing the Huntsman returned home, and the Prince went deeper into the wood.

A short time afterwards three waggons laden with gold and precious stones came to the King's palace for his youngest Son. They were sent by the three Kings in token of gratitude for the sword which had defeated their enemies, and the bread which had nourished their people. At this arrival the old King said to himself, "Perhaps, after all, my Son was guiltless;" and he lamented to his courtiers that he had let his Son be killed. But the Huntsman cried out, "He lives yet! for I could not find it in my heart to fulfil your commands;" and he told the King how it had happened. The King felt as if a stone had been removed from his heart, and he caused it to be proclaimed everywhere throughout his dominions that his son might return and would again be taken in to favour.

Meanwhile the Princess had caused a road to be made up to her castle of pure shining gold, and she told her attendants that whoever should ride straight up this road would be the right person, and one whom they might admit into the castle; but, on the contrary, whoever should ride up not on the road, but by the side, they were ordered on no account to admit, for he was not the right person. When, therefore, the time came round which the Princess had mentioned to the youngest Prince, the eldest Brother thought he would hasten to her castle and announce himself as her deliverer, that he might gain her as a bride and the kingdom besides. So he rode away, and when he came in front of the castle and saw the fine golden road he thought it would be a shame to ride thereon, and so he turned to the left hand and rode up out of the road. But as he came up to the door the guards told him he was not the right person, and he must ride back again. Soon afterwards the second Prince also set out, and he, likewise, when he came to the golden road, and his horse set its fore-feet upon it, thought it would be a pity to travel upon it, and so he turned aside to the right hand and went up. When he came to the gate the guards refused him admittance, and told him he was not the person expected, and so he had to return homewards. The youngest Prince, who had all this time been wandering about in the forest, had also remembered that the year was up, and soon after his Brothers' departure he appeared before the castle and rode up straight on the golden road, for he was deeply engaged in thinking of his beloved Princess that he did not observe it. As soon as he arrived at the door it was opened, and the Princess received him with joy, saying he was her deliverer and the lord of her dominions. Soon after their wedding was celebrated, and when it was over the Princess told her husband that his Father had forgiven him and desired to see him. Thereupon he rode to the old King's palace, and told him how his Brothers had betrayed him while he slept, and had sworn him to silence. When the King heard this he would have punished the false Brothers, but they had prudently taken themselves off in a ship, and they never returned home afterwards.

The Peasant's Wise Daughter

There was once upon a time a poor Peasant, who had no land, but merely a little cottage, and an only Daughter, who one day said to him, "We must ask the King for a piece of waste land."

Now when the King heard of their poverty, he presented them with a corner of a field, which the man and his daughter tilled, and prepared to sow in it corn and seeds. As they turned the land about they found a mortar of pure gold, and the Peasant said to his daughter, "Since his Majesty the King has been so gracious to us as to present us with this acre, we ought to give him this treasure."

But to this the Daughter would not agree, saying, "If we have the mortar, and not the pestle, we must procure the pestle for it; therefore be silent."

However, the Father would not obey her, but took the mortar to the king, and said he had found it while tilling the ground, and asked the King if he would accept the offering. The King took it, and asked if he had found nothing more. "No," replied the Peasant. "Then," said the King, "you must procure the pestle for it." The Peasant said they had not found that; but it was of no use, he might as well have spoken to the wind, and he was ordered to be put in prison until he discovered it. The keepers had to bring him daily bread and water, which is all one gets in prison, and when they did so they heard the man always lamenting, "Had I obeyed my daughter!" and would neither eat nor drink. His Majesty commanded them to bring the prisoner before him, and then he asked him why he was always crying out in this manner, and what his Daughter had said.

"She told me," said the man, "not to bring the mortar to you before I had found the pestle."

"What! have you such a wise daughter? let her come hither at once!" said the King. So the girl came, and the King asked her if she were so wise as was said, for he would propose a riddle, which if she solved he would then marry her. "What is that which is unclothed and yet is not naked, that moves along and yet neither rides nor walks, and that goes not in the road nor out of it?"

The girl said she would do her best, and went away and pulled off all her clothes, so that she was not clothed; then she took a large fishing-net, and set herself in it, and wrapped it round her, so she was not naked; then she bought an ass, and bound the net to its tail, so it dragged her along, and thus she neither rode nor walked. The ass, too, had to trail her along in a rut, so that she was neither in the road nor out of it, for only her big toes touched the ground. Now, as the King saw her coming towards him, he said she had solved the riddle, and fulfilled all the conditions. Then he let her father out of prison, and made the daughter his bride, and committed to her all the royal possessions.

Several years had passed away, when once, as the King was walking on parade, it happened that several peasants, who had sold wood, stopped before the palace with their waggons: some of them had oxen yoked and some horses, and one peasant had three horses, one of which was a young foal, which ran away, and laid itself down between two oxen who were in front of a waggon. Soon the peasants grouped together and began to quarrel, wrangle, and dispute with each other: the peasant with the oxen would keep the foal, saying that it belonged to him, while the peasant with the horses denied it, and said the foal was his, for his horses went with it. The quarrel was brought before the King, and he gave judgement that the foal should keep where it was, and so it passed into possession of the man with the oxen to whom it did not belong. So the other went away weeping and lamenting for his foal; but he had heard that the Queen was a very kind woman, because she had herself been born of peasant folk, so he went to her and asked her to help him that he might regain his own foal. The Queen said she would do so, and if he would promise not to betray her she would tell him now. Early in the morning when the King was on the watch-parade he was to place himself in the midst of the path by which he must pass, and take a large fish-net, and pretend to fish and shake the net about over the terrace as if it were full of fish. She told him, also, what to answer if the King asked any questions; and the next day, accordingly, he stood there fishing in a dry place. When the King came by, and saw him, he sent his page to ask who the simpleton was, and what he was about. The peasant merely replied, "I am fishing."

The page asked how he could fish where there was no water; and the man replied,

"So well as two oxen can bear a foal, so well can I fish in a dry place."

With this answer the page left him, and told it to the King, who bade the peasant come before him and asked him from whom he had the answer he made, for it could not be from himself. The man refused to tell, and replied to every question, "God forbid! I had it from myself." At last they laid him upon a heap of straw, and beat him and tortured him so long till at last he confessed that he had the answer from the Queen. As soon as the King returned home afterwards, he said to his wife, "Why are you so false to me? I will no longer have you about me; your time is over; go away to whence you came – to your peasant's hut."

He gave her leave, however, to take with her what she considered dearest and best to herself, and the Queen said, "Yes, dearest husband, I will do as you bid me," and she fell upon his breast and kissed him, and said she would take her leave. But first she made a strong sleeping-mixture to pledge him in, and the King took a long draught, but she drank only a little. Soon he fell into a deep sleep, and when she perceived it was so, she called a servant, and, wrapping a fine white linen napkin over her lord's face, she caused him to be laid in a carriage, and drawn to the cottage from whence she first came. There she laid him in a bed, where he slept a night and a day, and when he awoke he looked round him amazed, and called for a servant, but none answered the call. At last came his wife to the bed, and said, "My dear lord and King, you commanded me to take out of the castle whatever I thought dearest and best, and, because I had nothing dearer or better than you, I have brought you with me here."

At these words tears came into the King's eyes, and he said "Dear wife, you shall be mine and I will be thine!" and so he took her back again to the palace; and there they are living still in the full enjoyment of health and happiness, for aught I know to the contrary.

The two wanderers.

The Two Wanderers

It is certain that hills and valleys never meet; but it often happens on the earth that her children, both the good and the wicked, cross each other's path continually. So it once occurred that a Shoemaker and a Tailor fell together during their travels. Now, the Tailor was a merry little fellow, always making the best of everything; and, as he saw the Shoemaker approaching from the opposite road, and remarked by his knapsack what trade he was, he began a little mocking rhyme, singing, –

"Stitch, stitch away with your needle,
Pull away hard with your thread,
Rub it with wax to the right and the left,
And knock the old peg on the head!"

The Shoemaker, however, could not take a joke, and pulled a long face, as if he had been drinking vinegar, while he seemed inclined to lay hold of the Tailor by the collar. But the latter began to laugh, and handed his bottle to the other, saying, "It is not ill-meant; just drink and wash down the gall." The Shoemaker thereupon took a long pull, and immediately the gathering storm vanished; and, as he gave the Tailor back his bottle, he said, "I should have spoken to you roughly, but one talks better after a great drinking than after long thirst. Shall we travel together now?" "Right willingly," answered the Tailor, "if you have but a mind to go into some large town where work is not wanting to those who seek it." "That is just the place I should like," rejoined the Shoemaker; "in a little nest there is nothing to be earned, and the people in the country would rather go barefoot than buy shoes." So they wandered away, setting always one foot before the other, like a weasel in the snow.

Time enough had both our heroes, but little either to bite or break. When they came to the first town, they went round requesting work, and, because the Tailor looked so fresh and merry, and had such red cheeks, every one gave him what he could spare to do, and, moreover, he was so lucky that the master's daughters, behind the shop-door, would give him a kiss as he passed. So it happened that, when he met again with his companion, his bundle was the better filled of the two. The fretful Shoemaker drew a sour face, and thought, "The greater the rogue the better the luck;" but the other began to laugh and sing, and shared all that he received with his comrade. For, if only a couple of groschen jingled in his pocket, he would out with them, throw them on the table with such force, that the glasses danced, and cry out, "Lightly earned, lightly spent!"

After they had wandered about for some time, they came to a large forest, through which the road passed to the royal city; but there were two ways, one of which was seven days long, and the other only two, but neither of the travellers knew which was the shorter. They therefore sat down under an oak-tree, to consult how they should manage, and for how many days they could take bread with them. The Shoemaker said, "One must provide for further than one goes, so I will take with me bread for seven days."

"What!" cried the Tailor, "carry bread for seven days on your back like a beast of burden, so that you can't look round? I shall commit myself to God and care for nothing. The money which I have in my pocket is as good in summer as in winter, but the bread will get dry, and musty beside, in this hot weather. Why should we not find the right way? Bread for two days, and luck with it!" Thereupon each one bought his own bread, and then they started in the forest to try their fortune.

It was as quiet and still as a church. Not a breath of wind was stirring, not a brook bubbling, a bird singing, nor even a sunbeam shining through the thick leaves. The Shoemaker spoke never a word, for the heavy bread pressed upon his back so sorely, that the sweat ran down over his morose and dark countenance. The Tailor, on the other hand, was as merry as a lark, jumping about, whistling through straws, or singing songs. Thus two days passed; but on the third, when no end was to be found to the forest, the Tailor's heart fell a bit, for he had eaten all his bread; still he did not lose courage, but put his trust in God and his own luck. The third evening he laid down under a tree hungry, and awoke the next morning not less so. The fourth day was just the same, and when the Shoemaker sat down on an uprooted tree, and devoured his midday meal, nothing remained to the Tailor but to look on. He begged once a bit of bread, but the other laughed in his face, and said, "You are always so merry, and now you can try for once in your life how a man feels when he is sad: birds which sing too early in the morning are caught by the hawk in the evening." In short, he was without pity for his companion. The fifth morning, however, the poor Tailor could not stand upright, and could scarcely speak from faintness: his cheeks, besides, were quite white, and his eyes red. Then the Shoemaker said to him, "I will give you to-day a piece of bread, but I must put out your right eye for it."

The unhappy Tailor, who still wished to preserve his life, could not help himself: he wept once with both eyes, and then the Shoemaker, who had a heart of stone, put out his right eye with a needle. Then the poor fellow recollected what his mother had once said to him when he had been eating in the store-room. "One may eat too much, but one must also suffer for it." As soon as he had swallowed his dearly-purchased bread he got upon his legs again, forgot his misfortune, and comforted himself by reflecting that he had still one eye left to see with. But on the sixth day hunger again tormented him, and his heart began to fall in. When evening came he sunk down under a tree, and on the seventh morning he could not raise himself from faintness, for death sat on his neck. The Shoemaker said, "I will yet show you mercy and give you a piece of bread, but as a recompense I must put out your left eye." The Tailor, remembering his past sinfulness, begged pardon of God, and then said to his companion, "Do what you will, I will bear what I must; but remember that our God watches every action, and that an hour will come when the wicked deeds shall be punished which you have practised upon me, and which I have never deserved. In prosperous days I shared with you what I had. My business is one which requires stitch for stitch. If I have no longer sight, I can sew no more, and must go begging. Let me not, when I am blind, lie here all alone, or I shall perish.

The Shoemaker, however, had driven all thoughts about God out of his heart, and he took the knife and put out the left eye of his comrade. Then he gave him a piece of bread to eat, reached him a stick, and led him behind him.

As the sun was setting they got out of the forest, and before them in a field stood a gallows. The Shoemaker led the blind Tailor to it, left him lying there, and went his way. From weariness, pain, and hunger, the poor fellow slept the whole night long, and when he awoke at daybreak he knew not where he was. Upon the gallows hung two poor sinners, and upon each of their head sat a Crow, one of which said to the other, "Brother, are you awake?" "Yes, I am," replied the second. "Then I will tell you something," said the first Crow. "The dew which has fallen over us this night from the gallows will give sight to him who needs it if he but washes himself with it. If the blind knew this, how many there are who would once more be able to see, who now think it impossible!"

When the Tailor heard this he took his handkerchief, spread it on the grass, and as soon as it was soaked with dew he washed his eyeballs therewith. Immediately the words of the Crow were fulfilled, and he saw as clearly as ever. In a short while afterwards the Tailor saw the sun rise over the mountains, and before him in the distance lay the King's city, with its magnificent gates and hundred towers, over which the spires and pinnacles began to glisten in the sunbeams. He discerned every leaf upon the trees, every bird which flew by, and the gnats which danced in the air. He took a needle out of his pocket, and, when he found he could pass the thread through the eye as easily as ever, his heart leapt for joy. He threw himself upon his knees and thanked God for the mercy shown to him, and while he said his morning devotions he did not forget to pray for the two poor sinners who swung to and fro in the wind like the pendulum of a clock. Afterwards he took his bundle upon his back, and, forgetting his past sorrows and troubles, he jogged along singing and whistling.

The first thing he met was a brown Filly, which was running about in the fields at liberty. The Tailor caught it by its mane, and would have swung himself on its back to ride into the city, but the Filly begged for its liberty, saying, "I am still too young; even a light Tailor like you would break my back; let me run about till I am stronger; a time, perhaps, will come, when I can reward you."

"Run away, then," replied the Tailor; I see you are still a romp!" and with these words he gave it a cut with a switch, which made it lift its hind-legs for joy, and spring away over the hedge and ditch into a field.

But the Tailor had eaten nothing since the previous day, and he thought to himself, "The sun certainly fills my eyes, but the bread does not fill my mouth. The first thing which meets now must suffer, if it be at all eatable." Just then a Stork came walking very seriously over the meadow. "Stop, stop!" cried the Tailor, catching it by the leg, "I don't know if you are fit to eat, but my hunger will not admit of choice; so I must chop off your head and roast you." "Do it not," answered the Stork; "I am a sacred bird, to whom nobody offers an injury, and I bring great profit to man. Leave me alone, and then I can recompense you at some future time." "Be off, Cousin Longlegs," said the Tailor; and the Stork, raising itself from the ground, flew gracefully away, with its long legs hanging downwards. "What will come of this?" said the Tailor to himself; "my hunger grows every stronger, and my stomach yet more empty: what next crosses my path is lost." As he spoke he saw a pair of young Ducks swimming upon a pond. "You have come just when you were called," cried he, and, seizing one by the neck, he was about to twist it round, when an old bird, which was hid among the reeds, began to quack loudly, and swam with open bill up to the Tailor, begging him pitifully to spare her dear child. "Think what your poor mother would say if one fetched you away and put an end to your life!" "Be quiet!" replied the good-natured Tailor, "you shall have your child again;" and he put the prisoner back into the water.

As soon as he turned round again he perceived the old hollow tree, and the wild bees flying in and out. "Here at last I shall find the reward of my good deed," said the Tailor; "the honey will refresh me." But scarcely had he spoken when the Queen Bee flew out, and thus addressed him, "If you touch my people, and disturb my nest, our stings shall pierce your skin like ten thousand red-hot needles. Leave us in peace and go your own way, and perhaps at a future time you shall receive a reward for it."

The Tailor perceived at once that nothing was to be had there. "Three empty dishes and nothing in the fourth is a bad meal," thought he to himself; and, trudging on, he soon got into the city, where, as it was about noon, he found a dinner ready cooked in the inn, and gladly sat down to table. When he was satisfied he determined to go and seek work, and, as he walked around the city, he soon found a master, who gave him a good welcome. Since, however, he knew his business thoroughly, it very soon happened that he became quite famed, and everybody would have his new coat made by the little Tailor. Every day added to his consequence, and he said to himself, "I can get no higher in my art, and yet every day trade gets brisker." At length he was appointed court tailor.

But how things do turn out! The same day his former comrade was made court shoemaker; and when he saw the Tailor, and remarked that his eyes were as bright and good as ever, his conscience pricked him. But he thought to himself, "Before he revenges himself on me I must lay a snare for him." Now, he who digs a pit for another often falls into it himself. In the evening, when the Shoemaker had left off work, and it was become quite dark, he slipped up to the King, and whispered, "May it please your Majesty, this Tailor is a high-minded fellow and has boasted that he can procure again the crown which has been lost so long."

"That would please me much!" replied the King; "but let the Tailor come here to-morrow." When he came the King ordered him to find the crown again, or to leave the city for ever. "Oho! oho!" thought the Tailor; "a rogue gives more than he has. If the crusty old King desires from me what no man can produce, I will not wait till morning, but this very day make my escape out of the town." So thinking he tied together his bundle, and marched out of the gate; but it grieved him sorely to give up his business, and to turn his back upon the city wherein he had been so fortunate. Soon he came to the pond where he had made acquaintance with the ducks, and there sat the old one whose children he had spared by the shore, pluming herself with her bill. She recognised him, and asked why he hung his head so. "You will not wonder," he replied, "when you hear what has happened;" and he told her his story. "If that be all," said the Duck, "we can assist you. The crown has fallen into the water, and lies at the bottom, whence we will soon fetch it. Meanwhile spread your handkerchief out on the shore." With these words the Duck dived down with her twelve young ones, and in five minutes they were up again, carrying the crown, which, resting on the old bird's wings, was borne up by the bills of the twelve ducklings who swam around. They came to the shore and laid the crown on the handkerchief. You could not believe how beautiful it was; for when the sun shone on it it glittered like a hundred carbuncles. The Tailor tied it up in his handkerchief and carried it to the King, who was so much pleased, that he gave its finder a chain of gold to hang round his neck.

When the Shoemaker found his first plan had failed he contrived a second, and, stepping before the King, said, "May it please your Majesty, the Tailor has grown so high-minded again, he boasts he can model in wax the whole castle, and all that is in it, fixed and unfixed, indoors and outdoors." The King thereupon caused the Tailor to be summoned, and ordered him to model in wax the whole castle, and everything inside and outside; and if he did not complete it, or even omitted one nail upon the wall, he should be kept prisoner underground all his lifetime. The Tailor thought to himself, "It comes harder and harder upon me; no man can do that!" and, throwing his bundle over his shoulder, he walked out at the gate. When he came to the hollow tree he sat down and hung his head in despair. The Bees came flying out, and the Queen asked if he had a stiff neck, because he kept his head in such a position. "Oh, no!" he replied: "something else oppresses me!" and he related what the King had demanded of him. The Bees, thereupon, began to hum and buzz together, and the Queen said to the Tailor, "Go home now, but return in the morning, and bring a great napkin with you, and about this hour all will be ready." So he returned home, and the Bees flew to the Royal Palace, right in at the open window, crept into every corner, and observed all the things in the most minute manner. Then they flew back and formed a castle in wax with great speed, so that it was ready by the evening. The next morning the Tailor came, and there stood the whole beautiful building, with not a nail upon the wall, or a tile upon the roof omitted, but all was delicately white, and moreover, as sweet as sugar. The Tailor wrapped it carefully in his cloth and took it to the King, who could not sufficiently admire it, and gave him a house made of stone as a reward.

The Shoemaker, however, was not satisfied, and went again to the King, and said, "May it please your Majesty, it has come to the ears of the Tailor that no water springs in the castle-yard; and he has, therefore, boasted that it shall gush up in the middle clear as crystal." The King ordered the Tailor to be summoned, and told him that if a stream of water was not running the following morning, as he had said, the executioner should make him a head shorter in that very court. The poor Tailor did not think very long, but rushed out of the gate, and, as he remembered his life was in danger, tears rolled down his cheeks. While he sat thus, full of grief, the Filly came jumping towards him, to which he had once given liberty, and which had become a fine brown horse. "Now is the hour come," it said to the Tailor, "when I can reward your kindness. I know already what you need, and will soon assist you; but now sit upon my back, which could carry two like you." The Tailor's heart came up again, and he vaulted into the saddle, and the horse carried him full speed into the town, and straight to the castle-yard. There it coursed thrice round as quick as lightning, and at the third time fell down. At the same moment a fearful noise was heard, and a piece of the ground of the court sprang up into the air like a ball, and bounded away far over the Castle; and at the same time a stream of water, as high as the man and his horse, and as clear as crystal, played up and down like a fountain, and the sunbeams danced upon it. As soon as the King saw this he was astounded, and went up and embraced the Tailor before all his court.

But this fortune did not last long. The King had daughters enough, and each one

When the Beast was tired, the little Tailor produced a fiddle and played a tune on it. (The Valiant Tailor.)

"I am drumming to show the way to the many thousands who follow me." (The Drummer.)

prettier than the other, but no son at all.

Now the wicked Shoemaker went for the fourth time to the King, and said, "May it please your Majesty, the Tailor is as high-minded as ever. Now he has boasted that, if he might, he could bring the King a son down from the air." Thereupon the King ordered the Tailor to be summoned, and said, "If you bring me a son within nine days, you shall have my eldest daughter as a wife." "The reward is immense," thought the Tailor; "and one may as well have it as another; but now the cherries hang too high for me, and if I climb after them the branches will break beneath me, and I shall fall down." So thinking, he went home, set himself with his legs crossed under him upon his work-table, and considered what he should do. "It is of no use," he cried at length; "I must be off, I cannot rest in peace here!" So he tied up his bundle and hurried out of the door; but just as he arrived upon the meadow, he perceived his old friend the Stork, who, like a world-wise man, walked up and down, a while stood still, and considered a frog nearer, and at length snapped it up. The Stork came up and greeted him. "I see," said it, "you have your bundle upon your back; why have you left the city?" The Tailor told the Stork what the King had commanded of him, and how, as he could not do it, he was grieving at his ill-luck. "Do not let your grey hairs grow on that account!" replied the Stork, "I will assist you out of your trouble! Sometimes already I have brought infants into the city; and I can also fetch a little prince out of the spring. Go home and keep quiet. In nine days return to the Royal Palace, and I will come thither also."

The Tailor went home, and on the right day went to the Palace. In a short time the Stork came flying through the air, and knocked at the window. The Tailor opened it, and cousin Longlegs marched gravely in, and, with stately steps, passed over the marble floors, carrying in his beak a child, as beautiful to look at as an angel, and already stretching out its hands towards the Queen. The Stork laid it upon her lap, and she embraced and kissed it, almost beside herself with joy. Before he flew away, he took a knapsack off his shoulder and handed it to the Queen; and therein were dates and coloured bonbons, which were divided among the Princesses. But the eldest received none, because she took instead the merry young Tailor as husband. "It seems to me," said the Tailor, "as if I had won a great game. My mother rightly said, "He who trusts in God and his own fortune, will never go amiss."

The Shoemaker had to make the shoes in which the Tailor danced at the wedding, and as soon as he had done them he was ordered to leave the city. The road from thence to the forest led past the gallows; and, from rage, disappointment, and weariness with the heat of the day, he threw himself on the ground beneath it. As soon as he had closed his eyes and prepared to go to sleep, the two Crows flew down from the heads of the two criminals, and with loud cries pecked out the Shoemaker's eyes. Insane with rage and pain he ran into the forest, and there he must have perished; for nobody has seen or heard anything of the wicked Shoemaker since.

The Experienced Huntsman

There was once upon a time a young Lad, who, after he had learnt the trade of a locksmith, told his Father he wished to go and seek his fortune in the world. "Well," said the Father, "very well, I am content;" and gave him money for the journey. So he set off, looking about for work; but after a while he determined to follow his trade no longer, for he had got tired of it, and wished to learn the art of hunting. While he was in this mood he met a Huntsman, dressed in green, who asked him whence he came, and whither he would go. The Youth told him he was a locksmith, but his business did not suit him any longer, and he had a wish to learn how to shoot, if he would take him as a pupil. "Oh, yes!" replied the other, "come with me." The Youth accompanied him, and for several years abode with him while he learnt the art of hunting. Afterwards he wished to leave, but the Huntsman gave him no further reward than an air-gun, which had the property of missing nothing at which it was fired. With this gift he went off, and by-and-by came to a very large forest, to which he could find no end the first day, so he perched himself upon a lofty tree where the wild beasts could not reach him. Towards midnight it seemed to him that a light was glimmering at a distance, and he peeped through the boughs in order to mark more exactly where it was. Then, taking his hat he threw it in that direction

The experienced huntsman.

that it might serve as a guide for him when he had descended the tree; and as soon as he was down, he ran after his hat, and, putting it on again, he walked straight ahead. The further he went the larger the light appeared; and when he came nearly up to it, he discovered it was caused by a great fire, round which three Giants were sitting, watching the roasting of an ox, which hung on a spit above it. Just at that moment one of the Giants said he would taste and see if the meat were done enough; and, tearing a piece off, he was going to put it into his mouth, when the Huntsman shot it clean out of his hand. "Now, then," cried the Giant, "the wind blows the meat out of my hand!" And, taking another piece, he was about to bite it when the Huntsman shot that out of his hand. Thereupon he gave the Giant next to him a box on the ear, saying angrily, "Why do you snatch my piece away?" "I did not take it away," replied the other; "it was some sharp-shooter who shot it away." So the Giant took a third piece, but that also he could not hold, for the Huntsman shot it away. "This must be a good shot," cried all the Giants; "a man who can shoot away the food from one's mouth would be very useful to us." And then, speaking louder, they called to him, "Come, you sharpshooter, sit down by our fire, and eat till you are satisfied, and we will do you no harm; but if you don't come, and we have to fetch you, you will be lost."

At these words, the Huntsman stepped up to the fire, and said he was an experienced Huntsman, so much so, that whatever he aimed at, he shot, without ever missing. The Giants said, that if he would go with them he should be well treated; and they told him, besides, that out of the forest there was a large piece of water, on the other side of which was a tower, wherein dwelt a beautiful Princess, whom they desired to possess. The Huntsman said he would willingly fetch her; and they further told him, that outside the tower lay a little dog, which would begin to bark as soon as it saw anyone approach, and immediately it did so, everybody would wake up in the royal palace; and it was on that account they had never been able to enter, and therefore he must first shoot the dog. To this the Huntsman assented, declaring it was mere play; and soon afterwards he went on board a ship, and sailed over the water; and, as he neared the land, the little dog came running down, and would have barked, but he, aiming with his air-gun, shot it dead. As soon as the Giants saw this done, they were very glad, and thought they had the Princess for certain; but the Huntsman told them to remain where they were until he called them, for he must first see how it was to be accomplished. He went into the castle, and found everybody as still as mice, for they were fast asleep; and as he entered the first room he saw a sabre hanging up made of pure silver, and ornamented with a golden star and the king's name. Below it stood a table, whereon laid a sealed letter, which he broke open, and read that whoever possessed the sabre could bring to life whomever it passed. The Huntsman took the sabre down from the wall, and, hanging it around him, walked on till he came to a room where the King's daughter lay asleep. She was so beautiful that he stood still and looked at her, holding his breath while he thought, "How dare I deliver this innocent maiden into the power of these Giants, with their evil intentions?" He peeped out, and under the bed espied a pair of slippers; on the right one was marked the King's name with a star, and on the left his Daughter's, also with a star. She had also a large handkerchief over her, woven of silk and gold, having on the right side her father's name, and on the left her own, all done in golden threads. So the Huntsman took a knife and cut off the right corner, and then he took the slipper with the King's name in it, and put them both in his knapsack. All the while the Princess remained quite passive; and, as she was wrapped up in a sheet, the Huntsman cut off a piece of that, as well as the handkerchief, and put it in his knapsack with the others. All these things he did without touching her, and afterwards went away without noise. When he got outside he found the three Giants, who were waiting in expectation that he would bring the Princess with him. He shouted to them to come in, for the Maiden was already in his power, but he could not open the door, and therefore they must creep through a hole which was in the wall. The first Giant came, and, as soon as he poked his head through the hole, the Huntsman seized him by the hair, and chopped his head off with the sabre. Then he pulled the body through, and called to the second, whose head he chopped off likewise, and then the third Giant shared the same fate. As soon as this was done he cut out the tongue of each and put it in his knapsack, rejoicing to think he had freed the Princess from her enemies. He resolved next to visit his Father, and show him what he had done, and afterwards to travel again about the world; "for," said he "the fortune which God apportions to me will reach me anywhere!"

Meanwhile the King of the castle, when he awoke, had perceived the three Giants lying dead in the hall, and, going into his daughter's apartment, he awoke her, and inquired who it was that had destroyed the giants. "I know not, dear father," she replied; "I have been sleeping." But when she arose, and wished to put on her slippers, she found the one for the right foot was missing; and her handkerchief also wanted the right-hand corner, which had been cut off, as well as a piece out of the sheet. The King thereupon caused the whole court to be assembled, soldiers and every one, and then put the question, who had freed his daughter, and put to death the giants? Now, the King had a captain, a one-eyed and ugly man, who said he had done it. The old King, therefore, declared that, since it was he, he must marry the Princess. But as soon as he said so the Princess exclaimed, "Rather than marry him, dear father, I will wander over the world as far as my feet will carry me!" The King replied she might do as she pleased; but if she would not marry the man she must take off her royal clothes, and put on peasant's clothes to travel in, and, also, she must go to a potter and begin business in the earthenware trade. So the King's daughter drew off her royal clothes, and went to a potter, from whom she hired a crate of earthenware, and promised that if she had sold them by the evening she would pay for them. The King commanded her to sit at a certain corner of the market, across which he ordered that several waggons should be driven, so as to crush in pieces all the crockery. By-and-by, therefore, when the Princess had stationed herself in the appointed place, the waggons came driving past, and smashed her goods. Thereupon she began to cry, saying, "Ah, heaven! how am I to pay the potter?" But the King hoped by this means to have compelled his daughter to marry the captain: instead of which she went to the potter and asked if he would trust her with another crate. He refused till she should pay for the former one; and so the Princess was forced to go crying and groaning to her father, that she wished to wander into the wide world. The King said, "I will cause a cottage to be built in the middle of the wood, herein you shall sit your lifetime, and cook for anybody who comes, but without taking money for it." When the house was ready, a sign was hung over the door, on which was inscribed, –

"Gratis to-day: To-morrow, payment."

There she sat for a long time, while it was talked about in the world around, that a maiden sat in a cottage in the wood; and cooked gratis, as was stated on a sign over the door. This the Huntsman heard, and he thought to himself, "This is good news for me, who am so poor, and have no money." So he took his air-gun and knapsack, in which he kept all the memorials he had brought away from the castle; and, going into the forest, came soon to the cottage where was written up: –

"Gratis to-day: To-morrow, payment."

Now, he had the sword buckled round him which he had used to execute the three Giants; and he stepped into the cottage and ordered something to eat. The Princess asked him whence he came and whither he was going; and he replied, "I am wandering about the world." She asked next where he procured his sword, on which she perceived her father's name. "Are you the daughter of the King?" he inquired; and, as she nodded assent, he said, "With this sword I have cut off the heads of three Giants!" and he held up the three tongues for a token, together with the slipper, and the pieces which he had cut off the handkerchief and sheet. The Princess was glad indeed to see these things, and told the Huntsman it was he who had saved her. Then they went to the King; and the Princess led him to her chamber, and declared that it was the Huntsman who had delivered her from the three Giants. The King at first would not believe; but as soon as he was shown the tokens he could no longer doubt; and, in order to show his pleasure and his gratitude, he promised his daughter to the Huntsman as his wife, which pleased the Princess very much. Afterwards the King ordered a great banquet, whereat the Huntsman appeared as a distinguished stranger. When they sat down to table, the Captain took his place on the left hand of the King's Daughter, and the Huntsman, whom the former believed to be a visitor of rank, on the right. When they had finished eating and drinking, the old King told the Captain he would propound a question, which he must answer, and it was this: "If one should say he had killed three Giants, and was asked, therefore, where the tongues of the Giants were, and should then go to seek them and find none, how would he explain that?" "By saying that they had none!" replied the Captain. "Not so!" said the King; "every creature has a tongue; therefore, what should such an one deserve for his answer?" "To be torn in pieces!" said the Captain boldly.

"You have pronounced your own sentence!" said the King to the Captain; who was first imprisoned, and afterwards torn in four pieces. But the Huntsman was married to the King's daughter; and, after the wedding, he invited his father and mother to live with him; and, after the old King's death, the Huntsman ascended the throne.

BEARSKIN

There was once upon a time a young fellow who enlisted for a soldier, and became so brave and courageous that he was always in the front ranks when it rained blue beans.* As long as the war lasted all went well, but when peace was concluded he received his discharge, and the captain told him he might go where he liked. His parents meanwhile had died, and as he had no longer any home to go to he paid a visit to his brothers, and asked them to give him shelter until war broke out again. His brothers, however, were hardhearted, and said, "What could we do with you? we could make nothing of you; see to what you have brought yourself;" and so turned a deaf ear. The poor Soldier had nothing but his musket left; so he mounted this on his shoulder and set out on tramp. By-and-by he came to a great heath with nothing on it but a circle of trees, under which he sat down, sorrowfully considering his fate. "I have no money," thought he; "I have learnt nothing but soldiering, and now, since peace is concluded, there is no need of me. I see well enough I shall have to starve." All at once he heard a rustling, and as he looked round he perceived a stranger standing before him, dressed in a grey coat, who looked very

*Small shot.

stately, but had an ugly cloven foot. "I know quite well what you need," said this being; "gold and other possessions you shall have, as much as you can spend; but first I must know whether you are a coward or not, that I may not spend my money foolishly."

"A soldier and a coward!" replied the other, "that cannot be; you may put me to any proof."

"Well, then," replied the stranger, "look behind you."

The Soldier turned and saw a huge bear, which eyed him very ferociously. "Oho!" cried he, "I will tickle your nose for you, that you shall no longer be able to grumble;" and, raising his musket, he shot the bear in the forehead, so that he tumbled in a heap upon the ground, and did not stir afterwards. Thereupon the stranger said, "I see quite well that you are not wanting in courage; but there is yet one condition which you must fulfil." "If it does not interfere with my future happiness," said the Soldier, who had remarked who it was that addressed him; "if it does not interfere with that, I shall not hesitate."

"That you must see about yourself!" said the stranger. "For the next seven years you must not wash yourself, nor comb your hair or beard, neither must you cut your nails nor say one pater-noster. Then I will give you this coat and mantle, which you must wear during these seven years; and if you die within that time you are mine, but if you live you are rich, and free all your life long."

The Soldier reflected for a while on his great necessities, and, remembering how often he had braved death, he at length consented, and ventured to accept the offer. Thereupon the Evil One pulled off the great coat, handed it to the soldier, and said, "If you at any time search in the pocket of your coat, when you have it on, you will always find your hand full of money." Then also he pulled off the skin of the bear, and said, "That shall be your cloak and your bed; you must sleep on it, and not dare to lie in any other bed, and on this account you shall be called Bearskin." Immediately the Evil One disappeared.

The Soldier now put on the coat, and dipped his hands into the pockets, to assure himself of the reality of the transaction. Then he hung the bearskin around himself, and went about the world chuckling at his good luck, and buying whatever suited his fancy which money could purchase. For the first year his appearance was not very remarkable, but in the second he began to look quite a monster. His hair covered almost all his face, his beard appeared like a piece of dirty cloth, his nails were claws, and his countenance was so covered with dirt that one might have grown cresses upon it if one had sown seed! Whoever looked at him ran away; but, because he gave the poor in every place gold coin, they prayed that he might not die during the seven years; and, because he paid liberally everywhere, he found a night's lodging without difficulty. In the fourth year he came to an inn where the landlord would not take him in, and refused even to give him a place in his stables, lest the horses should be frightened and become restive. However, when Bearskin put his hand into his pocket and drew it out full of gold ducats the landlord yielded the point, and gave him a place in the outbuildings, but not till he had promised that he would not show himself, for fear the inn should gain a bad name.

While Bearskin sat by himself in the evening, wishing from his heart that the seven years were over, he heard in the corner a loud groan. Now, the old Soldier had a compassionate heart, so he opened the door and saw an old man weeping violently and wringing his hands. Bearskin stepped nearer, but the old man jumped up and tried to escape; but when he recognised a human voice he let himself be persuaded, and by kind words and soothings on the part of the old Soldier he at length disclosed the cause of his distress. His property had dwindled away by degrees, and he and his daughters would have to starve, for he was so poor that he had not the money to pay the host, and would therefore be put into prison.

"If you have no care except that," replied Bearskin, "I have money enough;" and, causing the landlord to be called, he paid him, and put a purse full of gold besides into the pockets of the old man. The latter, when he saw himself released from his troubles, knew not how to be sufficiently grateful, and said to the Soldier, "Come with me, my daughters are all wonders of beauty, so choose one of them for a wife. When they hear what you have done for me they will not refuse you. You appear certainly an uncommon man, but they will soon put you to rights."

This speech pleased Bearskin, and he went with the old man. As soon as the eldest daughter saw him, she was so terrified at his countenance that she shrieked out and ran away. The second one stopped and looked at him from head to foot; but at last she said, "How can I take a husband who has not a bit of a human countenance? The grizzly bear would have pleased me better who came to see us once, and gave himself out as a man, for he wore a hussar's hat, and had white gloves on besides."

But the youngest daughter said, "Dear father, this must be a good man who has assisted you out of your troubles; if you have promised him a bride for the service your word must be kept."

It was a pity the man's face was covered with dirt and hair, else one would have seen how glad at heart these words made him. Bearskin took a ring off his finger, broke it in two, and, giving the youngest daughter one half, he kept the other for himself. On her half he wrote his name, and on his own he wrote hers, and begged her to preserve it carefully. Thereupon he took leave, saying, "For three years longer I must wander about; if I come back again, then we will celebrate our wedding; but if I do not, you are free, for I shall be dead. But pray to God that he will preserve my life."

When he was gone the poor bride clothed herself in black, and whenever she thought of her bridegroom burst into tears. From her sisters she received nothing but scorn and mocking. "Pay great attention when he shakes your hand," said the eldest, "and you will see his beautiful claws!" "Take care!" said the second, "bears are fond of sweets, and if you please him he will eat you up, perhaps!" "You are must mind and do his will," continued the eldest, "or he will begin growling!" And the second daughter said further, "But the wedding will certainly be merry, for bears dance well!" The bride kept silence, and would not be drawn from her purpose by all these taunts; and meanwhile Bearskin wandered about in the world, doing good where he could, and giving liberally to the poor, for which they prayed heartily for him. At length the last day of the seven years approached, and Bearskin went and sat down again on the heath, beneath the circle of trees. In a very short time the wind whistled, and the Evil One presently stood before him and looked at him with a vexed face. He threw the Soldier his old coat and demanded his grey one back. "We have not got so far as that yet," replied Bearskin; "you must clean me first." Then the Evil One had, whether he liked it or no, to fetch water, wash the old Soldier, comb his hair out, and cut his nails. This done, he appeared again like a brave warrior, and indeed was much handsomer than before.

As soon as the Evil One had disappeared, Bearskin became quite light-hearted; and going into the nearest town he bought a fine velvet coat, and hired a carriage drawn by four white horses, in which he was driven to the house of his bride. Nobody knew him; the father took him for some celebrated general, and led him into the room where his daughters were. He was compelled to sit down between the two eldest, and they offered him wine, and heaped his plate with the choicest morsels; for they thought they had never seen any one so handsome before. But the bride sat opposite to him dressed in black, neither opening her eyes nor speaking a word. At length the Soldier asked the father if he would give him one of the daughters to wife, and immediately the two elder sisters arose, and ran to their chambers to dress themselves out in their most becoming clothes, for each thought she should be chosen. Meanwhile the stranger, as soon as he found himself alone with his bride, pulled out the half of the ring and threw it into a cup of wine, which he handed across the table. She took it, and as soon as she had drunk it and seen the half ring lying at the bottom her heart beat rapidly, and she produced the other half, which she wore round her neck on a riband. She held them together, and they joined each other exactly, and the stranger said, "I am your bridegroom, whom you first saw as Bearskin; but through God's mercy I have regained my human form, and am myself once more." With these words he embraced and kissed her; and at the same time the two eldest sisters entered in full costume. As soon as they saw that the very handsome man had fallen to the share of their youngest sister, and heard that he was the same as "Bearskin," they ran out of the house full of rage and jealousy.

The Valiant Tailor

There was once upon a time an excessively proud Princess, who proposed a puzzle to every one who came courting her; and he who did not solve it was sent away with ridicule and scorn. This conduct was talked about everywhere, and it was said that whoever was lucky enough to guess the riddle would have the Princess for a wife. About that time it happened that three Tailors came in company to the town where the Princess dwelt, and the two elder of them were confident, when they heard the report, that they should without doubt be successful, since they had made so many fine and good stitches. The third Tailor was an idle, good-for-nothing fellow, who did not understand his own trade; but still he likewise was sure of his own powers of guessing a riddle. The two others, however, would fain have persuaded him to stop at home; but he was obstinate, and said he would go, for he had set his heart upon it; and thereupon he marched off as if the whole world belonged to him.

The three Tailors presented themselves before the Princess, and told her they were come to solve her riddle, for they were the only proper people, since each of them had an understanding so fine that one could thread a needle with it! "Then," said Princess, "it is this: I have a hair upon my head of two colours: which are they?"

"If that is all," said the first man, "it is black and white like the cloth which is called pepper and salt."

"Wrong!" said the Princess; "now, second man, try!"

"It is not black and white, but brown and red," said he, "like my father's holiday coat."

"Wrong again!" cried the Princess; "now try, third man; who I see will be sure to guess rightly!"

The little Tailor stepped forward, bold as brass, and said, "The Princess has a gold and silver hair on her head, and those are the two colours."

When the Princess heard this she turned pale, and very nearly fell down to the ground with fright, for the Tailor had guessed her riddle, which she believed nobody in the world could have solved. As soon as she recovered herself, she said to the Tailor, "That is not all you have to do; in the stable below lies a Bear, with which you must pass the night; and if you are alive when I come in the morning I will marry you."

The little Tailor readily consented, exclaiming, "Bravely ventured is half won!" But the Princess thought herself quite safe, for as yet the Bear had spared no one who came within reach of its paws.

As soon as evening came the little Tailor was taken to the place where the bear lay; and, as soon as he entered the stable, the beast made a spring at him. "Softly, softly!" cried the Tailor, "I must teach you manners!" And out of his pockets he took some nuts, which he cracked between his teeth quite unconcernedly. As soon the Bear saw this he took a fancy to have some nuts also; and the Tailor gave him a handful out of his pocket; not of nuts, but of pebbles. The Bear put them into his mouth, but he could not crack them, try all he might. "What a blockhead I am!" he cried to himself; "I can't crack a few nuts! Will you crack them for me?" said he to the Tailor. "What a fellow you are!" exclaimed the Tailor; "with such a big mouth as that, and can't crack a small nut!" With these words he cunningly substituted a nut for the pebble which the Bear handed him, and soon cracked it.

"I must try once more!" said the Bear; "it seems an easy matter to manage!" And he bit and bit with all his strength, but, as you may believe, all to no purpose. When the Beast was tired, the little Tailor produced a fiddle out of his coat, and played a tune upon it, which as soon as the Bear heard, he began to dance in spite of himself. In a little while he stopped and asked the Tailor whether it was easy to learn the art of fiddling. "Easy as child's play!" said the Tailor; "you lay your left fingers on the strings, and with the right hold the bow; and then away it goes. Merrily, merrily, hop-su-sa, oi-val-lera!"

"Oh! well, if that is fiddling," cried the Bear, "I may as well learn that, and then I can dance as often as I like. What do you think? Will you give me instruction?"

"With all my heart!" replied the Tailor, "if you are clever enough; but let me see your claws, they are frightfully long, and I must cut them a bit!" By chance a vice was lying in one corner, on which the Bear laid his paws, and the Tailor screwed them fast. "Now wait till I come with the scissors," said he; and, leaving the Bear groaning and growling, he laid himself down in a corner on a bundle of straw, and went to sleep.

Meanwhile the Princess was rejoicing to think she had got rid of the Tailor; and especially when she heard the Bear growling, for she thought it was with satisfaction for his prey. In the morning accordingly she went down to the stable; but as soon as she looked in she saw the Tailor as fresh and lively as a fish in water. She was much alarmed, but it was of no use, for her word had been openly pledged to the marriage; and the King her father ordered a carriage to be brought in which she and the Tailor went away to the church to the wedding. Just as they had set off the two other Tailors, who were very envious of their brother's fortune, went into the stable and released the Bear, who immediately ran after the carriage which contained the bridal party. The Princess heard the beast growling and groaning, and became very much frightened, and cried to the Tailor, "Oh, the Bear is behind, coming to fetch you away!" The Tailor was up in a minute, stood on his head, put his feet out of the window, and cried to the Bear, "Do you see this vice? if you do not go away you shall have a taste of it!" The Bear considered him a minute, and then turned tail and ran back; while the Tailor drove on to church with the Princess, and made her his wife. And very happy they were after the marriage, as merry as larks; and to the end of their lives they lived in contentment.

Snow-White and Rose-Red

There was once a poor Widow, who lived alone in her hut with her two children, who were called Snow-White and Rose-Red, because they were like the flowers which bloomed on two rose bushes, which grew before the cottage. But they were two as pious, good, industrious, and amiable children, as any that were in the world, only Snow-White was more quiet and gentle than Rose-Red. For Rose-Red would run and jump about the meadows, seeking flowers, and catching butterflies, while Snow-White sat at home helping her Mother to keep house, or reading to her, if there were nothing else to do. The two children loved one another dearly, and always walked hand-in-hand when they went out together; and ever when they talked of it they agreed that they would never separate from each other, and that whatever one had the other should share. Often they ran deep into the forest and gathered wild berries; but no beast ever harmed them. For the hare would eat cauliflower out of their hands, the fawn would graze at their side, the goats would frisk about them in play, and the birds remained perched on the boughs singing as if nobody were near. No accident ever befell them; and if they stayed late in the forest, and night came upon them, they used to lie down on the moss and sleep till morning; and because their mother knew they would do so, she felt no concern about

Snow-White and Rose-Red.

them. One time when they had thus passed the night in the forest, and the dawn of morning awoke them, they saw a beautiful Child dressed in shining white sitting near their couch. She got up and looked at them kindly, but without saying anything went into the forest; and when the children looked round they saw that where they had slept was close to the edge of a pit, into which they would have certainly fallen had they walked a couple of steps further in the dark. Their mother told them the figure they had seen – doubtless, the good angel who watches over children.

Snow-White and Rose-Red kept their Mother's cottage so clean that it was a pleasure to enter it. Every morning in the summer-time Rose-Red would first put the house in order, and then gather a nosegay for her Mother, in which she always placed a bud from each rose-tree. Every winter's morning Snow-White would light the fire and put the kettle on to boil, and, although the kettle was made of copper, it yet shone like gold, because it was scoured so well. In the evenings, when the flakes of snow were falling, the mother would say, "Go, Snow-White, and bolt the door;" and then they used to sit down on the hearth, and the Mother would put on her spectacles and read out of a great book, while her children sat spinning. By their side, too, lay a little lamb, and on a perch behind them a little white dove reposed with her head under her wing.

One evening, when they were thus sitting comfortably together, there came a knock at the door, as if somebody wished to come in. "Make haste, Rose-Red," cried her Mother; "make haste and open the door; perhaps there is some traveller outside who needs shelter." So Rose-Red went and drew the bolt and opened the door, expecting to see some poor man outside; but, instead, a great fat bear poked his black head in. Rose-Red shrieked out and ran back, the little lamb bleated, the dove fluttered on her perch, and Snow-White hid herself behind her Mother's bed. The Bear, however, began to speak, and said, "Be not afraid, I will do you no harm; but I am half-frozen, and wish to come in and warm myself."

"Poor Bear!" cried the Mother; "come in and lie down before the fire; but take care you do not burn your skin;" and then she continued, "Come here, Rose-Red and Snow-White, the Bear will not harm you, he means honourably." So they both came back, and by degrees the lamb too and the dove overcame their fears and welcomed the rough visitor.

"You children!" said the Bear, before he entered, "come and knock the snow off my coat." And they fetched their brooms and swept him clean. Then he stretched himself before the fire and grumbled out his satisfaction, and in a little while the children became familiar enough to play tricks with the unwieldy animal. They pulled his long shaggy skin, set their feet upon his back and rolled him to and fro, and even ventured to beat him with a hazel-stick, laughing when he grumbled. The Bear bore all their tricks good-temperedly, and if they hit too hard he cried out: –

"Leave me my life, you children,
Snow-White and Rose-Red,
Or you'll never wed."

When bedtime came and the others were gone, the Mother said to the Bear, "You may sleep here on the hearth if you like, and then you will be safely protected from the cold and bad weather."

As soon as day broke the two children let the Bear out again, and he trotted away over the snow, and ever afterwards he came every evening at a certain hour. He would lie down on the hearth and allow the children to play with him as much as they liked, till by degrees they became so accustomed to him, that the door was left unbolted till their black friend arrived.

But as soon as spring returned, and everything out of doors was green again, the Bear one morning told Snow-White that he must leave her, and could not return during the whole summer. "Where are you going, then, dear Bear?" asked Snow-White. "I am obliged to go into the forest and guard my treasures from the evil Dwarfs; for in winter, when the ground is hard, they are obliged to keep in their holes and cannot work through; but now, since the sun has thawed the earth and warmed it, the Dwarfs pierce through, and steal all they can find; and what has once passed into their hands, and gets concealed by them in their caves, is not easily brought to light." Snow-White, however, was very sad at the departure of the Bear, and opened the door so hesitatingly, that when he pressed through it he left behind on the latch a piece of his hairy coat; and through the hole which was made in his coat Snow-White fancied she saw the glittering of gold, but she was not quite certain of it. The Bear, however, ran hastily away, and was soon hidden behind the trees.

Some time afterwards the Mother sent the children into the wood to gather sticks, and while doing so they came to a tree which was lying across the path, on the trunk of which something kept bobbing up and down from the grass, and they could not imagine what it was. When they came nearer they saw a Dwarf, with an old wrinkled face and a snow-white beard a yard long. The end of his beard was fixed in a split of the tree, and the little man kept jumping about like a dog tied by a chain, for he did not know how to free himself. He glared at the Maidens with his red, fiery eyes, and exclaimed, "Why do you stand there? are you going to pass without offering me any assistance?" "What have you done, little man?" asked Rose-Red. "You stupid, gazing goose!" exclaimed he, "I wanted to have split the tree, in order to get a little wood for my kitchen for the little food which we used is soon burnt with great faggots, not like what you rough, greedy people devour! I had driven the wedge in properly, and everything was going well, when the smooth wood flew upwards, and the tree closed so suddenly together, that I could not draw my beautiful beard out; and here it sticks, and I cannot get away. There, don't laugh, you milk-faced things! are you dumb-founded?"

The children took all the pains they could to pull the Dwarf's beard out, but without success. "I will run and fetch some help," cried Rose-Red at length.

"Crack-brained sheep's-head that you are!" snarled the Dwarf; "what are you going to call other people for? You are two too many now for me; can you think of nothing else?"

"Don't be impatient," replied Snow-White; "I have thought of something;" and, pulling her scissors out of her pocket, she cut off the end of the beard. As soon as the Dwarf found himself at liberty, he snatched up his sack, which laid between the roots of the tree, filled with gold, and, throwing it over his shoulder, marched off, grumbling, and groaning, and crying, "Stupid people! to cut off a piece of my beautiful beard. Plague take you!" and away he went without once looking at the children.

Some time afterwards Snow-White and Rose-Red went a-fishing, and as they neared the pond they saw something like a great locust hopping about on the bank, as if going to jump into the water. They ran up and recognised the Dwarf. "What are you after?" asked Rose-Red; "you will fall into the water." "I am not quite such a simpleton as that," replied the Dwarf; "but do you not see this fish will pull me in?" The little man had been sitting there angling, and, unfortunately, the wind had entangled his beard with the fishing-line; and so when a great fish bit at the bait, the strength of the weak little fellow was not able to draw it out, and the fish had the best of the struggle. The Dwarf held on by the reeds and rushes which grew near, but to no purpose, for the fish pulled him where it liked, and he must soon have been drawn into the pond. Luckily just then the two Maidens arrived, and tried to release the beard of the Dwarf from the fishing-line, but both were too closely entangled for it to be done. So the Maiden pulled out her scissors again and cut off another piece of the beard. When the Dwarf saw this done he was in a great rage, and exclaimed, "You donkey! that is the way to disfigure my face. Was it not enough to cut it once, but you must now take away the best part of my beard? I dare not show myself again now to my own people. I wish you had run the soles off your boots before you had come here!" So saying, he took up a bag of pearls, which laid among the rushes, and, without speaking another word, slipped off and disappeared behind a stone.

Not many days after this adventure, it chanced that the Mother sent the two Maidens to the next town to buy thread, needles and pins, laces and ribbons. Their road passed over a common, on which, here and there, great pieces of rock were lying about. Just over their heads they saw a great bird flying round and round, and every now and then dropping lower and lower, till at last it flew down behind a rock. Immediately afterwards they heard a piercing shriek, and, running up, they saw with affright the the eagle had caught their old acquaintance the Dwarf, and was trying to carry him off. The compassionate children thereupon laid hold of the little man, and held him fast till the bird gave up the struggle and flew off. As soon, then, as the Dwarf had recovered from his fright, he exclaimed in his squeaking voice, "Could you not hold me more gently? You have seized my fine brown coat in such a manner, that it is all torn and full of holes, meddling and interfering rubbish that you are!" With these words he shouldered a bag filled with precious stones, and slipped away to his cave among the rocks.

The Maidens were now accustomed to his ingratitude, and so they walked on to the town and transacted their business there. Coming home they returned over the same common, and unawares walked up to a certain clean spot, on which the Dwarf had shaken out his bag of precious stones, thinking nobody was near. The sun was shining, and the bright stones glittered in its beams, and displayed such a variety of colours, that the two Maidens stopped to admire them.

"What are you standing there gaping for?" asked the Dwarf, while his face grew as red as copper with rage: he was continuing to abuse the poor Maidens, when a loud roaring noise was heard, and presently a great black bear came rolling out of the forest. The Dwarf jumped up terrified, but he could not gain his retreat before the Bear overtook him. Thereupon he cried out, "Spare me, my dear Lord Bear! I will give you all my treasures. See these beautiful precious stones which lie here; only give me my life; for what have you to fear from a weak little fellow like me? you could not touch me with your big teeth. There are two wicked girls, take them; they would make nice morsels; as fat as young quails; eat them, for heaven's sake!"

The Bear, however, without troubling himself to speak, gave the bad-hearted Dwarf a single blow with his paw, and he never stirred after.

The Maidens were then going to run away, but the Bear called after them, 'Snow-White and Rose-Red, fear not! Wait a bit and I will accompany you." They recognised his voice and stopped; and when the Bear came, his rough coat suddenly fell off, and he stood up a tall man, dressed entirely in gold. "I am a King's son," he said, "and was condemned by the wicked Dwarf, who stole all my treasures, to wander about in this forest in the form of a bear till his death released me. Now he has received his well-deserved punishment."

They they went home, and Snow-White was married to the Prince, and Rose-Red to his brother, with whom they shared the immense treasure which the Dwarf had collected. The old Mother also lived for many years happily with her two children; and the rose-trees which had stood before the cottage were planted now before the palace, and produced every year beautiful red and white roses.

THE DRUMMER

One evening a young Drummer was walking all alone on the sea-shore, and as he went along he perceived three pieces of linen lying on the sand. "What fine linen!" said he; and, picking up one of the pieces, he put it in his pocket and went home, thinking no more of his discovery. By-and-by he went to bed, and just as he was about to fall asleep, he fancied he heard some one call his name. He listened, and presently distinguished a gentle voice calling, "Drummer, Drummer! awake!" He could see nothing, for it was quite dark; but he felt, as it were, something flitting to and fro over his bed. "What do you want?" he asked at length. "Give me back my shirt," replied the voice, "which you found yesterday on the sea-shore."

"You shall have it again if you tell me who you are."

"Alas! I am the Daughter of a mighty King; but I have fallen into the power of a Witch, who has confined me on the glass mountain. Every day I am allowed to bathe with my two sisters in the sea; but I cannot fly away again without my shirt. Yester-eve my sisters escaped as usual, but I was obliged to stay behind, so I beg you to give me my shirt again."

"Rest happy, poor child," replied the Drummer, "I will readily give it back;" and, feeling for it in his pocket, he handed it to her. She hastily snatched it, and would have hurried away, but the Drummer exclaimed, "Wait a moment, perhaps I can help you!"

"That you may do," said the voice, "if you climb up the glass mountain and free me from the Witch; but you cannot get there, nor yet ascend, were you to try."

"Where there's a will there's a way," said the Drummer. "I pity you, and I fear nothing; but I do not know the way to the glass mountain."

"The path lies through the large forest, where the Giants are," said the child; "more I dare not tell you;" and, so saying, she flew away.

At break of day the Drummer arose, and, hanging his drum round him, walked straight away without fear into the forest. After he had traversed some distance without perceiving any Giant, he thought to himself he would awake the sleepers; and so, steadying his drum, he beat a roll upon it, which disturbed all the birds so much, that they flew off. In a few minutes a Giant raised himself from the ground, where he had been lying asleep on the grass, and his height was that of a fir-tree. "You wretched wight!" he exclaimed, "what are you drumming here for, awaking me out of my best sleep?"

"I am drumming," he replied, "to show the way to the many thousands who follow me."

"What do they want here in my forest?" asked the Giant.

"They are coming to make a path through, and rid it of such monsters as you," said the Drummer.

"Oho? I shall tread them down like ants."

"Do you fancy you will be able to do anything against them?" said the Drummer. "Why, if you bend down to catch any of them, others will jump upon your back; and then when you lie down to sleep, they will come from every bush and creep upon you. And each one has a steel hammer in his girdle, with which he means to beat out your brains."

The Giant was terribly frightened to hear all this, and he thought to himself. "If I meddle with these crafty people they will do me some injury. I can strangle wolves and bears, but these earthworms I cannot guard against." Then, speaking aloud, he said, "Here you little fellow, I promise for the future to leave you and your comrades in peace; and if you have a wish tell it to me, for I will do anything to please you."

"Well, then," replied the Drummer, "you have got long legs, and run quicker that I, so carry me to the glass mountain, and I will beat a retreat-march to my companions, so that for this time you shall not be disturbed."

"Come hither, you worm," said the Giant, "set yourself on my shoulder, and I will bear you whither you desire."

The Giant took him up, and the Drummer began to beat with all his might and main. "That is the sign," thought the Giant, "for the others to go back." After a while a second Giant started up on the road, and took the Drummer from the shoulders of the first, and put him in his button-hole. The Drummer took hold of the button, which was as big as a plate, to hold on by, and looked round in high spirits. By-and-by they met with a third Giant, who took him out of the button-hole and placed him on the rim of his hat. Here the Drummer walked round and round observing the country; and, perceiving in the blue distance a mountain, he supposed it to be the glass mountain, and so it was. The Giant took only a couple more strides and arrived at the foot of the mountain, where he set down the Drummer. The latter desired to be taken to the summit, but the Giant only shook his head and went away, muttering something in his beard.

So there the poor Drummer was left standing before the mountain, which was as high as if three hills had been placed upon each other, and, withal, as smooth as a mirror. so that he knew not how he should ascend it. He began to climb, but it was in vain, he slipped back every step. "Oh that I were a bird!" he exclaimed; "but of what use was wishing? wings never grew for that." While he ruminated, he saw at a little distance two men hotly quarrelling. He went up to them and found that their dispute related to a saddle, which lay on the ground before them, and for the possession of which they were contending. "What fools you are," he exclaimed, "to quarrel about a saddle, for which you have no horse!"

"The saddle is worth fighting about," replied one, "for whoever sits upon it, may wish himself where he will, and may even go to the end of the world if he so desire. The saddle belongs to us in common; but it is now my turn to ride, and this other will not let me."

"I will soon end your quarrel!" exclaimed the Drummer, walking a few steps forward, and planting a white wand in the ground; "run both of you to that point, and whoever gets there first shall ride first."

The two men started off at once, but they had scarcely gone two steps when the Drummer sat himself hastily down on their saddle, and, wishing himself on the top of the glass mountain, was there before one could turn his hand round. On the summit was a large plain, whereon stood an old stone mansion, and before its door a fish-pond, and behind, a dark wood. The Drummer saw neither man nor beast, all was still, but the noise of the wind among the trees; while, close above his head, the clouds were rolling along. He stepped up to the door of the house and knocked thrice, and after the third time, an old Woman, with red eyes and a brown face, opened it. She had spectacles upon her nose, and looked at him very sharply before she asked what his business was.

"Entrance, a night's lodging, and provisions," replied the Drummer boldly.

"That you will have, if you promise to perform three tasks!" said she.

"And why not?" he replied, "I am not afraid of work, be it ever so hard!"

So the old Woman let him come in, and gave him supper, and afterwards a good bed.

The next morning when the Drummer arose, the old Woman handed him a thimble off her withered finger, and said, "Now, go to work and empty the pond out there with this thimble, but you must finish it before night; and, besides that, you must take out all the fishes, and range them according to their species upon the bank."

"That is a queer job!" said the Drummer; but, going to the pond, he began to thimble out the water. He worked all the morning, but what could he do with a single thimble, if he had kept at work for a thousand years? When noonday came he stopped and sat down; for, as he thought, "It is no use, and all the same whether I work or not." Just then a Girl came from the house, and brought him a basket of provisions. "What do you want?" she asked, "that you sit there so sorrowful?"

The Drummer looked up, and, seeing that the speaker was very beautiful, he replied, "Alas! I cannot perform the first task, and how I shall do the others, I cannot tell! I have come here to seek a King's daughter, who lives hereabouts, but I have not found her, and I must go further."

"Stop here!" said the Girl, "I will assist you out of your trouble. You are tired, so lay your head in my lap and go to sleep; when you awake again the work will be done."

The Drummer need not twice telling; and, as soon as his eyes were closed, the Maiden pressed a wishing-ring, which she had, and said, "Out water, out fishes." Immediately the water rose in the air like a white vapour, and rolled away with the other clouds; while the fishes all jumped out, and arranged themselves on the banks according to their size and species.

By-and-by the Drummer awoke, and saw, to his astonishment, the work completed. "One of the fishes," said the Maiden, "does not lie with his companions, but quite alone; and so, when the old Woman comes this evening and sees all that is done she will ask why this fish is left out, and you must take it up and throw it in her face, saying, 'That is for you, old Witch'"

So when it was evening the old Woman came and asked the question, and he immediately threw the fish in her face. She did not appear to notice it, but only looked silently and maliciously at him. The next morning she said to him, "You got off too easily yesterday, I must give you a harder task; to-day you must cut down all my trees, split the wood into faggots, and range them in bundles, and all must be ready by night."

With these words she gave him an axe, a mallet, and two wedges; but the first was made of lead, and the others of tin. When, therefore, he began to chop, the axe doubled quite up, while the mallet and wedges stuck together. He knew not what to do; but at noon the Maiden came again with his dinner and comforted him. "Lay your head in my lap," said she, "and when you awake the work will be done." Thereupon she turned her wishing-ring, and at the same moment the whole forest fell down with a crash, the timber split of itself, and laid itself together in heaps, as if innumerable giants were at work. As soon as the Drummer awoke, the Maiden said to him, "See, here is all your wood properly cut and stacked, with the exception of one bough which, if the old Woman, when she comes this evening, asks the reason of, give her a blow with it, and say, 'That is for thee, old Witch.'"

Accordingly, when the old Woman came, she said, "See, how easy the work is; but for whom is this bough left out?"

"For you, old Witch!" he replied, giving her a blow. But she appeared not to feel it, and, laughing fiendishly, said to him, "To-morrow you shall lay all the wood in one pile, and kindle and burn it."

At daybreak he arose again and began to work; but how could a single man pile up a whole forest? The work proceeded very slowly. The Maiden, however, did not forget him in his troubles, and brought him his usual midday meal, after eating which he laid his head in her lap and slept. On his awaking he found the whole pile burning in one immense flame, whose tongues of fire reached up to heaven. "Attend to me," said the Maiden to him; "when the Witch comes she will demand something singular, but do what she desires without fear, and you will take no harm; but if you are afraid, the fire will catch and consume you. Lastly, when you have fulfilled her demands, take her with both hands and throw her into the midst of the flames."

Thereupon the Maiden left him, and presently the old Woman slipped in, crying, "Hu! hu! how I freeze! but there is fire to warm me and my old bones; that is well; but," she continued, turning to the Drummer, "there is a log which will not burn, fetch it out for me; come, if you do that, you shall be free and go where you will, only be brisk."

The Drummer plunged into the flames without a moment's consideration; but they did him no harm, not even singeing a single hair. He bore the faggot off and laid it beside the old Witch; but as soon as it touched the earth it changed into the beautiful Maiden, who had delivered him from his troubles, and he perceived at once by her silken shining robes that she was the King's daughter. The old Woman laughed fiendishly again, and exclaimed, "Do you think you have her? not yet, not yet!" And so saying, she would have seized the Maiden; but the Drummer, catching her with both his hands, threw her into the middle of the burning pile, and the flames closed in around her, as if rejoicing in the destruction of such a Witch.

When this was done the Maiden looked at the Drummer, and, seeing that he was a handsome youth, and that he had ventured his life to save her, she held out her hand to him, and said, "You have dared a great deal for me, and I must do something for you; promise me to be true and faithful, and you shall be my husband. For wealth we shall not want; we have enough here in the treasure which the old Witch has gathered together."

Thereupon she led him into the house and showed him chests upon chests, which were filled with treasures. They left the gold and silver, and took nothing but diamonds and pearls; and then, as they no longer wished to remain on the glass mountain, the Drummer proposed that they should descend on the wishing-saddle. "The old saddle does not please me," said the Maiden, "and I need only turn the ring on my finger and we shall be at home."

"Well, then, wish ourselves at the city gate," replied the Drummer; and in the twinkling of an eye they were there. "I will go and take the news to my parents first," said the Drummer; "wait here for me, for I shall be back soon."

"Ah! I pray you, then, take care not to kiss your parents when you arrive on the right cheek, else will you forget everything, and I shall be left here all alone in this field." "How can I forget you?" said he, and promised her faithfully to return in a very short time. When he entered his father's house nobody knew him, he was so altered, for the three days which he had imagined he had spent on the glass mountain were three long years. He soon recalled himself to their remembrance, and his parents hung round his neck, so that, moved by affection, he entirely forgot the Maiden's injunctions, and kissed them on both cheeks. Every thought concerning the Princess at once faded from his mind, and, emptying his pockets, he laid handfuls of precious stones upon the table. The parents could not tell what to do with so much wealth, till at length they built a noble castle, surrounded by gardens, woods, and meadows, and fit for a prince to inhabit. When it was done the mother of the Drummer said to him, "I have looked out for a wife for you, and you shall be married in three days' time."

Now, the Drummer was quite content with all that his Parents proposed; but the poor Princess was very disconsolate. For a long time after he first left her she waited for him in the fields; but when evening fell she believed that he had kissed his Parents on the right cheek, and forgotten all about her. Her heart was full of grief, and she wished herself in some solitary forest that she might not return to her father's court. Every evening she went to the city and passed by the Drummer's house, but although he saw her many times he never recognised her. At last she heard one day the people talking of the wedding of the Drummer, and she thereupon resolved to make a trial if she could regain his love. As soon as the first festival-day was appointed, she turned her wishing-ring, saying, "A dress as shining as the sun." Immediately the dress lay before her, and seemed as if wove out of the purest sunbeams! Then, as soon as the guests had assembled, she slipped into the hall, and everybody admired her beautiful dress; but most of all the bride elect, who had a passion for fine dresses, and went up to her and asked if she would sell it. "Not for money," she replied; "but for the privilege of sleeping for one night next to the chamber of the bridegroom."

The Bride elect could not resist her wish for the dress, and so she consented; but first of all she mixed in the sleeping draught of the Bridegroom a strong potion, which prevented him from being awakened. By-and-by, when all was quiet, the Princess crept to the chamber-door, and, opening it slightly, called gently, –

"Drummer, Drummer, O list to me,
Forget not what I did for thee,
Think of the mountain of glass so high,
Think of the Witch and her cruelty;
Think of my plighted troth with thee:
Drummer! Drummer! O list to me!"

She cried all in vain, the Drummer did not awake, and when day dawned the Princess was forced to leave. The second evening she turned her wishing-ring, and said, "A dress as silvery as the moon." As soon as she had spoken it lay before her; and when she appeared in it at the ball, the Bride elect wished to have it as the other, and the Princess gave it to her for the privilege of passing another night next to the chamber of the Bridegroom. And everything passed as on the first night.

The servants in the house, however, had overheard the plaint of the strange Maiden, and they told the Bridegroom about it. They told him, also, that it was not possible for him to hear anything about what was said because of the potion, which was put into his sleeping-draught.

The third evening the Princess turned her ring and wished for a dress as glittering as the stars. As soon as she appeared in the ball-room thus arrayed, the Bride elect was enchanted with its beauty, and declared rapturously, "I must and will have it." The Maiden gave it up, like the former, for a night's sleep next to the Bridegroom's chamber. This time he did not drink his wine as usual, but poured it out behind the bed; and so, when all the house was quiet, he heard a gentle voice repeating:–

"Drummer, Drummer, O list to me,
Forget not what I did for thee,
Think of the mountain of glass so high,
Think of the Witch and her cruelty;
Think of my plighted troth with thee:
Drummer! Drummer! O list to me!"

All at once his memory returned, and he exclaimed, "Alas! alas! how could I have treated you so heartlessly? but the kisses which I gave my parents on the right cheek, in the excess of my joy, they have bewildered me." He jumped up, and, taking the Princess by the hand, led her to the bedside of his Parents. "This is my true Bride," said he; "and if I marry the other I shall do a grievous wrong." When the Parents heard all that had happened, they gave their consent, and thereupon the lights in the hall were rekindled, the drums and trumpets refetched, the friends and visitors invited to come again, and the true wedding was celebrated with great pomp and happiness.

But the second Bride received the three splendid dresses, and was as well contented as if she had been married!

Classic Library Titles

Alice's Adventures in Wonderland
Through the Looking-Glass
by Lewis Carroll
Illustrated by John Tenniel

Black Beauty
by Anna Sewell
Illustrated by Cecil Aldin and Glenn Steward
Rebecca of Sunnybrook Farm
by Kate Douglas Wiggin
Illustrated by Glenn Steward

Little Women
Little Men
by Louisa May Alcott
Illustrated by Clara M. Burd

The Secret Garden
by Frances Hodgson Burnett
Illustrated by Jan Burridge
A Little Princess
by Frances Hodgson Burnett
Illustrated by Louise Hill

The Water Babies
by Charles Kingsley
Illustrated by Jessie Willcox Smith
Peter Pan
by J.M. Barrie
Illustrated by Mabel Lucie Attwell

Treasure Island
by R.L. Stevenson
Illustrated by Eleanor Plaisted Abbott and Wal Paget
Kidnapped
by R.L. Stevenson
Illustrated by David Price

Pride and Prejudice
Sense and Sensibility
by Jane Austen
Illustrated

Andersen's Fairy Tales
by Hans Christian Andersen
Illustrated by E.H. Wehnert and W. Thomas
Grimm's Folk Tales
by The Brothers Grimm
Illustrated by E.H. Wehnert